Dedicated to my wife and my two beautiful children.

And to my parents. All of whom have made me who I am today.

To my wonderful brother and sister, who remind me how blessed I am

each and every day.

Kindle Link: http://www.amazon.co.uk/gp/product/B00SEK47B6

Atticus and the Orb of Time

Prologue

2500BC

"Kill the elders, take the child," says Alvarez, "Those are our orders," the demon stands hooded and cloaked in black garments, as if Death himself has come to Earth without his Scythe. He feels his heavy robe caress the sand as the wind swirls around him. This Earth realm smells revolting to him, the stench of blood and death tainting the night air, so stained is his attire of perished innocence, it is the only thing stopping him from vomiting onto the contrasting purity of the desert.

So many souls swallowed by order of his master, the symphonic screams of his victims, these tasks handed to him have always been met with glee. Alvarez relishes in these memories, his piercing red eyes, pupils pulsating, betray his humanoid form as he joyously reminiscences on each begging voice, each drop of blood. The hunt for his latest prey is different though. This one he cannot harm, for his master wants that honour.

Alvarez turns and addresses his group of unworldly creatures within the moonlit shadows. Their faces are clothed with the blackness of night; their skinless, dog-like shadows are all that is visible. He gazes at them as they stand. Some are hunched; some stand tall, their silhouettes reminding him of the charred stumps and branches of a burnt-out woodland, such is their number. The desert sands are slightly misty, as a light breeze blows the loose grains across the plateau of rock Alvarez stands upon, and around the dunes that sit, jutting out of the desert surface. The effect is soothing, almost as if the wind is comforting the sand, reassuring it that the sun's torture ends with the night.

Alvarez breathes deeply, taking in the air as he stares at his target. Not too far in the distance lies the silhouette of a small, makeshift home. Candles flicker and shine out a faint beam of light from the windows. The front door of the home is made from wood, its smooth finish and carvings telling all who see it that it is the work of a skilled carpenter. Visitors' suspicions are given further weight when they view the wooden horse and elaborate fencing. An area outside the rear of the single level house can be seen to contain a makeshift play area. Another, much smaller wooden horse lies on the ground, not quite finished, along with wooden balls and sticks.

A clear night sky aids visibility as the Moon's light skims the ground. Behind the house, barely a mile away, lie the walls of the great ancient Persian city of Aria. Its skyline blends into the distant mountainscape. Candles flicker from tall steeples, and the town folk can be heard faintly in the distance. Domes and citadels all make their presence felt as darkness against the faint blue of the moon's light, their lifeless nature betrayed by speckles of light and movement behind their open windows.

"We must be sure Alvarez; our King does not look kindly upon mistakes," whispers a figure who hides himself deep within the darkness.

Alvarez snorts, "You humans never fail to amaze me, in your willingness to betray your entire race, your very existence for power or profit. Still, *my* King offers his thanks for your information, and will reward you accordingly."

"We still need to be sure. We get just one chance at this. The Majjai will not be fooled twice, they will not allow this intrusion again."

"Our King has given us this to be sure," responds Alvarez as he pulls a large opaque globe out from his robe.

"What is it?" asks the person hidden in the shadows.

"Its name is not important. What is important is that it will show us if this child is the one we seek," Alvarez holds the globular object high above his hood, revealing pale, human-like hands with pinkish veins protruding outwards. He regards this traitor, this human with him on this dark night with contempt — the urge to destroy this pest is great, but the knowledge of the punishment if he does so is enough to divert his thoughts elsewhere. He chants something that the person in the shadows is unable to hear. It's an old language, archaic enough to only be known to a few scholars of the dark arts. As Alvarez finishes the chant, a tiny stream of blue light shoots outwards from the globe and onto the ground. It heads towards the house, slithering through the sand and up onto the walls until it gets to a window. The light ebbs faintly, barely affecting the candlelit ambience of the room. Almost alive, the light actively seeks what it is looking for. The room is square and small, draped in coloured blankets. A wooden crib sits in the centre with various shelves leveraging on the walls. The light pauses for a moment as it detects movement just outside, knowing it is safe to continue, it carries on its journey, snaking, towards the crib and latches onto a sleeping baby.

# # #

The maid of the house is tidying just outside the baby's room. She sweeps quietly trying not to wake her masters who are sleeping further down the hall.

She opens the door to the nursery very carefully and walks towards the baby; she doesn't notice the blue light as she softly strokes his head.

"Sleep well little one."

She covers his arms with a blanket, and proceeds to blow out the candle. The room is immediately imbued with a blue hue, and she sees it, the baby's birthmark, a small circle entwined with a vine like line on his left forearm, begins to glow as the snake-like blue stream pulsates outwards.

The maid snatches the baby from the crib and runs out of the room, breaking the connection of the light, which dissipates with a hiss and a fizz. She runs as fast possible, trying to focus in the low light. She grapples against the walls; all she can think is to alert the parents.

Awakened by the commotion, the boy's father appears first. He stands in his robes, wearing sandals, heavily bearded but still with a youthful appearance. His face is stoic and strong, but it does not hide the fear in his eyes.

"What is wrong, Sima?" he asks hurriedly.

Sima explains what she saw, and the sense of danger is all too apparent in his reaction. Waking his wife and trying to escape is all he can think about.

"Quickly, Nasreen, get dressed. We have to leave," he pleads to his wife, desperate to escape the confines of the house where he knows they will be easy pickings.

Startled and scared she listens and prepares herself, "What is wrong? What is happening Omar?" she asks.

"They have come for him. I do not know how they found us," the father replies

"Betrayal − it is the only answer − but who?" Nasreen tries to query as they attempt to sneak out. But it is too late. Alvarez and his demons have already surrounded their home.

Omar signals to Sima and his wife to stop; knowing that there is no way out for all of them, he turns to his wife, "There is only one chance, we must hold them."

The parents both look towards Sima, "You must use the tunnel to get to Aria. Find a Majjai named Elric Griffin, show him the mark. Our son is your responsibility now, keep him safe," says the father.

The mother cries as she strokes her son's head for what she knows is the last time, "Goodbye my sweet Atticus, may angels keep you safe."

Before Sima can stop them, they run outside with a makeshift blanket, pretending they are holding the baby. Sima knows what she must do. She goes to the tunnel, and closes the hatch behind her. She follows the cold stone walls taking her to the outer edge of the city of Aria in the darkness. Her hands sense the coolness of the walls; they feel soothing compared to the hot, desert air. Slowly she makes her way, making sure Atticus is safe in her arms. She hears strange noises above her, explosions, roars from large creatures. She knows she has to carry on; the impending sacrifice cannot be in vain. Suddenly all is quiet above her, in the silence she hears two screams, one male, one female and recognises them instantly. A tear falls from her cheek onto Atticus, "Goodbye my friends," she says to herself, "I will keep him safe, at all costs."

She finally reaches the end of the tunnel and looks around; in the far distance she can see the demons ravaging the house. She hears them shout in anger.

"Where is he?" shouts Alvarez, "He was here!"

The demons ransack the home. Sima spots one of them breaking off from the pack and run towards Alvarez, suspecting they have found the tunnel entrance in the debris, she tries to hurry again to the city, cursing that the tunnel has not taken her far enough.

"Alvarez! Out here!" screams the betrayer, from his hiding place in the shadows.

"What is it?" Alvarez demands.

Sima turns to see the traitor point in her direction and senses his betrayal go further.

"In the distance, close to the city, a woman."

Alvarez calls to his demons and points at Sima, "Bring her to me."

Sima is filled with dread, knowing she has been spotted. The demons whelp and howl into the night air as they charge over the two smoking, charred human bodies. Sima hears them but is too scared to turn around. The city walls are still too far for her to run, but in vain she tries, willing for a miracle to save her. Sharp stones jutting out from the surface cut into her feet as her sandals fall away, but still she carries on. Her feet bleed into the sand, leaving a red trail as she struggles forward.

She runs, faster, as fast as she can. But the demons are too quick, and in moments are upon her.

They grab her clothes, taunting her, tearing small bits and pieces, yet she does not let go of the baby. She can see one or two of them eating the sand where her blood has stained it, rabid with glee, as if they have not eaten for weeks.

Sima can see Alvarez walking slowly and patiently towards her and the child, looking nonchalant, confident that his prey is well and truly within his grasp. Sima closes her eyes and prays. As she does so, a faint breeze swirls around her and grows stronger. The sand whips up from the ground and surrounds her like a whirlwind. She looks up and can see a formation of clouds growing in size in the night sky above her. The clouds swirl faster and harder. The demons try to grab Sima through the wall of sand, but the force of the wind throws them back.

Another funnel of wind appears, this one is much more violent. It crashes into the group of demons and smashes them against each other. They try to run, but the funnel grows larger and more violent, sweeping them all into the air.

Sima can see Alvarez shield himself, sensing his fear that if he gets too close the same fate will befall him.

"Majjai," the demon mutters with disdain as he looks towards the betrayer, "Our master will not be pleased."

He holds up the globe, "This will have to do for now." Alvarez raises one hand while the other touches a hidden object concealed within his garments; in front of him an oval red circle appears, it grows larger creating a portal into which he and the traitor quickly disappear.

Sima closes her eyes tightly, praying for the end or a saviour, not knowing if she is now alone or still being hunted.

# # #

Minutes go by before Sima finally finds the courage to open her eyes. To her surprise she finds herself deep within the city of Aria, that the baby, Atticus, is fine and her own scrapes are fully healed. She notices an extra weight to her side, a heavy pouch; she peers inside to find a large number of gold pieces and a note.

"You are the guardian, and it is your time to watch over the chosen one."

Sima sighs, "Thank you, whoever you are."

She stares thankfully into the night sky for several moments before starting out on her quest, to seek out the Majjai known as Elric Griffin.

Chapter 1

Gooyeh Partaab

Present Day

Wysardian Manor lies silent. None of the hustle and bustle that is present during school hours is apparent at this very early phase of the morning. The air hangs heavy and the sky remains confused, still haunted by the night and its moon as it slowly crawls against the dark blue canvas. Only a single lit window is visible on one of the higher tower floors of the inner courtyard shows any sign of activity. The four towers that corner the structure impose themselves as dark shadows, tainting the moonlit landscape.

A spider climbs the wall just to the left of the lit window. It scurries and pauses, wary of any noise in the area while sensing for its next meal. Attracted by vibrations coming from the lit room it veers closer, actively sensing the area around it for any signs of danger or prey, it stops as it detects a powerful vibration; spying two large creatures in the room, it lies still, observing their movements.

Another powerful vibration rattles the window as one of the large creatures slams a goblet onto a table. The spider continues to lie still, watching the large creatures in the room. It appears that the two creatures are trying to communicate with each other, the sounds coming from them become louder.

"Are you sure Elric?" one of the creatures says, waving its arms in an agitated fashion.

"I am sure, Geoffrey, I was there remember," replies the other creature, this one has silvery hair hanging from his face and head and is sitting in a large chair, facing away from the window. In front of it lies a large desk. The spider finds a better place to hide as it moves closer to the bottom of the stone window frame; it has seen many brethren squished by similar creatures, simply for wanting to say hello.

The room is covered wall-to-wall with antique-looking shelves and cupboards filled with hundreds of books, some old, some new. Their spines vary in colour, age and size. Other shelves are heavy with strange ornaments and scrolls while some contain vials and an assortment of strange containers.

"I know you were there, my friend, but, how can you be sure? You know how much is dependent on this − the birthmark could just be a coincidence."

"Yes, it could be, but there are other elements to the prophecy that are known only by myself and those that are no longer with us. Many things have been hidden for the boys' safety," the hairy creature pauses for a moment. It raises its hand, and at the hint of a wave a book floats towards it from a nearby bookcase, "Look here, Geoffrey, if you need more convincing, there is a way for you to be sure − a chant you must use while the boy is in contact with the *Gooyeh Partaab*."

The other creature steps towards the book that now lies open upon the table, "And if this reveals that he is not the one, what then? We never searched for a possible alternative; and how is it *he* hasn't found him yet?"

"On the contrary my dear fellow, *he* actually *has* found him, but thankfully, he is too weak to act on his discovery, and is unable to be sure."

"How do you know all this Elric? If he has found him, surely he should be protected? The *Partaab* is limited in its power, it can be fooled," says the standing creature.

"He is being protected, he has been protected ever since he

entered this time. And as for the Partaab, yes, it can be fooled – but not when it is mine," another wave of the arm coincides with the opening of a large, dragon-encrusted cupboard door on the far side of the room.

The standing creature turns and walks towards the cupboard, then lifts an object covered in a purple fabric, "Is this the first? But, how?"

"Full of questions today, Geoffrey," says the seated creature; "I hope you keep this up when you quiz him tomorrow?"

"Sorry, it's just, well, you must have sensed it too; he may be weak, but he is getting stronger every day. If he finds the *Quantorbium*, then, all of this will have been for nothing. Our spies tell us that he has found a scripture left by the orb's creator and…"

"Enough, Geoffrey," the sitting creature with silver hair says calmly, "I already know; you forget who I am sometimes. The scriptures are known to me. I found them a long long time ago, and let's just say, whatever was left in their place will benefit us all in wasted months for our friend over there." The creature chuckles, and coughs harshly.

"Easy old man, have you been taking the medication that Madam Healsey has prepared for you?" the standing creature ventures over to the older one, placing its hand on the others shoulder to comfort them.

"Yes Geoffrey, it's been working well, but, my last *adventure* has taken a rather large toll. I'm not as young as I used to be," still sitting, it pats the standing creature's hand in thanks, "I may not actually be around forever, after all."

"Exactly why we need to be sure if we are right. Who has been protecting the boy?"

"That will be revealed in good time; for now, it must remain a secret. But rest assured, he is known to you, known to us all."

The standing creature walks to a fire in the wall at the far side, picks up a metal stick, and rummages the stones within the fire forcing the flames beneath to breathe new air, "It will be difficult for him, he has no knowledge of our ways; the others, they knew of us through heritage and through fighting a war they knew existed, because it directly entered their lives." It breathes a sigh, and turns back towards the silver-haired creature, "If he is the one, it means the final battle will be near. I fear we are not ready. From what you have told us, the other side may be too strong this time − he knows what to expect, and he will be ready."

"This is why we must assemble them, we must train them, and quickly. The power is within them all, we just have to show them how to utilise it. Olof − he will be invaluable − he knows the way of Norse Magic already, he needs little time to learn how to unlock his potential."

The seated creature reaches for a large stick. The spider fixates all eight of its eyes towards the room. It watches everything, trying not to be distracted by the dancing shadows cast by the flicker of the fire. The seated, silver-haired creature uses the stick to stand and walks towards the window. The spider quickly darts to a shadow in the corner.

"The others Geoffrey, they will need more guidance, it may be time for the chosen one to meet me. The true face of Wysardian Manor has been hidden for too long. He will complete them, and eventually lead them. But what I have sensed for him in the future will make things difficult for him, for all of us. Even now, he is dreaming, he crosses over without knowledge of doing so, mistaking everything for a dream, he does not realise the danger."

"Do not worry Elric, we will train him, the *Gooyeh Partaab*; with this, we may have hope. I know not of how you obtained the first,

13

my friend, I suspect it is how you obtained your latest injuries – you shouldn't keep going off on your own. You should trust us more. We are here to help, as well you know."

"No, you and the others that know you are here to protect the school, it is all important. My duties also lie here it is true, but I must complete these tasks. Until they are trained, I am the last... the last!"

The spider spots water seeping from the eye of the silver-haired creature now standing at the window, one of its eight eyes follows the spot of water fall and splash at the base of the window. The large creature sighs, turns away and follows a path back to the chair to sit, "Our numbers grow Geoffrey, but numbers may not be enough, this is why he is so important. The *Gooyeh Partaab* will prove to the doubters that the prophecy exists, and in turn give us all hope that we will save not just this realm, but all of them. If we fail, the fate of all that is good will be showered in darkness. It cannot happen. Evil cannot win!"

"We will need the scriptures, do you still have them? Were you able to decipher them?" asks the standing creature.

"Unfortunately not, they have been locked by their creator. Only the chosen one is able to open them. But fear not, they are perfectly safe, hidden by the chosen one's protector," replies the seated creature.

"I hope tomorrow's revelations will not be too much for him. Once the powers within him are awakened, there will be no turning back – providing you are right, of course. When he touches the *Gooyeh Partaab*, the power could be too much for him. If you are wrong... he could die if the link is not broken in time."

"Perhaps. That is why I chose you, Geoffrey," says the silver-haired creature, "You are one of my most trustworthy members. I have faith that you will be able to keep him safe while on school grounds;

stay close to him, at all times."

"What of the reports of beasts to the north? We will need to dispatch a team to deal with them; if the boy needs convincing, maybe he should join them?" says the standing creature.

"Could be dangerous, we know not of the beasts we are dealing with here, their numbers, or where they came from. But, the others need to go; they have had enough training, and should be ready. We'll send Benjamin Morgan with them, too, he is learned enough, and will protect them. It may be dangerous to take the chosen one, his powers will only just be awakened, he will know not of control – and, if the prophecies are correct, the consequences could mean disaster for us all."

"What you say is true, but we must remember that time is short here. In the demon realm, he will have almost infinite time to prepare with the runes that he stole; his powers will grow at a much faster rate than we can. It may be beneficial for the chosen one to go… if you are right of course. To accelerate his own learning's."

"The runes of *zamaan* are limited in power – not as powerful as the stone he seeks, far from it – but your points are noted… and I agree, which is why that matter is already in hand. I will send word to Atticus' protector to stay close to him. Let's hope his body is ready, I would have preferred to wait a little longer, but as you say Geoffrey, time is short. How have the others progressed?"

"The girls have been fine, progressing nicely. Olof is ahead of the other men, the others are still a little physical in the implementation of their skills."

"Indeed," The seated creature pauses for a moment, and turns towards the window, "Do you sense that we are being watched?" the air in the room turns cold.

The standing creature rushes towards the spider's window, it tries to creep further into the shadows, sensing a threat.... then nothing, the standing creature looks upon it and merely chuckles, "Your senses are too finely tuned, my friend, it's just a little spider, probably wants to come in from the cold."

"No, there is something else."

The standing creature peers out of the window, trying to catch a glimpse of something, "I see nothing Elric, nothing evil could trespass on these grounds without our knowledge, we have seen to that already, and surely they would not be foolish enough to open a portal so close?"

"I know," the seated creature joins the standing creature at the window, "It must be further away, they are getting braver." The spider senses another increase in tension, and furiously searches for a nook, a cranny, anything to squeeze its tiny body into to hide "There! On the hillside Geoffrey!"

"I'm on my way!"

In a flash the creature that was standing disappears, then another flash appears upon the distant hillside banks. At this point, the spider feels it better to run away, and it does so, scurrying down the walls as quickly as its eight legs can carry it.

# # #

Not so far away in the still slumbering town, a young boy wakes, wondering if what he just experienced was real, or just a dream. Rubbing his eyes, grateful to find only two, and not eight, he nonchalantly dismisses the strange dream as he returns to the comfort of his blanket.

Chapter 2

Dreams

Geoffrey quietly walks in the shadows of the hillside, stepping on the crisp grass, edging ever forward, avoiding making too much noise against the frost-covered ground, "We know you are here, show yourself." He senses the presence of something, as the chilled air tingles against his bare neck. A bead of sweat begins to crystalise on his brow, as the heat of the chamber he was in moments ago ebbs away, giving in to the cold. He checks his neck, to ensure his enchanted medallion, the source of his powers, is on his person.

"No." A voice emanates from the darkness, rasping, hissing, and deeply toned, "I want to play this game my way... Majjai Geoffrey!"

"Ha, so you know who I am, and you still hide?"

"My master will reward me greatly for your scalp, your head on my claws will be a trophy to savour," the beast's voice slithers in the air, surrounding the space around Geoffrey, making it difficult to pinpoint its origin.

Geoffrey knows he must not show fear, even when being faced with the unknown, his training has taught him this, "You speak with such confidence, yet lack the bravery to reveal yourself. Geoffrey Sprocking is nobody's fool, but, it seems that you are." Geoffrey hears a bush rustle behind him, and swings around, confident that the beast will soon betray its location.

"You are wrong, I am merely biding my time. I sense your fear, I can smell it − it beautifies the air around you. Your blood will flow soon, followed by the old man's, and then the chosen one. We are too powerful for you, and we are coming."

"You may be coming, but you have no idea what you are up against. Our army is complete, and its leader will soon be among them. It's not too late for you to leave your master. I offer you this as salvation," says Geoffrey.

"Salvation you say? Ha! I'm saved. I offer you the same. Come, and join us to rot in the malevolence of your true master, or die... I'd prefer you die!"

A low growl, deep enough to send vibrations through the ground begins to ring around the trees, the earth shakes violently as the movement becomes stronger.

Geoffrey catches his balance as the ground moves away beneath him, steadies himself, and calmly folds his arms behind his back as he looks towards the ground, then closes his eyes. He mumbles something under his breath, and from his feet strands of blue light appear, they follow the ground around him like ripples on a pond, hugging the grass, seeking the demon and touching all around Geoffrey, "Show yourself beast," he says.

"Never!" the beast growls harder and deeper; the ground beneath Geoffrey shakes with even more vigour, and the ripples of light are bounced into the air and disappear into the distance.

The shaking unbalances Geoffrey once more, he falls backwards, but before hitting the ground, he extends his arms, mutters something else under his breath and catches himself mid-air, the blue light now emanating from his open hands. He floats back to a vertical position, the blue light again appearing under his feet, but this time surrounding them as a circular platform, vapours of light rising upwards levitating his body. He closes his hands into a fist, clenching them, squeezing more ripples of light from his entire body illuminating the immediate area.

He sees it.

The beast, almost three meters tall, is trying to hide behind a tree not too far away. It growls again, the ground shakes, but this time, Geoffrey is not connected to it.

"Your party tricks won't save you from harm, human!" threatens the hidden beast.

"On the contrary, I have more than party tricks to show you," replies Geoffrey.

"As do I!" the beast roars and leaps from its hiding place. Disfigured from prior battles, one shoulder is lower than the other, claws longer than its forearms; its crooked back cracks as it lands, shaking the ground. Its dog like-face with a boil-covered hairless snout salivates, saliva seeping over the pockets of hair and bare skin on its chest, blending with the pus dripping from its scars.

The beast slowly rocks its head back, then thrusts it forward, letting out a bellowing roar, emitting sound waves of such force and power that they toss the very earth and smaller trees around the beast towards Geoffrey.

Geoffrey is prepared, his forearms crossed like a shield. The blue light encases him as the sound wave throws its might against it, pushing him back some distance with only a tree stump saving him from being thrown into the blackness of the night. Silence soon regains control of the hillside as the demon walks slowly over to its opponent.

Geoffrey falls to the ground, he checks his back is still intact, thankful it was not worse as he curses himself for not preparing his defense in a more timely manner. The beast comes and stands over him, breathing heavily, drained from the attack.

Geoffrey hears it try to growl once more to finish the job, but it is too tired. He grasps the opportunity and flips over, sweeping the beast to the ground and moving away to make space between them.

"You truly are as strong as they say," the beast says under its heavy breath as it stands, "But I can still kill you with my bare hands!"

It snarls, and leaps into the air towards its prey.

Geoffrey watches the beast as it arcs towards him and raises an arm. The beast stops mid-air, as if an invisible net of energy has caught it. It looks puzzlingly towards Geoffrey, flailing its arms in its efforts to escape this grasp on its body.

"My turn," says the Professor. With a wave of his hand, the beast is thrown back to the ground with an impact such that, after the debris clears, the beast can be seen coiled in a small crater.

The beast tries to stand. Geoffrey is ready, a blue ball of electricity appears in his hand, and he throws it towards the beast.

Engulfed, the beast screams in agony, its skin and flesh burning as the ball of energy consumes it. One last cry of agony rings into the night air, and then there is silence.

A flash of light appears next to Geoffrey, "Is it done?" asks Elric.

"Yes, a Screamer demon; they usually hunt in packs, so why just send one this time?" asks Geoffrey.

"Must be a scout. With the beast not returning, I doubt others will come," says Elric.

"Do you think it heard anything?" says Geoffrey.

"Heh, even if it did my friend, I think you have made sure it won't be telling anyone," Elric says as he checks the area for any would-be onlookers, "I cloaked the area, so no-one should have seen this. Quickly now, we must repair the damage," Elric mutters a few words under his breath, and the surrounding foliage and trees instantly repair themselves; the Screamer's body turns to ash, and is blown away on the wind, "We need to find the portal and close it before the school opens in the morning. Where was it hiding?"

Geoffrey points towards the tree where the Screamer stood earlier.

"You think the tree could be the portal?" he asks.

"Only one way to find out I guess." Elric taps the tree with his staff, and it glows a dim blue, "This is not the portal, hmm, let's see if we can pick up our dead friend's trail." Elric slams the bottom of his staff into the ground, and this time a red glow emits from the hole that is left, slowly moving towards where the Screamer died. The red glow illuminates the Screamer's paw prints. The two men follow the trail.

"This may be a trap you know?" says Geoffrey.

"Perhaps, but we need to discover how they are creating these portals'. We destroyed their only means of doing so many years ago, and besides, you are here to protect me," says Elric with a wink to his friend.

"As if you need any form of protection against a Screamer," Geoffrey replies as he follows Elric across the hilltop.

They venture over the crest, towards the tree line of Echo Forest, an old, protected piece of woodland, usually teeming with life. The forest has much history, many stories to tell, but this night it is strangely silent. Geoffrey senses this, and quickens the pace with the feeling that all is not well this night, "You think the portal originates from within the forest?" he asks his mentor.

"We'll find out when we get there. But we must be careful, Screamers are much more dangerous in packs," says Elric as the pair trek towards the forest.

"Should we call the others before we venture further? The forest is neutral territory, the trees ally with no one," asks Geoffrey.

"No, I think we should be quite safe, I may be old, but I think I can handle a few Screamers."

"One more thing, since when did Screamers learn to speak our tongue?" asks Geoffrey.

"The Runes must have slowed time by a massive degree, long enough for them to evolve to this level of intelligence. We can speculate later, right now, finding that portal is vital," answers Elric.

They venture into the forest together using the glowing red trail ahead of them as their guide; the light fades as they walk past each footprint to ensure no evidence is left. The foliage thickens and Elric uses his staff to force a path through it as the trail becomes more difficult to follow, "It appears that the Screamer took a rather athletic route," he says, pointing to the marks high up on the tree trunks.

"Looks like they have evolved to be more agile than before," comments Geoffrey.

"The runes can only be used in a singular area at a time," replies Elric, "It is probably a good sign that the Screamers have gained these skills; he hasn't had the Runes long enough to influence his entire realm. It seems our friend has become smarter, Geoffrey. He started with his foot soldiers, he will probably move to his larger demons soon. We need to find this portal!"

"I do wish you would stop calling him 'our friend,' he deserves no such accolade, he is pure evil, and the sooner we find a way to defeat him, the better," scoffs Geoffrey.

"Defeating him isn't our job; remember, it's their task now, our time has passed. Our job is to merely protect them while they learn, and pass on our knowledge and skills. The *Partaabs'* we have at our disposal will help with this, and the one you will use in your meeting will be the key to unlocking the power within the chosen one. The other *Gooyeh Partaabs* have another purpose, I am sure of it."

The two adventurers soon come to a circular clearing deep within Echo Forest. Geoffrey spots something in the centre.

"Over there Elric, in the clearing, there is the portal!"

Geoffrey and Elric approach the edge of the clearing carefully, taking refuge within the foliage. In the centre is a red glowing ring standing tall enough to allow a large animal through. Elric taps his staff into the ground once more, and the Screamer's trail dissipates.

"We'll wait here, observe the ring. I want to know what they are up to. See – it looks like someone is about to come through," Elric taps his staff into the ground again, transforming both himself and Geoffrey into giant oak trees.

"I wish you'd warn me before you do that," Geoffrey hisses as leaves and branches sprout from his ears.

The ring of light glows brighter, the centre changing from a bright red to a light grey, darkening as it reaches the red outer ring. Suddenly a cloaked figure appears in the centre of the ring. Its hood is large, and the being's entire body is covered in a dark, heavy robe. It turns towards the portal, raises an arm and fires a small beam of light through it beckoning several Screamers; one by one they exit the portal until the eighth squeezes out.

"My Lord," calls out another Screamer, running toward the hooded figure from the forest, "It is done my Lord," the beast walks towards the new arrival, carrying a sack, which it hands to the hooded figure, "Here are the *items* our master requested."

"You have done well," the hooded figure acknowledges the lone Screamer's achievement with some glee, "And what of your brother, did he return?" he asks.

"He must mean the one we encountered," Elric whispers to Geoffrey.

"No my Lord, he ventured toward the Manor, I have not seen him since. I fear he became too foolish," says the Screamer who retrieved the sack.

"Indeed, he may have been more than foolish, he may have alerted them to our mission; perhaps ambition was a step too far in your evolution?" the hooded figure beckons to the other Screamers, "Come, gather, we must return before we are discovered, this portal will be useless shortly, we may have starved it, until we know the level of which we can travel, we should be careful."

The Screamers begin to head towards the portal when a large branch is flung into their path. They halt as they see two giant great oaks move towards them.

Elric and Geoffrey, still in their tree guises, rip through the soft ground towards the now perplexed Screamer pack. The hooded figure dives for cover. With their branches the two trees pummel the demons. Geoffrey has recently learnt the art of juggling, and decides to see how many Screamer demons he can keep in the air at any one time. Elric, on the other hand, is a little more direct and hammers the skulls of each Screamer demon that crosses his path. It is over in a matter of moments. The Screamers lie broken in a heap in front of the portal.

The hooded figure stands, "Not bad for a pair of inanimate objects. Show yourselves!"

Elric steps forward, "You are not welcome here, remove your hood, the forest does not invite strangers from realms unknown," he says, stubbornly sticking to his tree form.

The figure removes its hood to reveal a bald, human-like face; its eyes are a pure white, spoilt only by its red pupils strikingly matching the colour of its lashless eyelids. Its smooth, straight nose sniffs the air, its tiny slits opening and closing. It opens its mouth, stretching its slightly pocked and scarred face, "I am Lord Alvarez, servant to the Demon King. Your actions will anger him!"

"I think not," replies Elric, "We know only too well who you are. Your master knows the law, and he must follow it before he enters here. The rules apply to him and his minions. This portal is forbidden – and until your master has power over this realm, he cannot enter."

"This I know," Alvarez snipes with evil laughter "but who are you to stop us?"

Both Geoffrey and Elric transform back to their human forms.

Alvarez's demeanour changes to a worrying stance as he looks upon his foes.

"Leave this place Alvarez, while you still can – and the sack, as well. I think we'll be taking that, thank you," demands Elric.

Alvarez puts down the sack and slowly steps away from it, "You don't really want that, it's merely a few rocks and sticks, nothing to interest you at all," Alvarez creeps slowly back towards the sack, cowering, he reaches a hand towards it, trying his luck...

"Tut tut, I think not, *Lord* Alvarez," Elric taunts mockingly, stamping his staff into the ground forcing a shower of light to fire upwards, "I think *we* will be the judge of that. Now be gone with you!" he says, stamping his staff again. It shoots a beam of light at Alvarez, throwing him back into the air and through the portal with his screams fading through it.

Geoffrey approaches the portal and touches the outer ring. The colour changes from red to blue, and the vortex within closes in on itself with a fizz, a final blue flash, and a dance of light signalling that the portal is sealed, "Well, that was interesting, sending his number two with a light guard. And he didn't even put up a fight, but was eager to return home as quickly as possible. And what did he mean by 'starving' the portal?"

"Still asking questions Geoffrey? Well, for once, I don't have the answers; not all of them, at least, although I do have my suspicions," Elric replies before he picks up the sack "Maybe this will bring us something more concrete. We will need to monitor the forest for any more portals, but I doubt they will return here."

"I guess you want our little team to decipher this?" asks Geoffrey.

"It would be a good test old friend," replies Elric.

Elric walks over to some of the final pieces of broken branches and damaged foliage left after the fight and begins to heal them, "Come Geoffrey, apologise to the trees, we have much more to discuss, and *you* need to be ready for tomorrow," and with that, both Elric and Geoffrey disappear back to the Manor... after Geoffrey apologises to the trees, of course.

"Elric," says Geoffrey, "it's been another interesting night with your good self, but, I'm wondering if you felt it, too?"

"The presence?" responds Elric.

"Yes."

Elric turns towards his companion, "I did indeed; in fact, it, or, more importantly *he*, is still here," he holds a hand high in the air and snaps his fingers loudly. A flash of blue light appears and then...

# # #

BEEP... BEEP!!

Atticus wakes with a start, his bedcovers all over the place, dripping over the side of the bed towards the floor. He shakes his head to wake himself and wipes the sleep from his eyes, "Well, that was an interesting dream," he mutters to himself. He turns off his watch alarm and double-checks the time. Only a few minutes remain before he needs to leave for school, "But it felt so real."

He squints his eyes and puts on his glasses, still feeling tired. He knows he has a big day today, because one thing is definitely true from his overnight experience; his meeting with Professor Sprocking.

Chapter 3

The Problem with Bradley

Little Proudwater is a small town to the west of London. Forests and many lakes, with only a few main roads allowing escape to the capital, surround it. Some would say it is quite isolated for a town so close to the main city, others – mainly its inhabitants – think it isn't isolated enough. The isolation does have its benefits. The landscape is full of sweeping, unspoilt views with many hilltops. One hilltop in particular is very special. It sits overlooking the grounds of a regal, but ominous mansion.

Wysardian Manor stands tall, overpowering the horizon. The mansion, now used as a school for those with unique talents, is alive with activity. Silhouettes rush past windows, the grounds are filled with children playing, talking, running. The four towers encompass the school like rooks on a chessboard, their shadows observing the building like kings observing their lands. The leading wall contains an arch so tall it almost overshadows the four towers; in the centre of the structure is a statue of a giant sword and shield, as tall as the highest walls themselves.

The hillside behind the building is awash with a thousand shades of green and uneven slopes that all bow to Wysardian Manor. The only blemish is the arrival of a regular visitor.

Atticus sighs, knowing he will need to return to school before the bell sounds. It is a place where most of the other inhabitants appear not to welcome him, but also a place where he feels a connection, almost as if the building itself wants him there.

A bird settles a few feet in front of him, catching Atticus' attention, a robin red breast, picking at the ground. Atticus smiles, "At least you don't hate me," he whispers under his breath as the robin pecks at the ground once more before looking at Atticus; and then as quickly as it came, it flies away.

Atticus follows the robin's flight path, watching as it bobs in the air and then swoops down further up the hill. For a moment he wonders what it would be like to feel that sensation, the freedom of wings enabling him to fly through the air, cutting through clouds, and soaring into the deep blue sky.

Checking the time on his watch, Atticus begins to make his way down the hills towards the school. The main gates, represented by their tall, large iron bars, are the first things seen. They are embedded with circles in the middle of each. On one gate the circle contains the engraving of a griffin, and the other, what can only be described as the face of a dragon. The grounds empty quickly as Atticus walks through the main gates; students are rushing into the mansion as the bell begins to sound.

Atticus walks up a flight of steps that precede the main doors into the mansion, each tip-tap step echoing around the marble pillars that encircle the spiral stairs. As he reaches the top, he hears voices behind him; one in particular he knows all too well. Atticus runs to the main door, catching his school cloak on the door, tearing it slightly. He darts inside, spots the nearest pillar and waits silently behind it. The voices get closer, and Atticus breathes a quiet sigh of relief "Not today Bradley, not today."

Bradley Burrows is an old-fashioned school bully, stocky in stature, spiky crew cut hair, a little taller than the average 15-year old, and not the brightest in a not-so-bright group of likeminded individuals who relish each and every opportunity to make the lives of those around them utterly miserable. Their main target of the moment

28

appears to be Atticus.

"It's nice being in charge of this place," boasts Bradley to the others who nod in agreement, in awe of their 'leader', "the food everyone brings in is lovely," his minions laugh out loud at Bradley's comments, with the knowledge that if they didn't, they would be outcast from the group and become one of those they mock and hurt on a daily basis. They continue laughing as they disappear out of view.

Atticus cautiously steps out of his hiding place checks his timetable, and works out where he needs to be this period, "Maths, then ugh, P.E."

Physical Education is his least favourite subject. He loathes the teacher and the fact that he just isn't very good at sport − utterly hopeless, in fact − a point well-noted by his classmates. Atticus still remembers the bruises from last year's rugby sessions and tends to be the ball when playing football. There is one exception though. Fencing is the one sport that Atticus actually excels at, so much so that he is genuinely pleased to attend P.E. during athletics season. The fact that it also includes general swordplay is a huge bonus in Atticus' eyes, and those sessions are very much to his liking. He has also built a strong bond with the fencing tutor, Mr Callan.

Mr Callan has often given Atticus extra tutoring, which skips around the standard fencing practices, and includes lessons about movement and attack with a variety of sword types. Mr Callan has become not only a tutor but also a friend to Atticus, one of only a few he would regard in that manner.

As Atticus walks through the school to his math class, he soaks in the familiar architecture of the corridors on the way. Wysardian Manor is no normal school; it was commissioned by a private syndicate to coach and teach problem children, those that had a different outlook on life or garnered certain unique abilities. Its

29

publicity darkened somewhat after one journalist wrote about the institution teaching Para sciences, and dark arts. Unfortunately, more often than not, problem children were enrolled, rather than those with unique perspectives or abilities.

Atticus remembers his own school interview, a panel of eight judges, each firing questions at him in an indiscriminate manner. The questions were rather odd, Atticus thought at the time. They asked about Para-dimensions and mythical creatures, things an average 11 year-old boy would never really have a formed opinion on, but Atticus was no average 11 year-old when he was first interviewed. It was he who instigated the application to Wysardian Manor. Atticus remembers the very day the prospectus was delivered to his door, wrapped in what could only be described as charred feathers hammered into some form of papyrus with his name stamped onto a rectangular leather fastener.

He recalls the judges who were asking questions, but also remembers another, who stood further away in the shadows. Atticus remembers some of the judges showing an odd twitch at some of his answers, some were excited, and others glanced backwards towards the man in the shadows in a manner that was somewhat portentous.

His life at the school since has been somewhat normal by comparison; now 15, Atticus is busy thinking about what the school calls Para-class Qualification exams, a non-standard certification which contains a syllabus only those that qualify are able to see, and are forbidden to disclose its contents to anyone. Even the PQ exams themselves are only offered to a select few, and they are also sworn to secrecy. Atticus received his invite through the post in the same manner the prospectus was delivered to him. It contained a handwritten letter in the form of rolled parchment:

Atticus Jones

You have been cordially invited to take part in the honour that is the PQE (Para-class Qualification Exam). Sharing knowledge of this invitation is strictly forbidden. On Tuesday the 12th of September at 2pm, you have an appointment with Professor Sprocking, he will instruct you on the literature you need to be familiar with for these examinations. Should you qualify, you will be given a new syllabus to study. Only a select few are chosen for this honour, and your studious nature along with your performance at your panel induction impressed us enough to bestow this honour on you.

Should you disclose knowledge of the PQE or this invitation to anyone, you will be expelled and barred from entering the premises of Wysardian Manor forever.

Yours Sincerely

Elric Griffin

Apart from his strange dream last night, Atticus only heard the name Elric Griffin once before, during a conversation between two senior Professors when one quietly whispered his name and Atticus in the same sentence, while he was unknowingly in ear shot. One of the professors was Professor Sprocking.

All attempts at trying to source more information of Elric Griffin were thwarted in the most unusual manner. One search on the Internet came up with the scrambled words 'Prukulia gringlegott praa praa,' a search on that took him to an interesting site with instructions on how to make a prune like juice from apples. Another search in the library, in the book of *'Who's Who?',* revealed the name 'Blueberry Baboons Bottom,' with a description of bright blue baboons with bottoms that look like blueberries, right where the entry for Elric

Griffin should have been.

Atticus even approached one of the junior professors once to ask whom Elric Griffin was, and was promptly surprised when he was given detention for calling the professor a 'girly-faced spotty slug.' At that point Atticus decided to give up on trying to find out who Elric Griffin was, and resigned himself to probably never finding out – that is, until the invitation to the PQE arrived.

His latest dreams have also thrown more questions into the air. They seem more real each time, and last night's episode, with him watching through the eyes of a spider, was probably the strangest one. Well, it was until he remembered later that same night when he was dreaming about trees fighting demon-doggies.

Today is the 11th of September, and Atticus is looking forward to finding out what exactly the PQE will entail.

"You're *late* again Jones!" a voice suddenly bellows through the corridors.

Professor Morgan, Atticus' math teacher, a portly fellow with round glasses and a thin beard around his chin and cheeks.

"Sorry sir," says Atticus apologetically, trying to think of an excuse.

"Stop jabbering and get into the classroom!" says the Professor.

Atticus goes in and quickly grabs a chair at the back of the class.

"Right," says the Professor as he closes the door, "Turn to page 154, chapter 12. Today we are going to learn about balancing complex equations in relation to mechanics."

The class look around a little perplexed, apart from Atticus, math being one of his strongest subjects, along with Chemistry, he had already prepared for the class and sat attentively, soaking in every word that Professor Morgan was saying.

By the end of the lesson the rest of the students are eager to escape Professor Morgan's clutches and rush to the next class.

"OK class," says Professor Morgan, "homework for tomorrow is to complete the exercises in this chapter, and read the next so you actually *understand* what I'm talking about next time. Dismissed!"

The students quickly get up and begin to rush out.

Professor Morgan waits for most of the class to leave before looking at Atticus, "Except you, Jones. I need to have a word with you."

Atticus doesn't mind too much as his next lesson is P.E., and apart from his occasional lack of punctuality, Atticus enjoys a pleasant relationship with Professor Morgan. Although stern and authoritative, Professor Morgan is always fair in his judgement.

"I hear you have an appointment with Professor Sprocking tomorrow?" asks the professor.

Atticus looks a little confused, wondering if he should acknowledge the question after what is written in the invitation; maybe this is a test of some sort?

"Don't worry Mr Jones, I know all about the PQE's; in fact, I've studied for them myself," says the Professor.

Atticus breathes a sigh of relief and nods at Professor Morgan who continues.

"Good, well, I would just like to say that whatever happens in your meeting tomorrow with Professor Sprocking, you *must* remember to keep it a secret. There are many things in this world that are hidden from those that are not lucky enough to see it all, and the ones that are unable to see or understand these things... are not meant to."

A confused look returns to Atticus Jones's face, his eyebrows have literally rolled up into a ball at this point.

The professor spots the scrunching of eyebrows and tries to reassure him, "Don't worry Jones, all will be revealed tomorrow. In the meantime, I've taken it upon myself to give you these."

The Professor reaches under his desk. He pulls out a medium-sized rucksack and hands it to Atticus.

"What are these, Sir?" asks Atticus.

The professor chuckles, "Have a read of these tonight; they may very well become useful in the future," he gestures to the door, indicating that it is time for Atticus to leave for his next lesson.

As Atticus makes his way out of the classroom, the Professor says one last thing, "If you are successful tomorrow Jones, I have even *more* interesting things for you than what is in that bag. Good day."

And with that, Atticus gives an appreciative nod before running to his next class while trying to put his newly acquired rucksack into his oversized school bag.

On his way to P.E., Atticus decides to stop off at the bathroom to freshen up. Recent nights have been rather difficult, with the strange dreams and nightmares haunting him during his sleep, and although he doesn't remember waking up, he feels like he has hardly slept when the alarm sounds.

Rinsing his face he peers into the mirror. Atticus is a rather handsome young man, but more than often, doesn't really pay much attention to his appearance. His jet-black hair is particularly scruffy this day with a few strands sticking up from his left parting.

His ovular face sports some mild freckles, concentrated around his slightly undersized nose. Atticus also has an interesting shade of colour for his eyes, almost hazel, but rather light, hidden by a pair of lightly-tinted rectangular glasses, which Atticus proceeds to put back on. With one last sigh, he turns and leaves the bathroom to make his way to class.

Arriving at the changing rooms for P.E., Atticus finds that everybody else has almost finished changing. Athletics season isn't too far away, and Atticus hopes to make the fencing team again; unfortunately, fencing is not on the menu in today's session. Atticus' face turns white as he sees Mr Bronson bring out the rugby balls.

"Today, I'm going to turn you scrawny mongrels into men! We will walk onto that field, and run our little socks off, then, you will all take a partner, and a ball, and show me what a rugby tackle should be like!"

Mr Bronson is a very large but muscular young man with spiky hair, and a physique almost built for the sport he now loves. He has a taste for the theatrical. He is a passionate sportsman, and ever since England won the Rugby World Cup, he has had a fascination with the sport that just won't go away, no matter how long ago that win was. Even at the last school open evening he was found wearing a tight rugby kit, flexing his chest muscles at any of the single ladies that attended.

"Jones, you're late!!" bellows Mr Bronson.

"Sorry sir, but Professor Morgan kept me behind," Atticus replies quickly.

"Professor Morgan, eh? Hmmm, very well, get changed and we'll meet you outside, no fake sickness today, alright?" Mr Bronson eyes Atticus up and down with a raised eyebrow, knowing all too well how much Atticus hates rugby.

"Come on lads, on the field now, sharpish!" he says as he marches out like a general, not looking back, holding the expectation that everyone will follow him – and due to the presence of the man, everyone does.

It is a good five minutes before Atticus manages to exit the changing rooms and onto the playing fields. The fields themselves are large, surrounded by massive hedgerows. There are three rugby pitches in total, and two football pitches. The main rugby pitch is on an elevated section with the edges banking down onto the main part of the field. To the left of the changing rooms are the outdoor netball and basketball courts, and to the right, the indoor sports arena.

The grounds themselves certainly look larger from the outside, as Atticus remembers from where he was sitting this morning. The hedgerows in particular seem a lot closer than they appear from the hilltops; they tower over the borders of the field and are so dense that it is impossible to see through them. Another strange thing about the hedgerows is that they stay this way all the way through the year, and never shed a leaf over autumn and winter.

Atticus spots his classmates on the main rugby pitch and proceeds to run towards them. Out of nowhere he begins to feel his birthmark tingle.

"Atticussssssss…!" whispers a sinister voice.

Atticus stops in his tracks, as he hears this chilling whisper calling his name.

"Atticusssssssssssss…"

Atticus spins around expecting to see someone behind him, but no one is there.

"I can sssseeee yoouuuu…" the voice says again, startling Atticus who is now as white as a sheet.

He begins to hear roars from giant animals, and what sounds like ten thousand men marching on his very soul. Atticus' heart begins to pound. He can feel a pressure on his neck, as if someone is strangling him from behind. The pain is unbearable, but he can't scream. His mouth opens but the stranglehold is so tight he can't find the air to make any noise. He can feel the pressure of someone trying to push him to the ground, and heat from an unknown source burning against his skin.

Atticus is pushed to his knees, the burning and the pressure on his neck so great now, he can hardly breathe. His eyes begin to water and his vision is blurring. In the distance he can just about make out Mr Bronson, but it is no good, he can't speak. Atticus tries with all his might, all his will to try and break free, but is unable. Whoever, whatever has hold of him is just too strong. Things begin to get dark. Atticus starts to feel his legs and arms give way, he sees a light in the distance of the darkness…

"Atticus!!!" shouts Mr Bronson, "Come on lad, it's not that bloody cold now!" the voices and stranglehold disappear in a whoosh of sound.

Atticus gasps for air as he steadies himself, squinting his eyes, trying to make sense of what just happened. He experienced something similar just the other night in his nightmares, but this was far more intense, and more importantly, this time he was awake when it happened.

Scared, he looks around him once again, he touches his neck, expecting to find scabs from the burning, but there is nothing, the skin is smooth.

He stands up and again, surprisingly, feels no after-effects. Confused, Atticus looks up the field, and spots Mr Bronson beckoning him to hurry up.

"Could I have been dreaming while awake?" Atticus thinks to himself, a recurrence of what he is experiencing during all these sleepless nights? It is the only explanation that sounds plausible to him, and with no pain, and now feeling almost 100% again; he decides that it must have been just that, a waking dream.

Although worried, he is more fearful of what Mr Bronson will do to him if he doesn't make his way to the rugby lesson as opposed to what he thinks is just a strange dream.

Still a little dazed from his experience Atticus struggles to make it up the bank to the rugby pitch, it feels like the tip is 50ft in the air by the time he nears the top. He isn't too pleased when he gets there.

Everybody is standing with their partner for this Rugby session, everyone except Bradley.

Bradley smirks at Atticus, and has an evil but happy glint in his eye. Atticus reluctantly walks towards him.

"'Ello Jones," greets Bradley with a grunt, and a sidelong glance at his minions gives the feeling to Atticus that this was all planned.

Bradley stands a few inches taller than everyone else, including Atticus. His crew cut straight hair adding a further few inches, "You ready for some fun then, shorty?"

Atticus just sighs because he knows what is coming. He adjusts his glasses and turns towards Mr Bronson; as he does so, everybody else stands to attention and waits for their orders.

"Good, good, all strapping young lads," says Mr Bronson. It is a credit to his ability that the entire class is in good shape, even though Atticus hates P.E. he always joins in the activities, his motivation is that being fit here would keep him in good shape for his fencing classes, and ensure he is quick enough to run away from Bradley when needed.

Mr Bronson addresses the class, "Today, I want you to do two laps of the rugby pitch, passing the ball between your self and your partner. Remember, *no soft passes*! I want them to be quick, and accurate, if I see anyone performing an illegal forward pass, they will have to do ten push ups on the spot, and take their partner on a piggyback ride for another two laps! Understood?"

The students nod.

"Well what are you waiting for? Hut! Hut! Move it! Move it!

Move it!" bellows Mr Bronson.

The class quickly begins their laps of the pitch.

"You better keep up Jones," snarls Bradley

"Don't worry, I will, I just hope you can," retorts Atticus, slightly smugly as he starts his run. He knows he can certainly outrun and outmanoeuvre Bradley; it's just his sheer brawn he cannot match.

Bradley passes the ball to Atticus first who then runs in front to return the pass. This goes on for one lap without incident. Atticus is still thinking about the waking dream he just experienced. How can something in his mind feel so real? And surely, once one feels pain in a dream do they not wake up straight-away?

All of these thoughts are racing through his mind when, as he is distracted, Bradley throws the ball with such a force that it knocks Atticus down the bank. Halfway down, Atticus manages to get back onto his feet, ball in hand, and somehow, without thinking it, is upright, with his football boot studs digging into the mud slowing his descent to a standstill.

Atticus can hear Bradley laughing at the top. Bradley walks to the edge expecting to see Atticus in a heap on the ground, instead, he is shocked to see Atticus standing firm, holding the ball midway down the incline.

A few wolf whistles emanate from the netball courts. The netball team are out on practice and saw everything; they seem to be quite impressed with Atticus' acrobatics. The girls at the school mostly hate Bradley, as he displays a level of chauvinism that even a caveman would envy.

Upset, Bradley turns around in anger and walks straight into Mr Bronson, who, unbeknown to him, has seen everything.

"Having fun Mr Burrows?" asks Mr Bronson.

"No sir, ju... just saw Jones fall, sir," replies Bradley.

Mr Bronson, fully aware that Bradley is lying, gives him a stern look, "Oh really? And I suppose the torpedo that you threw at Jones's head had nothing to do with that?"

"Well, erm, I, erm, don't know, sir," replies Bradley, trying to avoid eye contact.

"Hmmm, I'm sure; this is Rugby, not bloody American Football!" replies the teacher, "Right, Jones, come here!"

Atticus runs up the bank and stands next to Mr Bronson.

"Burrows, 30 push ups now, and after you have finished that, I want you to give Jones a piggy back ride for two laps, if I see you stop or slow down I'll give you so much detention you won't know what daylight looks like until you are 40… years… old! Understood?" commands Mr Bronson.

"Y-yes, sir," whimpers Bradley.

"I can't hear you boy! *I said, understood?*" snaps Mr Bronson, sending a chill through Bradley.

"Yes, sir!"

Mr Bronson, pleased with his latest show of authority smiles with delight, "Good, good, I'll be watching you from over there. Chop–chop! Get started!"

Bradley drops to the ground to begin his push-ups.

"By the way, Jones," mutters Mr Bronson, "That was a good recovery from that fall, I'm impressed. The girls seemed to enjoy it, too," he finishes by pointing towards the netball court, where the girls quickly spin round after realising they have been caught looking on.

Atticus smiles, and nods towards Mr Bronson before turning his gaze towards Bradley. Finishing off the push-ups in double-quick time, he hoists Atticus onto his back with ease, and proceeds to complete his task.

Atticus is rather smug at this point, it isn't every day he gets the better of Bradley − or indeed, gets a compliment from Mr Bronson − this particular moment is one to savour.

"Enjoying this Jones?" snorts Bradley.

"A little," replies Atticus, smiling.

"You'll need all the enjoyment you can get right now, you little git. I'm going to get you for this!" threatens the bully.

"You'll still have to catch me first Bradley," replies Atticus.

The rest of the P.E. session ends without incident.

Atticus quickly showers and changes, knowing full well that he needs to get out of the sporting grounds before Bradley and his minions are ready. He runs into the main cafeteria hall, as it is almost time for lunch.

He sits on a table by himself as usual, and pulls out his lunch box, "Yeuch! Boiled egg and mayo sandwiches again," he says with a grimace. His foster mother, although very loving, really didn't have a clue about making a good sandwich. Sometimes Atticus is almost glad when Bradley stops to take his lunch box. Today, though, he knows that Bradley is after more than just a free lunch.

As Atticus eats away, he looks around the hall. It seems a bit small for the number of students that supposedly attend Wysardian Manor. It is a little more modern than the rest of the building; apparently it was renovated just before Atticus joined, and wasn't part of the main building.

The cafeteria begins to fill quickly, with hordes of students all entering in unison. Atticus ignores the rush, concentrating on trying to digest his sandwiches and thinking about the 'dream' he had during rugby. He wonders whom he could talk to about it, but he doesn't trust anyone enough. The first person he tells may very well toss him into the funny farm, and he can imagine Bradley being there with his big boot kicking him into the white van. He thinks he may be able to approach Mr Morgan, but with such a good, credible relationship built up there, one of few, he dreads the thought of that deteriorating.

"Hello, Atticus," a soft voice speaks next to him as he eats.

His heart races a little faster, he knows this voice all too well, the slight Australian accent and softness tells him exactly who it is.

"Joyce?" says Atticus.

"Yup, that's my name, do you mind if I sit?" replies Joyce.

Startled, Atticus nods his head, but try as he might, he can't stop his cheeks going slightly red.

Joyce is an Australian-born girl whose mother is originally from a remote island off the coast of China. Joyce stands a little shorter than Atticus, and her features are unique, exotic, with long, fine, straight hair, and completely jet-black.

Atticus knows a lot about Joyce already. She studied in Iran in her early years; her parents are known to be great travellers and explorers. Joyce travelled with them all over the world, but this is the first time she's ever journeyed towards Atticus.

"I saw you today, after Bradley threw the ball at you, very acrobatic," she says.

"Erm, thanks," replies Atticus "You were on the netball court?"

"Yes, for some reason, Miss Stevens likes to schedule netball practice alongside Mr Bronson's P.E. classes," both Atticus and Joyce laugh, "That's nice," she comments.

"What?" asks Atticus, puzzled.

"You smiling for once. You always walk around with this blank, expressionless face all the time," replies Joyce.

"Oh, I'm sorry, I haven't been sleeping too well recently," says Atticus, trying to make an excuse.

"Nightmares?" asks Joyce.

Atticus nods, and he can feel his heartbeat slow back down to a normal pace; he is surprised that Joyce is so easy to talk to. For years he dreaded even the thought of talking to her for risk of making a complete and utter fool of himself.

"I used to get nightmares when I first started here, something about this place is, well, different," says Joyce.

"I know what you mean, I've had some, uhm, *interesting* experiences recently," Atticus replies.

"Really Atticus? Well, let's just say, things may very well get even *more* interesting," says Joyce, almost with a tone implying that she knows exactly what Atticus is going through.

"What do…"Atticus tries to ask what Joyce means by this, but she cuts him off before he can finish his sentence.

"Sorry Atticus, I have to go now. Keep smiling, I like it," she says, and then leaves before Atticus can even think of something to say in return.

Atticus is rather pleased with himself, this day has treated him rather well so far, strange strangulation experiences notwithstanding, and with a big smile on his face, he makes his way towards his chemistry lesson.

Chemistry is another of Atticus' favourite subjects. He enjoys what he learns, if not the way he learns it. Professor Snugglebottom is head of Chemistry at Wysardian Manor, and he has interesting methods of teaching, preferring to drown his class in theory rather than allowing them many opportunities for hands-on, practical application of those theories. Atticus relishes the practical lessons, but unfortunately this is a theory day, and a particularly boring one at that.

A yawn and a snore from the back of the room catch the Professor's attention. One can see Professor Snugglebottom's right ear twitch beneath his long, frizzy, light brown hair, his teapot-like frame

43

turns slowly, and with his eyes scanning the class like a radar, he locates the source of the snore. With pinpoint accuracy he flings a small piece of chalk in the direction of the offending pupil. With a snort Colin Hayes wakes up, blurry-eyed and rubbing the top of his head. The class laughs as a piece of paper has stuck itself to Colin's mouth.

"Get that off your face and concentrate, boy!" Professor Snugglebottom snorts, a little red-faced himself. One thing that infuriates him is a pupil falling asleep in his class. Today's lesson is incredibly tedious, and during the 2nd hour even Atticus' mind begins to wander.

Trying really hard to focus on the blackboard, Atticus begins to squint, trying to fight off the dreaded doze, knowing full well that he is in perfect range of the professor.

Nevertheless, his eyes begin to feel heavier, and heavier. All of a sudden, he sees a strange mist begin to pour out of Professor Snugglebottom's trousers, out of his pockets, and even his shirt sleeves. The mist fills the room, and soon becomes incredibly dense.

"Atticus..." He hears another whisper, but this one isn't chilling or threatening, more comforting.

"Atticus, over here," says the voice as the strange mist fills the classroom.

Atticus turns to his left, and sees a tall figure of a man, standing in the darkness, wearing a deerstalker hat that only Sherlock Holmes could get away with.

The lighting in the class has mysteriously disappeared, and all that remains are the shadows of his fellow pupils. Atticus can see the silhouette but no defining features of this figure. The rest of the class are still active, but Atticus can only make them out as an embellishment of the shadow.

"Yes?" Atticus questions tentatively.

"Good, you can see and hear me, this form is difficult to maintain," the silhouette continues to whisper, gasping for breath after each sentence, "It's time, Atticus."

"Time for what?" asks Atticus.

"You will find out soon enough, but for now, you need to be careful," replies the shadow.

"Who are you?" quizzes Atticus

"Heed my warning: there are those who wish to do you harm, and those that wish to protect you. Use your judgment; use your heart and your mind to determine what is right and wrong. The ones that will try to deceive you won't stop there… you MUST be mindful of your surroundings. I'll be seeing you soon," says the shadow.

"But who are you? How can I trust… you?" asks Atticus, desperate for answers.

The silhouette does not speak, it merely sticks out a finger and taps Atticus on the top of his head, hard!

Atticus flinches.

Another impact is felt!

"Ouch!" Atticus wakes with a start, rubbing the top of his head. Looking down, he spots two pieces of chalk next to his open book, and as he gazes up, he spots Professor Snugglebottom doing a perfect impression of a tomato.

"Sleep again, Jones, and it will be more than chalk you will be shaking from your head!" says the now very angry Professor, against an orchestra of muffled giggles.

Needless to say, Atticus is wide-awake for the rest of the class.

Chapter 4

Loss

Joseph Jones is tending to his garden, a passion of his for many years. He stands as he admires his rose bushes and tulips on one side, and a row of daffodils on the other. He walks through the garden upon the central path to the end, where he sits on his newly constructed rockery. He has just finished shaping the edges to form a curve at the end closest to the house.

The sun is shining brightly in the sky, he can tell from the shadow on the sundial in the middle of the garden that it is almost 3.30pm.

"Atticus will be home soon, better get the food ready," he mutters to himself.

Joseph loves to cook, but that ability was borne out of a need to consume something edible or starve. Although he loves his wife dearly, Sophia is probably the worst cook on the planet, he cringes each morning as he watches her prepare Atticus' sandwiches for school and admires Atticus for actually coming home with an empty lunchbox each day.

Joseph is a tall man, very well built, chunkily handsome, with strawberry-blond hair, a slightly chiselled chin, and holds an aura of presence that not many men can command. It was this presence – and the chiselled chin – that first attracted Sophia, along with his general coyness, and the fact that Joseph knows not of the presence he commands in front of others sealed that attraction.

Joseph can hear Sophia rummaging upstairs. Both Joseph and Sophia run a rather successful Internet business importing and exporting Pashmina shawls, and more often than not, the house is littered with new designs and materials. Today is a tidy day though, and the tip-tapping alongside the delving informs Joseph that Sophia is busy ordering the next shipment.

The home is a large detached house, not mansion-like by any means, but sizeable enough to accommodate the family of three rather comfortably, and secluded enough to allow for lots of welcome privacy. There are five large bedrooms scattered along the landing, and three bathrooms, two of which are en-suite. One of the bedrooms is used as a storeroom, with piles and piles of boxes filled with colourful shawls, some multi coloured, some differing shades of the same colour.

Sophia and Joseph originally bought the house in anticipation of starting a family of their own, but as the result of peculiar and unfortunate circumstances 15½ years ago, they are unable to conceive. Joseph often has flashbacks to the incident; poor Sophia can hardly recall the events that led to the accident.

Joseph allows the memories to come back again.

# # #

It was a dark misty November evening; Joseph and Sophia had enjoyed a night out at a theatre in London and were making their way home. Sophia was looking radiant; her deep black hair glistened as the lights on the road passed by. At each set of red lights, Joseph watched as she slept, he felt blessed that he had found someone so beautiful, both inside and out.

He watched as her cheeks glowed red, trying to warm her face in the cold. He remembered the joy of when Sophia had told him they were about to have a baby, while the lights were still red he reached over and gently touched the large bump on her stomach while she was still sleeping, hoping to feel a kick or some form of movement.

They met many years previous in university. From the first day Joseph knew they would be together forever. The first time he felt whole was when Sophia said hello, he remembered the way his heart went silent and all he could hear was her voice…

BEEP!!!

A car horn sounded from behind them, Joseph didn't notice the lights had turned green. He slowly moved off and headed towards the country road that lead to their home. The road was dark and narrow, with trees bending over them forming a tunnel of branches and twigs. While Joseph drove, his mind returned to the early years of him meeting Sophia, the courage he had summed up to ask her on a date for the first time he still, up to that day, believed to be his greatest moment. He had managed to find her alone, walking out of the library, and as he walked up to her, every step seemed heavier than the last, his heart began to beat fast, hard, slow down, then beat fast again, he could feel himself about to choke, his hands began to sweat and he was so close to turning back, but he didn't. Everything around him began to speed up into a blur, everything apart from his quest.

"Sophia?" said Joseph, softly as he stepped just behind her.

Sophia turned to face Joseph, her smile radiant, her eyes glinting as the light in the hall caught them for a moment, "Hi, Joseph, how are you?"

"F-f-fine Sophia, how are you?" replied Joseph.

"Tired. End of semester exams are coming up, and there is just too much to do," Sophia said. But she noticed Joseph looked a little disappointed, and sensed a question which she had also been waiting for begin to turn around and run away… "I really need a break from the studying," she added quickly. The last words reignited the flame within Joseph.

"Sophia, I was, uhm, wondering, what are you doing tomorrow night?" he asked.

"Well, I was hoping for someone to take me out," Sophia replied, feeling this was the strongest hint she could give to her would-be suitor

"Really? Well, what if, someone like, erm, me... asked?" said Joseph

Sophia smiled, "Then I would graciously accept the invitation, Mr Jones."

A swell of courage flowed through Joseph; he knew that was more than just a hint, "In that case... would you like to go to dinner tomorrow night?"

"Took you long enough, JJ," replied Sophia, then she slowly stepped towards Joseph, moved her head forward, and kissed him softly on his right cheek.

After a moment that seemed like hours, Joseph leant back and softly said, "Erm, I take it that's a 'yes' then?" with a rather large grin on his face.

Sophia nods coyly, "That is a 'yes'."

Joseph shook his head, trying to revert his attention back to the road, the fog was becoming very thick, and visibility was low. The road straightened, and the trees overhead cleared for a moment – what happened next still haunts him.

The fog seemed to move, it swirled around, and sucked itself into a form of a whirlpool with a large opening in the centre, pointing upside down so the fog was sucked upwards. The opening became larger. Suddenly a massive flash of light appeared, and a crack of thunder so loud that the windows of the car shattered, and a wave of energy consumed the car, sending it into a spin. It flipped over three times. All Joseph could think of was Sophia, he tried to hold onto her, but the force of the car spinning ripped her from the seat.

The shattered glass sliced the belt holding her in place, the shards were that sharp to the touch. He grabbed her, shouted her name, but she wasn't awake. He felt her stomach, and tried desperately to find some form of movement, but felt nothing.

The car was pushed again by another wave of energy and flipped with an even greater force. The door was blasted off and Sophia was thrown from the car. Joseph grabbed her hand to try and stop her from flying from the confines of the car, but he had no grip – she was bleeding, the blood had covered her arms, and she slipped from his grasp. All he could think was to get to her, and without a care for his own safety, he undid his belt, and was thrown from the opposite side of the car. He landed with a thud. Dazed he slowly rose to his feet, but promptly fell back down again. He felt a pain in his leg, as he strained to look around for Sophia he saw a large chunk of metal had pierced his calf, the pain almost overcame him when suddenly, all around him was calm.

The fog consumed the sky again, the thunder stopped and the funnel of wind had gone. Joseph glanced the horizon of the roadside, searching for Sophia. He desperately tried to focus through the fog, gasping, trying to find air to call her name, "SOPHIAAAA!" he screamed. Achingly he waited for her to reply, needing a sign from her that she was ok, but there was no response. The air was still, nothing stirred.

With a mighty effort Joseph pulled the metal shard from his calf, screaming in agony. He threw the shard into the bush, tore his shirt, and quickly bandaged his leg. He then rose to his feet again, and desperately limped across the road, screaming Sophia's name again and again as his wound left a trail of red on the ground. The fog lifted slightly, then he saw her, lying on her side facing away from him, her body was still. He moved towards her as fast as he could, drowning out the pain from his mind with his will to reach his wife. He couldn't lose her, he felt she was slipping away, and was cursing himself for not being able to hold onto her, for not being able to save her from injury. All he could remember at that time was the blood on her arm – where was she hurt? He remembered the glass, it didn't crumble as it should, instead, the shattered glass turned into spears. He agonized over what may have happened, but held on to hope that she was ok.

He finally reached her and collapsed to his knees. Joseph leant over her limp body, "Sophia," he whispered into her ear as he searched her body for injuries. He turned her slightly and stopped.

Joseph was horrified with what he saw, and screamed out in pain, not from any physical injury, but an emotional one so great that any man would have fallen from its blow. Tears fell from his eyes, he held Sophia's head to his chest, "Nooooo, why?" he cried out "Why?"

He was so overcome with grief that he didn't hear another car screech to a halt just behind him.

The lone driver ran towards Joseph, "Everybody ok?" he glanced over to Sophia, saw her blood-stained arms and stomach, and Joseph's bleeding leg, "Don't worry, I have a car phone, I'll call an ambulance. Is there anyone else in the car?"

Joseph shook his head. The driver ran to his car and promptly called an ambulance. Joseph was busily searching for any sign of life from Sophia. His heart was beating so fast.

"You can't leave me," he whispered into her ear. A large lump formed in his throat, he couldn't find the time to breathe, he felt choked and his head was throbbing with the pain of losing his dearest love. He felt for a pulse, but could not feel anything. As it began to rain, the

51

pitter-patter of the raindrops gave him hope, for in time with the raindrops he caught the faintest of something – a heartbeat! He clung onto this hope and clutched Sophia in his arms.

The ambulance arrived within minutes, and only then was it revealed to the rescuers the true horror of what had happened. Sophia was barely alive, but she was alive, nonetheless. As the paramedics lifted Joseph away, they saw why Joseph was grief-stricken. One of the spears of glass had found its way into Sophia's stomach. The Paramedics dared not remove the glass in fear that they may do more harm than good, and rushed both Joseph and Sophia to the hospital.

Joseph awoke in the hospital a few days later, the doctors told him of how Sophia had survived and was in a stable condition, she was recovering nicely.

He remembered them telling him about the baby. The glass that speared Sophia's stomach went straight through to its poor heart, the baby died instantly, but probably saved Sophia's life. The glass had snapped into several other pieces, and caused a great deal of internal damage, there was no chance of this being repaired or healed, from that day, it would be impossible for her to bear a child. At this, Joseph asked if he could see Sophia, and even though she was still unconscious he demanded to see her.

He stayed with her until she finally woke up a day or two later. She knew what had happened before Joseph uttered a word. Nothing needed to be said, their tears told their own story. They held each other, and if anything, felt an even greater bond than ever before.

# # #

The beep of the oven timer gladly wakes Joseph from his daydream and drags him back into the present. He removes the chicken steaks and applies a special sauce he had prepared earlier. Atticus arrives on cue just as Joseph finishes the salad to go with the chicken.

"Hi dad, where's mum?"

"Upstairs son, why don't you get yourself changed and come down for food, tell your mum everything is ready, she's in the office ordering the next shipment from our suppliers."

Joseph watches as Atticus heads upstairs. Praising what he has now as being so so special.

Chapter 5

Gain

Sophia is just finishing up her paperwork when she hears a knock at the door.

"Come in," she says softly.

"Hi Mum, Dad says food is ready," says Atticus.

"Wonderful," replies Sophia, "How are you sweetie? Good day at school?"

"Yeah, wasn't too bad," Atticus says tentatively.

"I'll be down shortly, just have to email this order off and shut down the computer," says Sophia

Atticus nods and walks downstairs.

Sophia quickly finishes off her email and begins to shut down the PC. She looks around the room for her own shawl, as she gazes across the desk she spots a framed baby picture of Atticus. She recalls the night when they found him, in almost as strange a circumstance as the cause of the accident.

# # #

Sophia and Joseph were at the docks preparing to receive a very large shipment of shawls, it was a night they both wished they did not need to be there. Marcellus was also there. Marcellus was the lone driver who helped Joseph and Sophia at the accident site, and had been close to them ever since. Joseph felt indebted towards Marcellus; if it wasn't for his presence and speed of action, Sophia may well have died that fateful night. Both Sophia and Joseph now see him as their own personal guardian angel.

It was six months after the accident, the rain was pouring down, and cracks of lightning lit the night sky as the wind buffeted the rather oversized umbrella that Joseph was clinging onto. Sophia was holding Joseph tightly.

"Again, tell me why we had to be here today, JJ?"

"I have no idea, the customs guard called and told me we needed to be here to accept this particular delivery – something about clearing the goods and paying the charge in person, as their systems are down," replied Joseph.

"Stupid computers, they could have chosen a sunny day to break down," snorted Sophia

They waited for the last crate to be unloaded; the customs officer had just finished the paperwork in the office and handed it to Joseph to sign.

Sophia and Marcellus went to the van to begin loading the shipment.

Suddenly out of nowhere, first one flash of lightning and then another struck the warehouse behind them. Joseph and the customs officer ran outside.

From inside the warehouse, a baby's cry was heard. Puzzled, all four of them looked at each other, then rather gingerly entered the warehouse. They peeked through the dim light, trying to follow the cries, and moved cautiously toward the centre of the large room where they found a huge crater with smoke still emanating from within it.

They cautiously walked towards the centre of the basin, and to their astonishment, at the heart of it was a baby in a chocolate-brown straw basket, on the front of the basket was an engraved metallic emblem, with the name '*Atticus*'. The baby had one arm exposed, and on the left forearm there was a small birthmark, a circle surrounded by a spiral. A note was sitting beside little Atticus, but the calligraphy in it was not understood by any member of the quartet. Joseph handed the note to Marcellus who put it in his inside jacket pocket. In the excitement, they had all forgotten about it by the time the police arrived.

After the accident, Joseph and Sophia had registered to be eligible for both adoption and fostering; with some help from Marcellus, the relevant agencies agreed for it to be suitable for Joseph and Sophia to foster the child, and from that day, they brought Atticus up as their own.

# # #

Sophia makes her way downstairs and enters the dining room. Atticus and Joseph have already started to eat. Sophia takes her place next to Joseph and proceeds to put her food in her plate.

"Have you told him yet?" asks Sophia, her question directed towards Joseph.

"Told me what?" responds Atticus.

"No, not yet, Sophia. I was waiting for you to come down so we can deliver the news together," replies Joseph.

"What news?" asks Atticus, a little curious at his foster parents' secrecy.

"Well, Atticus," answers Joseph, "As you know, your mother and I have been trying to get the adoption finalised. Today the agency sent us the confirmation letter and certificate, so as of today, we are not only your parents in our hearts, but legally as well."

Atticus beams, ecstatic at this news. He knows it won't change how he feels about his parents, but he also knows how long they have fought to earn this status, and to be called 'parents' rather than 'guardians' means the world to them. Perhaps now, the loss of their child can be brought one step closer to closure.

Sophia stands first and walks over to Atticus, closely followed by Joseph. They both hug him tightly, and Atticus hugs back, they become a family all over again.

# # #

The Jones's converse jovially over their dinner; savouring every moment of it. When they finally finish, Atticus helps Sophia load the dishwasher before heading upstairs to his room. He has a lot of reading to do and is eager to prepare for his PQE interview with Professor Sprocking tomorrow. It then hits him, how is he supposed to prepare? He knows nothing of what is expected, the only clue he has is the old rucksack that Professor Morgan handed to him after class.

His room is typical of a teenage boy. His PC hums on a small workstation in the corner, a few shelves with CD's and books litter the walls, accompanied by several posters – one of his favourite football team, Aston Villa, proudly takes centre stage on the ceiling.

Sitting on his bed, which resides in the centre of the rear wall, he reaches for his bag and pulls out the rucksack. Cautiously he unzips it and pulls out three books; the first is entitled *The Myth of the Minotaur*, the second *Dark Realms Discovered?* and the third, *A Majjai History: Vol 1*.

All three are plain in appearance. The titles are embossed at the top of the cover, and a circular emblem in the centre, the emblem

contains the letter 'M' within it. He stares at it again. The emblem –
minus the letter 'M' – matches his birthmark identically. He quickly
rolls up the sleeve of his left arm and turns towards his mirror, and sure
enough, when holding one of the books alongside his arm, the two
marks match. Taken aback, he reaches for the first book. He wants to
tell his parents everything that is happening, but he feels something
within him advising him not to, as if these revelations are not ready to
be revealed yet, to anyone.

Atticus begins to read, fascinated by each page of the books',
he speeds through *The Myth of the Minotaur* in less than an hour, and
Dark Realms Discovered? in about the same time. He finally gets to *A
Majjai History: Vol 1*, and is captivated by this book. It details the
history of the Majjai – not just the '*Three Wise Men*' account everyone
knows about from biblical stories, but even further into the past, many
orders of millennia earlier. It tells of a war, between good and evil,
where the Majjai fought evil with powers only thought possible in
fairytales. The book reveals the presence of an evil demonic being, with
a gift not seen by any Majjai, the power to call forth demons from the
depths of hell itself and even its quest to manipulate the fragments of
time. The book goes further and talks about a select group of Majjai:
protectors, warriors, but didn't delve too deep into their origins or fate.

The book then begins speaking of meditation techniques and
chants, which Atticus finds difficult to pronounce. He practices some of
the meditation techniques for a little while, until a knock on the front
door disturbs his concentration and stops him from reading too much
more.

Chapter 6

The Note that Time Forgot

"Atticus," says Joseph from behind the door, "Marcellus is here, why don't you pop down for a few minutes?"

"Coming," Atticus answers quickly.

Marcellus is eager to tell of his recent exploits in and around Iran. He is an archaeologist, who specialises in ancient Persia, and is excited with what he has found.

Atticus makes his way downstairs, he likes Marcellus as he is always jolly and treats Atticus very well when it comes to Christmas and birthdays.

Marcellus excitedly beckons towards him, "Atticus, you must come here, come, come!"

Atticus sits down in the main living room; Joseph and Sophia are on the sofa opposite and Marcellus in a large single seated lounger. The log fire is blazing fiercely, lighting and heating the dimly lit room at the same time keeping the warm atmosphere alive, soothing its occupants.

"So Marcellus, how was your trip?" asks Joseph.

"Very good, Joseph. Remember that little note?" Marcellus inquires.

For a moment Joseph looks puzzled, then the realisation strikes him: the note that Marcellus is referring to is the one they found in Atticus' basket, "You mean…?"

"Yes Joseph, *that* note," replies Marcellus. At this point, both Sophia and Joseph are giving their full attention to him.

"What note?" asks Atticus, more confused than ever at this point.

"Well Atticus," Marcellus responds, making eye contact with Joseph and Sophia to ensure that it was ok to continue, "When you were found, there was a note… your father handed it to me…"

"Found?" at this point, Atticus is looking at both his parents and Marcellus, "You mean at the orphanage?"

"Erm, orphanage? Erm, not quite, Atticus." Marcellus looks at both Joseph and Sophia again.

"It's okay, Marcellus, it is time Atticus knew about how we found him," says Sophia, looking lovingly and worryingly at Atticus. Now Atticus gives Marcellus his fullest attention.

"Well, Atticus," continues Marcellus, "Your folks get a little, shall we say, *excited*, when recalling these events, so it is probably best you hear it from my wonderful, calm self."

"Get on with it, will you," ribs Joseph, who is also eager for Atticus to know, even if it is making him incredibly nervous.

Marcellus nods and looks back towards Atticus, "We found you at a disused warehouse about 15 years ago, it was a very stormy night, and you, well, literally appeared out of nowhere." Atticus' gaze never leaves Marcellus' face as he continues the story of how they found him, "…needless to say, we were all a little flabbergasted, and in the commotion, your father handed me the note. It was written in a language none of us understood. I thought it seemed familiar, but also thought it impossible that it could be what I suspected. Anyway, we completely forgot about the note, until earlier this year when I was clearing out my stock room and library. I mentioned the rediscovery to

Joseph, and that over the years of excavations and study in Iran, the note now made some sense to me. Obviously Joseph was very excited at this, and I said I would take it with me on my next trip."

Marcellus adjusts his seating position, takes a sip of his tea, and carries on.

"I recognised the calligraphy in the note to be very similar to an ancient Persian dialect," continues Marcellus, "Now, a contact I have in Iran knew someone who was well-versed in this particular dialect; it took a few days, but he managed to translate it."

All members of the Jones family are on the edges of their seats, eager to hear what the translation says.

"Hurry, Marcellus, you must tell us!" demands Sophia.

Marcellus clears his throat before beginning, "Well, loosely translated, it says this:

Within this basket lay the boy.

The boy with the mark of ring entwined

It is he who is chosen, chosen to be our saviour from the dark one

To the keeper of the boy, he who finds him, it is decreed that they be his protector

The time for the act to be done will be revealed at a time which only the chosen one will know, the revelation of the mark and the purpose of his calling will be proof of his destiny. The Majjai have protected him to this day; the keeper must carry on this duty until the day of the chosen one arises.

"Some of the grammar is a little weak, as the dialect has not existed for many millennia, but the core of its meaning is there," says Marcellus.

By this time, everyone is staring at Atticus, who himself is staring back at them.

"I delved deeper into this whole 'mark' business," Marcellus adds, "It turns out the mark is one held in high regard by an ancient sect of Majjai who have been thought to have been disbanded thousands of years ago. The very fact that it exists on your arm, Atticus, is really quite perplexing."

Atticus longs to show everyone the books, and the letter regarding the PQEs, but something tells him not to; a feeling that the time is not right, and after the revelation of Marcellus' discovery, it makes even more sense for him to trust his feelings.

Marcellus continues with other stories, but Joseph and Sophia are still concerned about the note and what it all means. Atticus is exhausted, and knows he has a long day ahead of him tomorrow. He says his 'good nights' and heads towards his bedroom, hoping for a night without nightmares.

"Goodnight sweetie," says Sophia, "We'll talk about this fully tomorrow," and with a peck on his cheek, Atticus continues towards his room.

Chapter 7

The Prophecy

Joseph stokes the fire as Marcellus helps Sophia clear the coffee table, "What do you think this all means?"

Marcellus pauses, "Well, I'm not entirely sure. It's obvious that Atticus is important, but for what purpose, I couldn't say. The friend I spoke to about this was very excited, seemed to think that this note had something to do with a saviour, someone destined to protect our world from a great evil. After the full translation, he was even more adamant, so much so he is planning to go into training to 'fight alongside' this chosen one."

Joseph returns to his seat, the fire still lighting the room with a warm glow, "You are right about one thing there – Atticus *is* very important, important to *us*. We didn't need a note to tell us that."

Sophia carries the tray of empty cups into the kitchen, and Joseph grabs the opportunity to talk to Marcellus privately. He waits until the clinking of the cups and saucers disappear from earshot.

"You're holding something back," says Joseph, "I have known you for far too long to miss the signs Marcellus. Now tell me, what else do you know?"

Marcellus checks the large, dark, oak door to the living room, peering outside to make sure Sophia is not returning early. Upon carefully closing it, he returns his attention towards Joseph, "Yes, there was more, but I didn't want to worry Sophia or Atticus. Sophia especially, she has been through too much," Marcellus sits close to Joseph, speaking softly as he continues, "There is a prophecy. I uncovered parts of it last year, but after this translation, it all fits."

"What prophecy?" asks Joseph.

"We don't have time to go into it all right now," says Marcellus, "but it talks of a war, and a man. This man, he will be the one to end the war. It has been waging for thousands of years, hidden from what the prophecy calls 'normals.' I'm assuming that means 'normal people.'"

"Normals?" quizzes Joseph, "Normal people?"

"Well, more specifically, it translates to 'The non-Majjai, mortals.' The Majjai were purportedly the creators of Magic," says Marcellus.

"Magic?" Joseph, now sporting a very quizzical face, with eyes wide open and mouth ajar, continues to listen.

"Yes, Magic. The words *Magic*, and *Magician*, were born from the word Majjai," replies Marcellus, "Remember, how you told me about the accident, and what happened, and then how we found Atticus. It never made sense until now. The prophecy also mentions a mark – the same mark that Atticus has on his arm. I was only able to translate that part of the prophecy on my last visit; the note I gave them had the same scripture, but I could not decipher it."

"So, you are saying that Atticus is the one who is going to stop this war?" asks Joseph.

Marcellus pauses again, then looks Joseph straight in the eyes "Yes!"

"Absurd," retorts Joseph, "If Sophia knew what you were saying, she would be petrified right now!"

"Which is why she must not know. I fear Atticus' destiny is

out of our control, and mothers tend not to accept that," Marcellus puts a hand on Joseph's shoulder to calm him, "Remember, when Atticus was just a baby, the strange things that used to occur? Glowing blue lights during thunderstorms, things moving around the room as if they were alive – you can't say you have forgotten these things. These things alone are proof that he may be a Majjai."

"Yes, Marcellus," replies Joseph, "but those occurrences have not taken place since he turned three; you saw to that with that medication you brought back from Iran. We trusted you then, as we do now."

Marcellus tries to reassure Joseph, "You must trust me for a little longer my friend; you know there is more to Atticus' existence than that of a normal child – how we found him is proof of that, and the birthmark confirms it. I fear there are challenges ahead, but I have no idea when they will begin. You have already been touched by this Magic. There is much we do not know of our own existence, let alone that of Atticus'. Our minds must remain open."

"Open for what?" asks Sophia.

Marcellus and Joseph didn't hear Sophia return to the room; they look at each other, wondering what else she overheard.

"Nothing to worry about darling," Joseph replies quickly, "Just talking about that note."

"Oh, that," Sophia takes a seat next to Joseph, "I'm sure it's all nonsense."

"But what if…"

Sophia stops Joseph before he can finish "But if it isn't, we'll be ready, as long as we are together, we are strong. We can only follow our destiny, if it's bad, hopefully Atticus can change it," and with a coy smile aimed at the two men, she sits back, grabs a cushion with one hand, hugging it to her belly and grabs Joseph's arm with the other, before pulling him back to lay her head on his shoulder.

"Uhum!" mutters Marcellus, "I think it's time for me to go, it's getting late. No need to get up, I know my way out. Joseph, perhaps we can meet for a late lunch tomorrow?"

"That would be good. The usual place, about 3.30 ok?" replies Joseph.

"Perfect, good night. I think I'll scamper off now before you two get too lovey–dovey," Marcellus knew he had to get out quickly, but still gets hit for his comment with a cushion aimed at his head by a chuckling Sophia.

Sophia waits for the door to close shut before confronting Joseph, "Ok, now what were you two *really* whispering about?" she gives Joseph what they both have learnt to call 'the look.'

"Nothing whatsoever; like you said, whatever we'll face... it will be together," replies Joseph.

"I trust Marcellus," says Sophia, "but I fear he his hiding something. Ever since Atticus started at that school, Marcellus has been so... well... concerned about him, his whereabouts, his classes, his teachers, everything."

"I know, sweetie, but like you said, we can trust him, he has been with us since the beginning, and he hasn't been wrong, about anything... Yet," Joseph comforts Sophia with a cuddle, "Would you like some tea?"

Sophia nods "You always know how to calm me, JJ, I know whatever we have to face, if we are together, we'll beat it... together," She lets go of Joseph's arm and hugs the cushion, "Now go make me some tea or I'll have to force you to kiss me."

"No force necessary, dear," Joseph gives Sophia a quick kiss on the cheek, but Sophia grabs his shirt and kisses him back passionately. Josephs caresses her hair before softly placing his warm hand on her cheek. He smiles, gently kisses her forehead, "I love you so much, you know," he whispers softly while Sophia's eyes are still closed. She sits back onto the sofa softly grinning while Joseph walks to the kitchen, taking care not to make too much noise as he passes the staircase leading to where Atticus is sleeping.

Chapter 8

The Realm Of Demons

Atticus' room is silent apart from a small fan whirring away in the background. His bed is centrally located on the far wall, with posters of his favourite movies and football team above him. His computer is in the far opposite corner, Sophia always tells him off for leaving it on all night, but Atticus finds the noise soothing, and prefers it on while sleeping.

The only sign of life in the room is the movement of the bed sheets in time with Atticus' breathing. Unbeknown to the sleeping Atticus, the rooms' temperature begins to fall; it becomes icy, each breath now steams out of Atticus' mouth, yet he still dreams, ignorant of his changing surroundings. The steam from his mouth doesn't disappear as it would normally, instead it gathers in the room. It begins to swirl around the bed, the rest of the room begins to pivot around the swirling cloud, but the bed remains still. The room turns faster and faster, blurring into a single circular wall of bleeding lines. The swirling mist engulfs the bed, creating an opening hole below it. The room suddenly stops spinning, and beneath the bed, with Atticus still sleeping, the floor opens up revealing an abyss. The bed drops into it, spinning wildly as it falls.

The spinning finally wakes Atticus, it takes him a moment to realise what is happening; he doesn't understand it, but instinctively grabs the corner post of his bed. Hanging on, he tries to look down into the darkness, but sees nothing. The spinning finally stops and the bed lands with a thud.

Atticus looks up, the only light source comes from above, where his dimly-lit room remains in the distance, and as he looks, he can see the opening closing. He quickly scrambles to open the drawer on the bottom of his bed, in it is a torch and his glasses. He puts his spectacles on, and manages to find the torch just before the opening above closes. He feels for the 'on' switch of the torch in the darkness, locates it, and switches it on. He points it to the ground first, to check if it was safe to get off the bed. The ground itself is dusty, stony, like a cave floor. He feels this is all another lucid dream, he knows he must journey through it, or remain in the dark.

Atticus moves the torch along the ground until the beam of light is horizontal, he makes out a wall, about twenty meters in the distance, again it resembles a cave wall of some sort, and strangely the colour is not dull grey, but more of a dull orange. He cautiously steps off the bed, making sure his feet find solid ground and not some illusion of a floor. Once happy that the floor is secure, he lays down his other foot, sweeps the surface with his bare feet, watching out for sharp stones, and slowly makes his way to the stone wall. He turns his back to it, then shines the torch around him, trying to get some sort of bearing. He locates his bed, shines the light on it, only to find it fading. It becomes transparent, and then just disappears, melting into the nothingness.

Atticus can feel his heartbeat quicken. He begins flashing the torch around the darkness to try and find some way out of where he is. He follows the wall until it reaches a stony stairwell that appears to spiral upwards along the face of the wall. Atticus lifts his right foot up onto the first step.

Out of the blackness he suddenly hears a snort followed by heavy, deep breathing. He stops in his tracks and flashes the torch around again, trying desperately to peer into the dark. The light from the torch is just able to touch something in the distance, something that is moving. Another snort and the entire chamber lights up revealing to Atticus that he is in some sort of enormous dungeon, fire bellows from the nostrils of a giant creature, from the flash of light it appears to Atticus' eyes to be what is only myth: a dragon.

Atticus remains frozen with fear, it seems the creature is asleep, but Atticus takes no chances. Quietly, step-by-step, he slowly moves up the staircase.

After what seems like ages, he finally reaches the top. Light is still in short supply and the torch is limited in its reach, but the staircase seems to open up to a chamber. It looks like a lab, but not like one Atticus has ever seen. There are bottles and vials, some bubbling over, some with steam pouring out from their containers, all are standing on stone-like furniture. The next thing to hit Atticus is the smell; it's putrid, stinking of rotting flesh, almost forcing him to vomit right there and then. He flicks the torch, shining it across the room, lighting shelf upon shelf filled with these vials and bottles. Atticus spots a ladder and he walks towards it, peering upwards into the room it leads to. Cautiously, Atticus climbs the ladder. He shines the torch as his head pops up through the hatch. The room is cluttered, but quite well-lit in comparison to the dungeon chamber and the vial room. The light appears to be coming from a window. Atticus slowly navigates around a clutter of stone tables and chairs towards the window; he looks outside. It takes him a few moments to absorb the landscape. The room he is in is attached to a massive castle, not quite as large as Wysardian Manor, but still very large.

Atticus studies the landscape further from the building within which he is standing. The horizon is filled with giant mountains and erupting volcanoes, the ground either charred black and glowing bright red with rivers of lava. There are other buildings dotted along the land, some larger than others, many are tiny, some resemble villages and others castles, but all are twisted in their design, with demonic creatures littering their architectures like gargoyles on a church, but unlike gargoyles, these appear to be moving. Towers are not straight, but bend in several directions as they reach towards the blackened flame ridden sky.

Atticus knows not where he is, but knows he does not belong there. He steps away from the window and starts to make his way towards a door he notices on the wall parallel to the window. As he walks towards it, he spots what appears to be candlelight getting closer, then footsteps and voices. He quickly runs behind some shelves in the room, his heart beats faster as the footsteps get closer.

"Masssster, Lord Alvarez has returned empty-handed; speaksss of an ambush," the voice hisses and rasps. Atticus switches off his torch and tries to squeeze deep into the shadows.

"It seems Echo Foressst has made itsss decision, the treessss, they side with the Majjai," continues the voice. He recognises the voice as the same one he heard on the rugby field.

"It matters not," says a second voice. This one is much deeper, it issues authority and Atticus could sense the one who spoke first cowering, "They will not have a choice. Soon, I will have control of both realms, and they will bow or burn."

"And what of Alvarezzz, masssster? Hisss Ssscreamer contingent did not return with him. All perissshed by the hands of the Majjai, defeated easily. He isss requesssssting more demons," says the first voice.

"The Majjai have become more than an irritation. I have

respected their rules for far too long. Now that my strength has returned, they will pay for their insolence," the deeper voice sounds hateful; Atticus hears something smash into the wall, the entire room shakes and dust falls from the ceiling and lands on Atticus' head, "Too long have I been imprisoned here, Herensugue, my powers faded after the intervention of the Majjai Six. Now only Elric remains, and he is a weak old man."

Atticus desperately tries to remember the name he just heard, "*Herensugue, Herensugue,*" he repeats it in his head.

"And what of the prophesssssy, Massssster?" asks Herensugue, "Do you ssssusspect this boy Atticussss to be the one? He did resssspond to the calling."

"I cannot be certain, he is protected from all planes of existence by a power I have not seen before, we can only wait and see. If he is this chosen one, he will be no match for me – there is no longer a Majjai Six, and on his own, he is nothing. He could not even fight off the chaos spell we projected to him for the calling."

Atticus, shocked at hearing his name, tries to edge closer to the door, feeling the need to try to soak in every word of this conversation. He creeps out from behind the stone shelf, and feels his way around the room. It is much darker now without the torch, and the light from the window is limited. Atticus suddenly feels a sharp pain on the outside of his left arm, he looks down and sees a dagger like shard of stone has pierced his skin. The trickle of a warm liquid tells Atticus that his arm is bleeding, he tries not to make any noise and attempts to wipe away the blood, but before he can do so, he hears the voices go silent, followed by the sound of something sniffing the air.

"What is it Herensugue?" asks the being with the deep voice.

"The air massssster, I taste blood in it," hisses Herensugue, "Human blood."

Atticus hears what sounds like several snake tongues flicking in the air, and a rasping noise that he can only associate with that of a rattlesnake.

"I sense a presence... there!" shouts the being with the deep voice.

Atticus turns, he tries to find the hatch he came through as the footsteps storm towards the room. One of them is massive, causing the room to shake with each step, the other footsteps are preceded by a strange sucking sound, but no less terrifying. Atticus scrambles to the hatch, slides down the ladder, switches on his torch and runs towards the staircase. As he runs down, Atticus hears his two pursuers crash through the lab room, the being with the deep voice shouts again.

"Draconus! AWAKEN!" screams the deeper voice.

Atticus turns white; he suddenly remembers why he tried to escape this chamber in the first place. In that moment, the deep rumble of giant wings flapping engulfs the dungeon, a bellowing roar follows, and the chamber is alight; flame fills the area with scorching heat. Atticus dares not look behind him or to the side of the staircase, all he can think is to run. The footsteps behind him become louder and louder, then he hears one of them speak.

"Die boy!" bellows the deeper voice.

Atticus looks behind him to witness a fireball being thrown by one of the beings, he can't make out their faces only their silhouettes, one extremely tall, the other appears to have several heads, but is much smaller. The fireball is blinding and bears down on Atticus, his only reaction is to jump. The fireball explodes on the steps; he is flung into the air with the force of the explosion and thrown over the side of the staircase.

He falls. Scared, cold, and confused, Atticus scrambles in the dark to try and grab something, anything to stop his fall. He thinks,

"This is it, this is the end!" but then he feels something else, an overwhelming surge of confidence, of power. Defiantly, he screams "No!" immediately Atticus' fall slows, blue light begins to surround him, strands wrapping around his body, and he stops mid air. Instincts tell him to move his arm, and a ball of electrical light forms in his palm; compelled to throw it, he sends it aimlessly at the staircase he was thrown from. The staircase explodes again, but this time with a blue flash. The two pursuers stop, and the larger one screams again.

"Draconus, seize him!"

The dragon flies up behind Atticus and attempts to grab him with one of its claws, Atticus flies out of the way and swoops behind the dragon, above its wings. He brings his hands together to fire a massive electrical bolt into the creature's back, and succeeds in dazing it, but only for a moment. The dragon turns to face Atticus, and with an almighty roar shoots a violent jet of fire at him. Atticus shields himself with his arms crossed, and out of nowhere a giant shield of blue light protects him dispersing the flames around the blue light. Atticus has no idea how he is doing any of this, it's as if his body is acting on instinct, he feels this power coursing through him, but is it him controlling this or something else? The dragon flies towards Atticus, drives itself hard into him, but just bounces off the shield of light, the force of the blow pushing Atticus back and the shield disappears.

The chase continues around the chamber, the dragon following Atticus as he dives and swoops through the air, dodging the uneven cave wall undulations and plinths, up, around, to the left – no matter which path Atticus takes, the dragon is able to follow, and it is gaining. He fires another electrical ball towards it, the dragon merely shrugs it off and flies to the top of the chamber to begin a swoop towards the now shieldless Atticus. Atticus flies to the ground, as fast as he can, the dragon is catching up. Atticus can see his torch, lying on the ground; he uses it to measure the distance to the cave floor and at the last instant pulls away. Draconus smashes into the cave floor with such force that the walls of the chamber begin to shake with rocks from the ceiling falling to the ground.

Exhausted, Atticus drops to his knees on the cave floor, breathing heavily, sweating profusely, and still bleeding. The sound of the heavy footsteps approaching him are drowned- out by his exhaustion; it is too late for Atticus to react before the imposing figure of the larger being is in front of him.

"Herensugue, attend to Draconus; I will deal with this imp," says the large figure in front of Atticus. Who gazes down towards his prize, this intruder who he seems to recognise, "Your resemblance to Kazmagus is uncanny."

'Kazmagus,' whispers Atticus under his breath, 'who is Kazmagus?'

The cave is littered with tiny fires after the fight with Draconus, providing enough light for Atticus to look around and see a very strange creature walking towards the fallen dragon. A serpent like beast, with seven heads and four arms. Herensugue. Its legs did not look normal, they moved as if it has no bones, squelching with each step, yet there are claws on its feet scraping the floor as it walks.

Atticus returns his gaze to the larger being, standing in front of him. Atticus' eyes scan its massive frame: its legs are red, and incredibly muscular, each calf is larger than Atticus' entire body, its thighs and above are covered in some form of hair, soft and smooth like horsehair. Halfway up the stomach, the red skin takes over again, revealing a muscular torso. Atticus' gaze continues upwards; the head is large, the eyes yellow, its chin is almost square, devilish, the bone of its skull can be seen to protrude the skin along the jaw line. The demon's forehead is smooth, but with large veins protruding from it and jet-black hair growing from the top. The creature's hair is long and falls behind the being to the level of its waist. The strands of hair are grouped together and bound by hundreds of sharp metallic spikes, which seem to have grown from the hair itself.

Atticus speaks, "What are you?"

"You mean you do not know? Your very presence here confirms to me that you are indeed the one that has been chosen, and yet this fact is hidden from you?" the being stands at least 6 meters tall, it bends to get a closer look at Atticus, "Impressive. You are not really here, are you? Your powers of projection surpass those of Elric himself, a Master Majjai could not hope to conjure such a realistic apparition, and even fight from it, you are indeed... curious; still, these tricks are not enough to harm me," The creature picks Atticus up in his giant hands, its massive knife-edge nails forming a prison around him, "My name, is Razakel, remember it well, Atticus, for when we next meet, I will crush you like this," Razakel squeezes his hand, and Atticus cries in agony, he can feel his bones crushing, each rib grinding against the other.

A growl to the right of him tells Atticus that the dragon has regained consciousness. Razakel throws Atticus towards the beast with great force, and Draconus opens its mouth in anticipation of a tasty morsel. Atticus covers his eyes, waiting for the bite, he sees the jaws in his mind, a flash of blue light, and then nothing.

Atticus squints, his eyes are brought to life by the sunlight forcing its way through the gap in his room's curtain, the PC is still humming away, and all seems normal. He checks his rib cage, no breaks; but for some reason, he can still feel pain. He next checks his arm, it isn't bleeding, but there is a scar in the very place where he cut it. He quickly reaches into the bedside drawer to get to his glasses, and the birthmark on his arm begins to tingle. Hurriedly, Atticus rolls up his left sleeve to above his forearm, exposing the mark, which is glowing a faint blue.

Atticus is frustrated. What is happening to him? Why does he feel pain in his dreams – and are they dreams or something else? What are these creatures, and how do they know who he is? So many questions rush through his mind, and no one answers them, or no one can answer them.

"Perhaps Professor Sprocking can throw some light on things; surely he knows who Elric is, and the creature calling himself *Razakel* mentioned Elric directly several times," Atticus thinks out loud, "I need answers!" in frustration Atticus slams his fist onto his desk.

"Atticus! Breakfast's almost ready!" Sophia calls from the kitchen.

Atticus opens his door to the fresh smell of warm pancakes, much more comforting than his experiences from moments ago. He rushes to get ready, brushing his teeth at the same time as taking a shower, gets dressed, and darts downstairs to tuck into the pancakes. They are wonderful as always, folded over with banana fillings with maple syrup and powdered sugar on top. Pancakes are the one thing Sophia knows how to make well, her sandwich-making skills however, have never improved; but nothing will distract Atticus from the joy of these pancakes, not even the sight of Sophia forgetting to butter the slices of bread on his roast chicken sandwiches.

"Your dad had the first batch of pancakes; he had to rush off this morning, so I'm taking you to school today," Atticus acknowledges Sophia with a grunt around a mouthful of pancake as he relishes every last piece. There is a knock at the door and Sophia goes to answer.

Atticus finishes his pancake and looks around the kitchen for another, he knows Sophia always makes a few spare and spots one next to the cooker, he quickly grabs the plate and starts to eat the pancake with his hands, trying to hurry so that Sophia doesn't find him eating extra.

Sophia opens the door to the kitchen, "Atticus, shame on you! I gave you three pancakes already."

Atticus tries to say 'sorry,' but just splurts as the words are unable to cohere due to the amount of pancake in his mouth.

"By the way, you have a visitor," Sophia says, still staring angrily at Atticus.

Horrified, Atticus spies Joyce peeking around the kitchen door, giggling at the sight of Atticus with pancakes stuffed in his mouth and maple syrup dribbling down his chin.

Sophia's frown turns to a smile, "Looks like you are walking to school this morning then; you need the exercise after eating so much this morning. Look after him, won't you Joyce?"

"Of course Mrs Jones," she replies, "Come on pancake man, hurry up or we'll be late."

Atticus swallows the mouthful of pancake, quickly washes his chin and grabs his school bags before walking out with Joyce, trying to avoid eye contact and keep his cheeks from glowing a bright red.

A Majjai History, Vol 1 Chapter 3: The Legend of Kazmagus

The legend of Kazmagus is one that is steeped in contradiction. Some say he was the first Majjai, others declare him as a tyrant, more dangerous than the entire demon realm with his experiments. His very existence has been debated for millennia. Yet all those that believe are sure of one thing: he was indeed powerful. Not much is known of his demise, some say he was banished to the Void by Asmodei. Some stories state he died in a climatic battle with the Demon Lord, thus beginning the reign of Razakel. Some demons even revere Kazmagus and regarded him as their king, although it is believed that most of these were slain by Razakel soon after he took the throne.

It is known that Kazmagus was able to manipulate both dark and light Magic; there are stories of battles where Majjai saw both red and blue being conjured by their leader. Some feared him for this, wondering how he could perform both evil and good, others admired him; but none were ever able to replicate his abilities.

The tomb of Kazmagus has been sought through the ages; it is believed Myrddin came closest to finding it. Scriptures have been found stating that great wonders have been left there. Many followers of Kazmagus believed he was powerful enough to return from the dead and so built his shrine to enable a comfortable return. The world missed his presence; though only Majjai and Demon knew of him, the mortal world suffered the most.

With Kazmagus' disappearance, the demon world grew in number, influencing many wars in mortal society in the hope that humankind would sink into oblivion. Those that doubted Kazmagus' allegiance to good soon turned and renounced their views. A rally of the remaining Majjai managed to thwart many demonic intrusions, but such were the numbers that until the emergence of the Majjai Six, led by Elric Griffin, the Majjai were fighting a losing battle.

During his last days of known existence, those close to him reportedly heard him speak of something called white Magic, something he believed to be more powerful than both good Magic (blue) and evil Magic (red). He locked himself away and became a recluse. He was rarely seen outside of his palace and often ventured on voyages by himself with no support from the Majjai armies of the time. His sanity was questioned several times as he began speaking to himself in prose. Conversing with his own being, not merely discretely, but many a time he was heard in full voice. Eventually he left Persian lands, becoming a nomad, wandering the globe. Human eyes have not set on him since.

Chapter 9

Secrets Revealed

Atticus and Joyce walk down the garden path to the large front gate; Sophia watches from the window, still wearing the same smile. Atticus closes the gate behind them and nervously walks with Joyce.

"How are you feeling today, Atticus?" asks Joyce, trying to break the ice.

"Erm, fine thanks, a ...a... and you?" stutters Atticus nervously.

"I'm fine too, just thought you could use the company today; you always come to school by yourself or your parents drop you," Joyce checks her watch, "We better walk quickly though, we don't want to be late."

"You have classes with Professor Sprocking, don't you?" asks Atticus.

"Sometimes, yes, why do you ask?"

"Just curious to discover what kind of person he is really," replies Atticus.

Joyce flicks her hair back and pauses, as if thinking of what to say, "Well, he is a little eccentric, but nice, fair, although..."

"Although what?" asks Atticus, eager to learn as much as he can.

"Nothing, I shouldn't say. Anyway, why talk about school, tell me about you," says Joyce making an obvious attempt to evade the topic.

"Erm, nothing much to say really, … err…" Atticus flusters slightly, desperately trying to find something interesting in his life to describe, but his mind just slinks away until he remembers fencing, "FENCING!" he screams, making Joyce jump, "Yes, I like fencing."

"Really? Any good then?" asks Joyce.

"Not bad. I follow this unique style Mr Callan has come up with, which treats it like a martial art."

Joyce giggles, "So you're like Karate Kid with a sword?"

"Not quite," laughs Atticus, "Mr Callan is a great teacher, but he hasn't taught me the 'wax on, wax off' method yet."

Joyce laughs as Atticus begins to go into a mass description of his favourite sport; Joyce listens on attentively as they converse together.

Atticus feels a warm glow inside as the nervousness disappears. He continues to be amazed at how easy this girl − whom he feared in the past − is to talk to. They continue to banter on their journey to Wysardian Manor until they reach the outskirts of estate upon which it lies.

"You still getting those nightmares?" asks Joyce.

Atticus nods, "You?"

"Not for a long time, they stopped soon after…" Joyce pauses again, as if withdrawing something she was about to say.

"I'm listening," Atticus says, determined to get the answers Joyce is trying to hide.

"Atticus," Joyce says softly, "There is something I need to say to you."

"Go on," says Atticus

Joyce leans towards Atticus to whisper in his ear, "I have faith in you."

Atticus looks confused, "Faith in me for what?"

"You'll see, but I can't say any more until tomorrow. Shall we meet again in the morning?"

"Sure, but, what do you mean? You like confusing me don't you?" Atticus says jokingly.

"Not at all; in fact, I can't wait until tomorrow, it will be fun," Joyce looks towards the main gates, and sees that most of the other students are already on the grounds, "There is something I do know I can tell you though."

"And that is?" Atticus raises an eyebrow, itching to hear some clue to Joyce's verbal cryptography.

"That I can beat you to the school gates," Joyce darts ahead, not even glancing back to see if Atticus will follow.

Atticus stands perplexed for a moment watching Joyce run towards the main gates, then murmurs under his breath, "No way," and immediately races after her.

They get to the gates just as the bell sounds. Joyce hands Atticus her phone number on a piece of paper, "Call me in the morning to let me know what time you want to leave for school," and with that they say their goodbyes and head towards their lessons.

Atticus can barely concentrate in any of his classes. Professor Snugglebottom using him as target practice almost persuades Atticus to focus on the lesson, but all he can think about is today's interview – and Joyce.

He thinks back to their walk, the comfort he felt then was soothing, but he can't shake the thought, "Why has she suddenly appeared to take an interest? What isn't she telling me? Who is Elric? Why didn't my parents tell me how I was found until now?" the questions race through his mind as it wanders between the PQE, last night's revelations, and Joyce.

Lunch passes quickly. Atticus realises he has some time before he has to meet Professor Sprocking, so decides to pay Professor Morgan a visit and thank him for the books.

Atticus peers into Professor Morgan's room, but there is no sign of him. Atticus thinks this strange, as he is fairly sure that the Professor has a class taking place in this period. Atticus shrugs and continues his journey to Professor Sprocking's office.

His destination is near the opposite end of the manor; it is an area that is rarely ventured towards by most of the students as not many lessons are scheduled there. As far as Atticus knows, only a few students head in this direction. The corridors are quiet, and Atticus tries to make his walk go by a little bit faster by counting how many times he can hear his footsteps echo. The walls in the manor are very tall, but not much adorns them − they are mostly stonework or marble, some have engravings of battles carved into them, but most are quite plain, with only the odd pillar to break up the monotony.

Atticus checks his watch, making sure he is not running late as he nears Professor Sprocking's office. The door to the entrance is, as with all doors in the manor, incredibly tall, and very heavy. Compared to the bland walls, the doors are a symphonic celebration of carvings, with exquisite shapes and intricate patterns. Atticus knocks twice. A voice calls out from the room.

"Enter!"

Atticus opens the door slowly, its creak echoes around the chamber it connects to and back through the corridor. Atticus can see Professor Sprocking standing on the left side of his room, staring out of a window onto the hillside.

"Hello Sir," says Atticus tentatively, "I have an appointment with you today."

"Yes, Atticus, yes," Professor Sprocking says quickly, still staring out of the window, "Please, take a seat, we have much to discuss."

Atticus ventures into the room, all four walls are covered in books and strange ornaments; the far wall is curved outwards, with a large wooden arch preceding it. Within that area is a circular table, upon which stands what appears to be a large globe covered by a silk blanket. The ceiling is dome-like, curving upwards into an inverted steeple at the centre. Candles are alight in various areas, some large, some small. Although daytime, the window that the Professor is standing at is the only inlet of outside light, and it fails to adequately illuminate the entire room; the candles, therefore, are welcome members to the cast of objects scattered around. The Professor's desk is situated just before the arched area. Atticus' footsteps echo as he approaches it, he gets to the large leather chair and sits.

"Any questions before we begin, Atticus?" asks Professor Sprocking.

Atticus thinks for a moment, can this be the opportunity he has been waiting for? Before he can finish this train of thought, his mouth opens, almost of its own accord, "Elric Griffin, sir. Who is he?"

The Professor turns his head towards Atticus, and smiles, "You can ask him yourself, he'll be joining us shortly. But before he does, we need to talk."

Atticus sits attentively; rather excited now, as he senses that he may finally get the responses he has been craving.

Professor Sprocking walks to his desk. He is wearing a rich, deep red cloak under which is a black suit and a matching deep, red, mandarin-collar shirt. He sits, staring at Atticus as if trying to analyse every part of him, "Usually, Atticus, we would be giving you questions to answer today, and you would have needed to go through various tests before I could even think of telling you what we need you to know. But unfortunately, recent events have forced our hand."

"So, there is no test for me today? What about this PQE?" asks Atticus, cautiously.

"Oh, there will be tests for you for the rest of your life, Mr Jones. Things change for you forever today, if…" Professor Sprocking pauses, and decides not to carry on down that particular path of conversation, "Actually, I'm jumping ahead here, what do you know of the Majjai, Atticus?"

"*Maj-eye,*" Atticus says, seeing it phonetically in his mind's eye, making sure he gets the pronunciation correct, "A little, sir; Professor Morgan lent me a book."

"He did, eh?" the Professor chuckles, "Benjamin always did have a soft spot for you; he speaks very highly of you. What if I told you the Majjai exist not only in the pages of that book, but are alive and well today?"

Atticus shakes his head, knowing not what to say.

"Well, *we* exist, Atticus," the Professor raises his right arm, opens his hand, and as he does so, sparks of blue electricity jump from one finger to the next. Atticus' eyes open wide, mesmerised by the dancing ribbons of light.

Atticus suddenly remembers that what he is looking at is exactly the type of blue light he was using in his dream last night. Atticus does not mention this just yet, eager to hear more.

"Elric thinks you are very special, Atticus," continues the Professor, "I trust him, and he has entrusted me to inform you of a number of things, most notably, how important you are to us."

"Important? What do you mean?" Atticus keeps hearing about being a 'chosen one,' first from Marcellus, then in his dream, and now, hearing he is important to Elric, the thirst for answers grows ever more.

"There has been a war going on between good and evil for longer than any of us remember. It's been hidden for thousands of years – hidden from the mortal world," says Professor Sprocking.

"Mortal, sir?" asks Atticus inquisitively.

"Yes, Atticus, mortals. We regard those without Magic as mortals," Professor Sprocking leans back into his chair while speaking, "There are those in the mortal world who know of this war, but they are few and are only aware due to our need to sometimes keep our secret safe. The world will never be ready for such truths to be fully known, not in its current state. You see, mythology, religion, culture, it is all intertwined. Norse, Egyptian, Islamic, Kabbalah, they all have a beginning. Demon lore from the books of religion, from Genesis and before, to the present day, there is substance to all of it – even vampires and werewolves – all these stories have a basis. Yes, it has changed through the perception and translation of man, but the essence is there. This war is born from all of this and is very real, but it hasn't been so forthright for a few millennia. Again, I wouldn't be normally be telling you all of this; we would usually follow the standard procedure, in that you would be sitting a test today and learning of this history over time. But as I have mentioned already, recent events have forced us to include you sooner, therefore we need to bring you up to speed straight away."

"Why me, sir?" asks Atticus, still not wholly convinced of everything he is hearing.

"Patience, I'll be getting to that bit soon," the Professor opens a drawer on his side of the desk, pulls out a piece of parchment and places it face down in front of him, "This war, like any other, has sides Atticus. In this case, we regard ourselves to be on the good side. Our counterparts however, have dark intentions. They seek to destroy and want nothing but chaos; we bring order to the chaos. We cure their disease when it encroaches into this realm. They embody evil, and have been fighting to try and find a way here for millennia. For all those years we have stood in their way, but it has only been through sheer luck that their leader has not been strong enough to make an impact for such a long time."

"Why is that sir?"

"Because a brave group of Majjai, called the Majjai Six, stopped him from invading our realm a long long time ago, and in doing so, weakened him. Unfortunately, he has now become stronger than ever. There is a way to defeat him, but only the chosen one will find that way. This brings me neatly onto you, Atticus."

Atticus prepares himself for what he feels he already knows, he has heard about the note left with him when he was found, he has seen the birthmark, he has seen the birthmark glow, and then there are his dreams, "The chosen one. That's me, isn't it?"

The Professor chuckles, "Perhaps," he says, trying to diffuse Atticus's anticipation, "Some seem to think so; I will wait before making that judgement. Unfortunately there is only one member of the original Majjai Six alive today, and to combat the new threat from the dark realm, we need to train those that have the gift of the Majjai – and in doing so, hope to find the successors to the original Majjai Six. It's been prophesied that the new Majjai Six will be formed at a time when the demon king is close to becoming strong enough to enter our realm. Each will be identified by a birthmark – a circular birthmark with a tiny spiral around the main ring – you have probably seen it on the books that Benjamin lent to you."

Atticus nods.

"We have found five of the successors, the one missing is the chosen one. The mark of the chosen one will also be a circle, but his will include a larger entwining around it. You should also know that you have been brought to our attention because it has been noted that you have certain abilities, which were revealed when you were very young. In fact, you were so gifted we had to bind your powers early on, Elric managed to create a potion to stem your abilities after learning of your guardians' search for answers. The downside to this suppression is that it can be rather uncomfortable by the time one reaches your age. Nightmares, blurred vision and excessive static can be witnessed by some subjects."

"I have dreams about Magic, strange dreams," says Atticus, suddenly feeling comfortable enough to reveal this after what he has just been told.

"Please, tell me about them," requests the Professor.

Atticus tells him of his experiences, including his waking dream on the playing field; he is just about to start talking about last night's dream, but thinks it worthwhile to show the Professor his birthmark.

"I also have this," Atticus pulls up his sleeve to reveal the circular mark. The Professors eyes widen, dancing between the birthmark and Atticus' face, "The most peculiar thing is that it glowed this morning. I had the strangest of the dreams last night, about someone who called himself *Razakel*, and another creature called *Herensugue*. In the dream I am cut, and when I woke up, I had this scar, in the exact same place," Atticus indicates towards the scar on his other forearm.

"Did you speak to Razakel?" asks Professor Sprocking

"Speak to him?" replies Atticus, "He was trying to kill me, and then spouted some strange comments about projection before he threw me into the mouth of a dragon. Professor, what the hell is going on?" Atticus becomes flustered, for the first time in the entire conversation, he sees concern and bewilderment within the Professors eyes.

Professor Sprocking is visibly disturbed, "Draconus?" he asks.
Atticus nods.

"So he lives," says the Professor, "Atticus, I must leave you
here for a moment — I need to get Elric a little sooner than we planned.
Don't touch anything; feel free to read any of the books, but do not
touch anything else," Atticus acknowledges the Professor as he
observes him leave the room hurriedly. Atticus closes his eyes for a
moment, intending only to gather his thoughts, and as he does so, he
finds himself looking out through the eyes of Professor Sprocking.

# # #

The professor heads down the corridor towards Elric's
chamber. The sight of the birthmark has sent him into a state of
confusion, he is blinking wildly and shaking his head, whispering to
himself, "How did Elric know for sure, what hasn't he told me?" he
approaches a massive pair of doors, *"Farasi Bakhwar,"* he murmurs,
his whisper is purposely low, as not to make any possible passer by
aware of what is said.

The doors open slowly to blackness. Checking behind himself
as he enters the room, he waits for the doors to close. As the two doors
meet to seal the world hidden behind them, the corridor they lead to
suddenly appears through the darkness and everything is alight.

"No need to go any further, Geoffrey," Elric stands just behind
the Professor, placing his hand on his shoulder, "I know why you have
come to seek me early, but you must understand, the boy's identity had
to be kept secret. Only one other knows, and that other is his current
protector."

"You should have trusted me, Elric, like I have trusted you

many times in many a battle," the Professor turns to face Elric, "He speaks of encountering Razakel and Herensugue in his dreams, and has seen Draconus revived. Atticus' awakening should have been sooner, perhaps we wouldn't have lost her then. Draconus will pay for his crimes."

Elric sees the pain in the Professor's eyes, he knows his story is a sad one, and understands the emotion all too well, "Atticus' early awakening would have had no effect on that outcome my friend, it would have been too soon, he was too young and the *Quantorbium* is still lost. His time is now, not the times of King Arthur."

"But we can awaken him now. That is why you have that particular *Gooyeh Partaab,* is it not? If he finds the orb to control the portal of time, as he is meant to, we could use it to save her, perhaps turn the tide of this war?"

"Not enough time has passed, you know the portal does not work like that, and she certainly wouldn't have wanted to risk your life and the lives of so many others in a quest such as the one you seek," Elric holds the Professor's shoulder again, "Focus, my friend, I knew not of Draconus' survival; this is news to me, too, Razakel has hidden that well."

Elric tries to divert Geoffrey's attention, "Did you learn the chant for the orb?" he asks.

Shaking his head to focus properly, the professor recites the chant he has learnt; as he does so, something strange occurs back in the room where Atticus is sitting.

# # #

With a start Atticus shakes his head, not knowing if that was another dream or was he really seeing things through the professor's eyes.

He grabs his left forearm as he feels his birthmark tingling, a gentle breeze flows around the room fluttering the piece of parchment that the Professor left face down on his desk and then flipping it over. Atticus stares at the picture revealed in front of him. On it is his birthmark, and written above, "The mark of the chosen one," his attention sways from the parchment when the covered globular object beyond the archway begins to hum and glow. Atticus stands, still clutching his arm, and walks towards it.

The cover falls off to reveal a large orb, held in place by an oxidised metallic stand with intricate detailing. It shows engravings of a massive dragon and next to it, the image of Razakel standing. Atticus instantly recognises the dragon as Draconus and he grabs his arm again, the tingling is so intense now. He doesn't understand what is happening, the realisation of truth overcomes him and he begins to panic.

"Chosen one," he gasps, "Me? It can't be! I'm just, nobody."

Atticus re-focuses on the Orb as it starts to glow, first a deep scarlet red, then a piercing yellow, then orange, and finally settling on a blue hue. Atticus peers inside, there is a blue flame flickering at the bottom. Suddenly, out of the flame he sees himself jump out of the fire and into the orb. He sees himself smashing his fist on the side of the orb's glass wall as if trying to smash his way out; at the same time the swirling breeze around him turns into a violent gust of wind. Atticus is astonished at what he sees, his orb version looks angry, desperate to get free, he makes out the words, "Help Me!" from the lip movement of his orb-imprisoned doppelganger. He reaches out, slowly moving closer to the orb, he places one hand upon it, then the other.

"ARRRRRGGGHHHHH!" Atticus screams in pain, his hands welded to the orb. Sparks of electricity fly everywhere, the entire room is alight in blue as flames pour out of the orb as it begins to hover. Flying like a long piece of velvet ribbon across the room, it circles around Atticus' head then moves away and shoots itself into his back.

"Arrrrgggghhhh!!!" Atticus screams again, and then the orb drops back to the table as it was before. Atticus falls, his eyes closed, smoke rising from all over his body and around the orb. He sleeps, as the smoke forms a blanket over him and slowly dissipates.

# # #

Hours pass by, but to Atticus it feels like moments. His eyes blink open, squinting when the light from the candles strike them.

"Easy there young lad, you've been through a bit of an ordeal."

It's a voice Atticus has not heard in person before, but he recognises it. It sounds old, but also authoritative, harsh but also understanding.

Atticus opens his eyes a little more and can make out an old but strong looking man. His long, silvery beard falls to his waist. His hair is also long and silvery, but tied into a tight ponytail. Professor Sprocking is also there looking down at Atticus as he wakes.

"I thought I said not to touch anything?" Professor Sprocking scolds the drowsy Atticus.

"Come now Geoffrey, even we were not aware that the *Gooyeh Partaab* would sense our words from such a distance. It seems our friend here is more powerful than we imagined, it's the only explanation," says Elric.

"You mean the orb tapped into the power within Atticus?" asks Professor Sprocking, "But how?"

"That I do not know," Elric returns his attention towards

Atticus, "Here you go," he says, handing him a glass of what appears to be water, "My name is Elric Griffin, I hear you've been asking about me?"

Atticus sits up wearily. He wonders if it was down to unwittingly looking through the eyes of the professor that caused the activation of the orb, but thinks best not to mention it yet, "What time is it?"

"Don't worry about the time, you have been excused from your afternoon timetable and your parents know you are staying a little late at school today. It's been taken care of," Elric helps Atticus up, "How are you feeling?"

"Tired. What happened to me?" Atticus wipes the weariness from his eyes before putting his glasses back on.

"It's a complicated thing to explain, but, the orb you touched is what we call a *Gooyeh Partaab*, loosely translated it means Orb of Projection," explains Elric, "As you have probably worked out by now, you are a very important person. We had to bind your powers when you were very young, lock them away until you were ready – or until they couldn't be hidden from you any longer. You may well have experienced strange occurrences recently. As your mind and body grew, the power that is within you grew, too. It was only a matter of time until you outgrew our Magic with your own."

"So what was that in the orb?" asks Atticus.

"You, Atticus, you were in the orb. Well, part of you, anyway. The Magical part. Geoffrey already explained to you that I concocted a potion, which was sent to a family friend of yours through Majjai placed in what used to be Persia. Once this was fed to you, your powers were fully projected into the *Gooyeh Partaab*, locked away until it was time for your Magical self to be awakened. Only two people in this world knew that you are the chosen one. I am one of them; the other, well, that person needs to be kept hidden for now. Although, knowledge of your existence will now be impossible to contain within the Majjai community."

"Fully projected?" asks a quizzical Atticus.

"That's another story," Elric strokes his beard before continuing, "For reasons unknown, a part of you was already there."

Atticus shakes his head, finally waking himself up properly, confused as to how part of him could have been placed into the orb before the locking away of his *powers*, but thinks that there has been so much information taken in, that question can be asked another time, "So what happens now?" asks Atticus, looking towards Elric.

"Well, it will take time for your body to readjust, especially because the transference of your powers was split. And you will need to learn some control, Geoffrey has told me of your dreams. Your last one was of great interest. What do you know of astral projection, Atticus?"

Atticus pauses, he thinks back to things he has read or learnt during all those Internet searches about the paranormal, "It's when someone projects their consciousness elsewhere, right?"

"Correct Atticus, I believe these dreams you have been experiencing must be a form of astral projection. Only experienced Majjai are able to harness this ability, and yet you managed it in your sleep," Elric stands and moves to Professor Sprocking's desk to collect the piece of parchment that was left there earlier. Returning to where Atticus is sitting, he beckons Geoffrey to join them, "Your birthmark was prophesised in scripture centuries before the great battle where we banished Razakel to the dark realm. The chosen one, the one who would be born to defeat the great evil, would bear it. This chosen one will be so strong in the way of the Majjai that he will be able to perform great feats with a mere thought, his abilities are willed, whereas most other Majjai manipulate their gifts through other means."

"How so?" quizzes Atticus.

Geoffrey responds to this particular question, "We use chants, amulets, and the teachings of the old ways, informing us how to tap deep into our own psyche. The mind is an untapped resource, Atticus. Teach it, and the possibilities are limitless. Great power lies within all, but only a few are able to use it. The other members of the Majjai Six are the exception, like you, they have a greater level of ability than the norm, though not as much as you. They are still limited to the aforementioned chants, amulets, and other trinkets. Although they also have key skills that need only a thought, just like you."

"So there are more Majjai?" asks Atticus.

"Many more, Atticus," answers Elric, "But I think this is enough for today, your parents will be here soon to collect you. Please, don't try to 'will' anything too strange tonight. It will take some time for you to learn control over your abilities, and your awakening process has one final stage remaining. There is a quest we would like you to go on. Report to Professor Morgan first thing in the morning, and he will fill you in."

"But... I need to ask one more thing," Atticus says quickly.

"Go ahead," replies Elric.

"Who are the other members of this new Majjai Six?"

Elric smiles, "Don't worry, you'll meet them tomorrow, although, you know one of them already."

"I do?"

"Yes. She says you like pancakes quite a lot," Elric winks at Atticus.

Before he can respond, the phone rings to inform them of Joseph and Sophia arriving. Atticus leaves with Geoffrey to meet them for his journey home.

The Majjai Journals:

I have watched him for a long time from far away. He is cute. He has no idea of his potential. Elric is quite adamant that we keep an eye on this one; but in watching him, I think I'm getting closer to him.

But what these feelings are I do not know. His mannerisms are quite unique, and those little freckles are just kissable, yet, there is something else in him. I sense his strength, as do the other Majjai, but there is more to him.

I do not know if I should tell Elric about the darkness I have also sensed within him, but do I mistake this darkness with emptiness? I do not know.

He possesses the gift of insight, but I believe he is unaware, mistaking the skill as either dreams or his unique astral projection ability that even breaks the binding.

Olof was teasing me again, telling me that I just can't stop talking about our new discovery. Elric keeps information about this new boy from us – what is he protecting us from? Could he be the sixth, the fabled 'chosen one'?

These new times are interesting, I want to get closer to this new one, not just because he is cute. He seems vulnerable, but also strong. He might need some coaxing and the like, but I think he will be able to handle this new world.

This new ability I am feeling, these dreams... Elric says that I may be a seer. I get glimpses now and then of things that might happen, so perhaps that kiss I dreamt with him is meant to be? I don't know, there are so many questions about our futures, things we do not understand about our enemies or ourselves.

There are other dreams, too, these are much darker. Razakel may not be our only foe, there will be another if these dreams are anything to go by, but this foe seems confused between right and wrong. I should speak to Elric about these dreams, but when the time is right. At the moment he seems so pre-occupied.

I wish he would ask us to do more, give us more responsibility, but he keeps saying that we need to save our strength for future tasks. He looks tired now.

Anyway, tomorrow is a new day, and hopefully, Atticus will know everything he needs to. I need to speak to Elric before going to see Atticus in the morning, no doubt he will be telling me how things have gone tonight.

Time to sleep now I think. Tomorrow will be very interesting.

Joyce Sparks.

Chapter 10

Unification

Elric watches from the window as Joseph and Sophia drive Atticus home. He turns to see Geoffrey sitting with his head in his hands.

"Come my friend, we should prepare for tomorrow."

Geoffrey looks up, "You know I have to go after him, don't you?"

Elric sighs, "I know, but the fact Draconus is still alive proves that we are unprepared to do so right now. The legend, it seems, is true. He can only die by the Sword of Al-Amir," Elric sits opposite Geoffrey, "The sword was lost long ago; I fear Razakel keeps it locked in his domain, to protect his pet."

"Draconus is no pet, he is almost as evil as his master. He is rabid and twisted. We need to be sure of the location of that sword," snaps Professor Sprocking.

"Enough, Geoffrey," says Elric, with a tone of authority, "These things will be done in time. More importantly, Razakel now knows of Atticus' existence, and that he is definitely the chosen one. Our main goal must be to protect him, and unify the Majjai Six."

Geoffrey looks sternly towards Elric, "Fine. But, when we do find the sword, Draconus is mine."

"I wouldn't have it any other way, my friend," replies Elric.

"Tomorrow will be interesting," says Geoffrey, "Word will soon spread throughout the Majjai students about Atticus. I hope he is ready for the fame and the world that is about to be presented to him."

"Don't worry Geoffrey. I sense something in Atticus that assures me he will be fine with this new world, almost like he has always known," replies Elric.

Geoffrey decides to change the subject, "Is Benjamin comfortable with his mission?"

"Yes, I spoke to him at great length," responds Elric, "His only reservation is that the team hasn't learnt control yet, and are still too eager to use their gifts without measure. This will be a good test for them. Our watchers tell us that the beasts of the north are few and not powerful enough to worry even our junior students. The quicker this team learns to work together, the better, which is why I'm sending them."

"Agreed," says Geoffrey, "let's hope our watchers have done their job properly; we can't afford any surprises on this one."

"You are right, Geoffrey, but I'm sure Benjamin will be able to handle any unforeseen circumstances. I think we should retire to our rooms now, we have a lot to prepare for tomorrow − as you said, word will spread quickly of the chosen one's discovery," says Elric.

Geoffrey and Elric exit the room and retire to their sleeping quarters.

Atticus opens his eyes on the drive home, realising he can almost see anywhere, through anyone else's eyes, just by thinking about them, "This one will be useful," he thinks to himself.

# # #

"BEEP!! BEEP!!"

Atticus' alarm clock shrieks into life, waking him with a start. Surprised at how fresh he feels this morning, he realises the reason is that he had no nightmares during the night. Atticus jumps out of bed, brushes his teeth, and decides to get on the phone to Joyce as quickly as possible.

He frantically searches the pockets of the trousers he wore yesterday for the phone number that Joyce gave to him. Running downstairs to get to the phone, he bumps into Sophia.

"You're in a rush this morning," she says as she dodges Atticus' sprint, "If you're running to call Joyce, she already phoned. She'll be here in ten minutes. Your cereal is on the breakfast table."

"Thanks, Mum, did… erm, she say anything else?" asks Atticus.

"No sweetie, nothing much. Quick, now, you don't want to keep her waiting," Sophia continues up the stairs. As she gets to the top she calls back down to Atticus, "By the way, I think she is lovely," she smiles down at Atticus and continues to her upstairs office.

Atticus wolfs down his breakfast, grabs his school robe, and waits for Joyce to knock on the door. He passes a mirror, double-checks his hair, and makes sure there are no embarrassing embellishments on his face. The doorbell rings. With a final check on his breath, Atticus ventures towards the door.

"Bye Mum, I'm off; might be at school late again today. Will call you from there!" shouts Atticus before opening the door to meet Joyce.

Joyce is already waiting near the end of the path, "Morning, pancake man. Good sleep?"

"Not bad, you?"

"It was pleasant enough. So, how did your meeting go yesterday?" replies Joyce.

101

"You knew about that, then?" Atticus finds it slightly annoying that Joyce threw so many hints without actually saying anything.

Joyce blushes a little, "Well, I knew you had a meeting, but... erm, you know I couldn't tell you and... erm, well, I *really* want to ask you something."

Atticus looks at Joyce, almost instinctively knowing what she will ask, "Sure."

"Is it true, then? Are you the chosen one?" Joyce asks, grabbing her chance.

"I assume so," says Atticus tentatively, "but to be honest, I don't have a clue what that means, and what I have to do."

Joyce stops their walk for a moment, and holds Atticus by the arm, looking into his eyes she says, "No one knows, Atticus, it's what we have to figure out. Did Elric get as far as to tell you about the Majjai Six?"

Atticus nods.

"So, are you going to show it to me then?" asks Joyce.

Atticus stares blankly at her.

She rolls up her sleeve to reveal her birthmark. It is the same as the one on the book cover: a ring, with a small spiral encompassing it. The Mark of the Majjai, "Right, show me yours, now; I've shown you mine."

Atticus rolls up his left sleeve, lays open his forearm with the palm of his hand facing upwards and shows his mark.

Joyce stares at it, and brings her own forearm forward to compare, "So it's true, you *are* the chosen one!" Joyce brings her other hand forward and touches the mark on Atticus' arm. He shivers slightly as the touch sends tingles down his spine. Her touch is warm, soothing. The hairs on Atticus' arm stand up as he closes his eyes.

Joyce continues to caress his arm around the mark, but stops as soon as she spots the scar, "What's this? I sense something dark here."

"I had a dream the night before last, about someone called Razakel," replies Atticus. Joyce's face grimaces at the mention of the name while Atticus continues, "I cut my arm in the dream, and when I woke up, this scar was here"

Joyce studies the scar, turning Atticus' arm around, and back again. She looks behind as if checking for anybody watching them, "Let me show you something," she pulls Atticus behind a nearby tree, "Hold still." Joyce closes her eyes and concentrates.

The mark of the Majjai on her arm begins to glow, it is a different slightly lighter shade of blue to what Atticus has experienced before, and as it glows, Atticus begins to feel pins and needles around the scar. Joyce's hand moves over it, her palm face down. Below her palm Atticus can see the same colour light that appears on her mark shine out. Too dazzling to watch, Atticus shuts his eyes as well, and waits for the feeling to disappear. A few moments pass and the light dims, Atticus opens one eye to see if whatever Joyce is doing is finished.

"There, that's better," she sighs

Atticus looks at his arm – where the scar from his dream once was, to find it completely vanished. Atticus immediately stares at Joyce, "What did you do?"

"It's my power, Atticus. I'm a healer," she continues to hold Atticus' hand, "I have other powers, too, and so do the rest of us."

"Rest?" Atticus asks quizzically.

"The rest of the Majjai Six, including you," holding hands, they continue their way to school. Atticus uses his other hand to touch the skin where Joyce healed him; it's as smooth as it was before the injury.

"Is it true Elric always knew about you?" asks Joyce.

Atticus nods, "Yes, and someone else, too, but Elric wouldn't tell me who that person is."

Curious about the Majjai powers, Atticus asks Joyce more questions, "So, what power do I have then?"

Joyce looks at Atticus again, "All of them, I think, well, it is said the *chosen* one can will almost anything, but it will take you time to learn control. Khan, one of the Majjai Six, almost blew out the hall in his first training session. Olof as well. He's a big guy, but a real softie at heart."

"Khan? Olof? Who else is there?" asks Atticus.

"You'll meet everyone later today," says Joyce.

"Do your parents know Joyce? I mean, about all this Majjai stuff?" Atticus longs to be able to reveal these secrets to his Joseph and Sophia, but has shied away from doing so for fear of such an act being forbidden.

Joyce nods, "They know, in fact, it was they who sought out Elric. My parents discovered that I was special many years ago. It's why they spent so much time on archaeology projects in and around Iran."

"Do you think I can tell my parents about this?" asks Atticus.

Joyce shrugs, "I don't know, Atticus, that is a question you should really ask Elric."

At this point, they both forget that they are holding hands. The rest of the journey is full of questions from Atticus, eager to learn about this new world. They reach the school gates in what feels like a few minutes.

Joyce turns to him, "I was so glad when I found out it was you?"

"Glad? Why?" asks Atticus.

"Well, I always had a feeling, and, well…" Joyce suddenly feels a little awkward, "You know, you better hurry to see Professor Morgan. I'll see you soon after that meeting anyway. The rest of the team are eager to meet you."

Atticus hates it when Joyce changes subjects so rapidly, but is now almost so used to it that he just sweeps every change of direction under the carpet. They part ways and Atticus makes his way towards the Professor's office. Before he gets to the entrance, he hears Joyce cry out. He turns, and to his horror, he sees Bradley and his minions are grabbing her.

"Oi, Jones!" screams Bradley, "We have business to discuss."

Atticus desperately looks around for help, but most of the courtyard is already clear, and the students that are left quickly scurry away, not wanting anything to do with this situation for fear of being Bradley's next target.

Bradley throws Joyce into one of his minions' arms. Jimmy grabs Joyce and holds her tightly from behind, forcing her to watch the action.

"Go on, Brad, kick his 'ead in," goads Jimmy.

The minions roar in unison, rabid with excitement of the impending fight.

Atticus, far from being a fighter of any sort, is confused as to what to do. He knows he can't let them hurt Joyce, but hasn't a clue on how to stop them.

He marches towards Bradley, trying to act confident, knowing full well he is ill-equipped to beat Bradley in a straight fight. He stands in front of him. Bradley towers over Atticus.

"Told you I'd be getting you, Jones," Bradley grabs Atticus by his jumper and punches him in the stomach, hard. Atticus falls to his knees, winded. Bradley doesn't finish there; he winds up his fist again, and thumps Atticus on the side of his face.

"No!" screams Joyce, "Leave him alone!"

Atticus falls to the ground, stunned, then gets up slowly to face Bradley again who leans towards the dazed Atticus and whispers in his ear, "This is my school, don't ever make me look like a fool again," then he knees Atticus in the stomach, sending him back to the ground. Atticus wheezes, gasping for air, his eyes water. He thinks to himself about this great power he is supposed to have, but doesn't know how to use it. He hears Bradley speak to his minions again.

"Get him boys!"

Bradley's followers pile into Atticus, punching him and kicking him on the leg, in the stomach. Jimmy is still holding Joyce; both he and Bradley stand there laughing as the other three beat Atticus.

"Hey!" another voice is heard in the distance, "What is going on here?" the accent is different, with a strong Middle Eastern slant.

The boys stop and turn to see two older students approaching them, "Who the hell are you?" Bradley demands.

The Arab-looking one replies, "My name is Abd al-Hakim Khan, and this is Olof Gilmar. More importantly, you are holding two of our friends; you should release them, now!"

Olof stands tall and silent, allowing Khan to take the lead.

Bradley laughs, "Who's going to make me? You?"

Khan steps up to Bradley, his hair is long and straight, with a light goatee beard and clean-shaven lines. He is wearing a long, thick cloak that conceals the rest of his body.

"Yes," Khan replies. He stands and just stares at Bradley directly into his eyes. Olof continues to stand menacingly behind his friend, steely silent. He wears the same robe as Khan, but his is pinned by a large clip in the shape of a Viking helmet.

Bradley responds the only way he knows how, with numbers. He beckons his minions to follow him, and attempts to throw a punch right at Khan's head. Khan sidesteps and the punch misses him and hurtles towards Olof, who is already prepared and grabs the fist mid air, holds it, smirks, and pushes Bradley back.

Jimmy is still holding onto Joyce. Atticus looks up to see Bradley's minions attempt to beat up Khan.

Khan is moving so quickly, dodging and blocking every blow. Olof stands and watches, as if confident that Khan can quite easily hold his own.

Khan responds only with light slaps across the cheeks of his attackers before throwing off his cloak-like robe and covering one of Bradley's followers with it, sending him into the ground. Without the cloak the rest of his attire is exposed. He is wearing Arabic-style clothes that cling tight against the body in differing shades of white, intricately detailed and crisp, almost as if they had just arrived from an Arabian tailor.

Bradley and his minions soon tire, and shortly they stand huffing and puffing. Jimmy, unsure of what to do, keeps hold of Joyce.

Olof speaks in a deep Swedish accent, "Are you ok, Joyce?"

"Just fine now that you guys are here," she replies. Looking around as much as she could, she sees Atticus get up onto his feet, waits for him to see her so that he knows she is ok. She winks at him.

Atticus smiles back, pleased that she is unhurt.

Joyce suddenly elbows Jimmy, winds him, forcing him to release his grip. She then spins and roundhouse kicks him in the gut before stepping back to stand beside Atticus and Olof. Together they watch Khan's acrobatics as the tired Bradley and minions continue to try and hit him. Khan retrieves his cloak, and in one swift movement, it fully covers him again. He steps back to stand beside Olof, staring at the group of boys who attempted to attack him.

Bradley looks at the numbers, five versus four is too close for him to even consider making a stand. He stares at Atticus with a look of pure hatred, the will to want to tear Atticus apart is apparent in his eyes and bulging veins, "You better hope your bodyguards are always around Jones."

"Do not worry, my friend," replies Khan, "We will be."

With disgust, Bradley grunts and signals his little gang to fall back and head into school.

The two rescuers wait until they see them disappear into the school doors before turning to face Joyce and Atticus, "Are you ok, Atticus?" asks Khan.

"F-fine, thanks for that. Who are you?" asks Atticus.

"This is Khan," replies Joyce quickly, "Remember, I told you about him."

"It was not the story about the training session was it?" Khan stares at Joyce with a raised eyebrow.

"Maybe," she replies cheekily, "And the quiet guy is Olof."

Olof stands taller than Khan, with a blindingly light shade of blond hair tied into a long, tight ponytail. He appears to be much older than Khan; in fact, he appears to be almost old enough to be a teacher. Atticus is surprised that Bradley even has the guts to contemplate taking on someone of Olof's size, even if all he did was watch by the sidelines.

Olof nods towards Atticus, "It is an honour to finally meet you Atticus; you are very brave to try and take on those boys without training."

"Err, thanks. I didn't do much, though," Atticus touches his lip and looks at the blood on his hand.

"Wait, you can't go to Professor Morgan looking like that," says Joyce.

Olof and Khan check the surrounding area to ensure no one is watching. Khan nods towards Joyce indicating it is clear.

She touches Atticus' forehead and a blue glow engulfs him. His wounds heal quickly, and the blood disappears, "There, how do you feel now?" she asks.

"Perfect," Atticus says, realizing that he feels 100% again. He touches Joyce's hand, "Thank you" he says softly.

Joyce blushes and looks away.

"Uhum," interrupts Khan, "We should all be getting into the manor now; Atticus, you are already late for your meeting with the Professor. Joyce, you need to come with us to see Elric, we have preparations to do."

They walk into the school together, in case Bradley is waiting anywhere. After walking to Professor Morgan's office, the others leave Atticus to see Elric.

"Enter," Professor Morgan calls from behind the door after Atticus knocks.

The professor is sitting at his desk, elbows on the table, and his hands are touching at the fingertips, "Please, Atticus, sit."

Atticus accepts the invitation and sits opposite the professor.

"So, now you know, Atticus. How do you feel today after having a night to let things sink in?"

Atticus shrugs, "I'm not sure, sir, I don't *feel* any different, but I'm aware things have changed."

Professor Morgan taps his fingers together, "I see, but how do you feel about the whole '*chosen one*' thing?"

"Oh, that, well, I'm a little unsure that I can be who people want me to be," replies Atticus.

109

"In what way Atticus?" asks the Professor

Atticus decides to tell the Professor of his encounter today

"Well, today, I was jumped by some boys, and couldn't even defend myself. Khan and Olof had to save me."

"Ahhh, so you've met them then?" says Professor Morgan, "I wouldn't worry, they have had years of training, and you have had nothing direct, apart perhaps from your Fencing lessons."

Atticus' eyes widen, "Fencing, sir?"

"Yes, your fencing coach, Mr Callan, is experienced in the ways of the Majjai, and purposely guided you towards his own style for a reason. It is in fact, the closest real-world martial art that you will need to learn to help you with combat in our world."

"So, Mr Callan knew all this time as well?" asks Atticus.

"Yes, but he was unaware of you being the chosen one, as was I until Elric called a late meeting with the elders last night. Mr Callan has been away on a very important mission for the Majjai. But we need not go into that right now."

"Are you a master as well?" asks Atticus.

The Professor chuckles, "Me? Far from it. I'm not at the level of Mr Callan or Professor Sprocking, and Elric is even more powerful. Although you wouldn't know it from looking at him. But, the new Majjai Six – it's prophesised that you will be the most powerful Majjai of all time. Olof, Joyce, and Khan have years of knowledge."

"So, who are the other two?" asks Atticus.

"You'll meet them very shortly," says the Professor, "but so that you are prepared, I should let you know of their abilities."

Atticus waits with anticipation, "I know about Joyce, she says she's a healer."

Professor Morgan nods, "Yes, Joyce Sparks is a healer, but she also has the power of speed and protection. Abd al-Hakim Khan is

110

a descendant of a proud race of Saracen warriors, he has the power of might and is able to sense weakness in adversaries, making him an ideal tactician. You'll have fun with Khan, as he is also an expert swordsman. Olof Gilmar is a master of Old Norse Magic; it is suspected that he is destined to reclaim the hammer of Thor. His Norse ancestry is traced back to the Norse gods. He is a very powerful Majjai, with the native ability to create and control ice. He is also the oldest of the group by some years," the professor pauses to take a sip from his glass of water, "Now, onto the ones you haven't met yet. Princess Safaya Mirza."

"Princess?" asks Atticus.

"Yes, Princess, although it will probably be more difficult for you to comprehend that she is actually from another time," says the Professor.

"But, how is that possible?" asks an astounded Atticus.

"There is an artefact, an orb, which is currently hidden away. This orb has the power to open time portals. It is what Razakel is after," says the Professor.

Atticus looks towards the Professor, "Why is he after it?"

"Well, he wants to go back to the beginning," replies Professor Morgan.

"The beginning of what?" asks Atticus

The Professor adjusts his glasses before answering, "To the beginning of time, dear boy. Where life began. He knows the only way he can have total domination is to rule from the start."

Atticus wonders for a moment, "But, what about... God?" he asks.

"I was wondering when you would ask that question," says the Professor, "Free will, Atticus, is a gift to us all. We as a race created the Orb, we as a race have to protect it, or destroy it. There are many beings and creatures you may have heard or read about, some will not interfere; unless free will itself is stolen or forced, we cannot expect help from the Angels'. Anyway, I digress. Safaya is a princess from ancient Persia, the last to be transported through time with the Orb that we know of, before its creator hid it. It is you, Atticus, as the chosen one, who has been prophesised to find it, and stop Razakel from taking what he sees as the ultimate prize. This realm of Earth."

"And how am I supposed to do that?"

The professor rests his hands on the table, "I have no idea, but I'm sure Elric will point you in the right direction, he knew the creator of the Orb."

"Ok, so, there is Safaya and someone else? And what can Princess Safaya do?" Atticus asks, curious to find out about the final members of the Majjai Six.

"Yes, Princess Safaya. She is an elemental; she has the ability to control the four elements of earth, fire, wind and water. Unfortunately, she hasn't mastered the ability to control them simultaneously… yet. Finally, there is Ju Long, a master of stealth with the power of invisibility, flight, and an expert in the martial arts. He also has a tendency to not actually be able to keep his mouth shut, I'm pretty sure he thinks that is an ability too."

All Atticus can think is, *"Cool!"* but he is also worried, how can he even think of being anywhere near as powerful as the people he has just heard about? He doesn't even understand what he has or how to utilise it.

"So, what about me Professor, what 'power' do I have?" he asks, hoping he will finally get an answer to this question.

"All in good time Atticus," replies Professor Morgan, "Your powers will come to you naturally. We may need to do a little coaxing to help you discover them, but hopefully not much. We have to be careful with you."

"Why?" asks Atticus.

Professor Morgan sighs, "Because it is said that your powers are to be greater than all other Majjai that have gone before; greater than the Majjai Six, past and present, put together. To unleash that much power without control could prove to be rather dangerous. Using Magic is dangerous as it is; there are always consequences, and one must be sure of the right time to use one's abilities. The drain on the self is quite severe."

Atticus is still unsure of what all of this means, "So when will they start to appear? My powers I mean," he asks.

"Ooooh, hopefully in about an hour's time," The professor smirks, "We have to meet the rest of the Majjai Six, and once you are all together, the awakening process for your powers will be complete, and the training will begin."

"But Elric warned me not to will anything strange yesterday – what did he mean by that?" asks Atticus, puzzled at why Elric would advise him in such a way.

"Purely a precaution, I'm sure," replies Professor Morgan, "Come now, it is time to unify the chosen one to his brethren. It is time to take the fight to Razakel and prove to him that the Majjai Six have truly returned. I have been assigned a mission, to take the Majjai Six, including you, to investigate strange sightings near the Scottish borders."

"What kind of sightings?"

"Beasts, Atticus, demons," says the Professor, "Small pockets of portals have opened up across the country, and some lower demons have been left behind," the professor spots a look of fear encroaching onto Atticus' face, "But don't worry, you'll be perfectly safe, you're just coming along to watch the team in action. It will be a good training exercise for them and for you; it is doubtful that we will encounter anything too dangerous."

Atticus gulps, "Erm, ok, then," part of Atticus is terrified, but other parts are strangely excited about this mission. He wants answers – his entire life he has had questions about belonging, he never felt that the truth about himself was ever told to him. This new turn of events excites him, but there is another reason for his excitement aside from the fact he will finally start learning about his abilities. The best thing, he muses to himself, is that he gets to spend some more time with Joyce.

"Professor?" says Atticus tentatively, wondering if he should reveal one of his new skills, "There is one thing I already appear to be able to do, and that is… well… I can see things in rooms when I am not there. I just need to think about the place, and I'm there, or I see it through another's eyes."

The Professor looks at Atticus up and down, "That is the gift of insight, dear boy, but be careful when you use it. If your presence is detected, your mind can be trapped there; your very thoughts may even be wiped completely from your memory. It is a dark road you will travel if you abuse that power."

The Professor gathers some folders from his desk and beckons Atticus to follow him, "We must hurry now, they are waiting for us."

Atticus follows Professor Morgan out of his office, down the corridor, and in the general direction of Professors Sprocking's chamber, the one he remembers waking up in after touching the *Gooyeh Partaab*.

Professor Morgan taps Atticus on the shoulder, "Remember, Atticus, what you are about to see, whatever you hear, it must be kept secret. Our world is very different than anything you have experienced before. It is a world not only of Magic, and wondrous things, but also one of real danger. Those that know not of our ways, or indeed the dangers, risk their very lives to even consider entering it."

They continue down several corridors, until they reach a pair of massive doors. Professor Morgan checks behind him, to ensure that no one has followed.

He looks at Atticus, "Remember this password Atticus."

Atticus nods as the Professor returns his focus to the large doors.

The Professor moves his head closer to the doors, *"Farasi Bakhwar,"* he whispers.

Atticus recognises the words from when he experienced Professor Sprocking using them. He watches as the doors open slowly to a pitch-black corridor, which they enter as the doors slowly close behind them. As the doors meet, the corridor illuminates. Compared to the rest of the Manor, this corridor is lavishly decorated, with giant marble statues, and row upon row of paintings of what Atticus can only think to be Majjai of the past.

They continue down the corridor until they come to another pair of huge doors. No password is needed this time, they open by themselves as the two approach.

Atticus is in awe at what he sees. Hundreds of students fill the massive chamber he and the Professor enter. They are all facing a stage, but as soon as they hear the doors, they turn to look. Atticus can hear the whispers ringing around every seat.

"It's him!"

"It's the chosen one!"

"Atticus is the chosen one, that's what they're saying!"

"Look, look, he's here!"

Atticus moves forward. With each step, someone starts to clap, until the entire chamber erupts. Atticus remains awestruck, he feels proud, but also nervous. The thought of so many people relying on him to be this 'chosen one' makes him anxious.

Professor Morgan indicates to Atticus to continue without him "It's time to unify the Majjai Six, Atticus; they'll show you what to do next," he says, pointing to the stage.

At the front he spots Olof, Khan, Joyce and two others he assumes to be Safaya and Ju Long. He walks towards them, the crowd still cheering, almost as if a hero has returned home.

Atticus gazes towards the five before him. Differing in height, shape, colour, and emotiveness. All five stare back before finally Khan speaks.

"Welcome Atticus, it is time to begin your training."

Chapter 11

Alvarez – The Destructor

Red lightning strikes the sky; the clouds erupt in flames of deep orange, scorching the horizon. Alvarez stands watch at his keep as someone knocks on the door to his chamber.

"Enter," says Alvarez.

A Screamer enters the room, "I bring word from Lord Razakel; he wishes to see you."

"Tell our King I will be with him shortly," replies Alvarez.

The Screamer backs out of the room and slowly closes the door.

Alvarez collects his cloak and adorns himself. He knows Razakel will want answers regarding the episode at Echo Forest. He secretly hopes for mercy, but knows his King well enough to realise that mercy is something Razakel does not understand.

He walks slowly towards the Demon King's chamber, as if expecting this to be his final walk.

The corridors are very different than the cold, charred rock of the chambers and dungeons. The walls here are a mixture of biological and stone. The organic sections resemble bloody flesh, all moving, pulsating as if alive. The stones are almost like massive scabs on the surface. Chains litter the walls, piercing the flesh and binding it with the rock.

Shrieks and wails fill the walkways, not allowing any chance of silent meditation or reflection.

Alvarez finally reaches the King's chamber. The doors tower above him, almost fifteen meters into the air. He knocks, the echo of each impact rumbles back and forth, surrounding not only the chamber it links to, but also the corridor behind him. The giant doors open slowly, creaking as they do so.

"Come forth, Alvarez," Razakel's deep voice resonates throughout the throne room chamber. Alvarez walks towards his King. Even seated on his throne, he is still a threatening sight; his power can be sensed by all around him. Herensugue stands to the left of Razakel. The throne room is gigantic, with its imposing dome ceiling, the centre of which is so high that it is almost out of sight. Many small creatures are dancing around the chamber, scurrying here and there, doing tiny errands. Some appear to be cleaning. Others are just waiting for orders from slightly larger creatures.

"You sent for me, my Lord?" Alvarez drops to one knee, and bows his head.

Razakel turns menacingly towards Alvarez, "Explain to me what happened at Echo Forest. How could such a simple quest be a failure?"

"One of the Screamers alerted the Majjai to our presence, my Lord," Alvarez replies keeping his head facing towards the floor.

"And what of the amulets?" asks Razakel.

"The Majjai have them, but they know not what they are. I transformed their appearance before they took them. Even Elric will not be able to reverse this Magic," replies Alvarez.

Razakel leans further forward from his massive throne, "So, how do we get them back now?"

Alavarez knows that a mission to try and infiltrate the Manor would result in annihilation for any who dare go, "The Manor is well protected, my Lord, a stealth operation would be the only way," Alvarez cowers, "I recommend…"

"ENOUGH!" roars Razakel, "You cower before me like a snivelling dog; is this how you faced the Majjai? What good is the power I have given you, if you are unable to complete a simple task such as this?"

"Forgive me, my Lord. The portal was weakening, I had to return before it lost all power," replies Alvarez, the pitch of his voice rising in a crescendo of fear.

"Pathetic," Razakel stands and walks towards Alvarez, "*You* will go to the Manor, and it will be *you* who will retrieve the remaining amulets. The ones we have will soon lose their energy."

"As you wish my Lord," whimpers Alvarez.

"But, do not worry, I know the odds of returning are slim," Razakel beckons to Herensugue, who promptly reaches behind the throne to retrieve a goblet, bubbling over with smoke pouring from it. Herensugue hands the goblet to Razakel, "Drink this," says the Demon King menacingly.

Alvarez piously takes the goblet, "What is it, my Lord?"

"DO NOT QUESTION ME, IMP!" screams Razakel, the force of which makes the inhabitants of the chamber cower into their shadows, "You will do as I say, or suffer the consequences!"

Alvarez remains silent, and drinks the contents of the goblet without pause. A strange reddish light appears out of his hands and quickly swirls around him, covering each and every area of his body. Alvarez screams in agony, his voice piercing the air. The red light grows into a massive cocoon like shape, forming a liquid lava shell, and finally solidifies into charred rock. The chamber goes silent.

Razakel calmly returns to his throne. Herensugue approaches

him as they leave the smoking, charred cocoon to its own devices.

"Massssster, it will take time for the transsssformation to be complete," Herensugue says, his seven heads all slithering and moving from side to side while speaking.

"Yes, but we have time. Remember, get me the Runes of Zamaan. I believe the Behemoth armies has evolved enough for now," Razakel's voice resonates around the chamber. The Runes are soon brought to him. Razakel walks towards the cocoon and places the runes around it. Stepping back, he stares at the first rune, then points to it with his right index finger. A tiny jet of reddish-white flame shoots out, hitting the small stone.

A cage of blue light surrounds the cocoon, each rune acting as the source of each bar of light forming a confine around Lord Alvarez's new prison.

"It is done," says Razakel, "now we wait. Bring me the prisoner."

A pair of Screamers drag in a hooded lady. Weakened, she can barely stand. Her cloak and trousers are shredded, with cuts that still have not sealed leaking blood onto the floor. Her legs are limp, and merely follow where her torso is taken.

"You are a watcher, yes?" asks Razakel.

The weakened woman simply nods.

"You were caught spying on my beasts at the northern portal, were you not?" says the Demon King menacingly.

The woman coughs, her broken body shivers at the sound of Razakel's voice.

Razakel continues, "What did you report back to the Majjai?"

The woman remains silent.

Razakel is angered at the woman's defiance, "SPEAK! Do not dare defy me, or your death will be welcomed by your very soul. The pain I will put you through will be so great that your body will beg to die."

The woman speaks faintly "Please. I can't... just let me go. I have a son..."

"You think I care? Very well," Razakel signals to the Screamers, "Draconus has been wanting a new toy, he'll enjoy a new rag doll. He likes to keep his toys fresh, so don't worry, he won't kill you... yet."

"F ...f... four. I told them there were four demons, Screamers, and an Orc," the woman groans in pain as her broken bones scrape against each other, "Now please, let me go."

"Take her to Draconus," commands Razakel.

"But, but... I told you," whimpers the woman.

"And you still live, that is my gift to you. Take her away," says Razakel.

The Screamers drag the woman away from the chamber, her protests, as weak as her body, falling on deaf ears. All that remains is the trail of blood still seeping from her wounds.

"Perhapssss, sssshe could become ussseful my Lord?" hisses Herensugue.

"In what way?" asks Razakel.

"A witnesssss my Lord. A witnessss of your power. What more to ssssscare the remaining Majjai than a witnessss of your power, let her ssssee the birth of the Dessstructor and take the messssage of their impending doom back to the Majjai."

"There is no need, Herensugue," replies Razakel, "There is another Majjai here, in this realm. I sense his presence and his intentions."

"Where, Massster? Allow me to dessstroy his filth for daring to enter our domain," Herensugue splutters and hisses, excited at the prospect of fresh human flesh to consume.

"Calm, Herensugue. He is here for the runes. It will soon be time. Meanwhile, let's prepare a surprise for our Majjai friends on their way to destroy these *four* demons," Razakel says as he and Herensugue leave the throne room, followed by all manner of strange creatures. The throne room is left empty and the cocoon is now alone, with only the hum of the runes to keep it company.

Chapter 12

Enter − Mage Callan

A lone figure skulks in the shadows of Razakel's castle, robed and hooded. The hood is large enough to keep his face well-hidden.

Two screamers emerge from a door on the side of the castle. The hooded figure steps back into the shadows to listen to their conversation.

"I'm glad he was sleeping, that dragon is becoming a nuisance" The first Screamer adjusts its stance and continues onwards.

The second Screamer follows, "I agree, but at least now he has something to chew on that doesn't include us. The watcher woman will keep him pleased for a while."

"True, but we should have killed her," says the first Screamer, "The Majjai rarely leave their own behind."

The hooded figure slowly slides along the edge of the wall, trying desperately to not make any sound. The walls are cold, uneven, and sharp. His hands follow every stipple, every crevice; his legs do the same, melting into the shadows.

The screamers walk further away, and stand to guard the area leading to the door. The hooded figure nears the entrance, eager to reach the entrance. Just as he gets to it, another screamer exits. The hooded figure quickly grabs it and twists its neck until it breaks.

The noise alerts the other two.

"Who goes there?" demands one of the Screamers, snarling and snapping.

Both of them approach the doorway and find the corpse of the third Screamer, "Show yourself!"

The hooded figure steps out from the shadows, "You have a choice, my friends: run... or die?"

The two Screamers charge at the hooded man, who mutters under his breath, "Die it is then."

The Screamers massive frames are almost upon him as he steps back and to the side. His movement is so fast that the Screamers smash into the wall with their momentum. Before they are able to recover, two quick flashes of blue light lash out into the darkness, and they both fall to the ground, dead.

The hooded figure readjusts his cloak and enters the side door, unlocking it with a wave of his hand. Sticking to the shadows, he searches for the Watcher Woman he overheard the Screamers talking about.

From within his cloak he takes out what looks like a compass with the inscription '*Detector of Life*' which is written below another set of calligraphic symbols, similar to the ones on the note that was left with Atticus when he was found. The hooded figure speaks to the compass and a small blue arrow appears above it, guiding him towards the imprisoned Watcher Woman. He walks cautiously, knowing that not only is Draconus alive, but he also sleeps alongside his prisoner.

The woman is in a cage, the hooded figure, swiftly but quietly heads towards it, his footsteps silent against the floor. Beyond, Draconus sleeps, unaware of what is going on around him.

The woman whispers slowly, "Who are you?"

"I'm a friend, shhhh, let me get you out of this cage; we must be quiet," the hooded figure says with his face still hidden, pointing towards the sleeping dragon. Another wave of the hand and the lock clicks open; he opens the cage door very slowly, and beckons the woman to follow him quietly.

"I can't move," she groans as she attempts to lift her leg.

The hooded figure pulls a vial from within his cloak, "Here, drink this," he says as he hands it to the watcher.

She takes a sip and is amazed as her wounds begin to heal enough for her to be able to walk.

"Thank you," she says gratifyingly.

"You're welcome; but now, we *must* hurry."

They reach the staircase of the dungeon and make their way to the top. The hooded man helps the woman climb each step, sensing her injuries are still grave, "What is your name?" the hooded figure asks the woman once they are out of earshot of Draconus.

"My name is Serenity," she whispers, "I'm a watcher. I observed these demons enter through a portal. I contacted the Majjai council, but before I could return to observe them I was struck from behind. The next thing I remember is waking up in their torture chamber," Serenity bursts into tears, "I thought I was going to die."

The hooded figure consoles her, before remembering exactly where they are, "Shhh, you'll alert the others. You will be safe once we get out of here. First, there is something I must do, but I need you to remain quiet and calm. Can you do that?"

The woman nods, wiping her tears from her face. They make their way to the throne room very quietly, slowly checking each corridor before they continue. The hooded figure pulls out the compass again. This time it shows one blue arrow pointing towards Serenity, and several red arrows in various directions with varying lengths.

Avoiding the guards and directions of the red arrows, the two soon reach the throne room. Its doors are wide open, almost inviting them inside.

"This is way too easy," says the hooded man after spying the runes he is after surrounding the cocoon.

Approaching it he realises the size of the thing – it is much taller than himself, probably standing about three or four meters high. He pulls out a small black sack from his cloak, opens it and the Runes of Zamaan shoot into it, breaking the hum and releasing the bars of light encompassing the cocoon.

He looks towards the woman, "Come, it is time we leave this place," holding out his hand, the woman grabs it and they both head towards a nearby window. The hooded man is about to climb out of the window when a deep laugh rings around the chamber.

"Foolish Majjai, did you really think I didn't know?" says a deep voice.

"Show yourself," demands the hooded man.

Razakel and Herensugue appear out of thin air.

"I have something to show you Majjai, but first, I'm curious to know which of you had the courage to take such a mission. Reveal your identity," orders Razakel.

The hooded figure steps forward, pulling back his hood to reveal a middle-aged man's face, with a scar on the side of his right cheek. One eye has a silver pupil with a slightly different shade of silver iris, while the other eye is a deep, dark brown, "The name is Mage Callan. You may have heard of me?"

Herensugue is almost visibly frightened, taking two careful steps back.

Razakel laughs again, "It's comforting to know that the Majjai fear me enough to send their chief assassin to me. Now, allow me to reveal my little surprise to you."

Razakel takes a step towards the cocoon, bends slightly, and

126

touches the tip of it. Red light fills the crevices and a beam shoots out from the top. When the light stops, the cocoon begins to rumble. Loud bangs come from within it, as if something is trying to get out. The impacts get louder, more forceful. Suddenly a massive fist bursts its way out. Mage Callan acts quickly, moving Serenity to the corner, and projecting a shield of blue light around her for protection.

The cocoon explodes outward, filling the throne room with smoke and the putrid smell of rotting flesh.

"Mage Callan," says Razakel, "I'd like you to meet Alvarez, the Destructor."

As the smoke clears, Alvarez stands in the middle of the wreckage, breathing heavily. But he is different from before, an aura of red light now surrounds him. He steps out of the rubble and walks towards Mage Callan, moving faster with each step.

"I've beaten you many times in the past, Alvarez; a little bit of red light will not make any difference," says Mage Callan.

Alvarez chuckles at Mage Callan's comment, "Ahhh, but there is more," he stops walking, pulls off his cloak and roars into the air. As he does so, his skin begins to ripple, expanding, transforming him into a massive, hulking beast. He roars again. His jaw juts forward, and his arms grow. His whole physique expands once more, consuming the aura of red light, "Come Mage Callan, do your worst," Alvarez snarls in his new form.

Mage Callan flicks his cloak back as he moves his right leg forward, preparing for the impending attack.

Alvarez jumps into the air, and falls downward towards Mage Callan who in turn back flips firing multiple shots of blue fireballs towards the beast hurtling towards him. Alvarez lands with a force so strong that the entire chamber shakes.

Mage Callan jumps into the air. He flies towards Alvarez, arm outstretched with a blue spear of light forming just beyond it. He strikes Alvarez hard, but there is no effect. Mage Callan just bounces off the thick hide of Alvarez's new form. He rolls back onto his feet, readying himself for the counter-attack.

Alvarez charges towards him. Mage Callan tries to form a shield but it is too late, Alvarez punches Mage Callan in the gut, sending him soaring into the air, slamming into the far wall next to Serenity.

"He is too powerful for you," she says to her rescuer quietly, "Let us escape while we still can."

"Perhaps you're right," groans Mage Callan, he reaches into his pocket and hands Serenity a crystal, "Contact Elric with this, all you need do is speak into it. Hurry."

Serenity takes the amulet as Mage Callan turns to face Alvarez again. He runs towards him, unsheathing his sword screaming as he charges. With a flick of his finger on the blade his sword splits in two and they begin to glow blue.

Alvarez begins his charge on all fours, roaring and stomping his hands and feet like a gorilla. The chamber shakes and rattles, bits of rock fall from the walls. They clash in the centre of the throne room, in a bright flash of blue and red light.

The room falls silent. Razakel begins to chuckle, as does Herensugue.

"Foolish Majjai," says Razakel. Alvarez emerges from the debris unscathed. Mage Callan lies broken on the floor.

Serenity screams as she looks on in horror, "Nooooo!"

Without warning, a portal suddenly appears next to her. Out of it shoot two massive grappling hooks, one whips around and grabs Serenity, and the other grabs Mage Callan. The hooks pull them both through the portal, which then seals itself.

Alvarez transforms back to his human-like form and walks towards Razakel. On bended knee, head bowed down, he thanks his master, "My Lord, this gift of power will never fail you, I am yours to command. Do with me as you wish."

"Rise Alvarez, the Destructor. Your time will come, but for now, we have more pressing matters to sort out," Razakel says before turning to Herensugue, "Come, we must finalise our surprise for the Northern Portal."

"Masssster, they have the runesss," hisses Herensugue.

"No matter," replies Razakel, "we no longer have a use for them. Our armies are ready. We just need to find a way to get them there – now we must retrieve the amulets and locate the *Quantorbium*."

As all three leave the chamber, hundreds of little creatures flood the throne room and set to work repairing the walls and clearing away the mess.

Chapter 13

Awakenings

Back at Wysardian Manor, Atticus is taken to a bare room. Safaya and Ju Long still have not spoken to him while Khan acts as his guide for the route he is taking.

"Come Atticus, you must stand in the middle," says Khan as the five form a circle around Atticus. They close the circle by joining hands, which instantly triggers a blast of blue energy soaring skywards, startling Atticus at first, forcing him to flinch. He feels Joyce's hand, just to his right, grasping tighter, as if reassuring him that this is ok, that he is no danger. Any tension Atticus had soon disappears, and Joyce returns her hand to the circle.

The ceiling disappears to reveal stars and space, with the blue energy blast soaring faster and faster. Planets rush past their heads. Atticus almost ducks as he sees the rings of Saturn approaching at lightning speed. The other five stare upward, and a light breeze begins to swirl around the room. Their speed increases again, blurring everything into lines of white as they are transported to what appears to be another galaxy altogether. The view flips around and Atticus can see the Milky Way disappearing into the distance. Suddenly Atticus finds himself and the other five in a strange, liquid-like universe, with a massive star above them. Out of nowhere, five beams of light fire down from it and strike the five Majjai in the circle. A loud humming sound

130

begins to ring around the chamber, then, a smaller, much narrower beam of light shoots from their joined hands and fires into Atticus. Startled more than anything, Atticus flinches slightly. The ceiling returns to normal, and the others release their hands. They look towards Atticus as Joyce steps up to him.

"How do you feel?" she asks.

Atticus shakes himself, "I feel a little tingly, but fine otherwise."

"Good, ok, let's try to get you to 'do' something now," says Khan. He points to a chair in the corner, "See if you can shoot it."

"How?" asks Atticus.

"Remember those beams of light in your dreams?" asks Joyce. Atticus nods.

"Try to imagine them, imagine you are in control of them," continues Joyce.

Atticus closes his eyes, he thinks back to his vision, the one where he was fighting Draconus. His hands begin to feel a little warm, he looks down and sees a blue light surrounding them. He remembers the instinctive feeling in the dream, and throws the light at the chair. The chair flies back into the wall and smashes into pieces.

"Cool!" says Atticus.

"Quite," states Safaya, she has a similar accent to Khan's but with distinct differences in tonality. From her manner and bearing, Atticus can easily recognise that she is royalty.

"Now you must learn more control, and more power," Safaya says as she stands opposite Atticus, "Defend yourself!"

Safaya shoots a blue fireball towards Atticus. Instinctively he crosses his arms and a blue shield of light surrounds him, absorbing the attack from Safaya.

"Not bad," Says Ju Long, "Now, how do you move?"

131

Before Atticus can reply, Ju Long is upon him, with a lightning fast spin-kick sweeping his legs away. Atticus is on the floor.

"You must be faster, Atticus," says Khan, "Remember what Mage Callan has taught you."

"Mage Callan?" Atticus thinks to himself, and remembers what Professor Morgan told him earlier; they are talking about his Fencing teacher, Mr Callan. He stands again and tries to recall what he learnt to do with his feet and how to move in his lessons.

"Too much thinking," says Ju Long before jumping into the air and aiming another kick towards Atticus. Atticus breathes deeply, he thinks about slowing time, and as he does so he sees Ju Long decrease in speed, along with everyone else around him. Their voices turn to a slur of noise. Atticus casually moves to the side, he sees Ju Long land and attempt another spin kick. Atticus ducks it, and sweeps Ju Long to the floor. Atticus relaxes and time appears to return to normal.

"Impressive," says Olof.

There is a loud knock at the door, and then it opens abruptly. Professor Morgan enters, panting, "Quickly," he says, "Elric needs all of you in his chamber urgently!"

They all hurriedly follow the Professor towards Elric's chamber. The main hall has emptied allowing Atticus to notice how lavish it is, the walls are all covered in massive robes of red, orange and blue garments. Each chair has sumptuous cushions and the stage is outlined in matte silver. Two large muted silvery statues resembling griffins stand on either side of the stage. A large conference table is to the rear of it, facing the rest of the hall.

Professor Morgan quickens his pace. Atticus wonders what the urgency is and taps Joyce on the shoulder.

"What's going on?" he asks.

Joyce shrugs, "I have no idea, but it is not normal for Elric to call us in such a manner unless something bad has happened, especially after an awakening ceremony."

Joyce and Atticus hurry up to keep pace with the others.

"Quickly, this way," says Professor Morgan.

He leads them to Elric's room. As they approach, the doors open automatically. Atticus and Joyce peer around the corner to find Elric standing over two other people, a woman and a man that Atticus immediately recognises as Mr Callan, his Fencing teacher.

Mr Callan rests unconscious on a leather sofa, and the woman is seated next to him, weeping, with her head in her hands.

"Quickly, Joyce, attend to Mage Callan, before it is too late!" says Elric, as he tries to calm the woman down.

Joyce walks towards Mage Callan, she sees his broken, battered body and almost winces at the sight of the cuts and bruises. She holds her right hand to his forehead, closes her eyes and concentrates. The same blue glow that healed Atticus earlier in the day consumes Mage Callan. In moments his wounds appear to heal themselves, the cuts disappear and the bruises vanish. He lies motionless, breathing easily, but his eyes remain closed.

"Thank you Joyce, now please, help Serenity here," requests Elric more calmly.

Atticus steps towards Mage Callan, then turns towards Elric, "What happened?"

"That I do not know, Atticus. All I know is that Serenity contacted me to help them, so I brought them here as quickly as possible. Mage Callan was on an important mission to retrieve these," Elric removes the pouch containing the Runes of Zamaan from Mage Callan's belt. He opens it to show the runes to the Six.

"Stones, sir?" asks Atticus.

"Runes, Atticus," replies Elric, "These are the Runes of Zamaan, and they have the ability to slow or speed up time, almost to the point of infinity. They are very powerful – and dangerous in the wrong hands."

Atticus' eyes widen; every bit of this new world opening up to him fascinates him. The thirst to learn as much as possible grows with each passing second.

Serenity speaks after Joyce's healing powers have taken away enough of her pain, and she begins to explain what happened, "It was Alvarez; he is stronger than ever now. Razakel did something to him. He was in some kind of cocoon, which was surrounded by the runes, and when he emerged from it, he turned into a strange, hellhound-like beast. Mage Callan tried his best, but was no match for him."

Elric strokes his beard as he returns to his seat, "This does not bode well. Having the stones in our possession will only slow him down momentarily. It's only a matter of time before he learns to quicken the transformation process to fortify the rest of his army. The ingredients he needs are rare however. We will need to secure the sites where they grow, and bring them here. Minimise his ability to source more of what he needs."

"You know of this Magic then?" asks Professor Morgan.

"Yes, a very old friend told me of this a long, long time ago," Elric's gaze turns to his window, he glances out towards it for moment, as if deep in thought, recalling memories from his past, he quickly shakes off the reminisce and re-averts his attention to those with him, "Olof, I think you will be best suited to this task; the ingredients all lie in Nordic lands. Take Ju Long with you. Time is of the essence. You will need to transport the items back here for protection. Unfortunately, they cannot be transported magically or they will wither and die. So you must return by mortal means - over land, sea, or air."

Elric walks to one of his many bookcases; his right index finger touches the spine as he observes the titles of each book. He locates the one he is searching for and takes it out carefully, blowing on it hard to clear the dust from its surface. Flipping through the pages, he stops about midway and as he is touching the page he whispers into the air. A spark of blue light appears in front of him forming the shape of a quill, followed by a piece of parchment underneath it. The quill frantically writes upon it, copying the contents of the page that Elric is touching.

Elric blows on the quill and it fades out of existence as quickly as it appeared. The parchment then hovers towards Olof.

Atticus watches in awe.

Elric notices his gaze, "Party tricks, Atticus," he smirks before returning his attention towards Olof, "The second site on that list could well be close to the location of *Mjolnir*."

Olof's eyes widen, his attention is sparked, "Are you sure?"

"It is very likely my dear boy. Your research was thorough enough for me to analyse, and I feel this is the most likely location. Ju Long can help you, as I'm sure there will be tasks where both of your talents will be needed," says Elric.

"Thank you Master Elric, I will bring it back with me to help us win this war," Olof says with a smile. He and Ju Long both bow their heads to Elric, and then to Atticus, before exiting the chamber to prepare for their journey.

Atticus, surprised at the fact they lowered their heads to him in the same manner they did to Elric, turns to Professor Morgan and whispers, "Why did they do that? I mean… bow to me?"

"Because you are destined to be their leader, Atticus," replies the Professor.

Before Atticus can respond Elric beckons to Professor

Morgan.

"Benjamin, are you ready for tomorrow's mission?" he asks.

"Yes, although, losing Olof and Ju Long may mean we will need to tread a little more carefully," Professor Morgan hands a piece of paper to Atticus, "This is for your parents, Atticus, just to let them know that we are going on a little field trip tomorrow," he winks as Atticus takes the note.

"Thank you, Joyce. I will continue to tend to Mage Callan and Serenity," says Elric, "You should get back to your training, Atticus. It is important that you are at least minimally prepared for tomorrow."

The remaining members of the Majjai Six, along with Professor Morgan, leave the chamber and return to their duties. Atticus, eager to learn more about his abilities, takes the lead back to the training room. He knows this part of the Manor now, almost instinctively taking the right direction.

They bump into Olof and Ju Long with their packed bags ready to leave. Ju Long fidgets with his backpack, trying to find a way to carry it comfortably.

"Good luck my friends," says Ju Long, "Come back safely"

"You, too," replies Khan. With that, Ju Long settles his backpack over his shoulders and he and Olof disappear in a flash of blue light.

Atticus spots Elric rushing up behind them, thinking he was probably hoping to say a quick good luck to Olof and Ju Long, but slows down once he realises that it is too late. Atticus waves back.

Elric stands next to Atticus and places a reassuring hand on his shoulder, "Do not worry about Mage Callan, Atticus, he will be fine."

"What did that to him?" asks Atticus.

"Something very dangerous; hopefully you won't need to find out the exact nature of this enemy for quite some time," replies Elric,

"Anyhow, Mage Callan will have a gift for you, something that has been the chosen one's destiny to receive, and Mage Callan's destiny to protect."

"What is it?" asks Atticus excitedly.

Elric chuckles, "You will find out soon, dear boy, and hopefully, when you hold it, any doubts others may have will disappear."

The Majjai Journals:

Chosen one? Is that who I am supposed to be? I know I've always felt a little different. These dreams I've had are a pretty good indication of that. Mum and Dad know more than they are letting on as well. It was good to finally hear the truth about the accident and how I was found, but why did they hide it from me in the first place? Knowing what I know now, it would have helped me through this. I could have told them about all of it.

I suppose one good thing has come out of all this, Joyce. Wow, she is so nice, easy to talk to, and she is a Majjai, too! Will have to grill her tomorrow, though; she didn't let anything on even though she knew so much. I wonder if she knows about my crush? Should I ask her out? Is it too soon?

Elric was nice, I'm hoping for some more answers soon. Tomorrow should shed more light on what I'm supposed to be or do. I hope so, because right now I'm confused. One thing I really need to be sure about is that these Majjai guys are really the good guys; I only have the word of some old guy and a Professor who let me get electrocuted by this Gooyeh Partaab thingy. Professor Morgan is nice, though; I trust him, but I wish Mr Callan were around. I hadn't seen him for a while, now I know why. I hope he heals quickly.

Bradley is also on the warpath. I heard from Colin Hayes that he was looking for me earlier, and that he wasn't happy when he couldn't find me. I worry about him, he is always on my case, especially recently. His efforts to hunt me down have increased, and I have no idea why. Tomorrow will no doubt involve dodging him again.

Atticus Jones

Chapter 14

The Other Prophecy

Atticus arrives home a little earlier than usual. Sophia and Joseph are in the kitchen preparing tea.

"You're back early?" says Joseph.

"Yeah, they let us leave quick today because one of the teachers was not well," replies Atticus, desperately trying to make it sound as believable as possible.

Joseph looks at Atticus as if scanning him up and down, "Hmmm, ok. Well, chop-chop. You can help with dinner."

Atticus runs upstairs to get changed. As with most school uniforms, Wysardian Manor's is not exactly the most comfortable of attire, and all students relish the moment they arrive home to change into something much more casual.

The upper year students do not need to wear the entire uniform, and many are thankful it is only the robe they have to wear, with their choice of respectable clothing underneath.

Atticus tidily folds his uniform away and reaches for a pair of stonewashed jeans and a t-shirt.

After changing, he sits on his bed and stares at his dressing table. Trying to practice his powers he concentrates on a bottle of his favourite aftershave. Using his mind he wills it to move.

Nothing happens.

He concentrates again, breathing slowly. He repeats the word 'move' to himself repeatedly as the bottle begins to vibrate, rattling against the dressing table. Atticus thinks 'left' to himself, the bottle obeys and shifts to the left slightly. He then thinks 'up', the bottle begins to hover in mid air, rising higher.

"Atticus!" Sophia calls from downstairs, "Dinner is ready!"

Startled Atticus loses concentration and the bottle begins to fall. He moves quickly to catch it, "Hmm, best use Dad's cheap aftershave for practice next time," Atticus then grabs the note that Professor Morgan gave to him and heads downstairs to the dining room.

Atticus helps his mum lay the table as his dad brings out a casserole from the oven. The smell fills the room with a glorious aroma of warmth – carrots, parsnips and gravy exciting the senses. Atticus can't wait to eat.

"Lamb casserole today, Atticus, hope you don't mind? Thought I'd try something other than chicken steaks for once," says Joseph.

Atticus smiles and nods with his knife and fork at the ready to devour the contents of the casserole dish. He only just realises how hungry he is; the day's activities have drained more out of him than he realised.

Sophia walks round the table and ruffles Atticus' hair, "You look hungry. Busy day at school?" she asks.

"Yeah, uhm... new classes today."

"New classes?" asks Joseph

"Yeah, fencing, and uhm, wildlife," replies Atticus.

Joseph looks at him with a raised eyebrow. Atticus senses Joseph's scan mode enabling itself again, so quickly finds the note and hands it to him.

"Professor Morgan gave me this for you to read. There is a field trip tomorrow, and I might be back a little late," he says, hoping he is convincing enough to fool his dad. Joseph has a way of knowing when Atticus is lying.

Joseph reads the note.

This note is to request permission to allow Atticus Jones to attend a Biology wildlife observation field trip on the 14th of September. We aim to return by 9.30 p.m., and request that you pick up Atticus from the school gates. If pick up is not possible, transport can be arranged. Please sign on the dotted line below. If for whatever reason the trip finishes later than planned, we will inform you as soon as possible by phone. Please leave a contact number below if you wish it to be different to the one we have on file.

Regards,

Professor Benjamin Morgan

"Hmm, since when have you been interested in Biology and wildlife?" asks Joseph.

"Come now, JJ, I have a feeling that girl, Joyce, takes the same class," says Sophia quickly, winking at Atticus at the same time.

Atticus turns bright red. Joseph looks at Atticus again and chuckles, "So, found a girlfriend have we, Atticus?"

Atticus responds with the standard, "She is just a friend," answer, followed by, "I like animals, so thought it would be interesting."

"Well, while you are out observing wild animals, your mother has enrolled herself in a ruddy ballroom dance competition, and dragged me into the proceedings, too, as her dance partner," Joseph says, moving his gaze away from Atticus and towards Sophia.

Atticus bursts out laughing, "But you can't dance, Dad!" glad

142

that the dancing revelation has distracted his father away from prying any further into the note.

"I know that; they used to call me 'Jiggle Legs Jones' whenever I tried to dance at school," Sophia and Atticus snort in unison.

"Don't worry sweetie, I'll teach you," says Sophia. Sophia's parents sent her to ballet and modern dance classes while she was young, and she loves to dance. Joseph on the other hand dances as if he has two left feet and is unable to string more than three steps together before stumbling.

"Only because you had those lessons from your mummy and daddy, I'm far too bulky to be prancing around a dance floor in tights," Joseph retorts. He has always resisted any sort of dancing in the past, but realises that this time there is no way out and grumpily eats his meal with Atticus still chuckling away.

# # #

The night passes peacefully, Atticus wakes with the sound of timed footsteps coming from downstairs. He washes and dresses quickly, then heads down to investigate.

"Ouch!" screams Sophia, "Please, wear your soft slippers until you get the hang of things!"

Atticus pops his head round the door of the kitchen to find Sophia hopping on one foot, while rubbing the other with her hands. Joseph stands perplexed and his hair ruffled.

"I did warn you dear, two left feet, you see, and rather large ones, too. Dad always said I was part seal with these flippers," says Joseph jovially, trying to help balance Sophia as she hops.

Sophia soon finds the nerve to trust her now flipper-damaged foot to have enough strength to support her body weight again and slowly returns it to the ground, "Slippers, now please!" pointing in the direction of the shoe rack in the hallway.

Joseph heads towards the lobby, catching glimpse of Atticus peering around the door, "Morning son, good sleep?"

Atticus rubs his eyes. Too lazy to take off his glasses, he lifts them slightly with his forefingers as he massages his outer eyelids, "Not bad, until the disco dancing woke me up."

"It's *not* disco dancing thank you very much," rebuts Sophia, "It's *ballroom* dancing, and by the end of this week, I will teach your father how to do it somewhat properly," she looks towards Joseph, "Got those slippers yet?"

Joseph shrugs towards Atticus and leaves the kitchen.

"Right, Atticus, sit down while I bring you some cereal." Sophia indicates for Atticus to sit, which he duly does, "Walking with Joyce again this morning?"

Atticus nods.

"Are you all packed for your wildlife field trip today?" she asks as she pours milk over Atticus' cereal.

Atticus splurts, remembering that today he is supposed to go on the mission, "Err, yeah. All ready – the school is supplying everything we need."

"Good good. You may need to ask them to drop you home as I'm taking your father to a professional teacher this evening. I don't think my feet can take too much damage."

Atticus smiles and tucks into his cereal. The doorbell rings soon after, Joseph opens the front door to see a young girl, who just can't help but stare at his rather large bunny rabbit slippers.

"Hello Mr Jones, I'm Joyce. Is Atticus ready for school?" she asks, trying to stop herself from giggling at the sight of this tall, well-

144

built man, who is wearing fluffy, pink bunny slippers.

Joseph's querying look disappears as he puts two and two together, working out that this is the girl that Sophia told him about, "Ahhhh, yes, he is just finishing breakfast. Please, come in."

Joyce follows him into the kitchen, still mesmerised by the footwear.

Atticus almost chokes when he sees the slippers himself. Joseph sees him and finally realises what Joyce has been staring at, "Mum's orders, only soft slippers I could find," he says with a shrug.

"My feet will be forever grateful sweetie," says Sophia thankfully, now sitting massaging her damaged foot.

Atticus finishes his breakfast and leaves with Joyce. Quite eager to get started and take on his first real assignment in this new world.

###

The day passes relatively quickly. Lessons take place as normal; Professor Morgan is in a rather jovial mood. Even Professor Snugglebottom's class is enjoyable, as it is a rare practical lesson.

Atticus is also in good spirits. Looking forward to the evening's events with every passing moment.

Joyce and Atticus decide to head off school grounds for lunch, and head for a park close to Echo Forest. They sit on the swings and tuck into their packed lunches.

"You ready for tonight, then?" asks Joyce

Atticus nods his head, "I'm actually looking forward to it. Have you been on one of these before?"

"A few times. It's mainly Khan, Ju Long and Olof who go as they are the fighters, but I've taken a few demons out myself," replies Joyce

"How big are they?" asks Atticus.

"Size is irrelevant, usually. But they can get very big; you've probably seen more in your visions than I have."

Atticus scuffs his feet on the gravel beneath the swings at each passing nadir of the arc. The park itself is quiet; most students opt to stay within school grounds during lunchtime, as they are large enough for them not to feel crowded. A few trees of varying types blot the landscape, and a small stream runs to the north, splitting the park, with small bridges providing links to the two halves. The day is warm, with an autumn breeze drifting through the blades of grass, whipping the scent of the ground into the air.

The sun bears down unthreateningly, providing contours of shadows around the two adventurers as they swing and laugh.

Atticus stops for a moment as he notices a figure in the distance watching them. Signalling to Joyce to divert her attention in the same direction they both stare at the person walking towards them.

"Bradley?" questions Joyce quietly to Atticus.

"No, too tall," Atticus replies, trying to get a better look. His look of curiosity soon clears the way to allow a smile of realisation to appear, "Uncle Marcellus!" shouts Atticus.

Joyce, looking confused, for she has yet to meet Marcellus, gazes at Atticus, "You know this man, then?"

Atticus nods, "Family friend," he says as he dismounts from the swing and walks towards Marcellus, with Joyce following close behind.

"My dear boy, I thought it was you," Marcellus comments as they approach him, "What are you doing out here during school hours?"

"Lunch break; thought we'd take a break from school for a little while," replies Atticus.

"You should really stay within school grounds you know, the world isn't as safe as it used to be. Come, I'll walk you both back," Marcellus says, with a tone that implies that this is not merely a request, but more of an order.

Joyce and Atticus walk with Marcellus, "Your mother tells me you are going on a field trip this evening. Anywhere exciting?" he asks.

"The school is taking us on a wildlife observation trip," Joyce steps in quickly. Atticus gives Joyce a quiet, appreciative nod for coming up with that answer so quickly.

"Ahhhh, you must be Joyce. Sophia and Joseph have told me about you, too," says Marcellus, he looks at the both of them and smiles. Joyce blushes and nudges Atticus, "So, who is taking you on this field trip?" Marcellus continues.

"Professor Morgan," replies Atticus.

"Professor Benjamin Morgan?" asks Marcellus.

Atticus nods.

"Good, I know of him. Good man."

Atticus and Joyce look at each other quizzically, wondering how Marcellus could know of Professor Morgan, but before they can ask the question they find themselves at the school gates.

"This is where I must leave you both. Now, chop-chop, in you go," says Marcellus, hurriedly ushering them through. He turns quickly as if eager to get away from school grounds. Atticus and Joyce make their way inside; lunchtime is still in full swing. The playgrounds are full with boys playing football, and groups of girls huddling together chatting about anything and everything.

"Atticus! Joyce!" Safaya calls out from the crowd as she

elegantly steps towards them, "I've been looking for you both everywhere. Where have you been?"

Atticus and Joyce stare back, poker-faced, trying to offer a good reason as to why they went off school grounds in the first place.

"Never mind, I've found you now," Safaya continues, "We should get together and prepare for later. Elric has arranged for us to be excused from afternoon lessons."

Atticus and Joyce beam at the news; more so Atticus as this means he gets to dodge P.E. without any excuses. As they walk, Safaya stays quiet.

Safaya is an incredibly beautiful young lady, regal as her stature suggests, and exotic. Her hair is long and straight, a deep auburn in colour, and extremely well-kept. She walks like a Princess, but not overbearingly so. She, more than anyone, is well aware of where she stands in the world today. As she leads Atticus and Joyce into the Majjai training rooms, she recalls how she ended up in this time, and reminisces back to her time in Persia.

# # #

She was to be married, forced to unify two kingdoms. Only her immediate family knew the power she holds within her. They tried to keep it a secret, but there was a betrayal. Her sister, jealous of Safaya for her beauty and powers, exposed her to the prince she was to marry. The prince, angry at this indiscretion, declared a war which raged for a year. Thousands on each side were slain, including Safaya's father. Her sister, Princess Attossa, turned the kingdom against Safaya, blaming her for the death of the king. The war, now over, and won by

Safaya's brother, Prince Ismail, brought many hardships to the kingdom. Civil war threatened to break out every day, so Safaya could do only what she thought was right – to save her kingdom, she had to leave it.

It worked. Peace was restored, and the kingdom prospered under the wise rule of the new King, King Ismail. The King kept secret contact with Safaya. He promised her that one day, when the time was right, he would welcome her back into the kingdom. Unaware of the contact the King had with Safaya, Princess Attossa organised a secret group of assassins to find and murder her sister. Unknown to both sisters though, was the fact that the King himself had already organised an elite faction of the royal imperial guard to secretly protect Princess Safaya, each marked by a secret tattoo on their back of an eagle's head inside a pyramid.

The assassination attempt failed, foiled by the Elite Imperial Guard. King Ismail sent Princess Safaya deeper into hiding, to the only place he knew would be safe... the future. He knew of a powerful sorcerer, one who was able to manipulate time.

The King sought out a hermit known as Elric Griffin, reputedly knowledgeable in the ways of the Majjai, to help find this sorcerer. The King, upon finding Elric, was astounded to discover that he had found a surviving member of the Majjai Six who fought against Razakel and saved this realm at the Battle Of Aria.

The story of the battle had been told to generations of royal heirs. Tales of Razakel were routinely used as a deterrent to young children – the ancient version of the Bogey Man. The King, in awe of his discovery, requested the presence of Elric Griffin. Elric would only meet the King on his own terms, and one of those terms was for the King to bring Safaya to him.

The King reluctantly agreed, and he and Safaya secretly met with Elric. Elric checked Safaya for the mark of the Majjai, and accepted the King's request to seek out the sorcerer who could control time. Unknown to the King though, was that the sorcerer had left this time a long while ago, and entrusted the Orb to control time temporarily to Elric himself.

Elric had been told by the creator of the Orb that a Princess would arrive one day, and that she would be the final person to travel through the time portal to a year which all the original members of the Majjai Six agreed would be the most likely time for Razakel to return. Elric had used the Orb once before, but Safaya was never told who was sent through before her. Only that she would be the last until the return of Razakel. Elric was then instructed to leave the Orb hidden for the creator of it to find at a time of his choosing.

There was something else that was unknown to the new King. His father had sought out Elric many years earlier, after recognising the mark of the Majjai on his newborn daughter, for there was another prophecy, passed down from King to King. That there would come a time when a Princess would be born to protect this realm in order to rule another. This Princess would bear a mark, an ancient mark of rings around a ring... the mark of the Majjai. Due to his father's untimely death during the war, this message was never passed on to King Ismail.

Elric revealed this prophecy to both King Ismail and Princess Safaya. Astonished at this revelation, King Ismail knew this could be the last time he would see his sister. He vowed to protect her, even after his death. He evolved the faction of the Imperial Guard that he formed to protect Safaya to carry this on throughout time. They would protect her identity, and her destiny. They prepared throughout the following millennia to be ready for her arrival in the future. King Ismail called them, The League of Aria.

Princess Safaya knew of the League from her brother, but when she arrived in her current timeline, she was never contacted. Only an older version of Elric greeted her, and he promptly took her to meet Olof and Khan.

The timing of the activation of the portal was vital, so before Safaya could step through, she had to be prepared and schooled on certain things before travelling.

Princess Attossa, furious at not being able to find her sister, created another group of assassins, with the sole aim to find her sister... and kill her.

A young Prince called Darius (the first cousin of Safaya, Attossa, and Ismail) found out about Princess Attossa's plans, and followed this group as they tracked down Safaya.

Darius silently sent word to the King of Attossa's plans. King Ismail quickly gathered his most skilled League members and met with Darius as they tracked the assassins. The King told Darius of the League he formed, and made him vow to carry it on if for any reason he himself could not.

After a day's travel, they reached the large valley where Elric was preparing the portal for Safaya to step through. The valley was littered with flamed torches, the orange hue of which flickered against the rock and sand.

Attossa and her group of assassins were close by, and engaged Elric in battle. Attossa, who was unaware that Elric was a member of the Majjai Six, tried to run away upon her realisation that her new enemy was far more powerful than she could have ever imagined. Before she retreated to a safe distance, Attossa caught a glimpse of Safaya, and before fleeing, she decided to take matters into her own hands and threw a spear, aimed directly at Safaya's heart.

King Ismail, fearing for Safaya's life, flung himself into the

151

path of the spear, which plunged deep into his chest. Safaya turned to see her beloved brother dying. Because Darius had been instructed to aid the League Of Aria soldiers in helping Elric destroy the assassins, he was too far to help the King.

The rage built up within Safaya. Using her power she commanded the flames from the torches to form a giant sword of fire, and then, without thinking, she killed her sister in one fell swoop.

She knelt next to her brother, tears streaming from her eyes, dropping onto the King's light armour. He held her hand and told her not to worry, "Our Father would be proud of you, my sister. And know that there are things about Attossa that you were never told. You will learn these things in time."

"Please, Ismail, do not leave me. You are all I have," cried Safaya, as she clutched his hand as hard as she could.

In his last moments the dying King saw a light, a glimpse of the future, Safaya's future. He smiled, looked Safaya deep into her eyes, and said, "Do not worry, you will never be alone…" Then his eyes closed as Safaya hugged him tightly, crying uncontrollably.

After Safaya had travelled through the portal, Darius took Ismail's place as King to rule the lands of Persia. The League of Aria continued to prosper, and prepared every day in anticipation of the arrival of the Princess throughout time.

# # #

Safaya shakes herself from her reminiscence and returns her attention to the task at hand, continuing to lead Atticus and Joyce to the Majjai training room. Khan and Professor Morgan are waiting, along with someone else, someone Atticus is very happy to see.

"Mr Callan!" screams Atticus, "You're ok now?"

Mage Callan approaches Atticus "Within these walls, you can call me Mage Callan. And yes, I'm fine, dear boy."

Atticus grins broadly, and listens to Mage Callan.

"Khan tells me you are learning your powers well," continues Atticus's mentor, "I always had a feeling about you. Remember your training; when you return, I will be stepping up your lessons to a higher level. You need to be ready for whatever the Demon Realm will throw at you. Especially since they now know of your existence."

Atticus nods.

Professor Morgan places a hand on Mage Callan's shoulder and looks at Atticus, "Are you ready?"

"Ready as I'll ever be," replies Atticus.

"Good. We leave in five minutes," says Professor Morgan.

A Majjai History, Vol 1 Chapter 10: The swords of power

It is rumoured that there are three swords of power: the Sword of Ages, the Sword of Al Amir, and a third sword whose name is still unknown. It is thought that when these three swords are combined, they will be powerful enough to defeat Razakel. It is also said that no human hand will be able to wield this combined sword, only a hand of stone.

The Sword of Ages is currently under the care of Mage Callan, he is pledged to guard it until the arrival of the chosen one. This person will take charge of the sword when his identity is known. The Sword of Ages was the known weapon of choice for Kazmagus, it is said he fashioned it with a fusion of blue and red Magic. The sword's power has never met an equal, and it is the only sword other than the Sword of Al Amir to be known as 'Dragon Slayer'. Both swords are cut from precious stones and magically infused as to never shatter. The Sword of Ages is made from diamond and emerald, while the sword of Al Amir is constructed from ruby, infused with dragon's blood.

The Sword of Al Amir is said to be the only sword capable of destroying Draconus, the most powerful of dragons, and who allies with Razakel. It is not fully known what happened to the rest of the dragon kingdom, they disappeared a long time ago along with many other Magical creatures. This will be detailed further in a later chapter, The Age of Transition.

154

Al Amir himself was a shadow king, hidden from mortal history but well-known in Majjai and Demonic circles. The exact time of his existence is unknown, as none of the scriptures found detailing his life were ever dated; however, carbon dating techniques of modern times put the scriptures themselves at about the time of Kazmagus. Some advanced research claims to have found evidence of a family relation, some hypothesise that Al Amir and Kazmagus were brothers, some even state they may be the same being. One thing is for certain, these two swords were fashioned with the same Magic.

The third sword is said to lie close to the tomb of Kazmagus, but no one has ever found the tomb, and hence the third sword remains lost.

Chapter 15

The Beasts of the North

Safaya, Joyce, and Atticus glance at each other confusingly. They were not expecting to leave until later in the day, so this new element of urgency takes them by surprise.

"There has been another sighting; the quicker we leave, the easier it will be to track them down," says Khan.

Professor Morgan walks towards Atticus, "You must stay close at all times, and do as I say."

Atticus nods, he can feel the adrenaline beginning to increase throughout his body. He was excited before, but that excitement soon starts to turn to fear. The stark realisation of the dangers before him is beating against his very soul. For a moment he almost decides to skip this opportunity, but then he looks at Joyce, and wonders what she would think of him if he did so. Beads of sweat begin to form on his brow, and then a welcome interruption to his doubts distracts him.

"Before you leave, Atticus, I have a gift for you," says Mage Callan.

"A gift?" replies Atticus.

"Yes, every generation of Majjai has a keeper, a guardian. This guardian's job is to protect a sword – the Sword of Ages. It is made from a Magical fusion of emerald and diamond. No-one knows exactly when it was created, but it has been in our possession for thousands of years," says Mage Callan as he walks towards a large stone chest in the corner of the room.

He opens the chest and pulls out a long object, wrapped in an old sack-cloth, "For this generation, it was I who was chosen to protect the sword for the chosen one, Atticus; it has been saved for you," he hands the wrapped object to Atticus.

"This is the sword?" asks Atticus. Mage Callan nods, and Atticus begins to unwrap it.

"You have learnt much from being my student, Atticus; this sword will tap into your knowledge. Trust it − for it already trusts you," Mage Callan looks intently towards his student with pride.

Atticus unwraps the final piece of cloth to reveal a ruby-emblazoned leather sheath, and a hilt with smooth indentations, perfectly formed for Atticus' hand. Also on the hilt is an emblem, one that Atticus knows all too well now − it matches the Majjai insignia on his arm. As he holds the hilt, he feels his arm tingle slightly, he rolls up his sleeve to reveal his mark, glowing blue, as if this union with this sword has been a long time coming.

The inhabitants of the room stare in wonder, and the realisation that Atticus is certainly the chosen one is clearly seen within Mage Callan's eyes.

Atticus pulls out the sword, to reveal an inscription on the side of the blade.

'K^ZM^GVS'

"What does this mean?" he asks.

"It is the first time we have seen it. Let me have a look," says Mage Callan as he takes a closer examination, "Kazmagus... it can't be!"

"Kazmagus?" says Safaya, "I have heard that name before − my father spoke of him. He was the first Majjai. Nicknamed 'The Dark

157

Hero' and banished to the Void by followers of Asmodei."

"Void? Asmodei?" says Atticus, as the now all-too-familiar look of confusion washes over his face again. He feels that whenever he is beginning to understand this new world, something else comes along to add more to it.

Professor Morgan places his hand on Atticus's shoulder, "Didn't you read that book I gave you? Anyway, that's too much to worry about for now Atticus, no-one really knows much about Kazmagus, or what happened to him, or if he even actually existed," he says, as he looks to the group in front of Atticus, "Mage Callan, contact Elric regarding this inscription. He may have some answers for us," Mage Callan nods as the Professor turns to Atticus and continues, "We need to leave now, gather round."

Mage Callan steps towards Atticus, "When you return, I will teach you how to use this sword properly."

Atticus, Khan, Joyce, and Safaya gather around Professor Morgan. He closes his eyes, and raises his arms, and as he says the words, *"Enteghaal be maghsad,"* he brings the palms of his hands together. As soon as the two palms touch, a bright flash of light forces the group to close their eyes, then a snapping sound cracks around the room. In a moment, the five find themselves on the outskirts of a large forest, just in front of the tree line. Behind them lies grassland as far as the eye can see.

"Ennerdale Forest," says Professor Morgan, answering the question before it is asked.

They enter the forest in a line, their feet stepping in unison. The rustle of leaves on the ground resonates through the trees with each step. The rest of the forest is eerily silent, the movement of its five new inhabitants the only sign of active life.

"Quieter," whispers the Professor. The other four immediately

158

attempt to walk more softly, avoiding the dry, fallen leaves. They continue onward for about fifteen minutes.

Each of them takes turn to lead the line, with Atticus taking the rear as he clasps his new sword for dear life. The fear-fuelled adrenaline continues to pump through his veins, as the Professor suddenly stops, and motions everyone to be still.

"There, in the clearing, do you see it?" asks the Professor very quietly, "Khan, any ideas?"

"Not yet. I'll go in for a closer look, wait here," Khan moves swiftly but silently towards the clearing, leaving the others to wait anxiously.

Atticus tries to peer into the distance, but all he can see is foliage and trees, and he is unable to make out anything that looks remotely threatening. Another fifteen minutes pass by before Khan returns.

"What did you see?" asks the Professor.

"It is strange," replies Khan, "There is something there, but it appears to go on for miles, I tried to go around, but it seems that there is no ending to it. A wall of some kind."

"Any demons on the way there?" asks Safaya.

Khan shakes his head, "No demons – stranger still, there appears to be no life at all."

The Professor puts his hand on Atticus' shoulder, "Stay close now, use your sword if you have to, but be careful if you do. Control and restraint will be important for you. Even *we* do not know the extent of your abilities yet."

Atticus clasps the sheath of his sword even tighter and follows the Professor as they all head towards the clearing.

"Another thing," says Khan, "It is night there."

"Night?" asks Safaya.

"Yes, the sky turned into night the closer I got to the clearing. It was strange. I fear we are dealing with more than just lower-level demon beasts here. The facade is strong Magic; I've not seen anything like it before," Khan replies ominously.

They finally reach the clearing to find themselves faced with what can only be described as a giant bubble, its southern hemisphere bounded by the forest floor. It stands so high that they are barely able to glimpse even the tallest trees over it. The mirrored surface ripples as the breeze swoops through the air around it. The five adventurers are dwarfed by the size of this strange object. The Professor approaches it first.

"This is interesting. I have read about these, but never seen one," says the Professor.

"What is it?" asks Joyce.

"A demon cage. But why it is here, I have no idea," replies the Professor.

"How do we get in?" asks Safaya.

"Ahhh, that's the thing you see," replies the Professor, "Getting in isn't the problem; getting out is where we may have trouble. For all intents and purposes, these things are designed to keep things inside, and not to let them out. Demon cages are used as training in the demon world – last demon standing, wins. The only way to unlock it is to either destroy the demons inside or destroy the key. This one looks quite fresh, it's only recently been created."

The Professor looks at the Majjai Six members with him, and slowly puts his right arm inside the bubble, "Arrrrrghhhh!" the Professor screams out.

Safaya and Joyce run to grab him, then stop as he quickly pulls his arm out, chuckling.

"Not funny!" says Safaya, sporting an unimpressed pout.

"Just trying to lighten the mood," Professor Morgan says quickly, "Looks like you are only locked in when your whole body has stepped through. On three, then?"

They all shrug their shoulders and follow the Professor through once he finishes his count down. Atticus looks around as they all walk through. He feels odd, as if he can feel the bubble's wall push them further in as they walk through the thick surface edge of the cage. Sounds are muffled and uneven, almost as if all the life in the forest is muted through this thick, mucus-like membrane. After only a few steps they are through.

The inside of this bubble is nearly as strange. It feels both dead and alive at the same time, the air so still and at first the smell is so stagnant that Atticus finds it difficult to breathe; but then, after a few more steps the air freshens, the floral scents of forest life sweetens it, and everything feels normal again.

There are active signs of battle, evidenced by charred and broken trees, large craters and shattered pieces of rock. Above them the large dome like ceiling is opaque, the strange, night-coated sky is just about visible, but misshaped, with ripples flowing around the uppermost parts.

Atticus keeps up as the group step forward with caution, waiting for any sign of movement. The area is still quiet, almost deafeningly so. They venture deeper and deeper into this strange bubble.

"How did you know that this is a fresh demon cage Professor?" asks Joyce.

"The size of it, my dear," replies the Professor, "It's large. As a demon cage ages, it shrinks. The older it gets, the faster it shrinks. If there is no winner in the trial, the owner of the key is able to collapse the cage, crushing all within it. Or, if the time runs out, again, anyone or anything surviving within it is crushed."

"So, it was not very safe coming in here then?" says Atticus.

The Professor smiles, "Perhaps not, but we don't have much choice. Our prey is somewhere in here. And we need to find it, or them. We are expecting four of them. The only way to collapse the cage safely is to destroy the key."

"Shhhhh!" says Khan, "I sense something."

Everyone immediately stands still, waiting for a sign from Khan. Atticus holds his breath; his heart is beating so hard it feels as if it is about to pump out of his chest.

"We are being followed, watched," Khan whispers, "Everyone, close to me, now."

In an instant, the group huddles close to Khan. Joyce creates a shield around them, "Just one of my little tricks," she says, winking at Atticus.

The ground begins to shake violently. A rumbling noise begins to reverberate around them, shaking the ground harder and faster. The Majjai steadfastly hold their ground.

"You arrive to your doom Majjai," says a deep, growling voice, "We have been waiting for you!"

"Show yourself demon!" shouts the Professor.

The ground shakes more vigorously and the Majjai try to find some stable footing.

Three Screamers and an Orc jump out of from behind the trees. Atticus winces slightly at the sight of them, it is the first time he has seen a demon outside of his dreams. The Screamers are large, salivating beasts with dog-like faces and broken skin looking every bit as unworldly as can be. The Orc is dull green in colour, with pocked skin and tattered clothing; it wields a large club, which is riddled with dents and bumps from previous encounters.

162

"Ahhhh, I see you bring us a gift," the lead Screamer says as he looks at Atticus, "The chosen one. Master will be pleased."

"Silence demon. You four are not a match for us. I ask you this, what is the purpose of this demon cage?" says the Professor in a demanding voice.

"Hah! Foolish Majjai. The cage is for your doom — we are expendable," says the Screamer.

The situation dawns on the Professor, who realises that they have walked straight into a trap.

The Screamer continues, "You may be more powerful than us four, but who said we are alone?" as soon as the Screamer finishes his sentence, another twenty or so demons emerge from hiding, howling and cackling, circling them like a pack of hyenas closing in for a kill.

The Professor turns to Khan, "How many?"

"I count thirty," Khan replies, "We have never fought this many before."

"Doesn't mean we can't," says Safaya

"Wait," says Joyce, "None of them are making the ground rumble!"

"No, something else is," replies Khan.

The ground shakes hard again, and again. The impacts get louder, and closer.

"Graigons!" shouts the Professor, pointing into the forest. Trees are being pummelled to the ground by massive hulking beasts with short stubby heads and huge arms. Their skin is rough, stippled and hard. They stand almost as tall as the trees, and Atticus suddenly realises it's their *footsteps* that are causing the ground to shake uncontrollably.

"Graigons?" asks Atticus worryingly.

"Behemoth-class demons, Atticus, very powerful," says

Safaya.

'Behemoth by name, *and* by nature,' thinks Atticus to himself.

"Khan, we need to find that key, and quickly!" shouts the Professor. As he finishes, a total of eight Graigons make themselves known, beating their chests violently and roaring into the air.

"The lead Graigon – he has the key," says Khan, pointing to a chain around the creature's neck holding a glowing gemstone, "We need to destroy it. Joyce and Safaya should take on the Screamers. Professor, you and I must battle the Graigons."

"Agreed. Atticus, find cover, and use your sword if you have to," the Professor orders.

"ENOUGH!" shouts the lead Screamer, "Take them!"

"Brace yourselves!!" screams the Professor.

The three Screamers that first appeared line up in front of Joyce's shield. They each take a deep breath, and release their huge roars, demolishing all around them and sending a massive pressure wave of sound towards Atticus and the other Majjai.

The wave of sound shatters the shield and sends all of them into the air, scattered as they drop to the ground. Safaya gets up first, followed by the others. The Screamers rush forward, roaring, screaming and jumping into the air. With a wave of her hand, Safaya commands the ground to shoot up, creating a temporary shield of mud and rock. Several crashes are heard as Screamers crash into the other side. Another wave of Screamers attack. Joyce uses her speed ability to run behind them in a flash, and takes three out with fireballs.

Atticus runs for cover as a giant Graigon crashes through a second wall of mud that Safaya creates. It is almost upon Atticus before Khan jumps in front of it. His fists are glowing blue, he spins and launches himself into the air, jumping onto the Graigon. With an uppercut he launches the Graigon high into the air. As it falls, Khan somersaults off and lands onto the ground. The demon crashes onto the forest floor causing a wave to roll through the earth.

Another Graigon launches itself towards Khan. The Professor steps in. He clasps his hands together, and in one swift movement, launches a massive blue fireball into the Graigon's back, smashing it to the ground.

Behind them, Safaya creates a whirlwind, scooping up Screamers left, right, and centre, as Joyce uses her speed to divert their lethal roars away from the Princess.

Atticus clambers to the tree line. He finds cover as he watches the others take out the demons. One by one they fall. Several Graigons stand off against Khan and Professor Morgan, smashing their huge fists into the ground, sending rubble and rocks soaring through the air at their enemy. Khan simply smashes the larger pieces of debris with his fists; he then crouches, moving his hands behind him, a blue glow begins forming in his palms, charging, waiting for the right moment. Atticus can see the strain in his face as Khan waits for the right instance. It arrives and he throws his hands forward launching a giant wave of blue energy forward, annihilating two Graigons instantly, almost disintegrating them. But the time taken to fire the wave of energy has given another Graigon the opportunity to get behind Khan and the Professor, and it smashes its fist into their backs sending them flying into the trees.

Safaya spots them and creates a cushion of air to break their fall. Khan sends an appreciative nod to Safaya, as he runs towards the Graigon that attacked them. He jumps on top of it, but the Graigon slaps him back into the ground. The Professor is battling another Graigon so is unable to help.

Atticus spies the lead Graigon with the key, he seems to be doing something to it. The Professor sees this, too.

"He is turning the key!" roars the Professor, "Quickly, before the cage collapses! Joyce, a shield, as high and as wide as you can!"

Joyce acts, as the lead Graigon finishes activating the gemstone, forcing the giant demon cage bubble to come crashing down. Joyce fires her shield into the air. It successfully acts as a barrier, halting the collapse as the cage crashes into it.

Joyce groans, "It's too powerful!" she screams, "I don't know how long I can hold it. HURRY!"

Khan gets up quickly and out of the way, just before another giant blow from the Graigon he is fighting hits the ground next to him, "Atticus! You have to get the key!" screams Khan.

"Your sword Atticus, use it!" shouts the Professor.

Atticus looks around him, he sees Joyce struggling, trying to hold the shield protecting them. Safaya is still battling the Screamers, sending mounds of earth and rock into their ranks with massive force. The Professor and Khan are battling the other Graigons.

"QUICKLY!" screams Joyce, she falls to her knees as the shield weakens slightly. Safaya stands by her side, protecting her from any Screamer attacks.

Atticus runs out of his cover. He unsheathes his sword. The Sword of Ages is glowing silver, then green, light reflecting through the diamond and emerald. Without thinking, he runs towards the Graigon holding the key. He leaps into the air, remembering the feeling he had when he flew in his dream, he tries to tap into that power once again. A blue light surrounds Atticus and he begins to soar upwards, towards the head of the lead Graigon. The Graigon spots him and swings a fist towards Atticus.

Atticus instinctively tries to protect himself with the sword. The two crash into each other with an enormous flash of light. The force of the blow sends both Atticus and the Graigon into the air. The

166

Graigon lands on its feet, while Atticus spins himself and flies towards the giant beast again. His flight path is aimless, but he tries his best to stay on course. The Graigon sends blow after blow towards Atticus, but with no effect. Atticus matches each attempt with a skilful block with the sword. The sword is almost guiding Atticus, using his inner knowledge. Atticus can feel its power as it searches his mind for the skills he has already been taught by Mage Callan.

Atticus spins again, and launches a fireball towards the key. He misses it but hits the chain and the key falls to the ground.

Atticus tries to dive towards it but the Graigon succeeds to knock Atticus out of the air mid-flight. Atticus loses concentration and falls to the ground. His sword lands a few feet away from him. He quickly rolls towards the sword to retrieve it, just before the Graigon smashes his fist into the ground, narrowly missing him. Atticus turns and lashes out aimlessly, somehow managing to strike and slice the Graigon's hand, driving the creature backs as it roars in pain.

Atticus looks up. The shield is weakening further. Taking advantage of the Graigon's distraction, Atticus launches himself towards the key, "Professor Morgan!" he shouts, throwing the key towards his teacher.

Professor Morgan sees the key in mid-air and quickly throws a fireball towards it, shattering it. The demon cage disappears in a crack of thunder, revealing the daylight sky.

Atticus, pleased with himself, almost forgets about the giant demon that wants to pummel him. He turns just in time to dodge another attempted blow. Atticus launches himself into the air again, but with no control, and the hulking beast has no problem striking Atticus down. As Atticus lands he launches a fireball, which strikes the ground just before the beast. The Graigon stumbles over the newly created crater of earth and falls towards Atticus, who holds the sword upwards, wedging the hilt into the ground. He desperately rolls out of the way, and the sword plunges deep into the Graigon's chest. As the beast falls, it launches one final attempt to hit Atticus. The blow sends Atticus flying into the treeline. Atticus slams his back into one of the massive trunks, and falls to the ground, unconscious.

The others finish off their opponents quickly and run towards their fallen comrade. Joyce gets their first, and tries to wake him. Atticus groans and slowly opens his eyes, "Ouch!" he groans, "I think my leg's broken!"

"I'm not surprised with an impact like that!" says Joyce angrily, "Be more careful next time!"

Atticus shrugs, "So, you going to fix me then?"

"Shh!" orders Joyce, "Not until you promise to..." Before she can finish her sentence, Atticus kisses her.

"Uhum!" says Safaya, "Looks like you are just fine after all, Atticus."

Khan merely raises an eyebrow, impressed with Atticus's tenacious bravery.

Joyce, stunned by the kiss, is silent. Atticus winces as the pain of the broken bone makes itself known again. Joyce heals Atticus without a word, and walks away.

Khan, Safaya, and the Professor decide to give Atticus and Joyce a little space, and begin to secure the area and clear the mess. Safaya uses her powers to quickly heal the ground and fix the trees, with Khan doing all of the muscle work.

The Professor seems to be fixated on something else. A tiny reflection catches his attention; he walks towards it, and picks up a strange-looking locket with ancient Nordic symbols. He stares at it, and senses instantly that this item has magical ability, "Hmmm," he says to himself, just within earshot of Atticus, "I think Elric will be very interested in this."

Atticus, now fully healed, walks over to Joyce who is staring out into the forest.

"Why did you do that?" asks Joyce.

"It just felt right," replies Atticus, "But, if you don't want me to do it again…"

"It's not that, silly," says Joyce, "I like you, but, I'm scared."

"Of what?" asks Atticus.

"Of losing someone I care about. I have these feelings, and they are scary; we've only spoken this way for a few days, and there is so much more to do," whispers Joyce.

Atticus puts his hand on Joyce's shoulder, "Guess we're scared of the same things then," he says, "But you don't have to worry, you will never lose me."

A tear slowly runs down Joyce's cheek. Just before Atticus turns away, she stops him, and returns the kiss.

77107

77700777

777

The Majjai Journals:

Damn this curse. I never asked for these powers. Now I have to trek to the middle of the coldest place on the planet and help Olof track down this damn hammer. Ok, so Olof isn't bad company, but it's so damn cold here.

Elric was also looking at me in a strange way before we left, does he know my secret? It is in my past, and it will not take over my soul again; my teacher saw to that a long time ago.

I hide my sadness with humour – perhaps I've been trying too much? Maybe I should tell Elric about my past, or what I know of it, better he hear it from me than find out himself. It is a burden, this darkness that I hide.

This curse may not be so bad I guess, it did save me after all, saved me from the fate of all demons, but would the others understand? Would they trust me, would they trust that the darkness no longer remains? Would they understand what I had to do to survive? Even I do not the full extent of my history.

I suppose the only way is to earn their trust, and this quest is definitely a good start. I like Olof, he is always direct, and is not afraid to say what he thinks, a bit like Khan, but I know he has secrets, too. I wonder if they are darker than my own?

If only it was a little warmer.

Ju Long

Chapter 16

The Quest For Mjolnir

Olof and Ju Long finally near the summit of Kebnekaise, the tallest of Sweden's mountains. The landscape is icy and extremely cold, with barren rock providing a contrast to the snow-ridden background. The mountain itself is so far north that it takes Olof and Ju Long to within the confines of the Arctic Circle.

Ju Long longs for the warmth of the log cabin situated at the base of the mountain, but that is just a mere memory now. He is just glad he has brought along his thickest woollen garments.

Olof manages to get to the summit quickly. He uses his powers to dig right into the rock using his fists and hoists himself up. Ju Long uses his power of flight to follow, taking many breaks as the air becomes thinner.

The icy winds cut through their clothing and stings their skin; Olof merely smiles, as he is more than used to this climate. His Norse Powers enable him to harness the power of ice and create it at will, so the cold barely affects him. In fact, he and Safaya enjoy many training sessions combining their abilities.

"How can anything live here?" complains Ju Long, shivering.

"Only strong things can grow here, my friend," replies Olof. He bends on one knee, touching the ground as if trying to sense their exact location, "This way," he beckons to Ju Long who duly follows.

They reach a cave that is just below the summit and enter. Ju Long slaps his hands together and creates a glowing blue ball, which hovers just in front of them as they walk. The cave walls and floor are littered with pockets of snow. Icicles hang precariously above their heads. The two of them walk carefully through the many turns, Ju Long always taking his lead from Olof.

"What is this *Mjolnir* that you seek, Olof?" asks Ju Long as they continue their walk.

"It's a hammer. A very special hammer," replies Olof.

"And what makes it special?"

"Have you ever heard of Thor?" asks Olof

"The Norse God of thunder, right?" replies Ju Long.

Olof nods, "It is his hammer – *Mjolnir* – that I seek, together with the great belt, *Meginjord*, without which I will be unable to wield *Mjolnir*. Master Elric has been helping me search for it for the last five years. It is said that the hammer is able to repel great beasts and render its holder virtually indestructible. Whether or not it is able to control actual thunder and lightning is unknown."

"And you think you have now found this hammer?" asks Ju Long.

"Perhaps. It seems that this map that Elric has given us also marks the burial chamber of Brokk, the one who, with his brother Sindri, created *Mjolnir*," explains Olof, "I found scriptures many years ago pointing to the possibility that the hammer returned itself to its creators and lies with them in their burial chamber, waiting until it is needed again."

Ju Long looks at the map, "But, that is in the sea!"

"No," replies Olof, "It's even deeper than that."

Ju Long is now more confused, but continues to ask questions, "So, why has no one found it yet?"

"Others have tried, but it is supposed to be guarded by a giant beast," answers Olof.

Ju Long rubs his arms, trying to keep warm, "So, instead of chilling at the Manor, snacking on some pizza and those yummy chocolate dessert tarts, I'm here, on top of a mountain, cold, in a dark cave, cold, with spikes of ice over my head, cold, chasing weird plants and a giant beast? Oh, and... *cold*?" he says jokingly.

Olof looks at him and smiles.

"Gotta love this Majjai crap, eh?" finishes Ju Long, as he continues to rub his arms to coax any amount of warmth.

They venture deeper into the cave, hooking their ice boots into the ever-thickening frozen floor. The blue light reflects through the opaque ice, refracting into the cavern walls. Ju Long spots an opening further down and signals Olof to follow.

"Thank goodness this is the final location, it's too cold here," complains Ju Long.

Olof kneels and gathers the final herbs and plants that Elric has requested, "Now we should search for *Mjolnir*; but I fear these plants may get damaged."

"Could we store them at the Inn?" says Ju Long, referring to the place they have been staying at the bottom of the mountain.

"Perhaps; but, what if we do not make it back? These are too important to be left to rot alone. No, I have a better idea," replies Olof, "I have friends here. Let us get back to the Inn and I will contact Elric for his approval for returning these herbs with them."

The climb down from the mountaintop is tedious and long. Descent without using their Magical abilities is long-winded. A day passes before they return to the Inn. Olof contacts Elric and then retires to bed. Ju Long has already slept. Olof grins as he counts the number of bed sheets Ju Long has covered himself with before closing his own eyes to rest and wait for the morning.

# # #

Dawn comes quickly. Ju Long is the first to wake, and meditates as he waits for Olof to rise from his sleep. They are both disturbed by a loud knock at the door.

Olof wakes with a start and stares at Ju Long, who moves quietly to the door. The knock sounds again as Ju Long peers through the spy hole.

"Two large men, blonde hair," whispers Ju Long, "friends of yours?"

"Olof, det är vi, öppna dörren," says one of the men on the other side of the door.

Olof smiles, *"Alvar, vänta, jag kommer,"* he replies as he moves to the door to open it. Two large men walk through, very similar in appearance to Olof, *"Alvar, Kalle, hur står det till? Det var länge sedan!"*

"Ja, alldeles för länge sedan broder," replies Alvar.

Ju Long scratches his head and looks at the three other men. By comparison, he is tiny, and to make matters worse, he doesn't understand a word they are saying, "Erm, any chance of a discussion in English guys?" he requests tentatively.

"Sorry Ju Long," answers Olof, "These are my friends, Alvar and Kalle!"

Ju Long waves, but quickly stops as he realises that his hand action appears a tad feminine. Alvar and Kalle laugh as they sit at a table in the room. Ju Long brings everyone some water while Olof shows them the herbs.

"We have a boat waiting; it should take you less than a days travel from the city," says Olof.

"And Elric will be waiting for us?" asks Kalle.

"Yes, I have agreed this with him. He will be joined by Mage Callan and they will escort you back to the Manor," replies Olof.

"And what of your tasks that remain here, my friend? You still seek the hammer and belt?" asks Alvar.

"Yes," says Olof, "We may have found the location," he pulls out the map and indicates the area marked out for him by Elric. Alvar and Kalle stare at each other, almost in horror.

"You realise what lies beneath the waves there, my friend? Even Thor himself would think twice about such a task," says Kalle.

"I know of a beast that dwells in the sea, but no more," replies Olof, as Ju Long joins them.

"It is more than just a beast, Olof," says Alvar.

"This monster is massive, it dominates the sea, breathing fire when it rises above the waves and is even more lethal beneath it. This is no mere sea serpent, Olof. It's rumoured to be Leviathan," says Kalle.

The room goes silent as Kalle finishes. Ju Long can see the worried look on Olof's face, "Leviathan?" he asks, breaking the silence, "I thought it was just a legend, a story told by sailors to frighten new recruits?"

"Far from it," replies Alvar, "The beast is real – and is far more dangerous than what is hinted at in those stories."

"Your powers are great; but alone, against Leviathan... I fear even you will not be strong enough," says Kalle.

Olof looks at Ju Long. He knows that this task is dangerous for one as inexperienced as him, "Ju Long, I want you to return to the Manor with Alvar and Kalle."

Ju Long stares at Olof, "I'm coming with you, Olof. I will not allow you to go after this thing alone."

"You do not have a choice. I am in charge of this mission; you will take this order, and you will take it well," Olof says as he stands and heads to the window looking towards the mountain's base, "Do you want me to contact Elric and ask him to order you?"

Ju Long remains silent, knowing full well that there is no convincing him.

"This is my quest," continues Olof, "I must do this alone!"

"We should go now," says Alvar, "Olof, may Odin guide you and protect you."

Kalle gathers the bags containing the plants and herbs, then beckons to Ju Long to follow them. The three exit the room, Ju Long still visibly upset that Olof will not allow him to join him.

The room is silent again as the door closes. Olof prepares himself, re-enacting his training and testing his powers of ice. He changes into warmer clothes, checks the map, and looks once more to the window, "It is time," he says to himself. He raises his arms, and brings his palms together in front of himself. With a flash of light, he finds himself at the edge of a huge cliff.

The seas are far from calm today. The waves below him crash into the cliff face, the wind is strong, buffeting against Olof and pushing the birds that dared to venture out off course. Olof looks down towards the bottom of the cliff, closes his eyes and leaps.

As Olof rockets towards the sea, he points his arms in front of him, opens his palms and shoots masses of ice to form a sheet, upon which he slides down, rolling onto his feet. He touches the water's edge and creates a tunnel of ice to continue his journey beneath the sea. He reaches the seabed, the frozen walls of the tunnel keeping the seawater at bay. Olof extends his tunnel, referring frequently to the location on his map, and walks along carefully, keeping one eye on the condition of the tunnel's ice walls and the other eye for any sign of the rumoured sea beast.

He walks for almost half an hour, until he finally reaches what appears to be a circular iron seal, set in the sea floor. The seal is riveted and about five meters in diameter, with a symbol in the centre that resembles a hammer. Excited, Olof kneels and tries to feel around the seal for some form of opening.

On the outer side of the seal he finds what appears to be a button. In that same moment, a drop of water catches his attention, 'The ice should not be melting yet,' he thinks to himself. Standing up, he checks the ceiling of his ice tunnel. The melting is not just above his head; it is everywhere. The seawater around the tunnel is increasing in temperature.

"Something is coming," he says to himself listening for any unusual sounds, but before he can react, a giant tail comes crashing down through the ice tunnel, and it floods with water. Olof creates another tunnel, leading upward, to try and escape from the flooding. He runs, creating giant steps in the tunnel that he leaps onto as it climbs.

A huge roar screams out from beneath the sea as Olof finally reaches the surface. He quickly creates a small island of ice with a spire in the middle. Climbing to the top of the spire to get a better view, he looks down into the sea. Peering into the murky waters, he tries to see beneath the waves. Olof attempts to locate the source of the noise and the heat melting his ice tunnels. Another roar screams out, this one is so close and powerful that the spire shatters, sending Olof crashing into the plateau of ice beneath him.

Olof struggles to his feet, his right arm bruised and cut, "Show yourself beast!" he demands. Another roar is followed by a giant spray of water, as if something gigantic is rising from the sea.

"Leviathan," Olof whispers under his breath.

A giant, serpent-like body, wider than ten massive oak tree

trunks is all he can see. The beast's head is too high in the air for Olof to observe properly. The body of the monster is riddled with mucus and its skin is ripped and scarred. The stench of rotten fish mixed with water and silt dragged up from the depths is almost unbearable. Along the body are masses of ribbon-like fins, some attached fully alongside the surface skin, some much longer and free flowing, like thin but massive tentacles. One of the tentacles flicks out and whips towards Olof. He jumps out of the way, but the force of the impact shatters the ice floor. The massive body of Leviathan bends and then Olof sees it, the beast's head. It is more dragon-like than serpent, and moves towards Olof.

Leviathan's two nostrils are so large than Olof could quite easily fit inside them. The monster sniffs Olof, trying to get a scent. The smell coming from the mouth of it is awful, spewing out the exposed old flesh of past kills. Olof stands still.

"I am not here to harm you; I seek something else!" shouts Olof.

Leviathan moves away from the island of ice and stares at Olof. Its eyes are a bright yellow, and its teeth are twice the height of the Norse Majjai. It pauses, as if thinking. Olof breathes more steadily, hoping, willing the beast to disappear beneath the sea and leave him be. Suddenly, without warning, Leviathan lashes out. The rear of its tail shoots out from the surface and smashes what remains of Olof's island. The tail is not flesh like the rest of Leviathan, but spiked and bony, with giant shards of hard, metallic, claw-like protrusions. It makes short work of the island of ice and in moments Olof finds himself under water.

Knowing that Leviathan is much more lethal beneath the waves than above it, Olof makes his way to the surface again, creating another plateau of ice. As soon as he jumps out from the sea, Olof creates several small ice plateaus for him to jump between, then turns and fires several giant ice spears towards Leviathan. The ice spears just shatter against Leviathan's thick hide. Olof tries to find some form of weak spot and aims for the beast's eyes, underbelly, anywhere he can think of, but all he tries ends in vain.

Leviathan moves swiftly, each movement causing massive undulations to the water.

Waves crash upon Olof; he stands and waits for one wave to reach him, then leaps into the air and turns the wave into ice before sliding along it, he then creates another track of ice for him to slide down, using one hand to maintain the ice and the other hand to shoot ice spears towards Leviathan, who retaliates by shooting massive flames from its mouth. Olof tries to dodge the jets of fire; he can feel the searing heat on the back of his neck as he masterfully swoops in and out of the frozen pathways he has created.

He finally lands on one of his plateaus and steadies himself. Leviathan leaps up high, and shoots a giant continuous flame towards Olof. The Norse Majjai counters with a giant stream of ice, but it is no good, the flame is too powerful. Soon what seems like a momentary deadlock of fire and ice turns into a one-way battle, with fortune favouring the flame. The stream of ice is shrinking. Trying desperately to shoot out as much ice as possible, Olof tries as hard as he can, calling on all of his strength, but it is futile, he can see the jet of fire getting closer, hotter, and larger. Finally, the strength of his defence takes its toll, and he falls to his knees, spent.

The beast ceases his attach and swims closer to its prey, Leviathan towers above Olof, and prepares another giant blast of fire to finish him. It opens its great jaws wide.

Olof looks up; the fire is close now, he can feel the heat. He watches, beaten. The flame gets closer. Olof closes his eyes waiting for the inevitable. But the heat doesn't come. Instead, all he feels is a tug on his coat and weightlessness. He opens his eyes to see Leviathan below him, the flame still pouring from its mouth as it destroys the ice plateau.

"You found that damn hammer yet?" says a voice above him.

He knows that accent, that tone, and smiles; he looks up and sees Ju Long grinning back at him.

"You didn't *really* think I was going to leave you behind, did you?" says Ju Long.

Olof smiles, "Glad to see you my friend. But, how?"

"No time for that now — will explain later. At the moment, don't we have something to find?" replies Ju Long.

"It is no good. Leviathan is too powerful; we need the hammer to even think of standing a chance," says Olof.

"Well, I don't have a hammer, but how about some friends?" Ju Long points to the cliff face from where Olof first leapt. Khan, Safaya, and Mage Callan all stand there.

"You have all come?" asks Olof in amazement as they land.

"Yes," replies Mage Callan, "Do not worry, Professor Sprocking, Atticus and Joyce have gone with Elric to meet your friends. He sent us to help once Ju Long spoke to him."

"I am glad, but I fear that Leviathan is too powerful an enemy for us alone," says Olof.

"We do not need to kill it, just distract it," says Khan, shaking Olof's hand as he does so.

"It is coming!" shouts Safaya, pointing out to the sea. The massive serpent heads towards the cliff, creating a giant wave as it hurtles through the water. Leviathan's head pops out and it fires a gigantic ball of fire towards them.

Safaya quickly uses her abilities to divert the direction of the fireball to the sea.

"Quickly, we do not have much time," says Khan, "Ju Long, you distract it from the air, Safaya, keep diverting those fireballs and call the earth to the surface so Mage Callan has a base from where to launch his attacks. Mage Callan, try to cut away the tentacles when you can," Khan looks at Olof, "Find that hammer. I doubt we will be able to hold off Leviathan for too long, but we should be able to give you enough time, my friend."

Olof nods, "And what will you be doing," he asks.

"I'm going surfing," replies Khan, as he slides down the cliff face. Olof creates more ice for Khan to slide down with a ramp at the end. Khan shoots into the air with the momentum just as Leviathan leaps from the sea. Khan grabs a tentacle and swings from it to grab another on the other side of the beast's giant body. He swings himself upwards and lands on top of Leviathan's head. Using his power of might he smashes a blow to the side of Leviathan's face, diverting its course away from the ice ramp. Mage Callan and Safaya then both slide down and leap into the air. Ju Long catches them as Safaya commands a massive area of seabed to rise above the water level. Ju Long throws Mage Callan towards it. Mage Callan somersaults as he lands and immediately begins using his sword to fire beams of energy towards Leviathan and its tentacles.

Safaya swings herself over Ju Long and holds onto his neck as he flies. Every fireball that Leviathan fires she directs away from Mage Callan and into the sea, where it vaporises into a jet of steam. Ju Long flies in between the giant beast's body and tentacles, launching fireballs, trying to get its attention.

They continue to battle Leviathan as Olof quickly finds his way back to the large metal seal using his power of ice to shield him from the seawater. He finds the button and pushes it. It opens instantly, blasting out a small cloud of dust as the air escapes from beneath the lid. It clears to reveal a dark tunnel. Olof throws down a small ball of blue light and follows it. He soon reaches solid ground and another tunnel. He follows it on the meandering path as the walls glow blue with his light. Soon the hue changes to a warmer orange.

The orange light flickers, dancing with the flames from the torches that appear further down. Olof pokes his blue ball of light and it disappears. He follows the flickering flames to an opening.

"I have been expecting you," a voice echoes out around the cave walls.

"Who goes there?" asks Olof, completely surprised that anyone or anything would be alive here.

"It is I, Brokk," says the voice. An old frail figure of a man steps out from the shadows, "You seek Mjolnir do you not, Olof?"

"I do. The battle for this realm is close. A demon born of evil from before the times of Thor wants to rule. The hammer is needed," says Olof.

"Yes, Thor told me that you would come one day. But you must first prove your worthiness to wield the hammer and the belt," says Brokk.

"How do I prove this? There is not much time; as we speak, my friends battle with Leviathan."

Brokk walks to a battered old chest and pulls out a small rock. He hands it to Olof, "Only the Norseman of ice will be able to penetrate the flame."

Olof holds up the rock, and as he does so it begins to burn in his hand. The rock forces itself out of Olof's fist, bursts into flame, and engulfs the chamber. The fire is intense as it burns his skin. Olof can barely take it. His fear of fire is intensified due to his very nature of being one with the ice. He quickly builds a wall of cold air, solidifying it to counter the fire.

He hears Brokk in the background.

"My work is done, I now go to join Sindri in Valhalla. Good luck young Olof. May Odin protect you," Brokk says with a sigh and suddenly disappears into his robes, which fall to the floor empty.

"It was an honour to meet you old man," says Olof. He looks around the room, his vision blurred by the poor opacity of his cocoon. There are two graves here, and two statues. Olof recognises the statues as Sindri and Brokk, "The Hammer is here, but where?" he murmurs to himself. He stops for a moment and takes a deep breath, calms down and looks around again. His protection is beginning to melt around him as the heat intensifies.

Olof spots the fire encircling the statue of Sindri more fiercely than the statue of Brokk. Thinking this must be a sign, he blasts a mass of ice to try and calm the blaze, but the fire just grows more aggressive. An arc of flame strikes the ice cocoon, melting a large portion of it, creating an inlet allowing the flames to begin to surround Olof again. The Norse Majjai encases himself again, knowing he must get to the statue. But the only way is to walk there. The only way to fight this fire is to make himself as cold as possible. Olof concentrates, he closes his eyes and begins to freeze his very being, his skin turns blue and the blood in his veins begins to slow. He knows he does not have much time, without the flow of blood he will surely die in a matter of moments. He smashes his cocoon and walks through the flame to the statue of Sindri. With an almighty effort he pushes the statue to the floor, shattering it. In an instant the flame in the room turns to dust, swirling away into a mini whirlwind before disappearing into the cracks in the floor.

Olof breathes as his body returns to normal temperature. His skin reclaims its colour and he stretches slowly, before trying to peer through leftover smoke.

The room clears slowly. Hovering around the air, where the heart of the statue once lay, is *Mjolnir*, in all its glory.

Olof, awestruck at the sight of the hammer, walks towards it tentatively, his long search finally over. He grabs the handle but it fades from view, revealing a belt instead.

"*Meginjord*," says Olof.

"Yes," says the voice of Brokk, "I apologise; the wizard told me not to reveal the truth until you had proven yourself."

Olof spins around, but only Brokk's voice has returned.

"Which wizard?" asks Olof.

"You will find out soon," replies Brokk, "Without *Meginjord*, the hammer will be too heavy to wield, even for you. The belt will be enough to escape from the beast. It will make you strong."

"The hammer was never here?" asks Olof.

"It was here, but it now lies with the Orb," says Brokk.

"The Orb?" says Olof, "You mean the *Quantorbium*?"

"The wizard said no more," replies Brokk, "Now, I must sleep Norseman. Good luck with your quest. Oh… and Thor wants his hammer back when you are done," the chamber goes silent, disturbed only by the distant screams of Leviathan.

Olof wraps the belt around his waist, then quickly exits the tomb, returns to his tunnel of ice and replaces the seal. Using the belt's great power, he launches himself through the ice, the sea, and high into the air. He sees his friends still battling with Leviathan.

Khan, holding two of the massive tentacles, stands on Leviathan's head, almost steering the beast. Mage Callan pounds it with beams of energy from his sword, while Safaya, still hanging on to Ju Long, is continuing to divert the beast's fireballs the best she can. Olof is still too far away, but heads to the direction of the battle as

184

quickly as possible.

Leviathan whips into a frenzy of rage, kicking and splashing. It finally manages to shake Khan from its head and grabs him with one of its long thin sinewy tentacles, then quickly snatches the others. It dives deep into the sea, creating a massive whirlpool above it.

Olof follows the beast down, fearful for his friends' safety. Safaya clears a path of water for Olof to follow, he must get ahead of the beast to deliver his blow. Firing a massive sheet of ice ahead of Leviathan's path, Olof forces the beast to change direction, giving him the chance to go in for the attack. He can feel the belt giving him strength; its power surges through him.

Olof dives forward, winds back his arm with his fist clenched, and smashes it against the side of Leviathan's face, knocking the giant hulking beast unconscious. It releases its captives who all scrabble to a plateau of ice that Olof creates for them. Olof lands next to them.

"That is some punch!" splutters Ju Long.

"Took you long enough," smiles Safaya.

"Come, we must get out of here before the beast reawakens, it won't be fooled a second time and will not stop until we are dead," says Mage Callan. The others agree and they all head to shore and as far from the sea as possible.

They all sit for a while to gather their breath and some strength. They spot Leviathan in the distance swim away and dive under the surface of the sea. Olof wonders about *Mjolnir*, and who the wizard could have been that had the knowledge to move the hammer to another location. Only a powerful being could have managed such a task. He spots the others hesitating, and senses that they want to ask the question, but are worried just in case he is upset about being so close to his goal and not reaching it.

"The hammer is yet to be found, but this belt is a step in the right direction," says Olof, hoping that will quell the others' apprehension, "What say Elric?" he asks.

"Nothing much − but he has said that he will finally reveal the occurrences at the Battle of Aria!" replies Khan.

"The Battle of Aria, finally!" replies Ju Long, "At last we get to see what we are up against. Can't be much worse than Leviathan, and we taught that overgrown snake a lesson."

"On the contrary, dear boy," says Mage Callan, "What faces us in the future is much, much worse than Leviathan."

Ju Long remains uncommonly quiet for the rest of the journey.

# # #

It's late into the afternoon before Olof and the others return from the retrieval of *Meginjord*. They enter Elric's chamber to find Alvar and Kalle telling stories of Olof when he was young. Atticus and Joyce are practically on the floor in hysterics while Elric, smoking a hookah, chuckles.

They turn to see Olof proudly wearing *Meginjord*. Alvar and Kalle run towards Olof.

"You have found it!" says Alvar excitedly.

"Not quite," replies Olof, wearing a huge grin as he does so, "But we do have *Meginjord*," he says jovially.

"Another step closer then my friend?" says Kalle.

Elric stands, approaches Olof, and puts his hand on his shoulder, "I am very proud of you, Olof," he says, "*Meginjord* will be a great help in this battle, and it is only fitting that you wield it. The hammer will surely follow."

Olof nods and embraces Elric gently.

"See, told you − big softie really," Joyce says softly to Atticus.

186

Olof pretends not to hear.

A Majjai History, Vol 1 Chapter 12: Demonic

Hierarchy

In the time of Kazmagus, the demon king was Asmodei. He led ruthlessly, but was also known to have a sense of honour. His direct subordinates included Razakel, and it is rumoured that it was he who put end to Asmodei's reign by using his master's sense of honour against him.

Asmodei's greatest failing, according to the demonic scriptures that have been recovered, was his ability to love, a trait that escapes the vast majority of demons. One mortal woman in particular caught Asmodei's interest, and he became besotted, obsessive even. The exact events are not known, but it is said that this woman sought out refuge with the Majjai of the time. Here a brave young Majjai soldier and this woman fell in love.

Asmodei, who was fed lies by Razakel, was led to believe the woman had been captured and was being held captive by the Majjai. In anger, he pursued the Majjai army, seeking out the woman he coveted, killing many innocents along the way.

Razakel was already many steps ahead, and it is thought he cast an illusion, powerful enough to fool Asmodei into believing the woman he loved was actually the Majjai soldier that had taken her heart. Asmodei killed who he thought was the soldier, and upon realisation that he had killed the very woman of his desire, he became enraged and cursed the Earth. He caused havoc across the globe, and it is then that it is rumoured that Kazmagus returned from his Nomadic life to do battle once more.

Neither were heard from since.

Razakel gleefully took charge of the demon realm, claiming it as his birthright. He and his subordinates, Alvarez and Herensugue, slew any demon still loyal to Asmodei. This was a dark time, for where Asmodei understood and promoted balance of sorts, he also accepted that the demon realm and the Earth realm could co-exist. Razakel saw differently.

Not much is known of Razakel and his rise through the demonic ranks. Some ancient scriptures said that he was human once, and that Asmodei turned him. The turning process itself is noted to be an incredibly agonising process, and one that few survive.

Razakel attempted his first invasion into the Earth realm at the Battle of Aria. Many brave soldiers and Majjai died that day, but in the end, with the help of the Majjai Six, the Earth realm overcame the forces of evil and defeated Razakel.

Alvarez and Herensugue both tended their king, healing him over time. At the time of this writing his condition is unknown, but what is for certain is that he will return.

Chapter 17

The Battle of Aria

Atticus stares out of the window while Professor Morgan tries to project the laws of friction into the minds of his students. Maths and all of the standard lessons are held in the mornings at Wysardian Manor, and those that are gifted in the ways of the Majjai attend special classes and tutorials during the afternoon.

The first few days after Atticus found out about his new world were extremely eventful. The next few weeks that followed were filled with a level of normalcy that almost bordered on boring by comparison.

Atticus is fairly pleased at the new arrangement of classes though, as most of his P.E. lessons are scheduled for the afternoon, and it means he gets to miss most of his encounters with Bradley, who continually tries to find any opportune moment to corner him. Luckily for Atticus, his newfound Majjai teammates are never too far away.

The afternoons are filled with wondrous new things. Every day brings a greater understanding of his abilities. He has learnt to fly − with better control but still a little aimless − and his telekinesis abilities have also strengthened by massive amounts. He is even learning how to utilise the powers of his teammates, albeit to a much lesser degree.

This afternoon's activities involve something that many of them have wanted to see for a long time, the events of the Battle of Aria. From what Atticus has read from the books given to him so far,

Aria was once a great city close to where Herat now stands. Thousands of years ago it was regarded by some as being one of the most important cities in the known world; and certainly the most significant in ancient Persia. What mortals are unaware of however, is that Aria was host to a battle that saved them all. To this day, only a select few Majjai elders have ever known the specific details.

The reasons the events of the Battle of Aria have been kept in secrecy are unknown – albeit until later today, Atticus hopes. He recalls the Majjai history book that Professor Morgan gave to him to read the day before his meeting with Professor Sprocking. Within its pages it describes a battle and the group of Majjai who faced a great evil, but it never went into specifics.

Safaya has told Atticus of a crystal that Elric keeps with him which holds the entire battle within it, and he has saved it for presentation upon the arrival of the chosen one. She also told Atticus that, in her time, the original Majjai Six were a fabled group of heroes, their identities not widely known, except for Elric himself. She continued to inform Atticus the most popular myth as to why the details of the battle have been kept secret were due to the requests of one particular original Majjai Six member. A Majjai who has existed in various times – the very Majjai who created the *Quantorbium*.

# # #

The training fields for the Majjai students are much larger than the standard fields. Atticus always wondered why the hedges surrounding the standard playing fields are so tall – now he realises they are there to hide this vast space for Majjai needs.

Elric has cloaked the grounds to keep them hidden from the outside world, Magically ensuring that the hedges remain thick and green all year around.

The afternoon sessions begin and the Majjai training grounds are filled with about one hundred or so students; some Atticus recognises, and some he doesn't. He does sense the attention he is getting though. Many eyes try to catch as much of a glimpse as possible of the chosen one, a few are even brave enough to point

Atticus is used to this now, and tries his best to ignore it. He spends most of his time with Joyce and the other Majjai Six members. Their training sessions are very intense, and more often than not end up with at least one member injuring either themselves or another. The team welcome the fact that Joyce's healing powers are increasing, and now that Atticus has learnt that ability to a lesser extent as well, he is able to treat minor wounds. Although one thing he is also beginning to feel is a huge drain on his energy levels after using Magic. The others feel this too, but manage to mask their fatigue. Atticus surmises that he must also learn to adapt; he practices regularly to become more precise with his powers so that he can recover his energy levels more quickly.

Atticus and Joyce have also become even closer, but still haven't had time to go on a first date. Both hope that situation is rectified on Saturday as they have a very welcome respite from all the chaos.

The field goes silent as Olof stands next to Elric. They stand alone as a pair facing the rest of the Majjai students. Elric has spent the last few weeks busily preparing this presentation, knowing that many questions will follow. Anticipation has also increased among all of the Majjai since word spread of the revelations of the Battle of Aria.

"Welcome!" says Elric, speaking into his cane, which glows blue and amplifies his voice so that everyone can hear, "This has been an eventful month. The chosen one has been found!" the crowd cheer and whoop, some of them chant Atticus' name. Elric waits for the cheering to subside before continuing, "We have also been blessed with Olof continuing to fulfil his destiny. His quest for *Mjolnir* grows ever closer with the discovery of *Meginjord*!"

Olof steps forward with the belt adorning his midriff, which brings another loud cheer and roar of approval from the other Majjai students.

"But," says Elric, "There is also a message here for all of us. These events have been somewhat foretold. They are but steps on a path − one which ends with one of our most important tasks as protectors of this realm. This path finishes at the end of Razakel's destruction… or our own," the crowd are deathly silent at these words, "Make no mistake, we are at war. A war that this world has only ever seen the likes of once before. A war that we almost lost," Elric beckons to Olof to bring him the crystal.

Olof holds his hands out to offer the large gem piece to Elric.

"I know many of you have been waiting to see this for a long time. Safaya, if you could help to make everyone more comfortable, we can begin."

The Princess raises her arms, and creates chairs for everyone on the field. The earth rises from the ground next to each student, forming perfect little perches from which they can all sit comfortably.

"For this revealing, we will be joined by Majjai leaders from across the globe," as Elric finishes his sentence, several portals open up around the field. Atticus can see through some of them, revealing groups of what he assumes are other Majjai − all of them waiting for the story of the battle of Aria to begin. Joyce points to one of the portals and whispers, "They are the Bhandari Clan, from India. Very secretive, and powerful. They trained Ju Long."

"Who are they?" asks Atticus, pointing to another portal.

"Mecha Knights. They have a rare gift − they can infuse a

Majjai soul with technology, things like cars, computers. Only trapped souls though, like giving a machine consciousness, we know of only one successful instance of this melding. I think they are based somewhere in North America. They are the scientists of the Majjai world."

"I never knew we were global," Atticus whispers to Joyce.

She smiles as she replies, "There are quite a few of us you know, and we don't stay students forever."

Elric steps forward and leaves the crystal on the ground. As his hand moves away from it, the gemstone begins to hover and spin. It spins ever more violently and begins to spout out a mist. Within moments a massive cloud builds up. Flashes of light spark inside it, and an image appears. Elric raises his staff and hits it into the ground. Sparks of blue light shoot out in six directions, surrounding the crowd at different points around everyone in the field. From the tips of the blue light 5 large gramophones appear; the sixth beam of light creates a giant tubular object with a port near the top.

Ju Long turns to Atticus and whispers, "Cool! Majjai home cinema," Atticus laughs, as murmurs of awe and approval ripple through the other students.

The image inside the cloud focuses properly, and a man can be seen. Everyone instantly recognises the figure to be a much younger version of Elric. They fall silent again as this young Elric begins to speak.

"Welcome. I hope I have the dialect correct for your time, forgive me if I do not. What you are about to see is a history that has been hidden; the final events during the Battle Of Aria. The reasons the events of the battle have been hidden for so long are for the protection of several Majjai, one of whom is the creator of the *Quantorbium*. However, before we begin, I should introduce you to the original

Majjai Six!"

Everyone in the field can be seen fidgeting, clearly excited at what they are about to see and learn.

One by one the audience is introduced to the Majjai Six of old.

First a muscular man wielding a giant axe steps into view, "I am Arshan. I am gifted with the power of might and weapon enchantment," he nods his head and steps back to allow the next. Asad, Barmak, and a beautiful lady called Zarileh follow Arshan.

"That makes five, where is the sixth?" whispers Safaya to Khan.

The rest of the audience are also wondering this and whispers between them begin to get louder, when the younger version of Elric reappears in front of the other four Majjai Six members, "Yes, there is another. He tells me you may know of him by a different name, we know of him as Myrddin Emrys."

A massive gasp echoes through the crowd. Those in the know quickly convey their knowledge to the others. Atticus strains to hear what they are saying when a sixth, tall figure steps into view.

"Yes, my name is Myrddin Emrys. And it was at my request these events be hidden from you," says the tall man. He looks into the audience, as if he knows exactly where everyone is sitting. His eyes stop when they point towards Atticus, who stares back at the projection, "Hello Atticus," says Myrddin.

The audience all turn their heads in unison towards where Atticus is sitting. Not knowing what else to do, Atticus waves towards the mist where the figures are standing. Joyce quickly moves Atticus' hand back down to his thigh.

"Who is he?" Atticus asks Joyce.

"Merlin," she replies.

"*THE* Merlin?" spouts Atticus, Joyce replies with a nod.

"Hello everyone," Myrddin continues, "Elric has already informed you of what you are about to see. So I think I've delayed things long enough. I know there will be many questions, but please, direct these to Elric after the presentation has finished. I wish you all the best of luck for the challenges ahead."

The mist holding the image before them fades out, and in place of the original Majjai Six there is now a massive, barren landscape. The flickering lights of a city can be seen in the distance, oblivious of what is happening near its borders. The view spins around to the opposite direction, more lights can be seen, but these are more than just flickering flames. Giant arcs of blue and red, explosions, flashes of lightning, they command the horizon with an orchestral display of colour. The view quickly zooms closer to the battle. Atticus recognises Herensugue and Draconus instantly.

They are both attacking Arshan. Arshan blocks Draconus's attacks with giant shields of blue light. He returns fire with massive arcs of energy spouting from his axe as he swings it. Barmak arrives to aide Arshan with the chaos of war surrounding them. Elric can be seen in the distance, battling against masses of Screamers and Graigons. Asad and Zarileh are facing a giant portal, and battling hordes of other demons streaming through it.

There are other Majjai too, and soldiers, all battling this giant demon army. Hundreds upon hundreds of demons are pouring through the portal.

Myrddin is sitting in the middle of the battlefield, chanting. Protected by an energy shield, fireballs and demons attempting to attack him merely bounce off it, shooting into the air. Myrddin appears to be preparing something within his shield.

The giant portal suddenly changes colour, it turns from red to white, and then a bright crimson. Zarileh screams to the others, "He is coming!!"

Elric runs to Myrddin, "We must hurry, Myrddin. How much time do you need?"

"At least five more minutes; do you think you can hold him?" replies Myrddin.

"We will try," says Elric as he turns to the other Majjai Six members and shouts, "Form a line, ahead of the portal! Hurry!"

The demons all break off their attack, waiting for their leader to step through. They gather around the portal, numbering in their thousands; almost four times the number of soldiers and Majjai opposing them.

Draconus hovers above the portal, his massive wings blowing the sand into the air. The demons stomp their feet, Screamers roar into the air, Graigons punch their massive fists into the ground forcing the earth to shake beneath the Majjai and human army. The portal changes colour again, this time to a bright, blinding green.

A giant foot steps out, followed by the rest of the body of Razakel. Atticus knows it is him from his dreams, but this version of Razakel is even larger than the one he saw.

The student crowd gasps – for most, this is the first time they have seen the demon king. He stands, observing the Majjai and human army with an obvious degree of nonchalance.

"Majjai, I declare this realm as mine. Stand down, or die!" says Razakel. His voice rings deep, rumbling through the air.

Elric steps forward, "You have no rights here, return to your hell and leave us be!"

Razakel looks at Elric, his stare thrusting forward, sharp and foreboding, "You dare address me! Foolish Majjai!"

Elric feels a force push him into the ground, his stomach burns as he screams in pain. As Razakel attacks Elric, Barmak runs forward.

He jumps high and flies towards the demon, his two feet aimed directly towards Razakel's chest. Barmak's entire body begins to glow blue, screaming as he nears Razakel. The impact is huge. Razakel's focus is on Elric and he is not prepared for the power of Barmak's blow, which pushes the Demon King back, almost right through the portal. Barmak lands on the ground in front of him. Razakel swings a fist towards him, which Barmak dodges, then throws beams of energy back towards Razakel as he grabs Elric, retreating back to the line of control held by the Majjai army.

"Is that all you have, Majjai?" asks Razakel, "You have no hope in winning this war," he moves his arms together quickly, slapping the palms of his hands with such force that a massive pressure wave fires forward towards the Majjai army. Their attempts at shielding themselves are futile, as the wave of energy throws the entire army into the ground or flying into the air.

The Majjai Six regroup quickly and fire energy beams, fireballs, anything they can towards Razakel. Their impact has no effect; the attacks just bounce off his massive body. Arshan storms forward and punches the ground with massive force, causing the very ground to shake and sending another large wave of energy through the sand towards Razakel. The impact destabilises him slightly, allowing Barmak to launch another attack.

The rest of the demons rejoin the battle as the Majjai army who survived Razakel's assault charge forward.

Finally Myrddin stands and walks towards the giant portal, beckoning Elric to follow him.

Elric sends a signal to Arshan, indicating that he is joining Myrddin, before he too makes his way.

"Have you finished the key?" he asks Myrddin.

Myrddin nods, "Yes, but first we need to destroy his ability to create any more portals into this realm!"

"Agreed," Elric says as he puts his hand on Myrddin's shoulder.

"Are you with me Elric? Do we dance into hell for our last stand?" asks Myrddin.

"Always, my friend!" replies Elric.

Razakel spots them and commands Draconus and Herensugue to stop them. Myrddin and Elric jump into the portal, quickly followed by the dragon and the serpent. As Myrddin and Elric land on the other side, they drop white glowing crystals onto the floor and wait for their pursuers to venture through.

Herensugue and Draconus land on the barren landscape, spot Myrddin running towards Razakel's castle, and give chase. Elric steps out of hiding and plants several more crystals just behind them, which create a giant cage, holding the two demons. He smiles at his captives before following Myrddin towards the castle.

They reach the castle in a matter of moments. Myrddin pulls out a compass directing him towards a large room. They carefully navigate the corridors, trying to avoid contact with any possible demons still lurking within it.

Elric follows Myrddin for some way, until he senses something strange behind one of the doors, "Myrddin, over here, quickly," he whispers, "Do you sense it?"

"Yes," replies Myrddin, "this presence is strong. Do you think...?"

"It's Majjai, that is for certain; but I have never felt one as strong as this," Elric replies as he approaches the door.

"It could be a trap," says Myrddin.

"Perhaps, but there is only one way to find out," Elric replies as he flings open the door.

Two Screamers are guarding what appear to be six globular objects. Atticus has seen the largest one before – the *Gooyeh Partaab* in Professor Sprocking's chamber. Myrddin and Elric dispose of the Screamers quickly, and approach the row of *Gooyeh Partaabs*.

"I never knew these actually existed," says Elric.

"I knew of them, but did not think they would be here, in this realm," replies Myrddin as he approaches the smaller *Partaabs*, "These are empty."

"This one is not," says Elric as he nears the largest one and peers into it, "A baby? Why trap a baby's powers?"

"Look at his arm, Elric, he has the mark," says Myrddin, as they both peer down and see the mark of the Majjai, "It is the mark of the chosen one. There is a traitor; the only way this child could have been placed here is through betrayal."

"But who? The chosen one is unknown to us. But… can we use this to find him?" says Elric.

"Yes, but we don't have much time right now. Those crystals won't hold Draconus and Herensugue for long. Quickly, let's gather these and find the source of the demon's portal."

Elric stretches out one arm and transforms it into a large sack, which drops off his body, being replaced by another arm as it does so. They quickly put the *Partaabs* into the sack.

"I must say, I do admire your powers of transformation, Elric. Very useful at times like this," Myrddin says to Elric.

"Indeed," replies Elric as he quickly creates a portal back to his home and gently passes the heavy sack through it, "I will have to rejoin with myself later; I already feel like I'm falling to pieces," he jokes as the portal closes.

Myrddin winces before looking blankly towards his friend, "Although I'm glad I do not have your sense of humour."

They continue to follow the compass towards the source of the demon's ability to create portals into the Earth realm. It doesn't take long to reach their destination and they quickly dispose of the demon guards in and around the chamber. They walk to an altar near the centre of the room; the dome-like ceiling reaches high into the air, and the flesh and stone walls are just how Atticus remembers.

"We cannot destroy it straight away," says Myrddin as he reaches into his robes and pulls out a large pouch, "Something I borrowed from the future. Fabulous invention — the mortals call it gunpowder."

"Are you sure they cannot just rebuild this Altar?" asks Elric.

"No, the Magic used to create this is dead; once destroyed, there is no way back into our realm for these demons. This portal pillar will just become a black hole for any life force that tries to repair it," replies Myrddin, "We need to time the explosion properly or we will also be trapped. Quick, light these candles."

Elric shoots a small fireball to ignite the wicks, and watches as Myrddin ties some string to a stick, which in turn is tied to one of the other candles.

"When the string burns, the other candle should drop and ignite the gunpowder."

"How much time do we have?" asks Elric.

"About ten minutes. Should give us enough time to return to the battle and put part two of our plan into action," Myrddin turns to Elric and puts his hand on his shoulder, "We will win this, I have faith."

"I know, but the *Gooyeh Partaab*, it... it changes things; well, what we saw within it changes things," says Elric.

"Yes, but we can discuss that after we deal with Razakel. Otherwise there will be nothing left to discuss."

201

Myrddin and Elric run back to the large portal. Draconus and Herensugue are still trapped within the white cage of light created by the crystals. They roar and scream at the two Majjai, but are unable to break through their makeshift prison.

As the two Majjai step through the portal a giant fireball heads in their direction. Quickly diving out of the way, the two head towards the centre of the battlefield, destroying as many demons as possible on their way. Razakel can be seen causing havoc with Alvarez right behind him. The Majjai standing up to Razakel do not stand a chance, without remorse he destroys each and every opposing soldier who stands in his way.

Barmak and the other Majjai Six members are trying to get to Razakel but he moves too quickly. Myrddin calls out to them.

"We must tempt him towards us!" he shouts, "quickly, flank him, we must get him back through speedily, we only have a few minutes left!"

"But how do we tempt him?" asks Zarileh, glancing towards Elric with concern, as if to make sure he is ok.

"With this," replies Myrddin, as he retrieves the *Quantorbium* from within his robes.

"The Orb, you brought it with you?" questions Arshan.

"Of course," says Myrddin, "I cannot stay in this time. There is a certain future King who needs my services. I came here to help with this battle and prepare you for the next, nothing more. Now quickly – Asad, Barmak, take him by the flanks and become a distraction while I weaken him."

"And how exactly are you going to do that?" asks Zarileh.

Elric answers before Myrddin can, "The Void. You are going to use the Void, aren't you? That's what you were working on, that is what the keystone is for isn't it?"

202

"It is too risky!" says Asad.

"Do not worry, my calculations are precise, now go, trust me!" replies Myrddin.

Asad and Barmak run to flank Razakel as Myrddin holds the *Quantorbium* high in the air.

"Razakel!" screams Myrddin, forcing the battlefield into silence.

Razakel turns to see the *Quantorbium*. He growls as his red skin glistens in the desert heat. He begins to charge towards Myrddin and the others. Elric and Zarileh attack first, but they barely hinder Razakel. Arshan uses his Axe to send a giant arc of energy at Razakel; again, it doesn't even faze him.

Asad and Barmak attack from the sides and coax him closer to his own portal. Myrddin stands his ground, and waits. The other Majjai Six members regroup in front of him. Together they launch a simultaneous attack, five massive bolts of energy fire into Razakel, and finally, they slow his pace. Another attack is launched, and Razakel stumbles.

"Now Myrddin! You have to do it now!" shouts Elric.

Myrddin teleports behind Razakel and activates a black, charred keystone. It begins to create a large dark spiral, swirling inwards. Razakel turns, tries to step away from the spiralling whirlpool-like entity but it is too late, and his body is slowly dragged into The Void.

He drags himself forward, straining with every ounce of energy to pull himself away from the black entity, but it's no good; every step Razakel takes forward, he is pulled back by another two. Red light begins to swirl around his entire body creating a mist that is sucked straight into the abyss. It's as if his very essence, his very life-force, is being sucked out of his body and into this swirling whirlpool of nothingness shrinking both his size and power.

"You dare defy me?" screams Razakel, "I am your master! Satan himself... fears...meeeeeeee!"

Elric steps forward and shouts back at Razakel, "Make sure you say hi to him for us."

With those words Myrddin, collapses the keystone's whirlpool. The Majjai Six know Razakel is weakened enough now and launch one last massive attack, blasting Razakel back through his own portal. They all line up and fire as many fireballs and energy beams towards the Demon King as they can. Razakel cannot hold on, and eventually he is beaten back.

"No!" Razakel screams as he is blasted back through his own portal, which collapses in time with a large explosion from his castle.

Myrddin grins towards Elric, "Gunpowder."

"We won?" says Asad

"Not quite, there is a small matter of those guys," says Barmak, pointing to the remaining demon army.

It doesn't take long for the Majjai forces to destroy the remnants of their enemy that do not run away; all but a few are vanquished.

"Alvarez has disappeared, no-one has seen him since Razakel was weakened and sent back through the portal," reports one of the Majjai soldiers.

"His time will come," says Myrddin as the Majjai army celebrate their great victory. He turns to the other Majjai Six members, "We have more important things to discuss right now. Elric and I found something interesting while destroying the portal."

"What did you find?" asks Arshan.

"It could be the chosen one. Well, his essence more than anything else," replies Elric.

"The legend is true then?" asks Zarileh, "There will be another Majjai Six?"

"Perhaps," says Elric, "What makes things more interesting is the way we discovered his presence. The *Gooyeh Partaabs* were in Razakel's possession, and the essence of the chosen one was trapped inside one of them."

"The *Partaabs* exist? This truly is a day of discovery. But, how?" asks Barmak.

"This we do not yet know. And to what degree the essence of the chosen one is trapped within the *Gooyeh Partaab* is also something we need to ascertain. I fear this war is far from over; the real battle to end it is yet to come," replies Myrddin.

The Majjai Six give their final orders to the soldiers who remain behind, then Elric opens a portal to his chambers and the Majjai Six follow him through. Upon their arrival, he reveals the Partaabs' to the others.

The image in front of the Majjai students then zooms into the largest Partaab, holding the essence of the chosen one. The projection then fades and disappears, along with all of the massive horns.

"Damn," says Ju Long, "I was going to ask Elric if I could borrow those babies!"

Atticus does not respond. He looks towards the other Majjai students and all they can do is stare back at him. He can feel the questions flowing through their minds, together with the thirst for more answers that he himself requires.

"I know there will be questions," says Elric, pulling the focus away from Atticus and back to himself, "There will be a special assembly tomorrow; please, formulate what you wish to ask, and all will be revealed. For now, please, enjoy free periods for the rest of the day."

The Majjai students cheer and leave the field quickly before any of the professors can persuade Elric to change his mind.

Atticus and the other Majjai Six remain, along with Professor Sprocking and Mage Callan.

Elric walks towards Atticus, "It's time you knew the whole truth, Atticus," he turns to the others, "All of you, there are great challenges ahead. The war is nearing its end, and I have one more crystal to show you. What happened *after* the great battle."

A Majjai History, Vol 1 Chapter 17: Where do bad Majjai go?

All beings need a disciplinary model of sorts. The Majjai have many laws that govern their existence, but only a handful deal out the harshest punishment, one open to both Demon and Majjai. This prison is known simply as 'The Void.' No one has ever returned from The Void to explain what is inside, but it is thought to be pure emptiness, nothingness, not even darkness exists there, just nothing.

The Majjai Six are rumoured to have utilised the Void in the Battle of Aria, helping them overcome the force of Razakel and the demonic realm. Razakel survived his attempted imprisonment, but it weakened him immensely. Leaving the mortal world in relative peace, at least until Razakel recovered his strength. The time window available to access the Void was exhausted. Razakel was simply too powerful to completely absorbed.

To the best of our knowledge, The Void has not been used since the Battle of Aria. Some Majjai, desperate to discover the fate of Kazmagus, have been said to attempt access to the prison, but no one has succeeded in breaking through.

No one knows if this prison was created or if it is simply a natural phenomenon that appears between planes of existence. Some scholars have found evidence of ancient scriptures hinting at The Void being a form of living entity, a sentient being that exists simply to punish. The original scriptures have never been verified, however, and were rumoured to have disappeared around the same time as Kazmagus.

    Only senior Majjai have the knowledge to summon The Void. The only Majjai of modern times that are known to have this ability are Elric Griffin and Myrddin. It is rumoured that one other will also have this ability, the fabled Chosen One, whose identity is still unknown at the time of this writing.

Chapter 18

Truth

Elric waits for the playing fields to clear before continuing, "There is much more to this tale than what the first crystal showed," he beckons everyone to follow him.

"Isn't Professor Sprocking coming?" asks Safaya.

Mage Callan answers, "Elric has given him an important task; he will be joining us later, with guests... hopefully."

The professors, Mage Callan, Atticus, and the other Majjai Six members follow Elric towards his chamber. Atticus hasn't said a word since the end of the earlier presentation and just feels like he is in the midst of a cloud of information overload.

"I know, Atticus," says Elric, "There has been so much for you to take in over the last few weeks. I wish we could take things slower; but unfortunately, Razakel is a rather impatient fellow," Elric sits and pulls a small, lilac velvet pouch from his drawer, "You need to open this, Atticus. Myrddin has locked it so that only you are able to activate it."

"What do I do?" asks Atticus.

"You just need to touch it," replies Elric.

Everyone in the room watches silently as Atticus opens the pouch and tips it. A white crystal slides out, lands on the desk with a tinkle, and rolls towards him. Atticus sticks out his right forefinger and gently taps the upper most point of the quartz gem. As he does so, he can feel the now familiar tingle on his birthmark. The crystal hovers into the air and creates a mist, similar to the one seen on the playing fields, albeit much smaller.

# # #

Myrddin and the original Majjai Six members are in a dimly-lit room, looking at the *Gooyeh Partaabs*.

"The boy exists here?" asks Barmak, who stands steadfast with his muscular physique and full beard, "But, if the prophecy is true, this cannot be. Razakel is weakened. He will not return for a long time. Yet the chosen one is here now, in our time?"

"It seems that way, yes," replies Myrddin, "But we still need to find him and look after him."

Elric walks to a chest in the far corner of the room. From it, he pulls out an old and withered scroll, "This may help − I found it during my search for the tomb of Kazmagus. It didn't make sense until now," he hands the scroll to Myrddin, who quickly unrolls it.

"Yes, yes. This could work," says Myrddin, placing it on a table for everyone to see.

Zarileh, finding it difficult to observe, jumps up and down trying to find a way through the burly men around the table. Barmak lifts her up and puts her on his shoulder, "Thanks, that is much better," she says as she stares at the unrolled scroll, "Did Kazmagus write that?"

"We are not sure, we are not even sure of the origin of the *Partaabs* ', but we knew of their existence. The fact that this scroll refers to them directly may mean their creator also wrote this," replies Elric.

"Quiet, I need to translate this," Myrddin says, sending everyone into silent anticipation.

As Myrddin mumbles under his breath, Zarileh and Elric walk outside to patrol the immediate area.

"We won today Elric, against all odds," says Zarileh.

"Yes, we did, but only with Myrddin's help were we strong enough," replies Elric.

"That is why there are always six my friend, we are at our strongest when we are together. And now we know there will be another Majjai Six after we have gone."

Elric turns towards Zarileh, "It also proves that Razakel will return one day, stronger than ever before – and using the Void will not be an option again."

A cheer in the main chamber room interrupts them.

"Quick, Follow it!" screams Myrddin as he runs out, chasing a blue ball of light. The others quickly follow him, "Barmak, Asad, get the Prince, we will need his authority and presence to search the city!"

Elric shouts after Myrddin, "City? Which city?"

Myrddin turns his head mid-chase, "He is here, Elric, in Aria! Hurry, we must not lose the light!"

Elric and the remaining two Majjai run after Myrddin. Faster and faster, they race, through the streets of Aria. People are celebrating in every street after the victory; some recognise Elric and the other Majjai and cheer their name, but the Majjai do not hear them and do not stop. They are on another quest this night, to follow the light.

Zarileh uses her power of agility to leap above the crowds and onto the rooftops, she somersaults and dives over the buildings, keeping track of the light from above, guiding the Majjai below. They move faster, and the crowds become a blur. Finally they reach an old alleyway. Here it is dark, no party, and no celebration, just silence. The light shoots through a door at the far end.

"Do not enter here!" a voice screams from behind the sealed

doorway, "I will kill anyone who tries to enter!"

"A woman's voice?" asks Asad, arriving with the Prince and his Royal Guard in a crack of blue light.

"Your highness," says Elric, "We need your permission to enter this place."

"For what reason?" asks the Prince.

"Our future," replies Myrddin, stepping forward, "and the future of generations to come. Razakel is not defeated, we have merely slowed him down. The key to defeating him lies behind this door."

The Prince looks forward, and nods. He walks towards the door, "I, Prince Xerxus, hereby grant access to these premises. Open the door − or stand back and prepare for our entry."

"Whoever enters will be slain!" the woman's voice screams again from behind the door, "There is nothing for you here!"

Myrddin signals to Barmak to open the door. With a swift kick the door gives way revealing nothing behind it, just a darkened room. Barmak enters the room and the other Majjai follow.

The loud sound of a metal object resonates around the dark chamber, as a massive pot is slammed onto Barmak's head, shattering into several pieces. Barmak looks at the pieces on the floor, and then to the attacker, raising an eyebrow as he does so.

"We mean you no harm," says Elric, "We are Majjai. We sense the presence of a boy here."

A woman steps out of Barmak's shadow, her hair is wavy, dark brown. Her clothes show signs of struggle, with tears and holes, "Majjai? I search for one in particular, do you know him? Elric... Elric Griffin?"

"It is I − I am Elric Griffin," confirms Elric, as he creates a small ball of energy to light the room, revealing bare walls and a small, makeshift bed.

The woman falls to her knees, sobbing, "Finally! I have been searching for months, hiding from demons, protecting him from harm."

"Protecting who?" asks Myrddin.

Sima looks up at Myrddin, "Atticus, the baby," she says, "His parents' home was destroyed by the demons, and they were killed. Their final wish was for me to find the Majjai named Elric Griffin – they said that he would know how to keep the child safe. My name is Sima."

"You are safe now," says the Prince, "You have been very brave," he looks towards his royal guards, "Quickly, blankets and food for her, now!"

Zarileh walks towards Elric, and quietly whispers into his ear, "How can we be sure she is telling the truth?"

Myrddin overhears, "There is a way," he looks towards Sima, "Please, sit here for a moment, there is something I must do," he waits for Sima to sit, then places his palms on her temples. He closes his eyes, his lips move but the other Majjai are unable to make out what he says. A dazzling stream of light pours out from Sima's forehead, crystallises in the air and floats to the floor, landing gently with a light tinkle.

"What is it?" asks Zarileh.

Myrddin sighs, visibly tired from the exercise, "A thought crystal," he says, "It is a very difficult spell; takes away much of one's energy," he lifts the crystal from the floor, "A thought crystal holds certain memories, and is able to project them into the air."

Myrddin activates the newly-created device. The Majjai Six and the Prince all watch, jostling for position in the small room.

The memories start from Sima's goodbyes to Atticus's parents. Silently, they watch the events from Sima's memory of her plight and the demon's pursuit, until it ends with the mysterious whirlpool of sand vanquishing the remaining beasts.

"Interesting," says Myrddin.

"Indeed," replies Elric.

"No," replies Myrddin, "I mean, yes, the whole thing is interesting, but most interesting is that wall of sand."

"In what way?" asks Sima.

"That is my Magic," replies Myrddin.

The room falls silent as they all look towards him.

"The sky, it is the same as the one created by the *Quantorbium*, and the whirlwind of sand is a spell I have created quite recently in my own time. But, I have no recollection of performing it to save you," Myrddin says, looking towards Sima.

"Maybe you have yet to do it; you did say the *Quantorbium* was used, so perhaps you sent the spell through the portal?" asks Elric.

"Or *will* send it," comments Asad.

"Ugh, this whole time-travel thing gives me a headache," says Zarileh. The others chuckle as she stands and walks to the corner of the room and drinks some water from a bottle.

The sound of a crying baby catches everyone's attention. Sima stands quickly and walks to another corner of the room, uncovering a basket. She picks up the baby and walks towards Elric, "Elric, this is Atticus."

Elric holds Atticus in his arms; the other Majjai surround him and peer down.

"Check for the mark," says Myrddin.

Elric rolls up the sleeve on Atticus's arm, revealing the birthmark of a circle with an entwined line. The other Majjai look down with goldfish-like mouths, gawping at the baby.

"Now what do we do?" asks Barmak.

"I need to think, make calculations. We should head back to

214

Elric's chamber," says Myrddin.

Elric opens a portal and the Majjai Six, together with Sima and the baby Atticus, return to his chamber. While Zarileh and Barmak set about making Sima and the baby comfortable, Myrddin sits at his desk and begins to scribe on some parchment. Several hours pass by before he turns and speaks to the others.

"Listen carefully," says Myrddin, "I need a volunteer."

"For what?" asks Zarileh.

"Who wants to live a little longer than normal?" he replies, answering her question with another question.

The others look at each other, then return their gaze towards Myrddin, confused as to what he is asking.

"Let me explain," continues Myrddin, "Taking all of these calculations into account, together with findings from various scrolls prophesising the return of the Demon King, young Atticus should not be in our world until at least many millennia from now. I can transport him to the future, to approximately the time where Razakel will again attempt to return to rule this realm, but one of you will also need to be there ahead of him, preparing for his arrival, and making sure that, between now and then, the secret is kept safe."

"But how?" asks Elric.

"The Orb, I can use part of it to create a potion that will grant the drinker long life – long enough to live through to the return of Razakel, and hopefully beyond," says Myrddin. He wraps his black cloak around him, removing the *Quantorbium* as he does so, "Your knife please Barmak."

Barmak kneels down to the hilt tied around his ankle, grabs it, and pulls out a blade, which he hands to Myrddin.

Myrddin chants and carefully chips away a tiny shard from the Orb, which lands on the table with a tinkle. He then rushes to some shelves at the far side of the room and grabs a goblet, many herbs, and some vials, "Yes, this will do, and this, and this, and that too. And what about… ahhhh, there it is," he mutters as he quickly gathers his ingredients. Returning to the desk he grinds and chops and blends, adding various liquids and spices. After a little while, he adds the final ingredient, the piece from the Orb. A plume of smoke shoots from the goblet, hitting the ceiling and spreading across it. In a whoosh of sound, the plume of smoke is sucked straight back into the goblet.

"And you want one of us to drink that?" asks Zarileh.

"Of course," replies Myrddin, ignoring Asad gulping in the background.

Despite the pungent smell coming from the goblet, all of the Majjai step forward to offer themselves for this mission, but before anyone can take it, Elric speaks out.

"I'll do it," he says, "It is only fair I be put through this trial. The others deserve their rest now; they have families and lives to return to."

"I must warn you though, Elric," says Myrddin, "Once you drink this, your life will be forever bound to the Orb. While it exists, so will the potion in your blood continue to serve you."

Asad puts his hand on Elric's shoulder, "Are you sure my friend? Any of us would be more than willing to…"

Elric stops Asad mid-sentence, "No, this is my task. But I appreciate the gesture, old friend," he walks to where Myrddin is holding the goblet and grabs it with both hands. Before anyone can say anything, he consumes its entire contents.

At first nothing happens, then, in a flash, the room explodes in an eruption of blue light. Elric hovers in mid-air, then spins several times before coming to a rest on the floor. The others gather around him while Barmak helps him to his feet. Elric thanks Barmak before shaking his head and steadying himself.

"Interesting potion there, Myrddin," says Elric.

"Yes, but this is just the first phase of what we need to do. The next, well… it's a little more complicated. I know it must be done, but I've never sent a spell *through* a time portal before. I fear there may well be side effects," says Myrddin.

"You speak of the sand whirlwind that saved me?" asks Sima, who has been watching in silent amazement since they arrived in Myrddin's chamber.

"I do indeed," acknowledges Myrddin, "Stand back, everyone, while I activate the Orb," Myrddin waits for everyone to stand out of harm's way before holding the *Quantorbium* high in the air, then he taps it with his right forefinger and lets go. The Orb floats in mid-air and begins to glow a bright, light blue. Myrddin closes his eyes, taps the Orb again, and a huge portal emerges before him, filling the room.

The others in the room look on, as it is the first time most of them have seen the Orb in action. Through the portal they can see the plain of the desert where Sima is running. Several Screamers and other beasts that Atticus does not recognise are chasing her.

Myrddin clasps his hands together, and with an almighty push forward, sends through a jet of wind. It crashes on the ground and disposes of the demons below quickly and decisively. In the study, Myrddin is tiring from the Magical energy he is exerting, but he creates another whirlwind to transport Sima of the past into Aria.

"There, it is done," says Myrddin, physically drained from the ordeal, he stumbles slightly. Barmak and Elric rush to his aid, "The last few days have been taxing," he groans. Elric helps him to a small wooden chair in the chamber.

"Well, we can rest for a little while at least. Although there is still the small matter of Alvarez running loose in this realm," says Elric

"He can be contained; he will know not to show his face alone," says Asad.

# # #

The cloud holding the image that Atticus and the others are watching fades to white. Ju Long and Olof whisper to each other, thinking that the thought crystal had finished what it had to show, when Myrddin's face reappears.

"Unfortunately, there were a few side effects to that whirlwind spell. Elric will explain the main one to you. As for the Orb, it is now well hidden. You will need it soon. Atticus, Safaya, Olof, Joyce, Khan and Ju Long, there is a path that you need to follow," each Majjai Six member is taken slightly aback as their names are mentioned, "There are clues scattered along your journey. Some of you will make it all the way, and some may well not. I have helped you along your journey as much as I can, but there are rules when meddling with time, and I can only do so much. I cannot tell you what will happen, as the very knowledge of it may well change your actions – all part of the rules unfortunately," he sighs before finishing, "Who knows, we may even meet in the course of your adventures. For now, though, the path ahead is a dangerous one, for all of you. Good luck, trust each other, and you will prevail. Goodbye…"

The mist fades and fizzles out.

Atticus turns to Elric, "Side effects?" he asks.

"Yes. Your parents. The ones that have adopted you in this time, they have been through much in their lives yes?" asks Elric.

Atticus nods, "An accident, a long time ago."

"The whirlwind sent through the portal was not the only whirlwind that formed. There were always going to be risks with such an act. The consequence of this one was that it simultaneously created another portal, much closer to our time. In fact, it opened a portal right about the time your parents were driving down a certain country road..."

Atticus' concern grows, "You mean...?"

"Yes Atticus," responds Elric, "The accident was a side effect of saving you from Alvarez and his demons. The whirlwind that saved you created another, which forced your parents' car off the road. It was discovered – much later – that using the Orb so close together in terms of time creates tears in the fabric of space and reality, ripping open other passages. This is why we are unable to open portals too soon together."

Everyone else in the room is silent, not knowing whether to speak or to wait for Atticus to respond.

"They need to know the truth," says Atticus.

"Yes, but that is not your responsibility, for they were not your actions," says Elric.

As Elric says these words, the doors to his chamber swing open. Joseph and Sophia stand in the doorway, Professor Sprocking just behind them.

"Mum, Dad!" shouts Atticus.

Sophia runs towards her son and grabs him, sobbing, "It's ok, sweetie, we know... everything."

Joseph walks towards Atticus and touches his head with his palm, "I'm so proud of you son. Now, when are you going to teach me some of these magic tricks?"

The room empties quietly as the others leave to allow Atticus and his parents to talk privately. As Joyce looks back and gives Atticus a reassuring look, he knew at that moment that some things will be much easier now, but at the same time, others would be much more difficult.

The Majjai Journals:

I miss him. My brother sacrificed himself to save me, leaving a kingdom without its king. Today would have been his birthday. He would have loved this time. Alas the League of Aria no longer seems to exist. I have had no contact from them. At least there is the knowledge that Elric has kept me safe. My brother knew what he was doing when releasing me to his care.

These powers have strengthened more than ever recently; the help from Khan and Olof has been extremely beneficial, and Mage Callan is a fantastic tutor. Elric answers our questions as much as he can, as custodian of so much knowledge and with his gift of long life, I'm surprised he has managed to remain faithful to the cause for so many years.

This new language was difficult to learn at first, but I feel I am now fluent enough to converse with the natives of this time. Elric certainly seems to think so and has allowed me to leave school grounds many a time now. Khan is always around to make sure I'm ok as well, which is sweet. But I wish he would take more interest; our traditions are so similar, and I feel closer to him than anyone else, even Joyce. Yet he remains almost painfully distant. I sense a battle within him, one he fights alone. I'm sure my brother would have approved of Khan, they are much alike.

Attossa plays on my dreams. What did my brother mean when he said there is more to her? I guess I will find out in time, but right now, I'm just glad she is dead. She never loved anything but greed and power, and she tried to murder me. Oh, Ismail, I miss your guidance and your protection. Why did you have to leave me?

I also wonder more about this 'third realm.' We know of the demon realm and our own, but I have yet to find any more information about this prophecy I myself am supposed to fulfil. The dangers here are very real – Leviathan was a frightening experience, and then there are the demons we have to contend with. What dangers would a third realm bring?

I have reservations about this Atticus. His focus is not on what it should be, he merely chases Joyce wherever she goes. I hope the reality of what we are truly up against does not shock him; if the legend is true, he will truly be powerful.

My studies have also taught me about something else: white Magic. The Majjai use blue Magic and demons use red, but there is a fabled white Magic, which is most powerful. I found out about it in some obscure scrolls while researching Kazmagus. Some say he discovered this element of Magic, but never perfected it. Elric was quite interested in this and has tried to learn more, but even he has hit something of a wall. It seems much of this knowledge is held in the Tomb of Kazmagus, and this has never been found.

I should sleep now; I am having breakfast with Khan in the morning, so need to be awake early. Everybody is excited about the Battle of Aria, but I have heard this story from my father and brother, so know much of what to expect. I wonder if there will be any surprises in Elric's telling of it?

Princess Safaya

Chapter 19

Family

Three months have now passed by since the revelations of the battle of Aria. The students at Wysardian Manor are enjoying a well-earned rest from studies. Some however, have nowhere to go and remain within the confines of the Manor walls.

The Manor is encased in white snow, with the sun doing its best to try to melt everything away.

Atticus and Joyce have just completed a training session and are on their way to Elric's chamber when they spot Khan in the distance, racing ahead of them. They quietly follow him to Elric's chamber.

"You cannot send her alone on this quest. You know I am unable to leave her side," says Khan, bursting into Elric's chamber without waiting for an invitation to enter.

Elric and Geoffrey are sitting at Elric's desk, startled at Khan's intrusion.

"Khan, I know of your duties, but you cannot be there all of the time for her; you are needed elsewhere. Atticus and Joyce are still in training, they need your guidance. Olof and Ju Long will take good care of Safaya, there is nothing to worry about," says Elric, as softly as possible, trying to calm Khan down.

"What mission has she been sent on?" Khan asks forcefully.

"They are trying to track down a traitor," says Geoffrey

"Traitor?" asks Khan.

"Yes Khan, one we have been after for a long long time. The traitor who revealed Atticus' location to Alvarez all those years ago," says Elric.

"He still lives?" asks Khan.

"Apparently so. The watcher, Serenity, overheard the guards talking about a spy here. Someone linked to the Manor. Mage Callan has already gone to try to obtain more information from her," says Elric.

"And what about Safaya, what does she do?" asks Khan.

"She and the others are merely watching the staff, making sure nothing is untoward about them. I have requested they deliver letters on my behalf as a ruse, to try and analyse if there is any great threat we have not seen," answers Elric.

Geoffrey gets up and walks towards Khan, "Is there something else?" he asks, sensing that Khan has other reasons behind his question.

"No," he replies.

The door to the chamber creaks slightly. Atticus and Joyce realise they have been spotted and walk in, pretending they have not heard anything.

"Ahhhh, Atticus, how are you, dear boy?" asks Elric.

"Fine," replies Atticus.

"And how are your parents adjusting to the news?

"It took them a few weeks. Mum kept messing with my hair, even more than usual, and Dad keeps asking me to teach him how to make fireballs. But, apart from that, they have been quite calm about it – almost as if they always knew."

"That's good to hear. So, to what do we owe the pleasure of your company today? I thought we gave you two the day off?" says Geoffrey.

"Nothing much, we just wanted to see if Khan wanted to hang

out today?" says Joyce.

"Hang... out? What does this mean?" asks Khan.

"Come on, we'll show you," says Atticus.

Khan looks towards Elric with a puzzled face. Elric gives him a little nod.

"It'll do you good, Khan. Go on, get out and get some fresh air."

Before Khan can answer, Joyce and Atticus are dragging him out of the room.

"Wait!" shouts Khan, worryingly, "This doesn't actually involve *hanging* does it?"

Atticus and Joyce giggle as they drag Khan out.

# # #

Mage Callan reluctantly sits for a bowl of soup. Serenity is still so grateful for him saving her life that she took extra special care with his meal.

"I'm so glad you came today. I never had the chance to thank you properly since you saved me," says Serenity.

"It was my pleasure. How is your son? Joshua is his name, right?" replies Mage Callan.

"Good memory," says Serenity with a little smile, "Ever since his father passed away, I have been all he has had. The rest of the family don't particularly agree with our ways."

"The ways of the Majjai, you mean?" asks Mage Callan.

"Yes," replies Serenity.

"I know how you feel. I haven't spoken to my brother in 15 years. My parents forbade my presence at their funerals. They never understood. Called the Majjai ways 'evil,' when what we were doing was *fighting* evil," says Mage Callan, "Anyway, enough about me, I'm here to clarify what you heard from the guards."

"Are you sure you don't want any soup first? It's homemade chicken soup, with tender, roast chicken pieces," says Serenity, trying to waft the aroma towards Mage Callan.

Mage Callan tries to resist, "No time, unfortunately. I need to report back to Elric as soon as possible."

"Why not use one of those fancy crystals? Heck, we even have a telephone, you know," replies Serenity, teasing him, "Now, hush – just be quiet and keep me company. Then, and only then will I tell you what I heard."

Mage Callan looks towards Serenity; he can see a loneliness there that he is all too familiar with. The aroma of the soup, the warmth of the kitchen, and the attention of a beautiful lady are things he has been without for what seems a lifetime. This loneliness reasserted itself the day he saved her. The reason he jumped at this chance to question Serenity becomes all too clear to him, and at that moment, his loneliness seems to disappear.

With a smile he accepts the invitation to prolong this encounter, "Soup would be lovely," he says as he reaches for the freshly made bread. A puff of warm steam shoots out as Mage Callan tears a piece off and dips it into the hot soup that Serenity puts in front of him. She joins him at the table, their hands edge closer together until their fingertips touch.

"This is rather nice," says Mage Callan.

"Yes, it's been a while since I've had interesting company for dinner," replies Serenity.

Mage Callan looks at Serenity with a tiny smirk, "I was actually talking about the soup."

Serenity pauses a moment, looks towards Mage Callan, then

realises that he was joking as a cheeky smile appears on his face.

"So," says Mage Callan, "we really do need to talk about what you heard. I just need to clarify it."

Serenity sighs, she has tried to push her ordeal out of her mind; the torture she endured almost killed her, "I only remember bits. But what I do know is that Herensugue was talking about someone here, preparing a boy."

"Did they say any names?" asks Mage Callan.

"No, but he also said that this person is a traitor of old. The traitor was gifted with the cocoon of enhancement that Razakel used on Alvarez; he is very powerful," replies Serenity.

Mage Callan leans back into his chair, softly stroking his chin while he thinks, "Could they be preparing Atticus for something?"

"Perhaps," replies Serenity, "But, they also said the boy is 'almost converted to the side of the demons, his essence is evil.' That doesn't sound like Atticus."

"Razakel is very powerful, he may have planned this all along. But, we must not jump to any conclusions," Mage Callan is caught in a thoughtful state, and quietly helps Serenity clear the table, "I must leave now, I have a long journey back."

"Yes, well, it was nice seeing you, Ian," says Serenity, startling Mage Callan with the fact that she knows his first name.

"Who...?" he asks.

"Elric told me," she replies with a smile.

"Yes, well, I really must be off now," Mage Callan says. He walks to the door, but before he gets there, he realises that he actually enjoyed himself this evening. He turns, and decides to finish the evening with a question, "Serenity?"

"Yes, Ian?" she asks.

"Erm, I was wondering, well, you know. Tonight was nice.

So… I was wondering if you wouldn't mind accompanying me to dinner on Saturday evening?" Mage Callan says, with his eyes closed, hoping that he doesn't get a slap for his troubles.

Serenity smiles, "I would love to," she tip-toes up to Mage Callan's face, and places a little warm kiss on his cheek.

Mage Callan smiles, bows his head, and walks out of the door… still smiling.

# # #

"So this is *hanging out*?" asks Khan, perplexed at the thought of sitting down in a fast food restaurant, eating fries for a long period of time as being something fun.

"Not just this, we chat as well," says Joyce

"I have concerns with other matters at the moment," says Khan.

"Safaya?" Atticus says quickly, hoping Khan doesn't hit him.

Khan looks at Atticus with his right eyebrow raised, "Yes, but perhaps not for the reasons you think," Khan sighs, "There is much to me that you and the other Majjai Six do not know − and cannot know for some time yet."

They leave the fast food restaurant after realising Khan is simply holding the slim piece of meat that supposedly passes as a burger, and staring at his food rather than eating it.

They head towards the hills behind Wysardian Manor. The sun is already setting on the horizon when they sit, and they watch it dip below the furthest tower.

"Hmm, why don't you just tell her you like her?" says Joyce, completely ignoring what Khan said earlier.

He looks at Joyce, knowing full-well that she will not allow

227

the topic to pass by without a decent answer, "She is a Princess you know. Me, I'm just Khan, a Saracen; it can never happen. The laws prevent it."

"The laws are old, Khan," says Atticus, "I've researched into them – those Runes of Zamaan come in handy when you need to learn quite a bit in a short space of time. I also learnt that the order of Saracens that you descend from no longer exists; you are the last."

"Which is why it is important that I uphold their laws Atticus. Besides, there is another reason why it can never happen. My work here is not only with the Majjai Six, there is another task to which I am bound," Khan checks the time, "Come, it's time you guys went home, your parents will be wondering where you have got to. I'll walk you both, I've heard that Bradley Burrows is still eager for vengeance."

"He always will be," says Atticus, "Not worried though, he is just a bully."

#

Atticus closes the front door after waving bye to Khan and Joyce. He puts his rucksack on the coat stand and walks towards the lounge. Some music and tapping catches his attention. It seems to be coming from the conservatory. He walks towards it slowly.

"Ouch," squeals Sophia.

"That was your fault this time, you didn't move back at the right time," says Joseph.

Atticus pokes his head round the corner, the furniture has been cleared away and the large space has been turned into a mini dance floor. He remembers that the next dance competition is tomorrow night, Sophia and Joseph have been practising a great deal the past few evenings. Since the first dance competition, they actually improved enough to qualify for some big final.

"You're just jealous that I'm better than you now," says Joseph jokingly, not noticing Sophia sticking her tongue out at him while his back is turned.

"Hi, Atticus," says Sophia, "How is Elric?"

"He is fine," replies Atticus. He has been wondering whether or not he should ask a question he has been wanting an answer to ever since Sophia and Joseph were told the truth. They haven't mentioned it much, apart from the immediate few days' after the revelation. It's just been a quiet acceptance, with a few skirting queries.

"How was your day?" asks Joseph.

"Not bad. Mum, Dad, can I ask you guys something?" asks Atticus.

"Sure sweetie, go ahead," says Sophia.

"Are you guys ok with all of this? I mean, it was Myrddin's Magic that caused the accident," says Atticus.

"We've been waiting for you to ask us, Atticus; we wanted to be sure you were ready to talk to us about these matters," says Joseph, "Come, let's talk in the front room."

They all go to the living room and settle quickly. Sophia brings a tray of biscuits and tea. Atticus grabs a pile of Bourbon biscuits before anyone can stop him.

Sophia is the first to speak, "Obviously, we were shocked at first when Professor Sprocking explained everything. It was almost like we were watching ourselves in a television screen with that thought-crystal trick. Didn't believe a word of it until he started sparking up little balls of blue fire in his hands, and moving things around the room with his mind."

"Yeah, he likes doing that," says Atticus.

"To tell you the truth, Atticus," says Joseph, " yes, we were angry, very angry– at first. But then we realised it wasn't really the fault of the Majjai, more that son of a bitch, Alvarez."

"Joseph, no need for that language," snaps Sophia.

Atticus is shocked by his dad's words; he has never heard him curse someone before. In fact, he has never seen him this angry before.

"I know I shouldn't swear, but not only was he the real cause of our accident, he was also after you, Atticus. You saved us, you know," says Joseph. Atticus can just see a little shimmer of water forming in his eye, "You see, Atticus, your mother and I, we were only just barely coping with the accident. If it wasn't for Marcellus, I don't know what we would have done; we owe him a lot," says Joseph as he starts to pace around the room.

Sophia stands and puts a comforting hand on Joseph's shoulder, "What your father is trying to say is, although yes, we had a tragic accident and we lost a child, in those unfortunate circumstances, we also gained a son. One we are very proud of. And also one we are very worried about," Sophia sits back down and coaxes Joseph to do the same, "We learnt to cope with what happened through you, Atticus. You inspired us from the beginning to survive, to keep going, to believe that everything in life happens for a reason. Most importantly, you taught us how to be happy again."

This time, it's Joseph's turn to comfort Sophia, "So, yes, everything has been a huge revelation, but we have learnt not to take things for granted ever since we found you in the circumstances we did. We knew there was more to the story; but until Geoffrey spoke to us, we didn't know what it was. Having answers is comforting."

"I'm glad," says Atticus, "One less thing to be scared about."

"You don't have to be scared about anything, son," says Joseph, "We are always here for you. No matter what happens – even if we have to fight through hell itself – we will always be there."

For the first time, Atticus feels free from worry, from fear. He feels safer now more than ever, ready for the challenges ahead.

"We better get ready for that dance now dear," says Sophia, "Come on, Atticus, you can DJ the music for us."

They leave together for the conservatory, as close a family as they have ever been before. As Atticus goes through each CD, his mind begins to wander. He recalls the conversation between Elric and Khan regarding the traitor. The music fades into the background as Atticus' thoughts slowly drift away.

# # #

The moon shines through an upstairs window, at a house far from Atticus' home, dimly lighting the master bedroom. A lone figure sleeps, snoring loudly. The room is bare, with just a bed and a mirror, even the floor consists of splintered floorboards and little else.

The mirror is long, with a gold-carved bezel. On one side of the bezel is a carving of an animal with seven heads. On the other side, the carving of a dragon glints against the moonlight. The moonlight's reflection from the mirror shines on the bed, waking the lone figure.

With a cough and a splurt the figure rises from his slumber. Wiping the sleep from his eyes, he shuts the curtains to block the moonlight, returning the room to darkness.

"Isssssssssssss the boy ready?" a voice slithers out from behind him. He immediately spins around to see the face of a beast with seven serpent heads inside the mirror.

The lone figure hides his face in the darkness, "Not yet, Herensugue, but he is close. One more push and he will be ready for the ceremony."

"Ah. You realisssssse that our masssster growsssssss

impatient," hisses Herensugue.

"Yes, but I only need a few more days. We can then present the boy to our master," replies the lone figure.

"I'm sssurprisssed you have sssssurvived this long without detection. Do the Majjai sssssussspect?"

"Not at all, there are a few who have been tasked with searching for a traitor, but they are following a few false paths; I prepared for just such a situation. But it does mean we need to move quickly," the lone figure says, purposely keeping out of the light emanating from the mirror's projection, "Will you be accompanying Alvarez for the... uhum... surprise?"

"I sssssssshall. Have the boy there. We will usssse tomorrow'sss eventss asss a dissstraction," says Herensugue.

"Very good, I will ensure the boy is there. I will remain hidden until the time is right," the lone figure returns to his bed, "Now, leave me be, before they detect your Magic here."

The mirror pales to darkness again while the lone figure returns to his rest.

"I know you are here boy," says the traitor in the darkness, "I can sense you."

Atticus wakes instantly, finding himself in his own bed, but he still hears the voice in his mind.

"Your end will come, Atticus. You're weak, and so are your Majjai friends. The time for demons is near."

Atticus shuts his eyes tight, trying to push the voice out of his mind.

"You can't get away that easily," says the traitor.

"Leave the boy be, traitor!" another voice enters the fray, and Atticus feels his mind freed again. He looks around, searching for a clue to the identity of the voice that saved him, but there is nothing, no sign, no voices, just silence. Could that have been the protector? Atticus thinks to himself. His voice is familiar, he thinks it is the same one he heard when the shadow figure appeared to him in Professor Snugglebottom's class.

"Thank you," says Atticus, hoping the protector is able to hear him. Relieved with his rescue, Atticus promises himself to be much more careful with this gift of insight and sleeps soundly for the night, wondering how to inform Elric of this latest incident.

A Majjai History, Vol 1 Chapter 14: The Age of Transition

There have been many rumours of a third realm; one that is said is to be filled with creatures of fantasy. These creatures once existed in the Earth realm; mortals knew them as such creatures as unicorns, dragons, elves, fairies, and mermaids.

The Age of Transition fell just after the disappearance of both Kazmagus and Asmodei. The rise of Razakel forced these mythical creatures to find somewhere else to exist safely. It is rumoured that they left to nurture a new realm, hidden from mortal and demon, one where only mythical and Majjai may enter. The doorway to this realm has never been found − and though it has been prophesied that a Majjai queen will emerge to rule this realm, at the time of this writing, her identity is still unknown.

In the Earth realm, the Age of Transition brought many challenges. The demonic factions, led by Razakel, spread across the globe. They instilled hatred into man's hearts, causing conflicts born from prejudice and ignorance. Other intrusions were more direct; they often had running battles with Majjai soldiers, killing any mortal that stood in the way. These were dark times until the emergence of the Majjai Six. This small band of warriors united the Majjai. They began to take the fight back to the Demonic hordes. The tide had begun to turn, and stability found its way throughout the Earth realm.

Chapter 20

The Attack

The sports hall erupts in uniform applause. Joseph and Sophia danced and dazzled in a routine that surprised everyone, including Atticus. Joyce sits next to him, whistling and cheering as loud as anyone.

"They were very good, Atticus!" says Joyce, "Best of the night! If they don't win, it will be a travesty."

Joseph and Sophia soak up every ounce of the rapture surrounding them before exiting the dance floor beneath a large screen replaying their routine.

"You did soooo well, JJ, baby!" says Sophia, breathing heavily from the excitement of the crowd.

The Burrows' are also there. Bradley's dad looks like a much larger and meaner version of his son. Bradley's mum looks like her son, albeit with longer hair and a slightly puffier rosy-cheeked pout.

Joyce and Atticus leave their seats and head to the makeshift backstage to meet up with Joseph and Sophia. Navigating through the stacked benches and seats is not easy. When they finally reach the rear, Joseph and Sophia have changed into another set of evening wear, preparing for the announcement of the results.

Joyce gives Sophia a great big hug, "That was so cool. You guys owned that dance floor!"

Atticus does a strange handshake with Joseph, while Joyce looks at them both like they are fresh from the loony bin.

"Secret handshake," Sophia acknowledges to Joyce.

"Men!" replies Joyce.

"Indeed," says Sophia, "Joseph and I are going to go to dinner straight after this; think we deserve it after all the hard work. I've already spoken to your parents, Joyce, and they said they will pick you up from our house a little later. Marcellus is there already and has offered to stay until your parents arrive."

Joyce nods, glad that she will get some extra time to spend with Atticus. Sophia and Joseph return to the main arena. A gaggle of other contestants also take to the stage, all dressed in their finest. Sophia dazzles again; even her walk mesmerises Joseph.

Atticus is still a little taken aback. He was expecting a small amateur affair for this competition, but instead, the event is being held in a decent sized indoor auditorium − about three hundred seats filled with members of the local community who all now appear to be dance fans.

The host returns to the centre stage and begins his announcement.

"Ladies and gentlemen! Firstly, let me thank you all once again for coming, we are very impressed with the turn out, and your support for our charity this afternoon. The proceeds will all be going to the local children's hospital," the crowd claps in acknowledgement, "I now have an envelope here, with the names of tonight's winners," the crowd is silent, a few cheers come out for some of the dance couples, but Joyce and Atticus stay quiet, excited for the result.

"In 3rd Place, and winners of the 2-minute free shopping spree at the Fresco supermarket, Greta and Paul Green!"

The crowd claps and whistles. The host waits for the crowd to settle before continuing, "In 2nd Place, and winners of the Eurostar and weekend break to Paris, Sarah and Harry Trottleworth!"

The crowd applaud again, even louder, "In 3rd place... sorry, already done that," the audience chuckles and waits with baited breath for the announcement, "In 1st Place, and winners of a top-of-the-range home entertainment system including a 55" LED TV, surround sound system, Blu Ray disc player, stereo hi fi, and a weekend at a top London Spa..." Joseph and Sophia hold each other's hands tightly as they wait for the announcer to call out the names; all Atticus can think about is watching his favourite science fiction movies through the new home cinema, "...Joseph and Sophia Jones!!!"

The entire hall erupts in unanimous applause, whistles bounce off the walls and some people who brought party poppers make the reaction even more colourful.

Atticus and Joyce are jumping up and down, before running out to congratulate them, "Dibs on the TV, Dad!" says Atticus.

Joseph smiles, "Oi! Win your own dance competition, and then we'll talk."

The host hands the trophy to Joseph and Sophia as the audience continue to cheer. Atticus and Joyce lead them off the main arena floor before they all go deaf.

"Right, we'll see you guys later then," says Sophia her eyes still bright with excitement, "We're going to get changed and be off for dinner."

Joseph hands the trophy to Atticus to take home. Sophia calls to make sure that Marcellus is at their house, and gives Atticus a quick hug before seeing them out.

"Your parents are really sweet, Atticus," says Joyce as they exit the arena complex.

"Yeah, I'm lucky. Still haven't met yours though," replies

Atticus, "When did they get back from their trip?"

"A few days back, but I hardly see them. They are always so busy. Auntie Blossom is great though, and she is an awesome cook – you'd like her pancakes," teases Joyce.

"Well, I hope the school nerd in me doesn't embarrass you when I finally meet them," says Atticus.

"You're no nerd, silly," says Joyce, holding Atticus' hand, "Come now, we need to get back."

The late afternoon sunshine is crisp with the onset of the colder season; both Atticus and Joyce are wrapped warmly in scarves and thick coats. Winter is beginning to take hold, and the few animals that ignore the lure of hibernation can be seen busily scurrying for food to hoard. As Joyce and Atticus crunch through the frosted grass, some of the animals behind them scurry away, not for food, but to escape something else. The two young Majjai are unaware they are being followed.

Unbeknownst to Atticus, Bradley Burrows has managed to escape the watchful eye of his parents and has gathered his little team to track down Atticus and Joyce. They circle round ahead of them, and lie in wait.

Joyce pauses for a moment, "Shhhh, Atticus, I think I hear something," she whispers. She puts her hand on his arm, "Remember, our powers have to be kept secret."

"Oi, Jones!" screams Bradley as he and his little gang swarm out from behind a fence, "Your friends aren't around to save you now."

Atticus holds Joyce's arm, and guides her to stand behind him, "Go away, Bradley, we're not looking for any trouble."

"Well, trouble seems to be looking for you," replies Bradley.

Before Atticus can respond, Bradley throws a powerful punch towards him. Atticus sidesteps and pulls Joyce out of the way just in time. Bradley trips over Atticus' trailing leg.

"Look, Bradley, let's just call things even yeah?" says Atticus, quietly confident that the training he has had recently is just enough to keep his one-time nemesis at bay. The fact that Bradley's minions are giggling at the sight of their leader wriggling on the ground after being tripped already bolsters Atticus' own confidence of his ability.

Bradley gets up again, even angrier, throws another punch, and a kick, followed by several more punches. Atticus simply dodges them all, and blocks a few for good measure, always making sure that there is a safe distance between them and Joyce.

At this point Bradley is seething with rage − his little group are in hysterics at the sight of Bradley not getting anywhere, almost stripping away their own fear of him. Bradley sees this, and the loss of control begins to add fuel to the fire of his already angered state, "Jones!" he yells as loud as he can, "I'm going to *kill you*!"

With those words, everything goes silent; as Bradley's gang realises that Bradley has overstepped the mark. They turn and walk away without even looking back, Bradley hears the faintest of words as they disappear − "Loser," still angry, all he can think about is revenge. His head stays bowed, rage building, it soon reaches the summit of his ability to contain it, "Arrrrrggghhhh!" he screams, looking around him, Atticus and Joyce have long run away; he sees them in the distance, but before he can give chase, someone behind him startles him.

"Burrows!" says a sharp voice, "Causing trouble again are we?"

Bradley spins around to see a familiar figure, "No professor, just..."

"Jones annoying you again, eh? Should never have told you about that insulting picture he drew of you earlier this year," says the Professor.

"It's worse than that, sir. I hate him," replies Bradley.

"So I could hear. I think you need to calm down a little. I have something for you back at the manor; meet me there in half an hour. And here is one of those chocolate bars you like so much, make sure you finish it before you get to my office," the professor says, turning his back to Bradley and walking away before a response can be received.

Bradley kicks the ground and walks away, fists clenched, punching every bush on his route, but the anger remains unrelenting, in fact it grows ever more, with every tasty bite of chocolate.

# # #

Atticus and Joyce run around a corner, gasping for breath.

"Is he gone?" gasps Joyce.

"Yeah, he was talking to someone, couldn't see who it was, though," pants Atticus, "Whoever it was, they gave us the time to get away."

"We better get to your house in case he comes back," says Joyce.

They get home quickly. Atticus opens the door with his key and calls out to Marcellus, but there is no reply.

"Don't think he is here," says Atticus.

"Strange," says Joyce, "Your mum said she called to check he was here."

The phone rings before Atticus can reply. He rushes to it and answers.

"Hello?" he says, tentatively.

Joyce waits for Atticus to finish the call before asking who it was.

"Elric needs us at the manor straight away; some sort of revelation," says Atticus, "I'll leave a note for Mum and Dad. Elric says he is sending a car to pick us up."

"Really?" smiles Joyce, "I think you are going to enjoy this."

"What?" asks Atticus.

"Elric only ever sends one car," replies Joyce, "He calls it Spitfire."

Atticus raises an eyebrow. He quickly finishes his note, and changes into jeans and a black shirt. The huge roar of an engine catches his attention. He peers out of the upstairs window and spies a long black car, with giant air scoops and giant alloy wheels, "Cool," he thinks to himself.

"The car's here!" shouts Joyce from downstairs.

Atticus runs down, and almost rushes straight pass Joyce in his excitement to get a better look at Spitfire. He runs down the driveway, leaving Joyce to close the front door.

"Men," scoffs Joyce, a little more annoyed as she has now said that twice in one day.

Atticus stands in front of Spitfire, his jaw agape. He has never seen such a car before; it certainly isn't from any manufacturer known to him. The grille is large and of blacked-out metal, there are small strips of chrome on the side and the wheel arches protrude like a beefed-up muscle car. The wheels are also blacked out; the enormous brake callipers can just be seen behind the 20" multi-spoke alloys. Atticus walks around the back of the car and spies four large exhaust pipes, two on each side. The car rumbles, and a jet of flame shoots out of the pipes.

"Are you getting in or not?" says a deep, rumbling voice.

"Who said that?" asks Atticus.

"I did," says the voice again. Spitfire opens one of his doors.

241

Atticus & The Orb Of Time

"Hi, Spitfire, how are you?" says Joyce, nudging Atticus on her way into the car.

Atticus is gob-smacked, "The car talks?"

Joyce giggles, "Come on, Pancake Man, we have to get to the manor. Get in."

"The car talks," whispers Atticus, still amazed, as he steps in.

"I am honoured to finally meet you, Atticus," says Spitfire.

"Wow, this is so cool," says the young Majjai as he sinks into the sumptuous red leather seats, "So, are you like, alive?"

"I can explain," says Joyce, "Spitfire was created by Elric to embody the spirit of Barmak, one of the original Majjai Six whose spirit had been withdrawn from his body by an unknown energy and held in a state similar to limbo. Elric rescued Barmak and with the aid of the Mecha Knights, created this vessel for him to inhabit. There should be a chapter about it in the book on Majjai History that Professor Morgan gave you."

"Uhum," says Spitfire, "Yes, he chose my new name as well. Which I do rather like. Now, shall we take the low road or the high road?"

"Let's show Atticus what you can do," says Joyce, "The high road, please."

"Very well. I should cloak first, I think," says Spitfire.

"Naaah, it's quiet around here, let's make some noise," says Joyce.

"As you wish," replies Spitfire as he revs his engine to move off.

Joyce looks around to make sure no one is looking, "It's clear."

Spitfire roars down the road. Before they reach the end, a pair of wings morph out of the rear wheel arches; the vehicle body has turned into a liquid alloy state, fluidly changing form, with the rear spoiler growing taller. In a matter of seconds they are soaring through the air with Atticus screaming in delight.

They reach the manor in moments, Atticus still screaming. Spitfire lands on one of the towers closest to Elric's chamber, "I hope to be of service again one day, Atticus," he says.

"So do I," Atticus is unable to stop grinning.

Joyce tugs at Atticus' shirt, "Stop gawping, will you; we need to get to the chamber quickly."

They run so fast, that they find little time to wonder why the main doors to the Majjai section of the Manor are standing wide open.

"That's odd," says Joyce, "Those doors are never left open like that."

"We can ask Elric when we get there," replies Atticus, as they close the doors and continue their race to the chamber.

They finally reach Elric's room and knock.

"Enter," says Elric, who they see sitting at the head of a large oval table at the far end of the room. Professors Morgan and Sprocking and the rest of the Majjai Six are also there and waiting patiently for Joyce and Atticus to take their places.

"I trust Spitfire brought you here without incident?" asks Elric.

Atticus nods frantically, still overwrought.

"Good, although I suspect he did not do so in an austere fashion. No? He is far too extravagant; but that is Barmak's spirit showing through," Elric sighs.

"Everything ok?" asks Atticus, wanting to find out what is so urgent.

"Yes; but we have learned some interesting things which we need to act upon quite quickly," replies Professor Sprocking.

Atticus looks at the table close to Olof. In front of him lays a medallion, the same medallion that Professor Morgan found at Ennerdale Forest during their encounter against the Beasts of the North.

"The medallion is a forbidden item," says Olof, "My research led me to an old legend, one that is not widely known, which details the exploits of Loki, the Norse God of Mischief. He created a series of medallions that gave him the ability to open portals across realms. There are seven in total, six smaller ones, and one large. He used these medallions as a means to carry out his many games; but, to prevent the likes of the very powerful gods like Odin from using them, he booby-trapped them," Olof adjusts his position and levitates a book towards him. He opens the book at a specific page and lays it on the table. The page is written in Old Norse.

"What does it say?" asks Safaya.

"The medallions only allow a certain amount of energy through them, and the more powerful the being travelling through them, the more energy is used. As a result, once all of its energy has been consumed, the portal will close, trapping whoever is using it in the other realm. However, Loki made the seventh, larger medallion to counter this, just in case he himself ever became trapped. The seventh medallion is limitless, and I believe this is what Razakel seeks, to enter our realm."

"So he has been using the other medallions to send his demons through?" asks Khan.

"Yes," says Elric, "But, we think he only has two of the smaller medallions, as they are not to be found; they were stolen from a museum in Cairo about 800 years ago, allowing Alvarez return passage into his master's realm. It was not known what they were until too late."

"So where are the others?" asks Safaya.

"Well," says Olof, "We found one at Ennerdale Forest."

"Yes," says Elric, "And that leaves another four to find."

Professor Sprocking looks over at Elric alarmingly, "What about that sack?"

"Which sack?" asks Elric.

"Your memory, old man – the one we took from Alvarez in Echo Forest," replies the Professor.

"They are just branches, aren't they?" asks Khan.

"Yes," replies Elric, "But Alvarez is a master at transfiguration. There are three branches of equal size, and one branch noticeably larger. Looks like Alvarez is getting smarter as we…"

CRASSHHHHHHHH!!!

Elric is interrupted by a massive noise. They all storm to the window.

"Graigons!!" shouts Olof.

Ten Graigons are pounding the foundations of the Manor; each impact rocks the entire building. Before they can react, another explosion is heard.

"We are under attack!" shouts Professor Morgan, "That came from the Majjai Hall."

"Where is the sack?" asks Professor Sprocking.

"Near the hall," replies Elric.

Atticus and Joyce quickly remember that the great doors into the Majjai quarters were open.

"The doors were open when we came in," says Atticus.

"The traitor, this must be his work," says Professor Sprocking.

Elric nods, "Olof, Geoffrey, you're with me. Benjamin, you and the others investigate that explosion in the hall. We will take out those Graigons," Elric pulls out a small orb, and speaks into it, "Spitfire, my old friend, meet you near the rear."

Spitfire's voice emanates from the orb, "Already there, old friend," as the others look out of the window again, they see Spitfire flying into the heart of the first Graigon and sending him crashing into the ground, "You can pay for my next paint job."

Elric, Olof, and Geoffrey teleport outside and begin their fight against the behemouth monsters. The others race towards the Majjai Hall.

The corridors become a blur as they try to keep up with Joyce, who is using her speed ability to full effect. She pulls ahead, closely followed by Atticus.

They get to the hall to discover a lone figure: a hooded man looking away from them.

"Ahhh, the chosen one, and his little wench," says the lone figure, his back still to them.

"Who are you?" demands Atticus.

The hooded figure turns and drops his hood. Atticus and Joyce step back.

"Alvarez," says Joyce, "Quickly Atticus, MOVE!"

Alvarez begins to transform into his Destructor beast form, smashing his fists into the ground, "Prepare to feel the wrath of evil," he says as he fires a massive fireball that just misses Atticus and Joyce.

Joyce puts up a shield to protect herself from a second blast, but the force of it sends her crashing into the rear wall. Atticus sees Joyce drop to the floor, and fires three fireballs in quick succession towards Alvarez. Alvarez laughs them off and charges forward. Just as he is about to crash into Atticus, Khan rushes in and shoulder charges the demon out of the way, sending them both in opposite directions with the force of the impact. Khan groans and slowly gets to his feet. Alvarez is already standing.

The others reach the hall, Professor Morgan steps forward,

"What do you want here, demon, you can't take us all on. Leave now!"

Alvarez chuckles, "Who says I'm alone?" he flicks a look behind the Majjai.

Professor Morgan turns around; to his horror he spies Herensugue and twenty Screamers rushing forward. Before he can react, Herensugue smashes one of his heads into the Professor and sends him flying into the air, Ju Long is knocked to the ground by one of the Screamers, and Safaya tries to create a whirlwind, but is too late; a Screamer sends a sonic blast in her direction, taking her down as well. Only Atticus is standing. He tries to use the ability to slow down time that he has learnt, making everything move slowly around him. He rushes to Joyce first, heals her; and then to Khan, moving them both out of harm's way, before getting to the others.

A group of the Screamers try to rush Atticus but he evades them; what he doesn't realise is that Alvarez has already anticipated this and fires a fireball in Atticus' direction. He just about steps out of the way in time, but the force of the explosion knocks him to the ground. The other Majjai quickly get to their feet and regroup; Joyce returns the favour to Atticus and helps him up.

Herensugue rushes forward and spits acid from one of his heads towards Joyce, who blocks herself with a dome shield. She and Safaya then rush to take on the Screamers, but indoors it is much more difficult, as Safaya is limited to only the elements of wind and fire. The mini tornados she sends towards the Screamers have little effect.

Joyce shields her and creates a fireball for Safaya to use. Safaya immediately turns the tiny fireball into a wall of flame and picks off little bits to fire at as many Screamers as she can as another swarm of them pile through the doors.

Alvarez faces up to Khan, and charges forward. Khan blocks his first attack, but is caught by the second, he tries to throw a punch but it has little effect on Alvarez's thick hide and the demon throws him into the air like a rag doll; Herensugue doubles-up the attack by smashing Khan in the air with his tail. Atticus throws another set of fireballs towards Herensugue; one of them hits the demon and sends it into a spin. From the corner of his eye he spots Khan landing with a thud.

Atticus closes his eyes and calls the Sword Of Ages to his hands. Unsheathing it, he stands forward, and rushes into the battle. He slices through the Screamers, trying to reach Alvarez and protect Khan. Alvarez fires more fireballs towards Atticus who deflects each one with his sword. Atticus finally reaches Khan, and leaps into the air and snatches his friend from the clutches of another blow and rests him on the floor. Alvarez fires another fireball towards Atticus who deflects this one right back at the demon.

Alvarez is unable to move out of the way of his fireball in time and falls to the floor, roaring in pain as his thick hide sizzles from his own returned assault. Enraged, the demon jumps up, his eyes fiery red, and charges towards Atticus, who barely manages to move out of the way, dragging Khan along with him. Alvarez crashes into the wall, sending both Atticus and Khan flying from the shockwave of Alvarez's impact. Ju Long catches them mid-air as he soars towards the high ceiling of the hall, but the three are sent hurtling towards the ground by a sonic blast from one of the Screamers below. Joyce kills the Screamer with a huge fireball, while Safaya creates a cushion of air to soften their team members' fall.

Khan stands, charges a huge fireball, and hurls it towards Alvarez. The demon charges forward, deflecting the fireball into the air. Khan, Atticus, and Ju Long create their own shields in an attempt to try to block the impact, but just before the demon crashes into them, another foe enters the fray and knocks Alvarez into the floor.

248

"Mage Callan!" shouts Professor Morgan, "So glad you could join us."

"Pleasure my friend," Professor Morgan looks towards the young Majjai he just saved, "You three, help the others; Alvarez and I have unfinished business."

Mage Callan stands in front of Alvarez, "I underestimated your new abilities last time, demon. Trust that it will not happen again. Now stand and fight."

Alvarez gets to his feet and dusts himself down. He towers above Mage Callan, but the Majjai is not fazed. He stands tall and pulls out his swords, already glowing blue from the power surging through them. Alvarez throws a mighty blow towards Mage Callan, who blocks it with one of his blades. The Majjai immediately follows this up with spins and kicks, each with a determination that he will not be beaten. He forces Alvarez back with each blow, the demon is too slow to defend. Mage Callan steps back for a moment, crosses his swords together and sends a massive blue charge through them soaring towards Alvarez, the demon is thrown back and through the wall.

Atticus and the others battle with Herensugue and the remaining Screamers. Unbeknownst to anyone else, one of the Screamers sneaks away, making his way behind the main stage, and towards the room where Alvarez's sack is hidden.

The final Screamer falls to the ground in the main hall; Herensugue stands alone, the Majjai surrounding the serpent demon. Its seven heads snap at each of the Majjai who dodge the lethal bites. Confident that they have things under control, they forget that Alvarez is still around, though they are soon reminded.

The Destructor crashes through another wall and scatters the Majjai. Joyce is left standing in front of Herensugue alone; the demon takes the opportunity and bites into Joyce's right leg. She screams in pain, instinctively raising a shield around her, which severs the head that has just bitten her.

Herensugue screams in agony with his other six heads, and slithers back, bleeding green slime all over the floor.

Joyce looks helplessly towards Atticus as her eyes close slowly, and falls to the ground.

Atticus leaps towards her, "Noooo!" he screams, but it is too late; the bite has already done its work and the poison fills her veins.

The Screamer who slipped away soon returns, sack in hand. Alvarez looks towards it, "You have them?" he asks. The Screamer nods. Alvarez smiles and looks towards the Majjai, "Well, this has been fun, but it's time for us to go; kill you all soon," he transforms back into his humanoid form and uses a medallion to create a portal, which the remaining demons jump through. Before any of the Majjai can stop them, the portal snaps shut, leaving only a ball of smoke dissipating in the air.

Elric and the others rush back to the hall after destroying the last of the Graigons. They immediately surround Joyce. Atticus tries to heal her, but nothing happens. She lies still, though her warm hands give Atticus hope that she is still alive. However, it still doesn't stop a tear falling from his eye onto her cheek. Khan puts a hand on Atticus' shoulder.

"Come my friend, allow Elric to try," he says.

"There is nothing I can do, I'm afraid," says Elric, "It's her own healing ability that is keeping her alive right now, but it won't be able to do so for long. Herensugue's bite is very powerful, there is no cure, in this time."

"There has to be a way," says Atticus,

"There is, Atticus, but it means we need the *Quantorbium*, which in turn means you need to be ready for the challenges ahead," replies Elric.

Atticus looks around him at the other Majjai in the room, and then to the girl who owns his heart, "I am ready."

Chapter 21

The Year Of Solitude

Joyce is taken to the medical ward in the east wing of the Manor. Her parents, Dr. Victor Sparks and Dr. Wei Sparks, are both sitting beside her bed. Madam Healsey is doing her best to make Joyce comfortable, even trying to cool her with damp cloths to her forehead, but nothing is working. Her body temperature fluctuates between searing hot and icy cold.

"I give her a few days, possibly a week at best," says Madam Healsey.

"Isn't there something you can do?" asks Victor.

"Unfortunately, the ingredients needed for the cure no longer exist, and there is no way to magically recreate them," says Elric who is sitting a little further away.

"What about the Orb?" asks Wei, "Surely that could be used? She is Majjai, one of the Six. This is not her destiny."

Atticus waits outside the room, pacing up and down. The rest of the Majjai Six are with him.

"We don't have time for this," he says.

Khan looks towards Atticus with concern and anxiety, his face deep in thought he knows he must say what needs to be said, "The *Quantorbium* will help my friend. But we must find it quickly."

"They say it is guarded," says Ju Long, "By a horned beast; something that eats the dead."

Olof looks at Ju Long, "Where did you hear this?"

"My old master told me his version of the story, he called the guardian a dragon of some sort," replies Ju Long.

Olof strokes his golden beard, "That is disturbing. I know of such a creature in Norse legend. Perhaps *Mjolnir* truly lies with the Orb."

"I don't care what is guarding it," snaps Atticus, "I am going to find it."

"Wrong," says Olof, "*We* are going to find it, together."

Safaya laughs.

"This is not funny," says Khan.

"No," replies Safaya, "But *he* is not ready," she points towards Atticus, "He needs more training, and we do not have the time to do that now."

Mage Callan enters the corridor as they are talking, "What if I can give you the time?" he asks as he pulls out the bag containing the *Runes Of Zamaan*, "Elric has given his approval for their use. A year within the Runes' power should be enough."

Atticus grabs the bag and opens it, "How long will that be in normal time?"

"About half a day. It can be longer, but Elric believes that the ratio we have chosen is safer," answers Mage Callan.

Elric exits the Medical Ward and approaches the five Majjai and Mage Callan, "You are her last hope," he says with a sigh; he knows that the loss of the medallions means that it is only a matter of time before Razakel will attack in force, "Our enemy has the upper hand; this is where you need to be at your strongest, Atticus," Elric steps over to Atticus and extends his hand for the runes.

Atticus hands them over. His mind is split in two, he can sense the pain Joyce is going through, he wants to help her; but at the same

253

time, he does not want to leave her.

"Come now – we must go to the advanced training grounds. I will activate the runes myself and come with you," says Elric.

The Majjai and Mage Callan follow Elric to the depths of the Manor. Atticus has never been this deep underground before. The corridors are dark, musky; thin veils of cobwebs are hugging the walls, dancing in the breeze created by the adventurers' movements. The walls are covered in a skin of sweat; the warmth there also goes against Atticus' own assumptions of what should be this far down – it's almost as if the foundations are sweating. He senses something within the stone, something far from the dead soul of granite, more akin to the soul of something alive, he shakes this off, feeling the need to focus on the task at hand.

"We are here," says Elric.

A pair of large doors open automatically, revealing a massive chamber, filled with its own landscape and massive training platforms outfitted with combat dummies and various weapons. The ground is solid rock and uneven, the walls that Atticus can see are jagged, with dagger-like features.

"Stand back for a moment please," says Elric. He waits for everyone to get to a safe distance before pouring the *Runes of Zamaan* from the bag and into his palm. He holds them out, and blows. Immediately, the six runes blast away from his hand and fly into the distance, soaring out to surround the room. A massive bubble of light rises from the ground, covering the doorway. Elric turns to face the others.

"After me," he says before stepping through the doorway.

The others follow him a moment later. The sensation is strange, a moment of clarity followed by a massive influx of adrenaline; finally everything settles and they see the chamber clearly.

"Food and supplies will be generated inside the training grounds, Mage Callan will show you all how," says Elric, "Mage Callan will be with you. I must return to my chamber. Train well, for our war has now truly begun," he turns to Atticus, and gestures him to one side, "Before I leave, Atticus, I must speak with you."

Atticus nods and walks next to Elric; the others head for the main training ground, giving them privacy for their conversation.

"I know this will be hard for you, Atticus. Are you certain you are ready?" asks Elric.

"As ready as I'll ever be, I guess. I don't really have much choice," Atticus says, realising as he speaks that he will be away from Joyce for much longer than the time they have been together, "I have to save her."

"You don't *have* to do anything – everyone has a choice Atticus, and you must choose. This sacrifice should not be taken lightly. A year is a long time; I know, I have seen many of them," replies Elric.

"You doubt me?" quizzes Atticus, wondering why Elric is trying to dissuade him.

"Far from it, dear boy," says Elric, "*I* know you are ready, I just need *you* to believe it, too."

Atticus nods.

"These people here, as well as yourself, are all heroes. Everything that is good needs all of you to succeed – together. Listen to them, they can guide you and your abilities to heights that even I can barely imagine, and I have seen much," says Elric, "Mage Callan, the warrior. Khan, the Saracen. Olof, commander of Ice. Ju Long, the courageous. Safaya, the Queen of the Elements. These people will be your guides, Atticus. Trust them, as they trust you."

Atticus looks towards his compatriots and then towards Elric,

"But, what if I fail?" he asks.

"Think of her, if doubt ever enters your mind, think of her, the love you hold. It is the one thing we possess that Razakel will never understand. You fight not just for yourself, Atticus, you fight for us all – and every single life force on this planet, everything that is good, they are with you. We are your strength when you most need it, and we offer it freely," Elric says, "Good luck. And when you return, we will stand side by side and fight this evil that tries to take our lands."

Atticus looks at Elric, as a newfound confidence grows within him. He knows what he must do and why, "Side by side; I look forward to it," he says as he turns, and joins the others. He already feels older, and it has only been moments.

Elric smiles, "Train well, young Atticus," He turns and walks through the shimmering entrance, disappearing from sight.

"Are you ready, Atticus?" asks Mage Callan.

Atticus nods, focusing his energy and his mind towards the tasks ahead.

Mage Callan flips his cloak over his shoulder and hands Atticus a training sword, "Then let us begin."

# # #

Elric puts his hand on Dr Victor's shoulder.

"Have they begun?" asks Joyce's father.

"They have," replies Elric.

Dr Wei aids Madame Healsey in tending to her child, dipping a cloth in cooling water and brushing away part of Joyce's hair from her forehead before placing it down, "Will they save our daughter?"

"They are her only hope," says Elric, as he walks over to Joyce's bed. He sits alongside her parents, "In the morning we will know how the training has gone, and whether or not the chosen are ready."

"And if they are not?" asks Professor Morgan.

Elric lets out a deep, deathly sigh, "Then we, and every living thing in this realm, will die."

The Majjai Journals:

We age a year in this place. At least I know she will be safe in here. If only she knew why I can never get too close to her. She is a Princess, after all, and I am just a lowly Saracen, albeit one blessed with great powers. My focus must remain on this task – and that of ridding this realm of the demon threat.

If she knew about him, would she ever forgive me? But I have no choice; I must continue my mission, whether she likes it or not.

Atticus is learning quickly. I am very impressed with him. I think Mage Callan gives him much confidence, I am glad he is also here. The Sword of Ages is very powerful; the Magic used to make it is strong. Mage Callan is secretive about its origins. I know he was the sword's keeper, but now that it has been passed on, surely the secrecy should disappear? I believe there is more to the sword's history than what is written in books.

Olof is a good friend. I hope he finds Mjolnir soon, I see the torment it causes him. At least Ju Long offers him distraction. Elric calls him the courageous, but I do not think Ju Long knows how highly we regard him. He uses his humour to hide his true self. I see it, but does he know I do? He has abilities that could not come from Majjai teachings, so there are things that he is definitely keeping from us. It seems we all have secrets, in time maybe we will all trust each another enough to share them. One day.

Abd al-Hakim Khan

Chapter 22

Dragonclaw

"Elric!" Professor Morgan bursts through the doors of the medical ward, "I found him in the great hall, buried under some rubble."

"Who?" asks Elric.

"Burrows! Bradley Burrows," says the Professor, trying to catch his breath from carrying Bradley all the way to Madam Healsey.

"How did he get there?" asks Elric.

"I have no idea. Atticus did mention the doors being left open. Perhaps he snuck in then?" says Professor Morgan. He lays Bradley on a bed for Madam Healsey to examine, "How bad is he?"

Madam Healsey is a tall, elegant lady; a white witch with healing powers as well as a mild degree of telekinesis. Her hair is long, black, and straight and her skin is very light. The red lipstick she wears contrasts against her features, and a tiny beauty spot sits just above the right side of her mouth.

"He'll be just fine," she says, "It looks more like shock than any physical injury," she reaches over to her medicine cabinet and pulls out a bottle of smelling salts. Opening it carefully, she holds it slowly just below Bradley's nose.

"Ugh, ahh, eww!" he splutters. Looking around, he spies Elric, who he has never seen before. He pauses for a moment to take things in, before turning to see others in the room. His head continues to turn until his gaze meets that of Professor Morgan, "Freak!" he screams, and breaks free from the bed and storms out before anyone can hold him, "You are all *freaks!*" he screams at the top of his lungs as he runs through the corridors.

"Shall we stop him?" asks Professor Morgan.

"Probably not a good idea right this minute, we have to prepare for the Majjai to exit from the *Runes of Zamaan*," replies Elric, "There will be time to deal with Mr Burrows later. We need to know how he got into the Majjai quarters. For now, I think you should just follow him, make sure he is ok."

Professor Morgan twists a ring on his left hand, which first encases him in blue light, and then turns into a small, glowing sphere. Then, in his new form of transport, Professor Morgan flies out of the room and chases after Bradley, keeping just out of sight.

"Did the scrolls arrive?" asks Professor Sprocking, "Did the protector come?"

"He did indeed. And once Atticus and the others have returned from the *Runes*, we will get him to activate them," replies Elric.

Professor Sprocking, still eager to discover who the protector is, decides to ask once more, "You still hide his identity from us?"

"I do. An old friend told me that the protector will show himself when the time is right; and in order for that to happen, I must never reveal his name to anyone. There is much about him that I myself do not even know."

"Myrddin again, I presume?" asks Geoffrey, wondering again what else Elric is keeping from him.

Elric merely responds with a coy smile.

They gather the scrolls and walk down to the Majjai Training Room. Standing near the doorway, Elric holds out the palm of his hand and calls the *Runes of Zamaan* back to him. In a whoosh of sound, the six runes return, leaving just a thick mist behind them, hiding the chamber behind a curtain of fog. Elric and the others step back, awaiting the exit of the young Majjai and Mage Callan.

The mist around the door swirls as one by one they exit, first Khan, followed by Olof, Safaya, Ju Long, and Mage Callan.

Elric looks towards them, "Atticus?" he asks.

"He is coming," replies Mage Callan.

The mist swirls once more, and out of it steps Atticus. Robed in a thick garment, which trails the ground behind him, his hair is longer, tied back into a short ponytail. The rest of his attire consists of dark fabrics and leathers. The Sword of Ages is hilted to his side in its elaborate, ruby-encrusted sheath. The year has aged him well, he is more chiselled and more athletic in build. He looks towards Elric.

"I am ready."

Elric grins, "Indeed you are, dear boy, indeed you are."

Atticus feels strong. The year has served him well. Mage Callan advanced his sword fighting skills tenfold. The other Majjai taught him how to control his powers and tap into the energies around him. The abilities he has unlocked are just the beginning; he knows that there is more, much more that he can do. What he is capable of now is just the tip of the iceberg.

Elric walks them all to another room, once there he pulls a heavy key from within his robes and inserts it into the heavy, locked door. A rush of air surges out as the door is opened; this room has remained empty for a very long time. A large circular table sits in the middle.

The table has engravings at each seating point. The first six names at the crest of the table are very familiar: 'Atticus', 'Olof,' 'Khan', 'Ju Long', 'Safaya', 'Joyce'.

A rich gold emblem surrounds each name. In the centre of the table is a carving of the mark of the Majjai. Around the table are other names – 'Elric', 'Benjamin', 'Geoffrey' – followed by several unmarked placeholders. The final seat simply has the letter 'M' in front of it.

"We have our own 'round table' I see," says Elric.

The others look at him, puzzled.

"You did set up this room?" asks Professor Sprocking.

"No, I have never before entered it. Myrddin told me that he would leave me a castle to help in this war, and that in this castle there would be a door. He gave me the key for it, and told me that I would know when to use it," replies Elric, " *'The day the chosen ones return from their year of solitude, to save one of their own'* he told me. Today I knew it was time."

Atticus notices a cursory glance between Professor Sprocking and Elric just before the latter indicates everyone should sit at their place.

As they each sit down, a little glow of blue light shines on their position. Elric rolls out the scrolls he brought with him in front of Atticus.

"There is nothing on them," says Atticus.

"There won't be until you touch them," replies Elric.

Atticus reaches out a hand, and with the tip of his finger, he taps the edge of the rolled out scrolls. A jet of energy shoots out through his arm; Atticus is thrown back and onto the floor. He shivers and closes his eyes as intense visions cloud his mind. He sees a mountain, but it is no ordinary mountain. There are three tips to the base, each ivory white and pointing outwards at three different angles. Above the ivory white tips, there is sharp jagged rock, the only thing he can think it resembles is a dragon's claw.

Atticus opens his eyes and finds himself sitting on the floor; everyone stares at him, and then at the scrolls. As Atticus returns to his seat, the scrolls move until they are next to each other, a script appears on the surface. The script morphs and twists, forming an image, a map.

"That is the Khalakh mountain pass," says Professor Sprocking.

"In India?" asks Ju Long, "I know this place. Many monasteries, I trained there. The area is vast, it would take years to search it."

Elric looks at Atticus, "Did you see anything?" he asks.

Atticus nods, he describes the ivory white, claw-like mountain structure. Ju Long turns visibly pale.

"Dragonclaw Mountain," he says ominously, "It is forbidden land, no one has ever returned from there."

"Wait, there is something else, some writing below the map," says Atticus, "I don't understand it."

"It looks like ancient Persian," says Elric, "Let me see," Elric holds the parchment and analyses the text. After a moment he begins to read:

"Step in, step out... dare you find the dragon's snout?

Gifts of silver, gifts of gold, it is the lesser of two evils one must hold.

Step left, step right, the wrong choice means you lose the fight.

Step up, step down, the secret lays beyond the dragon's crown."

Myrddin's penchant for riddles seems to lighten Elric's mood, "He always loved a good puzzle."

"What does it mean?" asks Safaya.

"We'll have a better idea when we get there," says Atticus, "I want to see her before we leave."

There is a new aura about Atticus, a new confidence. The year within the *Runes* has given him the understanding he needs to eventually lead the Majjai Six, but also a fresh drive. He is almost accepting of this new role, this new responsibility, but also fully aware he is yet to experience the worst of it.

"Of course," replies Elric, "I'll prepare your things for this trip."

Atticus goes alone to the medical ward. Joyce's parents are sleeping just outside the room and Madam Healsey is in her office, typing away. Atticus opens the door slowly to avoid disturbing anyone, and goes over to Joyce who still sleeps. Pulling up a chair, he sits beside her, and takes her hand.

"I will save you," he whispers, "You are never alone."

He feels his hand being squeezed ever-so-softly – she hears him, and a faint hint of a smile appears on her face for just the briefest of moments. Atticus moves closer and gently kisses her cheek.

Then he quietly leaves the room and re-joins his companions.

"It is time," says Elric as Atticus enters. Elric hands him a sack of items, "These will be useful to keep you warm and to stay in touch."

Atticus, Olof, Khan, Ju Long, and Safaya all stand together. Out of the Majjai Six, only Olof and Ju Long have mastered the art of teleportation, so it is they that the others hold on to. With a crack of thunder and a flash of light, they are greeted with the sight of rock and snow. Safaya shivers.

"I thought India was supposed to be warm?" she says as she rubs her arms with her opposing hands.

"We are quite high up," replies Ju Long, "We have some walking to do, this way."

Khan requests the sack of items from Atticus and from it he hands round some robes and heavy coats. Safaya gladly takes a robe and thanks him. She quickly throws it around her and they both follow the others who have already started their journey. Atticus is just close enough to overhear their conversation.

"Khan," says Safaya as they navigate the cold mountain rock, "Tell me about your people."

"I am the only one left. I never knew my parents," replies Khan.

"What happened?" asks the Princess.

"I was never told. All I know is that from the time I was born, I was trained. The mark of the Majjai has been both a blessing and a curse to me," says Khan, "I only know this, how to fight. There is another mark that has scarred me, but it is one that I have gladly taken."

"You welcome hardship?" asks Safaya, curious as to the motivation for such an undertaking.

"This one has its plus points," replies Khan. Wanting to change the subject, he quickly begins another discussion, "Do you feel that you treat Atticus a little harshly sometimes?"

"Someone has to," snaps Safaya, "He has been slow to learn, although, I was very impressed with his progress within the *Runes of Zamaan*. His powers are undeniable, but I fear he lacks the maturity to use them. Well, he did until his awakening to what we are up against."

"You mean Joyce?" asks Khan.

"Yes," says Safaya, "Love is a great motivation, don't you think?"

Khan is taken slightly aback, "Whatever do you mean?"

Safaya steps close to her companion, "What motivates you Khan?" she asks, "I know how honourable you are, and how you are a mighty warrior; but what is the motivation behind your actions? Is there a reason you never allow me to go on missions alone?"

"Maybe this conversation should be held another day?" suggests Khan.

"No," says Safaya, "I need to know something. You are the closest to me here, the one that understands me the most. Yes, Joyce and I get on very well, but, my status requires me to shut out certain... feelings."

"As does mine," replies Khan.

"Now you are speaking in riddles," says Safaya.

"Perhaps," says Khan raising an eyebrow, "We should really try to catch up with the others, we cannot be far now."

Khan and Safaya soon re-join the other Majjai, who have stopped a short distance ahead. The three ivory-white sections stand before them, resembling a giant dragon's claw. There seems to be only one way in: the outline of a dark entrance stands out as a blemish on the central claw. A massive gust of wind shoots itself around the young Majjai and swirls above them before whipping up dust and dirt from the ground.

"I will go first," says Olof, "Stick behind me closely," the Norseman steps through the wind and examines the doorway before stepping in. The Majjai follow him into the darkness. The light from the entrance is unable to force its way into the chamber for any great distance. Khan lights up a fireball and tosses it in the air. Safaya spots some torches and uses Khan's fireball to light them.

The chamber is dim, even with the magical light. Cold walls surround the group, textured with crevices and sharp edges. A flight of spiral stairs stands at the far end. In the centre there is a large statue of a dragon with two great horns protruding from its forehead. Olof is visibly disturbed at the statue.

"What is it?" asks Ju Long.

"I recognise this dragon. It is *Nithhogr*. But other images of him have never had horns; those have been added."

"But why is his statue here?" asks Khan.

"I guess we'll find out eventually," says Atticus, "Look at the left horn, it has a jagged line around it, almost like it has been carved," Atticus points with his torch so that the others are able to see.

As they gather around the statue, the rock entrance behind them slams shut. The escaping vacuum of wind blows out the torches leaving the chamber in darkness. Khan quickly lights another fireball that Safaya uses to re-light the torches. She then tries to move the rock to the collapsed entrance, "I cannot move this!" she says as she strains.

"I guess we take the stairs then," says Olof, "it seems to be the only way out of this chamber."

They climb the spiral staircase to the next level, which opens to a massive armoury. There are weapons of both gold and silver scattered over the walls, all gleaming against the flickering flames of the newly-lit torches.

" *'Silver and gold, '* " whispers Atticus, "remember the riddle? *The lesser of two evils one must hold.*"

"Lesser... in what way? Weight, value, size?" asks Olof.

" *'Evils, '* most regard greed as an evil," says Ju Long, "I pick silver."

"So do I," says Atticus.

"Good enough for me," says Khan.

They each pick a weapon of choice made from silver. Olof favours a massive axe, Ju Long a pair of swords, Khan a large sabre, Safaya picks out a mace and a spear, while Atticus chooses a broadsword.

They continue up the next flight of steps. As they ascend, the torchlight dims and the staircase darkens. The air becomes musky and stale.

"It smells like death in here," says Ju Long, "Olof, you did shower before leaving, right?"

267

Olof gives Ju Long a little clip on the back of his head, "I wonder why the silver is so important?" he asks.

Khan is the first to enter the next chamber; he waits for everyone to enter before responding to Olof's comment, "In my experience, there were only two instances where silver was necessary," he tosses up a fireball for Safaya to light the torches in this room as he continues, "Werewolves, they hate silver, and the other time was for…"

"Vampires!" gasps Safaya.

The torches, now alight, reveal open caskets all around them, rising from them is the stench of the undead. There are twenty or so smaller, closed caskets, and one which is about double the size of the others standing at the rear of the room.

"Vampires," mumbles Ju Long, "I hate vampires."

Atticus moves slowly towards the nearest casket, "It looks sealed," he says as he checks it for any openings.

"Careful, Atticus," says Khan, "These beasts are very dangerous and incredibly strong; we must try not to disturb them."

Atticus steps away from the casket and back towards the others. He helps them all look for another exit out of the room, but the only one visible is the same way they came in. He spots Ju Long attempting to move a skeletal object out of his way, "Watch out!" he shouts, as Ju Long slips on another piece he did not see. He tries to break his fall, but in doing so he knocks one of the caskets to the ground.

They all stand still, trying to not even breathe.

Khan sighs, "I think we're ok," but just as he finishes speaking, the entryway into the chamber collapses and a shrill scream echoes around the chamber. The lids of the smaller caskets blow out to the ceiling, followed by several vampires bursting from their caskets.

"Shield yourselves!" shouts Khan, "Make sure they do not bite you!" he looks at Atticus, "Be careful, they are much quicker than normal demons."

The vampires circle the ceiling, screaming and hissing. They are not what Atticus has pictured vampires to be — their human features are far from familiar, they are more like twisted reptilian faces, but covered in slime instead of scales. Their ears are pointy and fangs protrude from their mouths without disguise.

One of them breaks off from their formation and heads towards the Majjai. Olof fires a spear of ice towards it, the vampire smashes through it and heads straight for Safaya. Khan steps in the way and stabs it with his newly-acquired silver sabre. The vampire squeals and screams in pain. It directs one last hiss towards Khan and then melts away, evaporating into charred dust.

More caskets burst open and the entire ceiling is filled with them, circling above the heroes.

"We need to find the master, this will continue until he is dead," screams Khan. He points with his sabre to the larger casket at the back of the room, "He will be in there."

"How do we get to him?" asks Ju Long.

"We have to kill enough of his children," answers Khan.

"Let's get started then," says Atticus as he leaps to the centre of the room and fires several fireballs to the ceiling, killing some of the fanged beasts; a swarm of the vampires head towards him. Using his telekinesis ability, he throws several back to the ceiling and decapitates the few that get through, always twisting and dodging their attacks, they burn to dust before their heads hit the ground.

The other Majjai join the fray. Khan stays close to Safaya, and Olof to Ju Long. Several more vampires head towards them. Olof creates a dome of ice, shielding them from the attack before smashing through with the axe and killing his aggressors.

269

Ju Long uses his combat skills and swords to bounce around the chamber, taking the fight to the vampires in the air, slicing and dicing his way through them.

Atticus feels strong, he has learnt much during his training, his abilities are more developed now, enough to hold his own against these dark creatures of the night. He uses the silver broadsword with deft skill, staying just far enough away from the deadly, infectious fangs of his foes.

The vampires are no match for the Majjai, and they are soon defeated.

"Any more?" asks Ju Long.

Before anyone can answer, the large casket at the rear of the chamber begins to move. Loud impacts can be heard and felt through the floor.

"Stick close," says Khan, "A master vampire is very, *very,* powerful. They can transform into many things, all of them deadly."

The casket bursts open, filling the room with dust and debris. As it settles, the Majjai try to peer through. The sight is horrid; the beast is massive, much larger than the casket containing it. Its fangs drip with saliva, the thirst for new blood is all-too-apparent. Its body is muscular, its skin pale. The hands of the master vampire are large, with huge claws at their ends.

"Its heart is its weak point, we need to pierce it with silver," says Khan to the others.

The beast stomps its feet onto the floor, roaring into the air; as it does so, a pair of large, dragon-like wings appear from behind it. It flexes them, slime dripping from the thin, bat-like membrane. It charges forward, rocking the chamber with each heavy step. The Majjai scatter, trying to surround it.

The master soars into the air, hovers near the ceiling and peers

270

down towards its prey. Focusing on their positions, the beast crosses its arms close to its chest and then flings them outwards, throwing five separate fireballs towards the Majjai. Olof immediately cancels out the fireballs with blasts of ice. The master roars again and swoops downwards towards Ju Long, who takes to the air himself just before the beast reaches him. The chase is on. Ju Long dives and turns, trying to shake the huge vampire off his tail, but to no avail. The master is quicker and more agile than Ju Long so Olof sends more spears of ice in the vampire's direction, trying to slow it down.

"Bring it here!" screams Khan.

Ju Long flies towards him, the vampire in tow. Khan leaps into the air and smashes into the back of the vampire leader using as strong a blow as he can with his Majjai powers. The beast crashes to the floor, sending rubble into the air. The beast is dazed, but far from out. It jumps up again.

"This bird's wings need to be clipped," says Atticus. Before the vampire can gain too much height, Atticus runs forward and slices at one of its arms. The beast screams in pain and crashes to the ground again. It charges towards Atticus who just manages to roll out of the way, dodging a swipe from the vampire's massive claws.

Khan hits his fists together, a blue aura surrounds them, and he charges towards the vampire leader. He blocks and punches into the beast, dodging its blows and counter-attacking it with guile. With one final blow, Khan jumps high and lays a devastating uppercut, sending the vampire into the air.

"Quickly, Olof, grab its arms," shouts Khan.

Olof swings round and creates a handcuff of ice holding the beast in the air, arms aloft.

Khan sends out another command "Now Safaya!"

The princess throws her spear with pinpoint accuracy, piercing the outer flesh of the vampire and stabbing its heart.

Olof relinquishes his grip and the master vampire drops to the floor. It emits one final deafening roar.

"Quick!" screams Khan, "Take cover! He's going to blow!"

The Majjai quickly hide behind anything they can find, caskets, rocks, and crevices. The roar from the Master gets louder and louder; the Majjai cover their ears as the scream overwhelms their senses. Then, in huge flash, the chamber is engulfed in a massive silver flame, with smoke and heat bellowing through any gaps in the chamber's rocky walls. As suddenly as it appeared, the fire and smoke rumble back towards the centre of the chamber, sucked into nothingness, leaving only a pile of ash behind; as a final gust of wind blows away the ash, the silver weapons that the Majjai accrued earlier, melt from their hands and disappear into the floor.

"Guess we don't need those anymore," quips Ju Long.

"Indeed," says Olof, "We should keep moving."

Behind the master vampire's fallen casket, they spot another staircase and walk up it. Another chamber lies at the top. This one has a smaller dragon statue, its two horns point to two separate tunnels. Both tunnels are dark, and look virtually identical.

"Now what?" asks Ju Long, "Do we split up?"

"No," says Atticus, "Remember the riddle again: *step left, step right, the wrong choice means you lose the fight. Step up, step down, the secret lies beyond the dragon's crown.*' If we take the wrong tunnel, we lose."

"Let me try something," says Safaya. She raises an arm towards the right tunnel, forcing a mound of earth to tear itself from the ground and fly through the entrance. Before the mound of earth can get too far, a massive jet of fire shoots out of the tunnel and burns it.

"Well, looks like it isn't that one," says Ju Long.

"Wait," says Olof, "try the other one as well Safaya."

Safaya does the same, and another mound of earth heads towards the left tunnel. The Majjai watch in anticipation, hoping that they are right. Just as they are about to cheer, another jet of flame appears, destroying their hopes along with the mound of earth.

"Damn it!" says Atticus, "We don't have time for this!!"

"Calm, Atticus," says Safaya, "We will save her. Repeat that last part again – the bit about the crown."

Atticus sighs, " *'Step up, step down, the secret lays beyond the dragon's crown.'* "

"But this dragon has no crown," says Khan.

"No," replies Atticus, "But the one at the entrance did!"

"The jagged line on one of its horns," says Olof.

"But which side was it on?" asks Safaya.

Atticus closes his eyes and thinks back to the entrance, "Left side!" he shouts, "We go left."

Atticus steps forward, but is stopped by Khan.

"Let me go first my friend," he says, "you are more important than any of us, If we are wrong, at least you get to make another choice."

Before Atticus can reply, Khan steps through the tunnel entrance. A jet of flame shoots out.

"Nooooo!" screams Safaya, thinking the fire is heading straight for Khan. But instead, the flame circles him as if judging his worthiness to enter. Then it soars into the ceiling of the entrance on the right side, collapsing it.

"You worry too much princess," says Khan, winking towards Safaya.

Safaya runs to him, "Don't do that again without my permission, ok!" she orders.

"As you wish," Khan grins, "Now, if you let go of me, we can hopefully finish this quest."

The Majjai all step through the tunnel tentatively. As they travel deeper, they begin to hear a constant humming sound, and notice a faint light. They walk in the direction of the light and reach the end of the tunnel in a few moments. The room is totally bare, apart from the far wall. A large swirling portal spins invitingly. The Majjai look towards each other, knowing what they must do. Standing side by side, they step through together.

Chapter 23

Fire Mountain

The portal opens and the Majjai step through and onto their next challenge.

"Hekla," says Olof, looking up at a nearby mountain.

"The volcano?" asks Khan.

"Yes," replies Olof, "We are in Iceland," he looks worried. Safaya wraps herself a little tighter in Khan's robe.

"What is it?" asks Ju Long, disturbed by Olof's reaction.

Olof looks to the top of the large volcano, "This is a dangerous place. This volcano is very unstable."

"So we should be careful and ready to teleport out just in case," says Atticus.

"It's more than that," says Olof, "During the Middle Ages, the people here had another name for this place – they called it the Gateway to Hell," Olof looks around ominously, "We should hurry. Hel herself watches over these lands, she is the guardian of the Underworld."

The others are visibly concerned at Olof's words, except for Atticus. He knows that he needs to return the focus to the quest at hand, "Ok," he says, "Which way now?"

A small orb of light has remained from the portal's closure; it hovers briefly, then shoots across the air, towards Hekla.

"Quickly, follow it!" orders Atticus.

The Majjai pursue the orb of light, the air is strange here, even though the volcano itself is not erupting, a strong smell of molten rock taints the air, making it heavy and unwelcoming, their pace slows as breathing becomes more difficult and by the time they reach the base of the mountain, they are almost spent.

The volcano itself is dark and dirty. The smell of burning rock surrounds them, more intrusive than ever. Knowing the poisonous nature of volcanic gasses, Olof tells everyone to steady their breathing and pace themselves.

The orb hits the side of the volcano and draws a circle, cutting into the blackened surface of the volcano's outer wall. The entire section fades and melts away, revealing an entrance. Atticus walks through first, followed by the others. Khan lights another fireball, which hovers just in front of them, lighting the immediate area. The entrance seals itself behind them as soon as the last is inside.

"So much for a quick getaway," says Ju Long, "Should have brought my camping gear and marshmallows."

Olof gives Ju Long another little clip on the back of his head, "I'm sure there is another way out," he says.

"Whatever you say, Goldilocks," replies Ju Long, rubbing his head, "Tell that to the three bears when they gobble us up. Or this dragon you keep worrying about. What is it with Majjai and dragons? They're not all bad you know!"

The Majjai all look at Ju Long curiously, wondering if he experiences with dragons other than bad, but before anyone can contemplate much further, Atticus pulls them all forward to follow the passageway into a large clearing. Khan fires a few more fireballs in the air to light the new chamber they find themselves in. There seems to be nothing on the walls apart from the entrance.

"It's empty," says Atticus.

"Perhaps not," says Safaya, as she kicks at the dirt on the floor of the chamber, "The surface is loose, from centuries of volcanic activity," she raises her arms and concentrates. A light breeze begins to move around the chamber, then the earth below them begins to shake, breaking up the loose covering of the chamber floor to reveal another layer. Safaya creates a small whirlwind, sweeping the free dirt to one side.

"There are markings here. Like the script on the scrolls," says Khan.

Olof reaches into his robes and pulls out a communication orb. He holds it up to activate it.

"Elric?" he says as a communications window opens back at the manor.

"Olof. How go things?" asks Elric, his face appearing within the window above the orb.

"We need another translation," he moves the orb around so that Elric can get a good look at the floor.

"Interesting," says Elric, then translates the lines:

"Walk through the door unseen, to reach the hidden dream.
Hammer and Orb, the goals as taught;
the weapon you need is speed of thought.
Below the wings of Pegasus lays their bed,
but take care not to wake, the Eater of the Dead."

"*Nithhoggr*," says Olof, "He sleeps here, and I can sense him. The 'Eater of the Dead' must refer to him."

"Maybe," says Elric, "As for the door unseen, maybe I can help you with that. Are there any rock formations that look out of..."

Before Elric is able to finish, a gust of wind blows through the chamber, smashing the communications orb to the ground.

"Hmmm," says Atticus, "I don't think he is allowed to help from the outside. This is our task alone, it seems."

"But how are we supposed to see the unseen?" asks Safaya.

"Maybe we can't, but what if the unseen are able to see the unseen?" says Khan.

"What do you mean?" asks Atticus.

Ju Long steps forward, "I know," he says, "My invisibility works differently from what one would consider normal. I move to a different phase of our dimension, and see things that do not exist – that are 'hidden' from our view. It also allows me to walk *through* things."

"Cool," says Atticus, "And you never told us, why?"

"That is dark Magic, how is it you are gifted with it?" asks Safaya pointedly.

"Didn't think much of it; only Khan knew," replies Ju Long. He disappears from view before giving anyone else to question further.

"Atticus, use your gift of insight to make sure he is ok," says Khan.

Atticus nods and closes his eyes; he thinks of Ju Long and suddenly sees exactly as if he were Ju Long.

He scans the chamber. Ju Long sees his friends, and pokes Olof cheekily in the ribs. His hand passes through the chamber walls as he feels for a change in density, a sure sign that there is something different about the fortification. It is not long before he finds it. Popping his head through, he sees another room and walks into it. Returning to his normal state, Ju Long examines the rock and finds a lever, covered in cobwebs, "Yeuch!" he splutters before pulling it.

The rock door opens outwards allowing the other Majjai access to this new cavern, as Atticus withdraws himself from Ju Long's vision, he becomes quietly more confident in his growing grasp of this ability.

Khan finds some torches at the entrance and lights them, handing them round once complete; Atticus completes his waking from his connection with Ju Long. Once they all gather together they inspect their new location and they find a strange sight.

"What is it?" asks Safaya.

"Looks like a sliding puzzle," replies Atticus, "I used to be really good at these, but this one… it just has different spots, no pictures or numbers."

In front of the Majjai fixed onto a wall stands a large square, with smaller squares cut out from it, all hinged together forming a random pattern, and each movable piece has a dot in a different place.

"And what are those?" asks Ju Long, pointing to a series of dots on the wall.

"I don't know," says Atticus.

They all move toward the puzzle; as they do so, the door behind them slams shut. A massive egg timer rises from the floor and flips over, triggering the sand to fall through the glass, beginning a countdown.

"Err, this doesn't look good," says Ju Long.

"I guess this is where the *'speed of thought'* bit of the riddle comes from," says Atticus, "Think, what else did it say?"

" *'Below the wings of Pegasus lies their bed,* '" says Safaya, "Stars!"

"Stars?" asks Khan.

"Yes, stars. I used to love looking at them when I was younger, and Elric gave me a telescope so I could continue to do so here. I studied the constellations. These dots, they each resemble a star, and this one," Safaya says, pointing to one of the patterns on the wall, "this is Pegasus."

"Quickly," says Olof, "We do not have much time, the sand is falling quickly."

Atticus runs to the puzzle and starts to rearrange the squares, trying to match it against the pattern on the wall.

"Hurry, Atticus, the sand is almost out!" shouts Khan.

The walls of the chamber begin to shake violently; small openings appear and searing hot lava starts to seep from the cracks.

Olof fires ice towards the molten rock, but it only slows it down for a moment before more lava appears.

"Just a few more seconds," says Atticus.

"I doubt we have many, my friend," screams Khan, "Faster!"

The egg timer runs out of sand. A larger opening appears, Olof tries to fill it with ice, but the lava is too hot and cuts through it easily.

"I can't hold it for much longer!" he shouts.

"Almost… there," says Atticus as he slides the last piece into place.

The chamber stops shaking and the lava tunnels re-seal themselves.

"That was close," says Safaya, "Well done, Atticus."

The others look at each other in amazement — a compliment from Safaya is rare, and this is the first time she has given one to Atticus so openly. Their focus returns to the task at hand as the floor beneath the puzzle gives way, collapsing into a spiral staircase moving downwards, revealing another chamber.

They peer through the opening beneath their feet and try to look into the darkness.

"We need to be careful here, the last part of that riddle refers to the Eater of the Dead. There is too much coincidence that his statue existed at Dragonclaw Mountain, and now the latest riddle refers to him via his alias," says Olof, "We must be silent."

"Guess that means me again, then," says Ju Long. He hovers

into the air and falls gently through the new opening. His torch dimly lights this new chamber, but he doesn't need it for long. A giant river of lava flows through a deep crevice. He lands lightly, looks around, and spots a large chest with a large hammer and an orb engraved on the front. Above the carvings lay two hand imprints', the one above the orb has *'Atticus'* written above it, and the other has the name *'Olof'*.

Ju Long flies back up to the other chamber and begins to help the others down. He carries Olof down last.

Ju Long pants on purpose, "Olof, my friend."

"Yes?" replies Olof.

"When we get back to the Manor, remind me to put you on a diet."

Ju Long lands and quickly steps out of the way of another clip to the back of his head.

The Majjai walk towards the chest.

"I guess we put our hands on it then?" says Atticus.

Olof walks with him and they both slide their hands onto the imprints. A light glows around them where they touch the cold metal, designed perfectly around them, and the lock clicks open. Olof and Atticus lift the lid together. Inside, they find masses of red velvet. On one side lies the *Quantorbium*, and on the other, *Mjolnir*, the hammer of Thor.

Between the two objects is a crystal. Atticus picks it up. As soon as he touches it, it begins to glow and hovers out of his hand. The image of Myrddin appears.

"Well done, Atticus and Olof," says the ghostly image of the wizard, "I'm sorry I had to move the hammer, Olof, it was not safe there. The guard here is much scarier than Brokk; be sure not to wake him. Atticus, you must take the *Quantorbium* to Elric, he will know how to activate it. Hurry now! Joyce does not have much time. Pass these words to Elric, along with the parchment within the chest. *'The hammer of Thor is both nemesis and ally to the orb.'"*

As quickly as the image appeared, it disappears, and the crystal drops back into the chest.

"Quickly, let's teleport out of here before whatever *is* here wakes," says Olof.

Safaya's curiosity gets the better of her, and she peers over the edge of the crevice to observe the lava flow beneath.

"Safaya, come, we must leave!" says Olof.

"Coming," she replies. As she twists around, a small piece of the fracture supporting her gives way and drops below. Safaya slips and screams loudly. Khan is quick to act and catches her arm before she falls too far. He pulls her up, and holds onto her until they are safely away from the edge.

Safaya doesn't let go of Khan; she stares into his eyes, as if daring him to make a romantic move.

"What game are you playing?" whispers Khan.

"It's no game," replies Safaya.

Atticus turns around to hurry them up, but as he moves towards them he stops.

"What's wrong, Atticus?" asks Ju Long.

"Shhhh, do you hear it?" replies Atticus, "A deep flapping noise?"

A gust of wind flows through the cave they are in, getting stronger with each passing moment.

"It's coming," says Olof, "Khan, Safaya... HURRY!"

The Majjai quickly gather themselves together, preparing to teleport out as the dragon Nithhoggr appears, roaring into the chamber.

"Nithhoggr," says Olof.

"Now!" screams Atticus, "Do it NOW!"

Olof and Ju Long begin the teleportation, a shimmer of light, a flash, and they disappear just as Nithhoggr shoots a jet of fire towards their position.

The Majjai reappear outside of Hekla.

"Why are we not back at the Manor?" asks Atticus.

"I do not know," replies Olof, "Perhaps the power of the hammer or the orb is limiting our ability to teleport far enough."

"It's coming!" shouts Safaya.

Nithhoggr blasts through the side of Hekla in a shower of lava. The dragon circles around. Its size is breathtaking, dwarfing what Atticus remembers of Draconus. Opening its massive jaws, Nithhoggr shoots a gigantic jet of fire towards the startled Majjai who scatter as fast they can. Safaya is able to divert much of the fire away from them, but she cannot control the intensity for long. Ju Long swoops in to save her, teleporting her away before the dragon's fire breaks out of Safaya's control.

Khan looks towards Olof, "You have to use it – it is the only thing that will have any effect," he says, pointing to the chest holding the hammer.

"This must be what Myrddin meant by *'ally'* – the hammer can protect the orb," says Atticus, "Ju Long, get to the Manor, tell Elric we need a portal back home, quickly."

Ju Long doesn't need to be asked twice; he gently returns Safaya to the ground and teleports himself away. Nithhoggr circles again, then lands just in front of the remaining Majjai.

"Atticus, your hand, now!" shouts Olof, his palm already in the indentation on the chest. Atticus quickly opens it with Olof, allowing the Norse Majjai to grab the hammer.

"I call forth the power of Thor!" shouts Olof as he holds the hammer above his head. The clouds above the volcano begin to darken.

Nithhoggr is all too aware of the power of Thor's hammer and is wary to attack. A huge bolt of lightning fires downward from the sky and strikes the hammer. Olof's hair turns from light blonde to a striking, blinding white. His eyes cloud over and his body begins to hover just off the ground. Olof soars towards Nithhoggr, striking the beast on his jaw. The dragon is knocked back. The others join the attack and launch as many powerful fireballs as they can. Safaya uses her command of earth and wind to send masses of rock into the beast's belly. Slowly but surely together they force Nithhoggr back.

Olof charges over and launches another attack with the hammer, hurting Nithhoggr once more. The dragon's anger grows; it slams its massive horned tail into the ground making it tremble beneath the Majjais' feet, then swings it towards the now unstable group. Khan is hit hard and flung backwards, his robes tearing as the force of the blow sends him sliding across the ground. Safaya looks around, and rushes to catch him. She drags his unconscious body away from the dragon's flames; as she does so, she notices some markings on his back she believes she seen before.

The dragon attacks again. Safaya has no time to ponder what she has seen, but she knows now that things are starting to make sense. She drags Khan to safety behind a rock and returns to the battle.

Atticus creates a blue shield below his feet and uses his telekinesis powers to levitate it. He surfs through the air on his new board of light, brandishing his sword, and blocks an attack heading towards Safaya, slicing one of the horns from Nithhoggr's tail in the process.

Olof holds the hammer high in the air and crashes it to the ground sending a massive wave of energy through the surface, forcing the dragon to stumble.

Nithhoggr takes to the air and launches several fire attacks.

284

Safaya manages to divert these smaller flames back towards the dragon. The Majjai are so distracted fighting the Norse dragon that they do not notice Ju Long's return.

"Quickly, this way!" shouts Ju Long standing next to the newly-opened portal.

Safaya and Atticus grab the chest while Olof grabs Khan. They race to the portal, barely avoiding another massive jet of fire from Nithhoggr. The portal disappears taking the Majjai with them. Mage Callan quickly grabs Khan and takes him to the medical ward. Elric stands with a look of concern when he sees Khan, he immediately goes to check on him, addressing the other Majjai on his way.

"I knew you could do it," he says, looking at Ju Long, Olof, Safaya, and Atticus, he waves a hand over the Saracen's body, trying to sense his condition, "Khan will be fine; he looks to be just a little stunned. Come, we must take the *Quantorbium* to our new meeting room."

Professor Morgan and Professor Sprocking join them. Safaya seems distracted as she follows the others. What she saw on Khan's back is still troubling her.

"Elric," she says, "Can we please talk. I have something on my mind."

Elric beckons the others to continue to the meeting room and stays behind with Safaya, "I'm all ears dear."

Atticus, curious as to what could be so important, invades their privacy. Closing his eyes, he thinks of Safaya and tries to see into the room.

"What do you know of the League of Aria?" asks the Princess, sensing that Elric knows something that he is keeping from her.

"All I know is that they are shrouded in mystery. Created to protect you throughout the ages. Their skills passed from generation to generation. Beyond that, I have no new knowledge that I am *able* to tell you," replies Elric, "Why do you ask?"

"I think I saw something," says Safaya, "Did the league disappear without a trace? Or is their secrecy so great that they will not even inform the one they are protecting of their existence?"

"What does your heart tell you, Safaya?" asks Elric.

"That my brother would never let me down," she replies.

"Then I think you have answered your own question," says Elric, "Now go, sit with him; the others should be able to handle this final task by themselves. I will send Mage Callan with them just in case."

Safaya nods and races to the Medical Ward. She informs Mage Callan that Elric would like him to join the others, and then sits down next to Khan.

He lays still, eyes closed. His shirt has now been removed allowing Madam Healsey to apply ointments to his wounds. The nurse returns, flicking her long black hair over her shoulder as she moves Khan onto his side. It is then Safaya sees it fully: the tattoo of an eagle's head within a pyramid. The mark of the League of Aria.

She waits for the nurse to finish dressing Khan's wounds before stroking his hair away from his forehead.

"You never told me," she whispers, "Do not worry, my prince. Your honour is safe with me," she moves towards him slowly and gently kisses Khan's forehead.

Atticus withdraws himself, "It's enough now, enough," he thinks, as he learns that some things must remain private. An overall guilt overcomes him; this power requires much discipline, it cannot be abused for it is wrong to do so. Atticus sighs and rejoins the other Majjai.

Chapter 24

Eye Of The Storm

Atticus follows his friends to the round-table room. As they walk he feels something, a tingle at first, then a tugging, as if his very soul is being ripped from him. He falls to the floor and drifts away. Atticus's mind is clouded, he sees nothing. Then the mist begins to clear and as it does so, he instantly recognises the people he sees.

"The boy has been prepared, my King," says Alvarez, his head bowing to the ground as he kneels.

Razakel breathes heavily, "Very good. How has Herensugue's healing progressed?" he asks.

"He has sealed the wound, but fears the head will never re-grow. I doubt he will be ready for the taking," replies Alvarez.

"Then you must go. Bring the boy to me – his turning will be our secret weapon," says Razakel. He stands from his mighty throne and steps in front of Alvarez, "You have done well. Redeemed yourself with the re-acquisition of the medallions. Now tell me of this new Majjai Six."

"They are no match for you, my lord. They are children, mostly. The Majjai elders overestimate their abilities," replies Alvarez.

"Or maybe you have underestimated them?" quizzes Razakel, "Elric is no fool, neither is Myrddin. These young Majjai could still pose a threat to our plans," Razakel returns to his throne, "Leave me."

The chamber empties at his command. Alvarez is the last to

leave and closes the massive doors behind him, leaving Razakel in silence.

The demon king ponders his next move. The medallions are in his possession, but he is still hampered. He tires of his reliance on those in the Earth realm, longing for total control, but his frustration is eased with the knowledge that absolute power is merely moments away in his relative existence. He takes the minute to smile, savouring his impending victory.

"They will never see it," he whispers to himself, his smile turning into a callous laugh, echoing around his throne room, "But you might... won't you, Atticus!"

# # #

Atticus shivers and wakes up, "They're after me," he says, looking at Elric.

"Who, Atticus?" asks Elric.

"Alvarez and Razakel. They're planning some sort of kidnapping."

"You saw them?" asks Ju Long.

"Yes, but it was strange. I didn't instigate it this time. It just happened."

Elric strokes his beard, "The gift of insight does not work this way, unless it has been overused. Atticus, you must be careful, there is consequence when power is abused. The doorway to your mind can work both ways."

Atticus remembers the other night, where he tried to use his power to find the traitor. He tells Elric about what happened. But keeps to himself his recent foray into Safaya's mind, an act he already feels shame for.

"You were warned of this, Atticus," Elric says sternly, "Razakel's traitor could have killed you. You are lucky the protector was there watching over you."

"I know, I'm sorry," replies Atticus.

"We'll sort this out later," says Elric as they all pick Atticus up off the floor, "Right now, we have more important tasks to take care of. While you are with us, you are protected."

Elric and the other Majjai continue to the table room, leaving Joyce, Safaya, and Khan in the medical ward. They take their seats at the round table. Elric carefully places the orb in the centre. Atticus opens the unlocked chest and hands Elric the parchment along with Myrddin's message about the hammer being both nemesis and ally.

As soon as Elric makes contact with the parchment, it shimmers into a fountain of light which circles around his forehead before resting on his skin and melting into him.

Elric closes his eyes.

"Are you ok?" asks Professor Sprocking.

"Yes," replies Elric, "It was a message, from Myrddin. There is one last task we must perform before we can use the Orb."

Elric stands and walks to the rear wall of the room. He touches some of the stone bricks, activating a glow of light, which surrounds the walls in the room. The light forms into shapes, bookshelves, drawers and chests, as it finishes, the shapes morph into solid objects.

Elric returns to his seat and makes himself comfortable, then he taps the edge of the table and a set of crystals morph into view on the surface. He moves one of the crystals forward. A map appears, hovering above the centre of the table.

"We need to go here," says Elric, "Myrddin's message states that the orb has been drained of all its power. It needs to be recharged."

"Recharged?" asks Atticus, "How?"

"Ahhh, this is why we need to go here," replies Elric, "There will be a storm, and we need lightening to strike the orb. Myrddin discharged all of its power to protect it."

"So the orb is useless?" asks Ju Long.

"Only until it is hit by a bolt of lightning," says Atticus, "Should be easy enough," he finishes with a wry grin, "But why can't we just get Safaya or Olof and his new toy to do it?"

"Their control of the lightening weakens it," replies Mage Callan as he walks into the room, "No doubt the lightening needs to be pure."

"Mage Callan will be joining you," says Elric, "Safaya is busy tending to Khan. The quicker we find the cure the better. We need Joyce and her advanced healing skills. Our numbers are already running short here," he pauses for a few seconds and then looks towards Atticus, "Yes, and because we miss her."

Elric waves his right hand in the air, creating a portal. The other Majjai see the storm raging on the other side.

"Err, Elric," says Ju Long, "You do realise that is in the middle of the sea, right?"

"*Ocean*, actually," replies Elric, "The Pacific Ocean, to be precise. Olof, we need a rather large plateau of ice, think you can manage that?"

"Of course," replies Olof, jumping through the portal, streaming ice from his hands onto the ocean's surface. He soon creates a mass large enough for everyone to stand on safely. Mage Callan, Atticus, and Ju Long step through.

"Good luck — and remember: keep the Orb between yourselves and the lightening," says Elric as the portal closes.

The sea itself is incredibly calm. As the Majjai peer upwards, they do not see a storm, only clear skies.

"Aren't storms supposed to be a bit more lively?" asks Ju Long.

"We are in the eye," replies Mage Callan, "Now, we just have to find a way to get the Orb up there."

"I'll do it," says Ju Long, "Only I can fly high enough. I can phase myself out so the lightening does not strike me."

Mage Callan nods, "We will wait for you on the ice plateau. I doubt we will remain within the eye of the storm for too long," Mage Callan points out to the sea, where a massive wall of water and cloud betrays the façade of calmness belonging to the storm's eye.

Ju Long grabs the orb and begins his ascent, shooting into the air towards the edge of the storm. The others wait patiently.

"Things are never this easy," says Atticus, "We wait, while Ju Long risks his life on his own?"

"Your flight ability still needs work, Atticus. You are fine in short bursts, but your concentration wanders," replies Mage Callan.

"I keep thinking of her," says Atticus, "My mind wanders, thinking of saving her."

Olof puts his hand on Atticus' shoulder, "We all feel her pain, Atticus, but we need to…"

Olof stops his words mid-sentence, and looks around, "They have found us."

"Who?" asks Mage Callan frantically, "Who has found us?"

Before Olof can answer, a giant, serpent-like head smashes upward through the centre of the ice plateau.

"Leviathan!" shouts Olof.

"He is not alone!" screams Mage Callan, as a massive jet of fire from the air, boiling the sea around them, "What the hell is that?" he says, pointing to the sky.

Atticus looks up, "Nithhoggr!"

"Norse demons!" shouts Mage Callan, "How did they find us?"

"They can sense the Hammer!" replies Olof, "Quickly, we must divert them away from Ju Long."

"Looks like you will be getting your flying practice after all, Atticus," says Mage Callan.

Atticus closes his eyes and concentrates. He crouches ever so slightly, as if charging himself. Then, in a bright blue flash, Atticus shoots into the air, leaving just a puff of smoke behind him. Nithhoggr immediately follows.

As he nears the edge of the eye of the storm, Atticus can see the massive waves in the distance and heads for them, the Norse dragon in tow.

Mage Callan cuts out a circular section of the ice plateau and uses his powers to levitate it, then begins to surf the air, following Atticus and Nithhoggr.

Olof stands alone against Leviathan, "Come beast, taste the hammer of Thor!"

Leviathan screams and launches an attack towards Olof. The Norse warrior slides out of harm's way before creating a path of ice in front of him. He builds momentum and shapes the path upwards, launching himself into the air. Hammer in hand, he smashes it against the head of Leviathan, dazing the massive sea serpent.

Leviathan crashes into the water, sending a huge tidal wave in Olof's direction. He leaps into the air again, creating another path of ice, trying to outrun the wave. Diving in and out of the undulations of the waves, he escapes it. Leviathan rises from the water again to give chase. Its massive body cuts a path through the ocean's surface, snaking towards its prey at great speed.

Olof turns and holds the hammer aloft. The eye of the storm

has now passed; lightning strikes spring downward from the clouds, some are brave enough to strike the water. Olof waits for the moment he knows is coming, when the lightning will seek out its master. As a huge bolt strikes the hammer, Olof roars, "Be gone beast! Or the hammer will strike your very soul!!"

Leviathan ignores the threat and launches another attack towards Olof, who throws the hammer with all his might towards the Norse beast. The hammer strikes Leviathan and a blanket of electricity cloaks it, sending the beast into spasms. Leviathan screams in agony, before sinking into the sea, its skin, searing hot from the blow, fizzes and hisses against the cold water.

Olof holds his hand in the air once more and catches the hammer, as it returns to him, "May you rest until the days of your calling," he says as Leviathan disappears from view. Olof then turns to seek out his allies who he sees in the distance.

Atticus is moving as fast as he can with the dragon still close in pursuit. He dives and swoops, before heading to the clouds, like a glowing blue bullet, changing direction leaving sharp lines of light in his wake.

Mage Callan shoots a series of fireballs in the dragon's direction, trying to grab its attention. The dragon turns and throws a look of disdain towards the Majjai attempting to divert its focus.

Olof is too far away to help, but in vain he tries to get to them, shooting streams of ice to aid his journey.

Atticus turns and looks behind him, throwing as many attacks as possible towards the massive dragon. They barely slow Nithhoggr down as the beast swoops toward its next perceived meal. The beast closes in, closer and closer, chomping at Atticus with its gigantic jaws. Atticus can feel the heat of the dragon's breath on the back of his neck. He looks back again and its jaws are nearly upon him.

Suddenly, out of nowhere, Atticus is pulled away, dragged from the dragon's mouth.

"Why do you guys keep getting into trouble without me?" says Ju Long, before reappearing, "Follow me."

Ju Long and Atticus head toward Mage Callan and Olof, who are already requesting a return portal from Elric.

Nithhoggr turns and gives chase. The clouds spin with him, and fall away in the beasts wake.

"Quickly!" screams Olof, who is already near the portal. He dives through, soon followed by the other Majjai who crash into the floor on the other side.

Elric quickly closes the portal before Nithhoggr can get close enough to launch an attack, "Did you do it?" he asks excitedly.

Ju Long opens his robes, revealing the *Quantorbium*. It is glowing a deep, violet colour. He hands it to Elric who gently holds the Orb for a moment before carefully placing it on a brass plinth. The Majjai follow Elric and the Orb to the Majjai Training Room.

"Here, this room should be large enough," says Elric, "Stand over there please. Time is literally of the essence," Elric points to an area just in front of the doorway. He waves his hand over the orb.

"Where are we going?" asks Atticus.

"Where is not important, and funnily enough, when isn't even as important as *who* we are going to see," replies Elric.

"What do you mean?" says Olof.

"There is only one person I know of who is able to create the cure we need," says Elric, who then bends, his face placed just above the glow from the orb as he softly chants. A giant portal opens up in front of the Majjai, with its circumference edged in flame. It lights up the room, reflecting off the stone brick walls.

Atticus looks around, he knows he will soon save Joyce. But

he is also worried. These missions are so dangerous, with so much at stake, how does one have time for love? Love without risk. Risk without danger. Joyce lies upstairs, suffering in agony, and after all the dangers they have faced, they still do not have a cure. His thoughts distract him for a moment as they have many times, before he is disturbed by Elric.

"Follow me," says the elder Majjai, "Professor Sprocking will remain here to guard the portal while we are away, we'll need to keep it open," and with that, he steps through.

Atticus follows straight away, eager to get on with this rescue mission. This portal feels very different than the teleportation portals. Atticus can feel his very soul being torn from the timelines. In brief flashes he sees his own memories, mixed in with glimpses of events with no context. The future perhaps? The past? Broken timelines? He does not know, but the chaotic voices add to his tension as he travels through time. And then in an instant it all stops.

They all arrive on the other side in what appears to be the same chamber they just left.

They all look at each other slightly puzzled, wondering if the orb has actually worked.

"Welcome fellow Majjai," says a voice from the shadows, "I have been expecting you."

Chapter 25

The Cure

"Myrddin, my friend, it is good to see you," says Elric.

Myrddin steps from the shadows into the faint glow of light from the portal.

"As it is good to see you as well," replies the wizard.

Atticus, Mage Callan, Olof, and Ju Long are all doing the perfect impression of a goldfish, gob-smacked that they are in the presence of Merlin himself.

"You know why we are here?" asks Elric.

"Of course," replies Myrddin, with a wry smile, "But, there is a problem. The cure you seek requires a special item: The blood of a Cantor Ogre."

"A Cantor Ogre?" questions Olof, "But they have not existed for thousands of years – since long before even the Battle of Aria."

"Can't we just use the Orb to go back to that time?" asks Atticus.

"Ahhhh, Atticus," says Myrddin, looking towards him, "I wish it were that simple. Come, let us sit down and I will explain."

The Majjai all follow Myrddin to the room they know as Elric's own chamber. The walls of the Manor are hardly any different than in their own time – a little colder, and with candles rather than electricity used to light the corridors, but otherwise identical.

Myrddin sits at his desk and beckons everyone else to take a seat around him.

"The *Quantorbium* is a powerful device," he explains, "It can only be activated once within a year of its usage. Using it again would cause an irreparable rift in space and time, our own world, it would risk implosion."

"So we have failed, then?" asks Ju Long slumping in his seat.

"Far from it," replies Myrddin, "You can all still save Joyce. I know of the existence of a vial of the blood we need – in exactly the right amount."

"Where?" asks Atticus.

"The Tomb of Kazmagus," says Myrddin.

Elric almost chokes with excitement, "You have found it?"

"Yes, but I have been unable to enter," Myrddin strokes his beard, in a very similar manner to Elric, and looks attentively towards Atticus, "But I suspect *he* can."

"Me?" asks the young Majjai, "Why me?"

"I have my reasons, Atticus. Unfortunately, it is not my job to tell you why. Another will reveal these reasons to you one day, I'm sure, unless you figure it out for yourself," replies Myrddin.

"So, should we not hurry then?" asks Olof.

"All in good time," replies Myrddin, "the portal will remain open for some while yet, so you will just return at the point you left," he turns to Elric, "How is Geoffrey?" he asks.

"Still troubled, my friend. His abilities have grown immensely, but memories of Jennifer still haunt him," answers Elric.

Myrddin lets out a sigh, "As they will. The Sword of Al-Amir; he will need this before confronting Draconus."

"We have yet to find it," replies Elric, "Although we have found something interesting on another sword, which has its own mystery," he points to the Sword of Ages that Atticus carries, "If you will Atticus. Please show Myrddin the unique engraving."

Atticus unsheathes his sword and lays it on the table. The name *Kazmagus* glows from the blade. Myrddin grins.

"What is it?" asks Atticus.

"Let's just say that my suspicions are now verified," Myrddin looks to all of the Majjai in the room, his gaze is always one of observance, as if he is constantly analysing everything around him, "The Sword of Ages and the Sword of Al-Amir, they are two of the Swords of Power."

"So it is true, then," says Elric, "The Swords of Power actually exist as they do in myth."

"Yes," replies Myrddin, "And during my search for the Tomb of Kazmagus, I came across scriptures indicating a third. Kazmagus himself created them. The Sword of Al-Amir was gifted to Prince Khalif, leader of a secret group of Majjai who were agents for Kazmagus; he was also a Dragon Slayer, hence the need for it against Draconus. But the location and identity of both it and the third sword are locked away, there was an inkling in something I read that Kazmagus himself reclaimed the blade," replies Myrddin, "The tomb will surely have more answers I hope."

"But I thought the Sword of Al-Amir belonged to Al-Amir himself?" quizzes Ju Long.

Olof and Atticus dart surprised looks towards him.

"I do study sometimes, guys."

"Yes," replies Myrddin, "The swords timeline is confusing. Some even state that Kazmagus and Al Amir were one and the same, but we do not know this for sure."

"So let's go then? Shall we head to the tomb?" says Atticus.

"My dear boy, Atticus," says Myrddin, "We do not have to go anywhere. Do you know where you sit? This is Kazmagus' palace; his tomb is here."

"But how did it get here?" asks Elric, as surprised as the young Majjai.

"That," replies Myrddin, "is still a mystery I'm afraid. Now, Elric and I must chat. Please feel free to explore the building. It's a little bare; I still have much to do to prepare it for your generation."

Elric and Myrddin leave the others in the room. Atticus turns to Mage Callan.

"Who is Jennifer?" he asks

Mage Callan looks at Atticus and smiles softly, "Jennifer Sprocking. Professor Sprocking's late wife."

"What happened to her?" asks Ju Long.

Mage Callan sighs, "It is time you were told, I guess. Elric actually asked me to do so some time ago; things have been quite busy, and I haven't had a chance. Jennifer was known to be a sweet young lady. She and Geoffrey were Myrddin's students, and very much in love. One day, the day after their wedding, actually, there was an intrusion. Geoffrey was sent to investigate. Jennifer, fearing for her husband's safety, followed him. The intrusion was a ruse, a trap. Both Geoffrey and Jennifer were captured by Razakel's forces and taken back to the Demon Realm. Draconus tortured Jennifer in front of Geoffrey. Keeping her just alive enough so that her pain receptors were still feeling the agony. He burnt her, cut her, and beat her. Geoffrey begged Draconus to stop, but the beast ignored him. Razakel was still too weak at that time, but it was believed the orders for the torture still came from him."

The other Majjai sit quietly as they listen to the story. Atticus, in particular, can relate in a small way to the pain Geoffrey feels. He is at the edge of worry, to have gone through the trials that the professor has endured, he does not dare to think about. Mage Callen takes a sip from a goblet of water before continuing.

"Finally a rescue party came, but it was too late for Jennifer, she died in Geoffrey's arms. Enraged, Geoffrey battled with Draconus – he severely wounded him, and believed he had killed him. He then returned Jennifer's body back to our realm, buried her, and asked Myrddin to make him sleep until the time came to battle Razakel once more. Elric woke him when he discovered this place, what you all know as Wysardian Manor."

"No wonder he hates Draconus so much," says Olof.

"Indeed," replies Atticus.

"Right. Now, enough stories of the past; let's have a gander at this place shall we?" Mage Callan leads the way out, walking briskly as to instil some urgency in proceedings, he too appears eager to resolve the matters at hand and return to prepare for what could be a battle at any time.

They exit the chamber and walk through the corridors. The layout is all too familiar, and they quickly reach what is now the Majjai Hall. Ju Long stands on the stage and attempts to make an impression of Elric giving one of his speeches.

"Shh!" says Atticus, "Do you hear that?" he whispers.

He pulls Ju Long from the stage. Olof and Mage Callan have wandered off in another direction. Atticus and Ju Long give up trying to get their attention, and follow the noise themselves. It soon becomes clear that they are overhearing the conversation between Myrddin and Elric.

"Are you sure Myrddin?" Elric is asking behind a closed door.

"I assume so; if Kazmagus was truly banished to the Void, then what we did at the Battle of Aria could have dire consequences," replies Myrddin, "If he ever finds a way out of the Void, we may have a threat greater than Razakel on our hands."

"Surely some good would remain?" says Elric.

"Perhaps," says Myrddin, "But, there is no way to be sure unless – or until – he returns."

"So if his body does not lie in the tomb, it is a good indication that he is still alive in the Void?" says Elric.

"Precisely," replies Myrddin.

"And how are you so sure that Atticus will be able to access the tomb?" asks Elric.

"His mark appears before the Entrance," replies Myrddin, "Why it is there, I do not know. But, if what I suspect about the Void is true, then the answer will come to Atticus one day."

"You have not seen it?" asks Elric

"No," replies Myrddin, "I have not been that far ahead as yet; knowing too much of the future is a dangerous thing, which is why I am not able to tell you of the many hardships that lay ahead of you and the others my friend. Atticus will grow up very soon, and you need to be there when he does."

"What do you mean?" asks Elric.

Myrddin looks at him, "You will know when the time is right," he says, "Now, we must get to the tomb."

Atticus and Ju Long quickly run back to the Majjai Hall before being discovered eavesdropping, and when Elric and Myrddin return, they act as if they have heard nothing.

"Come," says Myrddin, "This way."

He leads them to the furthest room behind the Majjai Hall; behind it lies what appears to be just a solid wall. Myrddin counts up five stone bricks from the floor and seven stone bricks across, places his palm against it and pushes. The wall moves back and slides behind the adjacent stonework out of view. A spiral staircase is revealed, and they all follow Myrddin downwards until they get to a large stone door.

Above the door is the mark of the Majjai, the same as Atticus' birthmark. On the right hand side of the door is a palm impression.

"Ahhh," says Elric, "Now I see where you got that wonderful idea for the chest."

Myrddin winks at Elric and beckons Atticus forward to put his hand in the impression. As soon as he does so, the doors slide open. When the dust settles, all they see is darkness. Atticus begins to step in, but the words he overheard earlier are playing on his mind and he hesitates. What did Myrddin mean by Atticus growing up soon? Could he be talking about Joyce? He fears the worst – will she die? Are they already too late? Before Atticus can move forward he is stopped.

"Careful now; we know not of what is inside, there could be traps," says Myrddin, "Stick close to me."

The Majjai follow Myrddin further in; he lights a torch, which allows them to see most of the length of the tomb. There is a casket in the middle, and several tables and cupboards. It is cold and damp, with the air tasting stale; this room has not seen life for a very, very long time. Atticus looks at the slab walls with shelves jutting out of them holding vials and makeshift tubes made from wood and metals, and he thinks to himself that this place is more of a lab than a tomb.

They soon reach an altar at the far end of the room. Above it is a flag bearing the Mark of the Majjai on a light blue background. Next to the flag is an engraving, a language that only Myrddin seems to understand. He begins to translate, reading aloud.

"Here lies the tomb of Kazmagus. In his spirit we build this place, for his followers and knights to grieve. May our descendants return to avenge us, and strike at the heart of Asmodei and his demon realm. Our knowledge is yours, use it well. Long live the King, long live Kazmagus."

Myrddin and Elric exchange knowing glances. Atticus peers

further into the darkness, and sees a thin track filled with fluid that looks like oil. He takes the torch from Myrddin and touches it to the upper part of the trough. The small flame soars across the oil's surface, lighting another chamber. Within it are row upon row of scrolls and scriptures and another stairwell heading down.

"I guess we have found the knowledge," says Ju Long.

"Yes, but it will take a lifetime to translate it all," says Elric.

"I guess I'd better get started then," says Myrddin, "Remember to return to this chamber when you go back through the portal Elric. Now, let's find that vial of Ogre blood."

"How did you know a vial would be here?" asks Olof.

"They used the blood to build this chamber. It's how I was able to locate it," replies Myrddin, "It has a distinctive trace. When mixed with a specific oil, it solidifies, and is how they fused the stonework. They left the vials to enable future Majjai to locate it, but the knowledge of how to do so was lost until I returned from the Battle of Aria."

"The master Alchemist, as always," jokes Elric.

"Yes," grins Myrddin, "I've learnt your shape-shifting trick as well."

"There are some vials over here," says Mage Callan, who has found some shelving with different vases and containers. Myrddin walks over to verify the discovery.

"Yes, yes, this is it here," he says, "Come, we must return to my lab. This tomb requires much investigation, which I will complete later, but we have more pressing matters to attend to at the moment."

Back in Myrddin's lab, he carefully adds the blood of the Cantor Ogre to the cure and hands the vial containing it to Atticus.

"Thank you," says the young Majjai.

"You're welcome," replies Myrddin, "Now come, the portal

does not have much time left, you must all leave," he looks towards Atticus, "Do not worry, dear boy. I'm sure we will meet again one day," he says with another wink.

They rush back to the Majjai training hall, and prepare to step back to their own time.

"Remember, you must keep the Orb away from Razakel. If he wins, then everything is lost," says Myrddin, "The time will come when you will need to decide what is more important, the Orb's survival, or your own. Good luck my friends. Trust your feelings, they will guide you."

One by one the Majjai step through the portal, and wave back at Myrddin as it closes in a hiss and a fizz.

Atticus wastes no time and uses his speed ability to rush to the medical ward. He hands the cure to Madam Healsey before waking Joyce's parents.

Khan is also now awake and sitting upright, his torso bandaged. He holds his left arm up, greeting Atticus. Safaya returns to the room with a glass of water for Khan.

"Good, Atticus, you have returned," she says, "And the cure?"

Atticus nods toward Madam Healsey as she administers the contents of the vial to Joyce. She holds Joyce in her arms, and coaxes her to drink it. Slowly Joyce sips at the concoction presented to her. Madam Healsey then gently lays her back down and orders everyone out of the ward, apart from Khan who is still healing from his own injuries.

They all wait patiently; seconds turn into minutes, and minutes turn into hours. Finally, the door opens and Madam Healsey calls Joyce's parents back in the room. Atticus and the others try to peer through, to catch a glimpse of whether or not the cure has worked. A further few minutes pass before the Sparks' exit the room. Dr Wei turns towards Atticus.

"She wants to see you," she says, beaming. She ruffles Atticus' hair, giving him the impression that things appear to be fine.

Atticus bursts through the doors and sees Joyce sitting up. She looks at him and smiles.

"I like the new hair, Pancake Boy," she says.

Atticus does not reply, he just hugs Joyce, tightly, "I missed you," he whispers softly.

"Thanks for saving me," Joyce whispers softly.

"It was more of a team effort," replies Atticus, "Even Ju Long helped," he says jokingly, making Joyce laugh.

Khan walks over from his bed, also now fully healed, "I fancy some pizza," he says.

"You know what," replies Atticus, "that's not a bad idea."

Elric enters the medical ward and overhears their idea, "Good, we'll all go," he says, "I'll call Spitfire. Tell him to be ready."

Before Elric can summon Spitfire, Professor Morgan returns and reports on Bradley's whereabouts.

"Sound asleep at home," he says, "His parents thought he had been drinking or something along those lines, so sent him to bed with a pretty severe ticking-off last night. He hasn't even left his room today."

"What happened?" asks Atticus.

"Long story," replies Elric, "Come, we'll talk about it over food. The last few days have been taxing; I think we deserve a little enjoyment."

The Majjai reach the main entrance of the Manor, they use the time to inform Joyce of their adventures. They soon arrive to where Spitfire is waiting. He has morphed into a large van to carry them all, but as always, he has done it with some style and found it appropriate to add some 22" chrome alloys to his attire.

Late afternoon turns into early evening, and after pizza, the Majjai Six decide to walk back, leaving Spitfire free to choose his more favoured sporty garb to take Elric, Mage Callan, Professor Morgan, and Professor Sprocking, back to the Manor.

They wait for Spitfire to roar down the street before starting their journey back.

"That was a close one," says Joyce to Atticus, "Now you understand what we are up against; that was a rare second chance. And that year you guys had for training, it, well, it's changed you. A good change."

Atticus blushes, "Thank you," replies Atticus, "But one other thing I learned was that together, as a team, we should not be afraid of anything."

"Well said, Atticus," says Safaya, "Maybe you will turn out to be a great leader after all," she continues, cheekily, playfully nudging Atticus.

"Another compliment," says Khan, "You sure you're feeling ok?"

Safaya aims a light kick towards Khan who deftly sidesteps out of the way. The young Majjai continue their journey back and decide to cut through the park near the manor. As they approach the main gates they notice some movement in the trees.

Olof holds his hand out, indicating to the others to stop, "Who goes there?" he shouts, "Show yourself!"

"Freaks!" screams out a voice.

Joyce looks at Atticus, "Bradley," she whispers with a concerned sigh.

Bradley Burrows steps out of the treeline, "I know what you are!" he screams, "I'm going to tell everyone about you freaks!"

"Bradley," says Khan, "That would be foolish. Now please,

calm down. Come with us to see Elric. He can explain everything."

"I'm not going anywhere with you monsters!" replies Bradley, "I saw what you are."

"Bradley," says Atticus, "You are making a mistake. Please, just come with us."

"You think I'll trust *you*?" shouts Bradley, "I *hate* you, Jones, I wish you would just die, you piece of shit!"

As Bradley finishes his sentence, a swirling wind builds up; then there is a bright red flash, which twists and turns into a portal.

"Bradley!" screams Atticus, "Run!"

Bradley turns around and peers into the darkness. Before he can react, Alvarez jumps out of the portal and grabs him.

"Foolish Majjai, your end is near," says the Demon, "We have our prize."

Alvarez transforms into his beast form and fires several fireballs in the direction of the Majjai before jumping back through the portal with Bradley tucked under his arm, screaming.

The Majjai Six dodge the fireballs and try to reach the portal before it closes, but it is too late.

"He's gone," says Safaya, puzzled, "Why do they want *Bradley*, of all people?"

Khan shrugs his shoulders, "We better report this to Elric."

The Majjai Six hasten their journey and quickly head to Elric's chamber to explain what has just happened.

"Do not worry," says Elric, "There was nothing you or anyone could have done. We have been betrayed."

"We have to rescue him," says Atticus, "He may be an idiot, but he is still human."

"Agreed," replies Elric, "But *human for how long?* Is the question we should really ask ourselves."

"If they turn him, that could be dangerous," says Professor Sprocking, "He knows the Manor, and the other students."

"Yes," replies Mage Callan, "But we do not have a clue where they have taken him."

Elric paces to his window overlooking the hills just before Echo Forest, visibly concerned over these new developments, but also realising of how futile a search would be right now; a rescue, although desired by every ounce of his being, would bring nothing; he turns back to his students and sighs solemnly, "Then there is nothing we can do apart from wait."

The Majjai Journals:

Finally! The hammer is in my possession. I thank Odin and Thor for guiding me. Some augmentation has been required to even hope to harness the power of lightning and thunder, only Thor himself can harness these commands natively it seems.

Leviathan and Nithhoggr were both formidable adversaries. It proves to me that Jörmungandr has influenced Leviathan. If this is true, then Thor will have more than one beast to battle, unless we destroy the serpent in a future encounter. I must ensure that Mjolnir is returned for Thor to use at the time of Ragnarok.

I must make time for Alvar and Kalle. They have been good friends and deserve to be shown the hammer. I wonder how they go with the task I have set them.

The other Norse Mages were always wary to allow me to join the Majjai Six. Their teachings are perhaps a little closed.

Elric has taught me to broaden my thinking, and I have learnt much under his tutelage. I know his sadness. The years have taken their toll. Professor Sprocking told me of a woman that Elric once loved, but he vowed never to love again after he outlived her.

The Professor himself has a story of his own and his hatred of Draconus is well-justified.

These Swords of Power appear to be our only hope – not only for destroying the dragon, but also the Demon King, once and for all.

My meditation has brought other things to the fore. Now that I now no longer seek the hammer, those visions have disappeared; but they have been replaced with visions of someone else, someone extremely powerful. A red mist, a fire around the demon realm surrounds this new being, and I fear that he may be even more powerful than Razakel, if that is possible.

This task that Elric has given me plays on my mind. I trust his judgement, but the actions he has asked me to take on could mean his end. I hope this is not the case. I must return to my training, I sense something on the horizon. I also smell death, lots of it, I fear this war will not end without despair and loss, but we must be strong.

Olof Gilmar

Chapter 26

The Turning

The stench chokes him first, as he lies in a damp dark dungeon. The flesh-covered walls pulsate as if they have a heartbeat, the chains feeding through them chink against the stone as they move. He does not know why he is here; all he knows is that he is frightened.

Bradley cowers in the corner, folding himself up into a little ball. He knows he is in a dungeon of sorts, but does not know how he got there. All he remembers is a flash of light and a man in a cloak grabbing him.

He calms his breathing as he hears footsteps outside of his cell. All night, the only things he has heard are deathly screams, strange animal like noises, and roars from giant beasts that sound so terrifying, he dare not look out of a tiny hole acting as an excuse for a window.

Then he remembers why is here, "Atticus!" the blame lies there. If it were not for his victim, he would not be here right now. The anger grows within him again, until he screams aloud the name that has caused him so much pain.

"Atticus!" he doesn't understand why his hatred has increased so much, all he knows is that he would do anything to exact revenge… anything.

A few levels higher, his screams are heard.

"The boy seems to be ready," says Razakel, as he looks towards Herensugue, "Is the potion complete?"

Herensugue looks back at his master excitedly, "Yessssss, and ssso isss the room massssssster."

"Good," replies the Demon King, "Take him there."

A group of Screamer demons march out of the throne room and make their way to the dungeon cell holding Bradley.

Without words, they burst in. Bradley backs into the corner, but to no avail. One of the Screamers grabs his left leg, and drags him out of the dungeon. Another grabs an arm and they carry him to another room where there is what appears to be a makeshift crucifix.

"Who are you?" Bradley whimpers, "Why are you doing this to me?"

The Screamers tie their prisoner to the cross and step to the side, their heads bowed.

Bradley can hear the sound of massive footsteps over his pounding heartbeat; as they get closer, they drown out any remnants of courage that remain. He squeezes his eyes closed trying to shut out the horror that is all around them, but out of morbid curiosity, he still peeks. Surely, if they wanted him dead, he would be so already. The realisation is all too clear to him, and in that moment, his fear lessens and anticipation increases.

Razakel enters, with Alvarez and Herensugue behind him.

Bradley's eyes widen, straining his neck as high as he can to take in the size of the being in front of him, "What are you?" he groans.

"My name is Razakel," says the Demon King, trying to act as non-threatening as possible, "Do not fear us. We wish to help you."

"Help me?" asks Bradley, "How?"

"We know you have been wronged. Humiliated even," replies Razakel, "We merely wish to give you the opportunity for... revenge. We know how Atticus has treated you, laughed at you, made you look the fool in front of your friends. He has ruined you in the eyes of those around you."

Bradley remains silent.

"What if I told you I could give you the power to defeat him and his companions?" Razakel continues, "All you need to do is drink this," he looks at Herensugue, who brings forward a goblet.

"What is it?" asks Bradley.

"Come now Bradley, I offer you a gift and you question it?" says Razakel, his voice holding more authority, almost as if it is an order for Bradley to drink the goblet's contents rather than an offer.

"I just want to go home," says Bradley.

"But what about Atticus, Bradley. You hate him don't you?" Razakel grows more impatient.

Bradley nods.

"Drinking this will make things clearer for you," says the Demon King, "I know you secretly covet the power they have. Yes, you say they are 'freaks', but I know, deep down, you want that same power."

"No, I just want to go home, to my family," says Bradley, hoping, praying that they will let him go.

"Very well," says Razakel, "We did ask nicely."

Razakel turns his back and looks at Alvarez, who needs no further invitation to do what he loves most: cause pain.

He transforms into his beast form, roaring loudly as he runs towards Bradley. He grabs his head and holds it head high, beckoning Herensugue to come with the goblet, the contents of which are forcefully poured down the prisoner's throat.

Bradley chokes and splutters, trying to spit the potion out, but he can't manage it. He feels it — in his veins, his blood is boiling. Bradley's head spins, his thoughts are being re-written, reprogrammed. He knows what is right, but that which is wrong is pulling him in the other direction. Finally the anger takes over, consuming every part of his mind and soul. The image of his hatred, Atticus, flows through his mind.

"Atticus!" he screams, "I hate Atticus! I want to tear him limb from limb!"

Razakel chuckles, "Good. Feel your morality being stripped away. Their world gives you confusion, Bradley, I give you clarity. Their world takes power away from you, I give you power," he walks back towards Bradley and leans down to him, "Now, you call *me* master."

Bradley, drained and exhausted, looks upwards, and whispers, "Yes master. I am yours to command."

Razakel turns to several Screamers waiting near the doorway and nods to them. They open the main doors to reveal a massive beast pulsating into a walking shadow and then into a physical form, almost like a werewolf, but much bigger. It takes five Screamers to hold the creature. They drag it closer and closer towards their captive human.

"Do not be afraid, Bradley," says Razakel, "This is all part of the gift I give to you," he looks at Alvarez, "Use the neck," he says, "The transformation will work quickest from there."

Alvarez heeds his master's orders.

The monster is brought closer, it looks at Razakel who smiles and nods, then it leaps at Bradley, biting into his neck. Bradley screams in agony. The beast writhes excitedly and roars, before biting his victim again.

Razakel laughs loudly in the background, "Behold the birth. The birth of Shadow Wolf!"

Alvarez and the other Screamers bellow and howl into the air. The strange werewolf like being turns into smoke and enters Bradley's body via the wound it has created, consuming him. Bradley screams again, louder this time; as he continues screaming it changes pitch and his body begins to transform. The scream changes pitch again, getting lower, turning into a growl, and the transformation is complete.

Shadow Wolf roars into the air, howling along with the Screamers and Alvarez. He then turns to Razakel.

"Master," he says, his voice deep and foreboding, "I thank you for this gift. My revenge will be your victory."

"Good," laughs Razakel, "But first, there is another task you must complete."

# # #

"Do not worry, Atticus," says Joyce, "Elric will find a way to save Bradley."

Atticus stares out into the front garden, "It has been a week now. We have heard nothing about any plans."

"Well, what do you suggest?" asks Joyce, "We can't exactly storm into the Demon Realm and save him ourselves, that would be suicide."

"But you have seen the missing person posters of Bradley around town," says Atticus, "We can't even tell his family we know where he is. They must be worried sick."

"I saw his mum yesterday, outside the school gates," says Joyce, "She was asking the students if anyone had seen her son. It was horrible to watch."

The night sky blankets the house. Sophia and Joseph are in the front room watching a movie. Joyce and Atticus decide to move to the back garden where things are a little quieter.

"I'm scared, Joyce," says Atticus.

"We all are," she replies.

"There are not many of us here. Razakel has hundreds of thousands of demons at his command," Atticus says, pacing up and down the garden path, "How do we fight an army like that? It's only a matter of time before he uses the medallion. A part of me wishes he would just do so and get things over with. Why is he playing this waiting game?"

"Arrogance," replies Joyce, "He is very powerful, he knows that no-one here is a match for him yet. Not even you, Atticus. He is probably enjoying the thought of us being scared, and wants to prolong that fear."

"Myrddin seemed confident enough," says Atticus, "He must have seen that we will win this. Translating the documents in the tomb of Kazmagus is taking longer than expected, too. Myrddin has changed the locking system and Elric has been busier deciphering that than planning a rescue. Perhaps the answer lies in there," he peers through the window into the living room. He can see Joseph and Sophia snuggling on the sofa. He looks at Joyce, and the night sky, clear but for a few scattered clouds.

Atticus holds out his hand, "Joyce, come with me," he says as softly as he can.

Joyce takes his hand and they float skywards. Atticus takes them both up into the night above the clouds. They soar through them, dancing between the star constellations and come to rest just above the mists over the River Thames.

"You see that there," says Atticus, "I bet that's Big Ben."

Joyce peers down, "Look, there's the London Eye," she says, pointing, before frantically grabbing hold of Atticus again, "I see your flying skills have improved, Pancake Man."

"Yeah, a massive dragon chasing you does seem to act as effective motivation," replies Atticus with a grin. He hugs Joyce

316

tightly, "We've grown a lot these last few months. Maybe a little too quickly."

"What do you mean?" asks Joyce.

"It was hard to be away from you for so long during my year within the runes," replies Atticus.

"Yes, but it does mean you managed to grow this funky new hair," giggles Joyce.

"Very funny," says Atticus, "What I'm trying to say is, during that year away, I did a lot of thinking. I know we are young, but it is strange, what I feel for you is so strong. You are the reason why I have pushed myself so hard, Joyce. Saving you was all I could think about. If anything had happened to you, I don't know..."

"Shhhhh!" says Joyce, she puts her right forefinger on Atticus' lips, before moving forward to kiss them softly.

At that moment Atticus realises something. That same drive that pushed him, that same feeling of love, this is their greatest weapon against Razakel. He thinks back to his parents, Joseph and Sophia, and how much love they have for each other. His mind then wanders to Mage Callan, whose all-too apparent blushes whenever Serenity is mentioned tell their own story. Then to the forbidden love that torments both Khan and Safaya. This drive to do whatever it takes to protect what they hold dear, it is this that will help them win the battle. Atticus breathes softly, as if new calm and understanding are giving him clarity.

"What's the matter, Atticus?" asks Joyce.

Atticus looks at Joyce, "Nothing," he whispers, "Absolutely nothing. We should head back now," as they start their journey back, Atticus realises the decision he must make; he senses the tension increasing within Joyce as they return as well.

They arrive back at Atticus's house fairly quickly. When they

317

get inside, they hear voices in the living room – Marcellus has arrived and has brought snacks. Atticus is both glad and frustrated. Glad to see Marcellus, but frustrated that he is unable to tell Joyce something he needs to.

"Atticus, my dear boy, please, come. And Joyce," says Marcellus, "So good to see you both."

Today Marcellus is dressed most strangely, in a chequered coat and a deerstalker hat. Atticus senses that he has seen that hat before, but can't quite place where.

"What is it?" asks Joyce.

"Lebanese food. They call it – *shar-waa-maa*," replies Marcellus, trying hard to get the pronunciation correct.

Atticus and Joyce each grab one of the take out bags and begin to devour their contents.

"So, where did you two disappear to the night of the dance competition?" asks Marcellus, "I must have left the house for less than half an hour; you two must have come and gone during that time."

"We had to go to the manor," replies Atticus, trying to speak through a mouthful of chicken sharwama.

"That school takes up so much of your time; I barely get to see you anymore," says Marcellus.

"Neither do we," says Sophia, "But I'm sure it is all for important things."

Marcellus strokes his chin, "Indeed," he says, "And Joyce, hope you are feeling better? I heard you were a little poorly."

"Better now," replies Joyce, "It was… erm, an allergic reaction to a nasty insect bite," she says coyly, not knowing if Marcellus knows the full story.

"Must have been some insect," says Marcellus.

"It was *this* big, according to her," quips Atticus, holding his arms out as far apart as they can go.

Joyce almost chokes on her food, before everyone is interrupted by the phone ringing. Sophia answers it. She soon returns to the living room and turns to Atticus and Joyce.

"That was Elric," she says, "He needs you both back at the Manor as soon as possible. Something about 'the room being ready.'"

Atticus and Joyce look at each other, stuff down their last few bits of food, and get ready to leave.

"Here, I'll drive you both," says Marcellus, "Just picked up a new car and need to run it in anyway."

They wave bye to Sophia and Joseph and head towards Marcellus's new car, a brand-spanking-new Jaguar XJR, decked out in black paint and huge wheels.

"Very nice, Uncle Marcellus," says Atticus.

"Many thanks," replies Marcellus, "Now, we'd better hurry; it sounds like this Elric fellow needs you back at the manor fairly urgently."

They reach their destination in a few minutes, but Marcellus does not drive all the way in, he simply stops at the main gates, "That's far enough, I think," he says.

"Not coming in?" asks Joyce.

"Err… no, not today, I have to meet someone in a few minutes. Perhaps next time," replies Marcellus.

As he drives off, Joyce turns to Atticus, "That is the second time he has come to the gates and can't wait to get away," she says, "Bit strange, that."

Atticus shrugs off the comment, "Marcellus is all right, just a bit busy. Haven't seen him much since my powers were awakened."

"Well, as long as you can trust him," says Joyce.

"I can," replies Atticus confidently.

They rush through the manor towards the Tomb of Kazmagus and find the rest of the Majjai Six there, along with Elric, Professor Sprocking, Professor Morgan, and Mage Callan.

"Quickly," says Elric, "inside," he steps into the tomb and lights several torches, "It took some time, as you know, but we have finally regained access to this chamber. Atticus, if you would be so kind."

Atticus steps forward and puts his hand in the palm impression to open the door. As soon as it opens, Elric ignites more torches so that there is enough light for everyone to see where they are going.

"We definitely need some new lighting in here," says Ju Long.

The others follow Elric in as he fires up the oil trough, which lights the rest of the chamber. They reach the main altar and find a thought crystal there.

Elric activates it and Myrddin appears.

"Glad to see you were able to get back in my friends," says the image, "I have found much here, and translated as much as possible before other duties became more urgent. There are, indeed, three swords of power, but the whereabouts of the third sword are unknown. What is clear, though, is that this sword is not to be wielded by any man. The texts were cryptic in this regard, and I *think* it means that no man is *able* to wield it. Regardless, we still need to find it, as some of the things written imply that these three swords are key to winning the war against Razakel."

Myrddin strokes his beard and looks down again towards the Majjai below him, "Glad to see you are ok, Joyce; hope my potion wasn't too bitter. As I was saying, there are many items within these walls: maps, clues, and information on many, many trinkets that Kazmagus was researching and creating. I have left instructions on how to translate the language. Good luck, my friends; who knows, we may meet again one day."

The thought crystal's image disappears, and the Majjai all look at each other.

"I guess we're supposed to look around, then?" says Atticus.

"Indeed," says Elric, "But perhaps tomorrow will be a better time for that. Let us rest today so we are fresh to look at these properly."

"But," interrupts Ju Long, "It's Saturday tomorrow. We should get paid for this."

Olof quickly knocks some sense into him with a quick slap on the back of his head.

They follow Elric to the Majjai Hall. The hall itself has been fully restored, and one would be hard-pressed to find any evidence of a violent battle within it.

"There have been some interesting intrusions into our realm the last few days," says Elric, "I have had watcher reports come in that state sightings of a werewolf, one unlike any other seen before. Some even say that the beast turns into shadow upon being discovered."

"How does this concern us?" asks Professor Morgan.

"This werewolf wears the dragon insignia, torn from the uniform of this school," replies Elric, "I fear Bradley has been turned."

"Turned?" asks Atticus, "What does that mean?"

Joyce looks down to the floor, sighs, then looks at Atticus, "It means he has been stripped of all humanity, Atticus. His morality will no longer exist – all he will feel is hatred and anger."

"Yes," replies Elric, "And there is someone here who he feels more anger against than anyone else."

"Me," says Atticus.

"Yes," replies Elric, "I suspect that Razakel was never actually after you. We miscalculated. Bradley was his target all along."

"But why?" asks Atticus.

"Another enemy for you − the more he can amass, the greater his chances. And this one is of particular interest, because the amount of hatred exponentially increases the transformation's strength. Bradley will be a formidable foe," says Elric, "We must be on our guard."

"Why is he waiting to attack?" asks Khan, "He has the medallions, surely he can enter our realm any time."

"Yes, but he needs to prepare his invasion," says Elric, "I doubt we have much time, but we will have to meet him wherever he appears. The Orb is locked away in the Majjai Hall, and should be well protected. I have put measures in place to prevent the traitor in our midst from getting their hands on it. Olof, can the Norse Majjai join us?"

"I will send a request to meet with them," replies Olof.

Elric looks at the others, "It's time we rally the troops. Begin your communications once we have finished here."

"Do we have any idea on who it is yet, this traitor?" asks Professor Sprocking.

"I have a suspicion," replies Elric, "And rest assured, it will be dealt with."

Elric stands, takes his walking stick and makes his way to one of his book shelves. As he reaches for one of the hardbacks he suddenly keels over in pain.

"Arrrrgghh!" he screams.

Safaya and Professor Morgan rush over to catch him.

"What is it?" screams Safaya.

"I sense something," says Elric, "No! No! It is too soon!"

"What is it?" shouts Professor Sprocking.

"The portals, they are opening," says Elric, "They are coming. It's time."

Chapter 27

Traitor

"Where Elric?" asks Professor Sprocking.

"We have to leave," screams Elric, "Now! We have to go back, Aria is about to see another battle."

The Majjai quickly stand together.

"Remember, bring all those who are able to fight; we meet outside Aria," says Elric.

Joyce looks at Atticus, "You ready?"

Atticus looks at Joyce, then the other Majjai, "Yes."

# # #

In a bright flash, the Majjai disappear, leaving just a puff of dissipating smoke. As the smoke clears, a shadow creeps out from behind the bookshelves. It slithers out of the room and towards the great Majjai doors. Once there it transforms into its beast form, still hidden in the darkness. It whispers the password *"Farasi Bakhwar,"* and the doors open.

"You have done well, Shadow Wolf," Says a figure standing in front of the beast.

"Thank you, Professor," Snarls Shadow Wolf, "Now I must continue with my own mission. I will see you at the rendezvous point."

"Very well," replies the traitor, "Did you find out where the

Orb is hidden?"

"It is in the Majjai Hall," replies Shadow Wolf before melting into the darkness.

The traitor heads towards the Majjai Hall. Once there he opens the entrance to the rooms behind it. Before he can go through, a voice shouts from behind him.

"Snugglebottom!" says the voice, "YOU are the traitor!"

Professor Snugglebottom quickly turns around, "Ahhh, so, you still live. It was wise that Elric hid your identity, protector – or should I use your real name? Marcellus! One of The Fallen?"

"Whatever name you wish," says Marcellus, "I will still be ending your existence!"

Professor Snugglebottom moves away from the door, and walks towards Marcellus.

"I should warn you, Majjai, I have been gifted the Cocoon of Enhancement!" says the traitor, "I should tell you my true name: Scourge!"

Snugglebottom's skin begins to bubble, his head and body begin to expand, while his face flattens then morphs into an ovular shape, with bat-like ears and fangs dripping with saliva.

Marcellus steps back, and fires several fireballs at Scourge, who catches each one and throws them back towards their origin.

Marcellus jumps out of the way and smashes his fist into the ground, sending a pressure wave towards Scourge.

Scourge stumbles to the floor, but leaps up again quickly. He is still growing, and he is now towering over Marcellus.

Marcellus pulls out an emerald-encrusted metal whip and creates a blue shield of light, "Die demon!" he screams as he leaps into the air, lashing at Scourge.

The whip cuts the demon's back. Scourge screams in pain and

retaliates by sending a massive jet of flame from his mouth.

Marcellus raises his shield to deflect the flame away from him before lashing his whip again. This time Scourge is ready and grabs it, pulling Marcellus towards him and throwing him into the air. Marcellus crashes into the wall and falls to the floor.

Scourge leaps upwards and aims his massive claws towards Marcellus as he descends. Just before Scourge lands, Marcellus raises his shield and protects himself from the attack. Using both of his legs, he kicks Scourge back into the air and flips himself back up.

Marcellus launches another attack, his whip causes another deep cut, but this time Scourge uses the attack to land a blow of his own. His massive fist punches into Marcellus's chest, sending him flying through the air again and crashing into the floor, dazed.

Scourge walks over to him and looks down, "You Majjai were so easy to fool for all these years. My King, Razakel, gifted me the cocoon all those years ago, when Atticus was first found. I am more powerful than you could ever imagine. It has been frustrating hiding my true form from all of you; but now, now you will feel pain and death like you never thought possible," says Scourge, "We chose Bradley, to turn him – it was my idea. His hatred was easy to focus. Diverting your attention away from our plan was just too easy; we've slipped him potions, prepared him for months, intensifying his rage. Razakel will reward me again, and you… you *Majjai* will cease to exist."

The beast stomps on Marcellus's head roaring as he does so, "I slept for thousands of years, waiting for Alvarez to wake me, and rejoiced when he finally came. I then infiltrated this school and assumed the Professor's identity. I am the traitor within. The Professor's family bled, the taste was enjoyable. But it will not be anywhere near as enjoyable as tasting the blood of the chosen one.

Atticus & The Orb Of Time

Bradley will get the first bite, of course; he is so looking forward to it."

Scourge throws another bone-crunching blow at Marcellus, who still lies on the floor, this time kicking him with enough force to slam him into the stage.

"You Majjai did all of the hard work for us – we knew the chosen one would retrieve the Orb. Your weakness is your compassion. If you had let the girl die, the Orb would still be safe. This Atticus is no match for Razakel – he will destroy him utterly," says the beast.

Marcellus groans, "I would not underestimate him. His power is still to be realised."

"FOOL!" screams Scourge, "What makes you think he will have the *time* to become so powerful? Bradley will tear him apart; and if not, Razakel will crush him easily. Heh, Atticus wasn't even a match for Alvarez, and his strength is dwarfed by our King!" the beast stomps forward, slamming one of his massive feet into Marcellus's head, pummelling it into the ground, "I hold you all in contempt! Now you will die."

Scourge walks back to the main stage area to access the rooms behind it, a few moments pass. Marcellus drifts in and out of consciousness, he sees Scourge return, the *Quantorbium* in his hands. The beast walks up to him and drags him by his collar.

Marcellus feels himself being lifted high into the air. Opening his eyes again, he looks upwards, Scourge has sprouted massive wings and flies high into the night sky, carrying him in his arms. His eyes close again.

Next all Marcellus feels is weightlessness, as if he himself is flying. His eyes open, and he sees the Manor as he falls through the air towards one of the towers. The last thing he sees is the stone wall of the rampart's stonework, then nothing.

Scourge flies south, happy with the knowledge that he has

dealt the Majjai a damaging blow by killing one of their most powerful warriors. He screams into the night like a banshee, and continues his journey.

The sky around Wysardian Manor falls silent. Marcellus lies still, a gentle breeze whispering around him. The quietness is soothing as Marcellus sleeps.

Suddenly, a pair of bright lights appear, followed by a deep rumble as a deathly black figure rolls into view.

A faint whisper floats towards the sleeping Majjai, "Marcellus…"

# # #

Olof stands outside a traditional pub in Sweden. At Elric's request, he has taken a slight detour on his journey. Two figures sneak up behind him; he hears their footsteps crunching on the snow and spins round quickly.

"Hey Olof," says Alvar, "No need to be so jumpy. You wanted to meet us? What do you need?"

Kalle steps forward, "I think I know."

"Where can we get an army?" asks Olof, "And quickly."

"Has the time come?" asks Alvar, "Is Razakel coming?"

Olof nods, "I do not have much time."

"We have already prepared something," says Kalle, "There was talk of the demons' retrieving Loki's medallions?"

"It is true," says Olof.

"Then, indeed, we do not have much time my friend," replies Kalle, "And it has taken you too long to come and show us this," he says, pointing to Thor's hammer.

"Time has been short," replies Olof, "We have also found the

Quantorbium. Razakel comes for it. You say you already have something prepared?"

"We do; come with us," says Kalle.

The three pass through a blizzard, fighting the cold winds for what seems like an hour before they reach their destination.

"In there," says Alvar, pointing to an old cave, "We have a little surprise for you," Olof follows the other two into the cavern and is amazed; over 200 Norse Majjai stand before him, chanting his name, "Olof! Olof! Olof!"

Olof stands on a higher plinth filling himself with pride, this show of acceptance that his fellow Norse Majjai finally unite and join him in his quest, "Fellow Norsemen!" he shouts, "Today is a day where we fight. Not just for ourselves, but for every living being in this realm. We walk into a dangerous battle. Do not be fooled into thinking otherwise; the demons we face are real. I come to you after facing the might of Nithhoggr and Leviathan, and yet I still stand!" a huge cheer erupts throughout the cave.

Olof holds the hammer of Thor above his head, "With *Mjolnir* guiding our path we *shall* be victorious! Or we will die a death of honour, only to rise from the grave and fight again! Until *every... last... demon... burns in flames*!!"

# # #

Serenity is putting her son, Joshua, to bed. For the first time in what seems like years, she is smiling as she does so. Mage Callan stopped by just a little earlier that day and brought four bouquets of flowers, which are currently throwing their scent gracefully around the house.

She ponders for a moment, for Mage Callan was not as jovial

as he usually is, but he still left with a kiss and some chocolate. Carrying on with her nightly routine she continues to make some hot chocolate for herself from some fresh cocoa. The aroma blends with the scent from the flowers to create a warmth that gently hugs her, almost as if Mage Callan is there in spirit himself.

"He was so tender this last visit," she thinks to herself, but some things he said have troubled her ever so slightly. This last visit seemed a little sombre, there was something hidden in his tone, but she ignores it and soaks in the velvety smooth memory of that final kiss. She pauses again.

It hits her finally – what if it's time? What if Razakel comes now and this is why he came to see her? The thoughts of happiness turn to fear.

She gets up and starts to search for the communications crystal that Mage Callan had given her. She tries to activate it, but there is no answer. Her heart sinks, and she kisses the small gemstone in the hope that it will send some luck her suitor's way.

#

Khan steps into the hot sand, the grains burn into his sandaled feet as he traverses the Dubai desert. It feels like he has walked for hours, but in truth the journey has lasted mere minutes such is the burden of the heat and dry arid air. He searches for the secret camp where he was trained all those years ago. Each step gets harder as the sun bears down. A voice calls out to him.

"Who goes there?"

Khan stops and speaks, "It is I, Abd Al-Hakim Khan. I seek council with the elders."

"Khan?" says the voice, "You have grown, my dear boy."

"Assaad?" says Khan, recognising the figure that emerges from the heat wave's glare, "It has been a long time, my friend."

"Indeed; the elders have been expecting you, we sense great danger," says Assaad.

"The demon comes," says Khan, "It will not be long."

Assaad nods and creates a portal, which both he and Khan walk into.

They step through to the League of Aria training grounds. Before them lies what appear to be ruins more than actual areas that could be used to train future generations. But the landscape is still imposing. Giant waterfalls are seen in the distance with tropical rainforest-sized trees dotting the horizon, their foliage thickening as they disappear into the distance. Birds and insects can be heard all around them, as well as the sound of the leaves rustling in the calm, warm breeze.

They stand on a makeshift wooden platform, high above the ground, attached to one of the taller trees.

"Always a breathtaking sight," says Khan, as his gaze takes in the wonders of the diverse landscape.

"Welcome home, Khan," says another voice.

Khan turns around and sees a very old man, but one who still has the strength to wield a mighty sabre. The body may be old, but Khan immediately recognises the face of his teacher.

"My Lord," says Khan, as he kneels to the ground.

"Rise, Khan. You know I see you like a son; there is no need to kneel," says the elder figure, "I am a king merely in name these days; I no longer have the wealth or power I once had."

"You still have our respect, my Lord," says Khan, "And my allegiance to my duties as the last remaining marked League member still hold true."

"I'm glad to hear it," replies the elder, "You do not need to worry. I already know why you are here, the demon's arrival is imminent. I have amassed a small group of fighters to help you in your quest."

"I see your wisdom is still as great as ever, my Lord," says Khan.

"Yes, well, Assaad has been keeping my mind sharp; he is a superb chess player you know," replies the elder.

"That I am all too aware of," replies Khan, "He has beaten me many times."

"How is she?" asks the elder, "How is my sister?"

"The Princess is fine, my Lord," replies Khan, "She is strong, and has learned to control her powers with the guidance from Elric. She misses you."

"I miss her, too," says the Elder, "But you know she can never know I survived; to lose me again would be devastating for her, and there is no telling how it will affect her. History sees me as dead, and therefore, that is how I, King Ismail must remain."

Khan nods reluctantly.

"Good; you and Elric are the only ones that know the secret outside of the League's circle," says King Ismail, "Maybe, one day, I will be able to reunite with my sister; but that time is not now. Long life is a curse, but Elric thought it wise that I receive a potion borne from the Orb. Time will indeed tell."

Khan looks towards his mentor. He sees the same wisdom in his eyes that he sees in Elric's, but also the same sadness. He does not question anything, dutifully moving the conversation on, "I suspect she knows I am from the League, my Lord. I fear the mark may have been revealed to her after our last battle."

"I wouldn't worry too much. I'm surprised it has taken her this long to figure it out," says the King, "Protecting her might be a little easier now."

"I need to leave now, the battle nears," says Khan.

"Very well," replies King Ismail, "The warriors I have amassed for you will join you; give the location to Assaad. You have the heart of a warrior. I will see you again, soon, Abd Al-Hakim Khan. Fight well. May Allah be with you."

Khan bows again and walks outside with Assaad. He gives Assaad the location of the other Majjai. He has missed his long-time companion; he cannot control himself and wraps his hands around his brethren-in-arms.

"Fight well, brother, I want to see you back here again soon," says Assaad.

"Do not worry. We will see each other again soon, in this life or the next," says Khan, before stepping back through the portal.

# # #

The night is cold in London. Most people are asleep in their beds or snuggled up indoors. Only shadows move in the moonlight. One shadow, in particular, is busier than most, moving between crevices and buildings. The quiet night aids its progress and it soon reaches its destination.

A small cocker spaniel wanders the streets, lost, trying to find its way home. It sniffs at this strange shadow that appears not to have an owner. Once the scent has taken hold the little dog freezes, and in a panic begins to bark loudly. The last thing it sees is a couple in the distance, through a window, who seem to be dancing. Then a claw severs its neck, and it sees nothing.

Chapter 28

The Return to Aria

The moon shines across the desert sands. Atticus and the other Majjai stand atop the highest dune they can find, and look towards where Aria once stood. Elric cloaks the area as much as possible, but is still visibly weakened from sensing the invasion earlier.

Atticus spots Mage Callan supporting Elric while he tries to regain his strength. Olof, Ju Long, and Khan all return from their travels and report straight to the others.

The tension is high. For the first time in all of this Atticus finally feels real fear. In all the previous battles he took solace in the confidence of his friends, his teachers, Elric. But now, all he senses is worry. A realisation that this battle has come too soon overwhelms him as he looks across the desert. There are only ruins now where there a grand city once stood, the stonework is all but broken, nonetheless, its still imposing. Citadels have fallen, houses and walls crumbled. To the west, the sunlight begins to give way to the night as the wind kicks up small ripples in the sand. Atticus times his breathing, trying to calm his soul. He slowly begins to take in the moment. He looks towards Joyce, he gains strength from her, his muse; he has found his something to die for, and in that moment, realises he has also found his reason to live.

"What word comes from the Norse Mages, Olof?" asks Elric. Atticus can see he is trying to break the tension.

Olof adjusts the hammer on his belt, to ensure it is ready when needed before answering, "They are willing to help and should be here shortly."

"And the Saracen Elders?" asks Elric, looking towards Khan who nods in confirmation.

Ju Long puts a hand on Elric's shoulder, "Do not worry, my guild will also be sending their most powerful Majjai."

"Good, good," says Elric, "Hopefully the portals will be narrow, and it will be easier to pick them off as they come through."

A flash of light indicates the arrival of the Norse Mages'; all of them are dressed in the finest battle armour, glistening against the dusk's ever increasing moonlight. They take their position behind the Majjai Six. Things seem calm, but then a spark appears, and then the skies cloud over, challenging the moon to break through.

"Here they come!!" screams Professor Morgan.

A portal forms in mid-air not too far from where they stand, it floats high and turns on its axis, now facing downwards it settles on the desert floor.

"What is happening?" asks Atticus.

"I'm not sure," says Khan.

The ground begins to shake violently, causing several dunes to collapse.

Khan spots something beneath the sand, "Slugs!" he screams, "They are coming through the ground!"

"Slugs!" shouts Atticus, "What the hell are Slugs?"

A giant, worm-like creature smashes through the desert surface and shows its ugly head. A large central mouth surrounded by tentacles, each with their own smaller mouths.

"That's a slug, Atticus," says Safaya.

Another Slug crashes through the Majjai, forcing them to

scatter.

"Hold your lines!" screams Khan, "They are trying to divide us. Atticus, just hit anything that's ugly!"

"Maybe *we* should divide *them*?" says Mage Callan, who hands Elric into Professor Morgan's care. He unsheathes his swords and throws one like a boomerang at the first Slug, slicing part of its body, before speeding on and slicing the other half of the Slug with his other sword. He picks his first sword from the sand and uses it to pierce through the Slug's head, killing it.

The remaining Slug circles round and leaps into the air, forcing the Majjai apart again. Another three Slugs make their presence known and attack the Norse Mages, who defend themselves with blasts of ice and fire.

Three more portals open, and hordes of Screamers begin to pour through and immediately launch sonic attacks towards the Majjai Six. Joyce throws up a huge shield to protect them, deflecting the sonic blasts into the air.

"My turn," says Olof, who holds Mjolnir high above his head and throws it towards the amassing Screamers. The blow sends a massive shockwave through their ranks, killing most of them instantly. The hammer swing around and returns to Olof's hand.

Another wave of Screamers stream through; nearby another larger portal opens sending through large numbers of Graigons.

Atticus freezes; the battle now is more real than ever, and he can sense the tension around him. The danger is of the worst kind, he knows there is more threat of death this time than ever before.

The Graigons smash their chests with their fists, roar into the air, and charge forward.

"This is it, my friends," says Elric, "This is the battle you have trained for. We must win it, for the sake of all that is good," he looks down at Atticus and reminds him of the promise he made, "Side by side, dear boy, side by side."

Atticus nods.

"Onwards!" shouts Mage Callan, "Die, Demons!" he screams and uses his blades to cut through the swathes of Screamers.

Atticus pulls out the Sword of Ages and follows his teacher into the battle. Khan and Olof head over to battle the Graigons while Ju Long helps the Norse Mages. Safaya and Joyce take on the flanking Screamers, while the Professors and Elric aid from afar with fireballs and shields.

They soon reach a balance of attack and defence, the numbers coming through the portals matched by the number killed at the hands of the Majjai, but they know they are unable to keep this up.

One more portal begins to form ahead of the battlefield, and Alvarez and Draconus appear.

Professor Sprocking spies his enemy, "Dragon!" he screams, "Come taste my wrath!"

Draconus hears him and heads towards his nemesis, shooting fire in his direction. Sprocking deflects the fire and launches a massive fireball with all of his rage towards the dragon. The blast sends Draconus high into the air, through the cloak of clouds and into the night sky beyond. The beast quickly recovers and darts towards the earth again, heading straight for Professor Sprocking, who by now has created a staff of light to do battle.

Alvarez heads straight for the Norse Mages, quickly morphing into his beast guise as he runs; without mercy he kills at least four in a furious rampage. Mage Callan heads over to assist but is blocked by a group of Graigons. They throw blow upon blow towards him, Mage Callan uses his swords and agility to dodge them, but is prevented from getting anywhere near Alvarez, there are just too many of the hulking beasts in his way.

More Slugs appear, aiming to flank Elric and Professor Morgan. Safaya steps in to aid them by creating massive whirlwinds of sand to throw the Slugs into the distance. Olof spots the Slugs in the air and spears them all with giant shards of ice blasting out from his hands.

Atticus is deep within the Screamer hordes, slaying as many as he can with the Sword of Ages and his telekinesis ability. His training is being utilised to its fullest as he twists, turns, slices, and shoots fireballs into the demon crowd. He can feel the sword tapping into his inner knowledge, but is fearful of allowing it to take full control. He can feel something else within him, not his own. The sword is acting of its own will at times, Atticus allows it to move, it drags him deeper into battle, as if its own thirst for blood is overpowering his intentions. Atticus wrestles control, and as he does so, the name Kazmagus glows brightly from the blade and the sword succumbs to its owner again.

Atticus pauses for just a moment, taking in the battle, he sees wounded and dead from both sides. Scared, for a moment he wishes he were home, he remembers his mum, his dad, what he wouldn't give right now for one of Sophia's sandwiches. Or just a warm embrace from them, telling him it will all be ok.

"Atticus! Watch out!" screams Khan as a Graigon breaks free.

Atticus snaps back into focus, he dodges the first Graigon blow and swings around before another smashes into the sand next to him, blasting a huge amount into the air. Atticus swings the Sword of Ages forward, thrusting it into the forearm of the demonic beast. He withdraws the sword and slices the hand of the Graigon clean off. The beast roars in pain before Khan kills it with a giant fireball. Atticus nods his appreciation and continues to fight, slicing his way as much as he can through the Screamer masses.

But the Majjai efforts are in vain, even with Ju Long aiding from the air with fireball attacks. The demon numbers grow; for every demon slain, another three appear in their place.

Just as the Majjai fear the worst, reinforcements arrive, the warriors sent from Khan's Saracen friends and Ju Long's own guild, the Bhandari Clan, teleport in. They join the fray immediately, sending fireball upon fireball into the demon packs.

Safaya whistles to Ju Long who swoops down for her to jump onto his back. When they take to the air she uses her powers to raise huge clumps of sand, then binds the grains together to create huge rocks, and uses them to plough into the Screamers.

Joyce is cleverly combining her powers by creating a spherical shield around her and using her speed to roll it into any demon she can find, firing fireballs through it to take care of any she misses.

Another wave of demons streams through, of a type Atticus has not seen before. They resemble the Screamers, but have bat-like wings. They take to the air and begin to chase Ju Long and Safaya.

Olof points to the winged beasts, "Draygoyles!" he shouts.

Khan looks to Atticus, "Help them!" he shouts, pointing to the air at the draygoyles pursuing Ju Long. Atticus immediately soars after this new threat.

"Safaya!" shouts Atticus, "Here!" he says, as he fires a large fireball up in the air.

Safaya sees it, and uses it straight away. She stretches the flame, turning it into a net of fire, which she launches towards the Draygoyles, killing several. Atticus chases the others, giving Ju Long time to turn and aid in the battle against this new aerial foe. Their flight path is briefly blocked by Draconus who is still battling with Professor Sprocking.

Draconus tries to burn Sprocking, who uses all of his ability and might to dodge the attacks. He fires a swarm of fireballs at the dragon, some hit their target, the others merely fly into the night sky.

"I WILL take your head, beast!" screams Sprocking. He forms a disc of light and throws it towards Draconus like a frisbee; it slices the skin on one of the dragon's wings sending it crashing to the desert surface, just missing Olof.

The Norse warrior still battles the Graigon forces alongside Khan; he uses the hammer of Thor to slay as many as he can. Khan uses his enormous strength to great effect, grabbing one Graigon, spinning as fast as he can and launching it with a force robust enough to kill the group of Graigons' blocking Mage Callan's path.

The Norse reinforcements aid Mage Callan who now has a clean line of sight towards Alvarez. Using his swords, he crosses them and sends bolts of energy towards the demon, knocking him off his feet. Alvarez roars at Mage Callan and charges toward him, allowing the surviving Norse Mages to continue their battle against the Slugs that continue to appear.

Elric has almost regained his strength and becomes more involved in the battle. He and Professor Morgan join the fight against the Screamers, filling in for Atticus who continues to help fight the Draygoyles with Ju Long and Safaya.

Another, much larger portal appears in the distance.

Elric looks towards it; he knows all-too-well who has opened this one, "Prepare yourselves!" he screams, "It is the seventh portal. *He* is coming!!"

The demons all fall back to the sides of the new opening, allowing the Majjai to regroup and stand opposite them.

The Majjai are outnumbered ten to one already, and Razakel is still to come. They are battle-weary and scarred, nevertheless, they continue to stand before the portal, prepared to take on whatever comes through.

The gateway changes colour, and first through is Herensugue. He glares directly at Joyce with his remaining six heads. The portal changes colour again, this time to a deep crimson. Razakel steps through. His presence fills the Norse Mages and the other reinforcements with dread.

"Ahhh, a welcoming committee," says Razakel mockingly.

"Return to your domain, demon, or we will destroy your forces and send you back to hell without remorse or mercy!" shouts Elric.

"You?" scoffs Razakel, "Your forces are a mere shadow of what you had before – a few hundred against two thousand? – and these are just the beginning. My armies stand behind me, and will tear your realm apart."

"You will never find the Orb," says Elric, "It is protected."

"Yes," replies Razakel, "about that," he pauses as a winged beast swoops down and lands besides him. It transforms into its human form and looks towards the Majjai.

"Surprise!" says the new arrival, with a contemptuous twirl and a bow.

"Snugglebottom!" shouts Mage Callan, "*You* are the traitor? How dare you! You betray humanity!"

"Who says I am still human?" says Snugglebottom as he transforms back into his demon form, stretching his wings as far as he can.

Razakel laughs into the night, "I introduce you to Scourge," he says, "And oh, there is another surprise," Razakel holds out his hand.

Scourge hovers high enough to put the *Quantorbium* in his giant palm.

"You see, I have the Orb," says Razakel, "It was never safe."

"But how?" asks Elric.

"Oh!" rumbles Scourge, "That Protector fellow, he is very much dead."

Elric looks on in horror, "No," he says under his breath, "Marcellus."

Atticus turns sharply, "Marcellus?" he says, surprised. At that moment the cold dark reality of this war hits home; the death of someone he knows and cares for sends an emptiness of emotion through him. How does he react? Does he break down? Does he rush in to avenge? Atticus does not know. Before he can decide anything, Razakel decides to reveal yet another surprise.

"Wait," says the Demon King, "I find I enjoy taking pleasure in your remorse even more than I thought I would. Perhaps I should add to it," he roars into the air, the act is answered by a howl, but it comes not from Razakel.

Shadow Wolf steps through the portal. He holds a rope in his hand and is dragging something behind him. He looks coldly towards Atticus, salivating and barking. The faces of the Majjai turn pale as they spot what is at the other end of the rope. Dragged behind Bradley's new form... Joseph and Sophia, pulled across the sand appear next from the demon's doorway.

"No..." says Atticus, "Leave them alone!" he screams.

"It's ok, Atticus," shouts Joseph, "We are ok!"

"Surrender, Majjai," says Razakel, "and I may just imprison your souls instead of destroy them. This battle is lost for you."

Atticus steps forward, but Elric stops him.

"We have a better chance alive, Atticus," he says.

"But they are my parents. My everything. They do not deserve to be part of this. You said earlier, that we must save all that is good. I do not know anyone more good than them," Atticus says, distraught. A tear slowly trickles down his cheek. He can't bear the risk of such a loss, "I must go."

Elric releases Atticus with a nod.

Atticus looks towards Razakel, "Release them and take me instead. I come willingly. Please, do not harm them!" he shouts across the battlefield.

Razakel holds the *Quantorbium* aloft, the demons cheer triumphantly, "We win. Ha! Foolish Majjai, foolish humans."

Atticus takes another step forward, trying to drown out the baying squalls from the demon horde. But Ju Long soon stops him.

"Wait, Atticus, do you hear it?"

The demonic cheers are also disturbed by the strange buzzing sound heard in the distance. Herensugue looks to the sky and turns to his master.

"My Lord," says the serpent demon, "What is that noise?"

It grows louder, the sound fills the air in the desert, turning into a deafening bellow, then a metallic roar. A flash of light appears, sending a powerful sonic boom vibrating downwards towards the demon army.

Joyce points to the air, "Spitfire!" she says.

Spitfire darts out of the night sky, and flies directly towards Razakel, knocking the *Quantorbium* out of his hands.

Atticus reacts quickly, using his telekinesis ability to shoot the orb towards Spitfire. Razakel roars in anger.

Spitfire morphs from his jet mode into his car form and uses his rear wheels to blast a wall of sand towards the demons. Safaya acts quickly and whips a forceful blast of air towards the enemy, blocking their view. Under the cover of the sand, Ju Long teleports to Sophia and Joseph, bringing them to the safety of the Majjai back line.

Spitfire spins around and joins the Majjai ranks.

"So," says Razakel, "you wish to die painfully."

Spitfire's driver's door opens, and out steps a bruised and battered Marcellus.

"You tried that once," says Marcellus, "I'm here to return the favour."

The demons stomp furiously, and Razakel orders them forward.

"Hold your lines!" screams Khan, as the demons' stomp turns into a charge. He looks to the newest member of the Majjai Six, "Fight well, Atticus, fight well."

"*For victory!*" shouts Khan as he charges forward, followed by the other Majjai. Elric heads towards Razakel, cutting a path in front of him using his staff. He slams it into the sand, sending a giant beam of light through the demon forces, killing all in its wake.

Joyce quickly heals Marcellus before she and Safaya engage in battle alongside the Norse Mages and the other reinforcements.

Atticus hands the Orb to his father, "Hold on to this," he says. Joseph nods. Atticus joins the others in the skirmish.

"Be careful, Atticus!" shouts Sophia.

Shadow Wolf spots his nemesis and runs towards him. Atticus is ready and creates a shield to block his attack.

"Bradley!" shouts Atticus, "I know it's you. Don't do this!"

"Idiot!" shouts Shadow Wolf, "Bradley is no more, and soon you will join him!" he leaps into the air and swipes a claw towards Atticus who blocks it with his sword. Atticus uses his telekinesis and throws Shadow Wolf into the air, and then slams him toward the ground. But before the demon smashes into the sand, he melts into shadow and slithers on the surface toward Atticus. The darkness consumes the young Majjai. Shadow Wolf cocoons Atticus, who tries to dart out of the lightless grip, but the demon is too quick and follows his every movement.

Atticus thinks, what can he do to drive the shadow away?
"Light!"

Atticus holds a hand high above his head and creates a
blindingly bright ball of blue fire. Shadow Wolf squeals and runs from
the piercingly luminous energy. Atticus launches the fireball in the
demon's direction. Shadow Wolf reforms to his werewolf state and
leaps out of the way, the beast then leaps a second time and lands
behind Atticus, clawing his back before he can turn to defend himself.

Atticus screams in pain, his back scarred and burning. Joyce
sees his injury and rolls her spherical shield to knock Shadow Wolf out
of the way, she then grabs Atticus and uses her power to heal his back,
but is unable to do so fully, leaving scars behind.

Razakel watches as various battles take place in front of him,
any stray attacks that come his way he merely absorbs, nonchalantly.

Marcellus hacks and whips his way towards Scourge. The
demon is brandishing his own weapon, a giant flaming mace. He
crashes the mace into the ground, sending a swell through the sand
towards Marcellus. The Majjai deftly dodges the attack and leaps into
the air, using his whip to slash at the monster.

Draconus, now unable to fly with his damaged wing, faces up
to Professor Sprocking once more. Using its tail as a weapon, the
dragon launches another attack. Professor Sprocking blocks it with a
shield and fires several fireballs to the beast's underbelly. Draconus
screams in pain and flicks his tail again, knocking Professor Sprocking
high into the air.

Spitfire has now morphed into a humanoid form, almost
resembling a metallic samurai warrior, he brandishes two large blue
glowing broadswords and begins to slice into the Draygoyles and
Slugs.

Elric finally reaches Razakel, "Demon, you have been

344

warned!" he shouts.

"And so have you... Majjai," replies Razakel. The Demon King fires a giant fireball towards Elric. The Majjai leader uses his staff to create a giant shield, deflecting the fireball back at Razakel, who sidesteps and runs towards Elric.

Elric smashes his staff into the sand, a glow surrounds him and he quickly morphs his body into rock and grows in size to match Razakel. They share massive blows as they fight, sending vibrations through the ground. Razakel is agile, belying his size, but Elric is able to match him.

"The Orb is mine Elric, you must gift it to me!" says the Demon King.

"Never!" shouts Elric, "We will fight you to the death if need be, but you will never have the Orb!"

"Look around you," replies Razakel, pointing to the fallen Norse Mages and the amassing bodies of the other reinforcements, "Your *army* is all but defeated. The Orb will be mine."

Elric pauses, indeed, Razakel is correct, their numbers are dwindling. He remembers the message left by Myrddin in the chest; the word 'nemesis' has always haunted him. He knows what Myrddin meant, but surely the time can't be now, so soon after finally finding the Orb.

He looks towards Olof, keeper of Thor's Hammer.

"Olof!" shouts Elric, "You have to do it now!"

Olof looks over and nods. He races to Atticus, "Where is the Orb?" he asks.

"My parents have it," replies Atticus as he dodges another of Shadow Wolf's attacks, "Why do you need it?"

"I have to destroy it," says Olof, who creates a massive shield of ice protecting Atticus from another attack from Shadow Wolf.

Khan runs towards them, "Do what you have to do; I will hold this wolf here."

Atticus and Olof race to retrieve the *Quantorbium*.

"But, what if we kill Elric?" says Atticus, "His life blood is linked to Orb."

Olof sighs, "I know, but the order comes from him directly."

"Wait for my signal," says Atticus "I must help him against Razakel, in case the Orb's destruction harms him."

Olof nods, "Be careful, Atticus," he says, "Razakel is a very powerful being."

Atticus flies towards Razakel, charging a massive fireball as he flies. Once close, enough he launches it at the Demon King. The fireball strikes the Demon on the shoulder. Razakel turns and looks towards Atticus and smirks.

"Is that the best you can do, *chosen* one!" snarls the giant monster. He returns fire with a much larger fireball, which Atticus dodges. The fireball lands in the middle of a group of Razakel's own Screamers, sending them like demon fireworks into the air. One of the dead Screamers knocks into Joyce, sending her crashing to the ground, unconscious.

"No!" scream Atticus, who takes the Sword of Ages into battle against the evil leader. He charges at Razakel, slicing with his sword; the Demon King creates a sword made from fire and a shield to battle Atticus. From the other side, Elric is launching attacks, the two Majjai flank the Demon King.

The tide of the battle is turning. The Majjai are beginning to get the upper hand, most of the portals have all lost their power, and no more demon reinforcements are coming through. But it is not without cost. Joyce is down, but alive; most of the Norse Mages and the other reinforcements are dead or wounded. Alvar and Kalle are tending to the

346

ones still alive and moving them to safety.

Olof looks to his fallen compatriots, "I will see you all in Valhalla one day, brave soldiers," he turns to Sophia, "I need the Orb."

"Where is Atticus?" demands Sophia as she hands over the *Quantorbium*.

Olof points to Razakel, "He battles the Demon King, alongside Elric."

"Come Joseph, we have to help our boy," says Sophia.

"That would not be wise," says Olof, "You should both stay here, where it is safe."

Atticus sends a fireball towards Olof, giving him the signal to destroy the Orb. The Norse Majjai raises *Mjolnir* above his head and smashes it into the *Quantorbium*, sending a bright flash of light through the desert. As he turns, he sees Sophia and Joseph running into the battle, towards Atticus.

Atticus looks towards Elric who pauses for a moment. Atticus can sense it himself, he can feel the gift of long life ebb away from the old Majjai leader.

Elric feels his body return to a normal aging process, and lets out a sigh, almost as if he is relieved of this burden no longer being upon his soul. He looks at Atticus, "I'm fine," he says, "Now, let's finish this fight."

Meanwhile, Professor Morgan tracks a lone Screamer skulking behind a sand dune with a large chest next to him.

"The medallions," whispers Professor Morgan. He creeps up behind the lone Screamer and slices his throat. The professor grabs the chest and heads back to cover, "I have them!" he shouts towards Elric.

Elric returns his focus to Razakel, "The Orb has been destroyed, Razakel!" he says, "You have lost."

Razakel roars, then lets out a massive wave of energy. It hugs the ground and knocks everyone to the ground, "Foolish Majjai!" he screams, "Now, you will taste the wrath of Razakel!" he sends a massive beam of light into the Majjai forces, killing a large remnant of their reinforcements. Khan rescues Safaya from certain death as she stands in the middle of the blast, while Ju Long barely escapes, flying out of range just as the beam burns the back of his cloak; he turns invisible to avoid being hit by another blast aimed his way.

"Stop!" shouts Atticus, "No more killing!"

Scourge, Shadow Wolf, Draconus, Herensugue, and Alvarez are the only demons left save for groups of Screamers and Graigons who flee the battlefield. They huddle behind their leader for protection.

"But we so much enjoy it Atticus," says Razakel, " This domain is mine, your pitiful powers cannot come close to what I possess. Stand down, or die."

"We will never stand down," says Atticus, "You will never rule us."

"Very well," says Razakel, and sends a spear shaped fireball straight at Atticus.

Atticus is too close, he cannot dodge the blast in time. His eyes close, but there is no impact, the fireball does not strike him, though he is sure he heard a muffled "No!" echo across the sands. He opens his eyes and sees Sophia standing in front of him.

"Nooooo!" screams Joseph.

Sophia drops to the ground, her midriff scarred with the impact of Razakel's attack. Joseph catches her, and kneels in the sand, cradling her in his arms.

Atticus stands still, shocked at first, then he feels a rage begin to build within him. He can't control it — his whole body begins to glow a bright white, all that can be seen are his eyes, which are also burning, but at an even brighter luminance of white. He can feel a new power pulsating within him, forcing its way out.

While everyone is distracted, Ju Long pops up, right in front of Razakel, "You won't be needing this," he says, and swipes the Loki Medallion from the demon's neck before disappearing again and flying away.

Atticus points his arms towards Razakel.

"Razakel!" he screams as he fires an enormous beam of white energy towards the group of demons. The blast is so powerful that it sends Razakel, Draconus, and Herensugue back through the main portal.

"Noooo!" shouts Razakel, his voice fading as the portal closes.

Scourge, Alvarez, and Shadow Wolf look at each other and escape into the desert. No one pursues them. The Majjai surround Joseph who is still holding onto Sophia.

"Sweetie," says Joseph softly, "Open your eyes. You can't leave me. You can't put me through this again."

Sophia slowly opens her eyes.

"Mum," says Atticus, "I'm sorry."

"Shhhh," whispers Sophia, "It's not your fault. It's no-one's fault," she groans slightly, "I had to save you."

"Stop talking," says Joseph, "Save your energy."

Atticus quickly looks around, "Where is Joyce?" he says, "She can save her!"

"She is unconscious, Atticus," says Safaya, pointing to Khan, who is holding Joyce in his arms.

"We have to wake her! Quickly!" shouts Atticus.

"It would not work, Atticus. This is the Demon King's magic, and its power is beyond even Joyce's abilities," whispers Elric.

"Sophia," says Joseph, "Please, hold on for a little longer, don't close your eyes, we'll find a way," he grabs her hand and holds it tightly.

"JJ," whispers Sophia, "Let me go. You have to look after Atticus now, keep him safe."

"Not without you," says Joseph, "I can't do it without you, I can't do anything without you," a tear echoing his emotion runs down his cheek and onto his hands, rolling onto Sophia's arm, and swims through the tiny undulations and hairs, finally dropping onto the sandy surface.

"You can JJ; you always could. I love you," whispers Sophia, "Promise me something."

"Anything," says Joseph.

"Remember me when you dance," says Sophia softly. Her eyes gaze upwards as her mouth breathes out one final sigh. It echoes into the darkness and blankets everyone in silence.

"Sophia," says Joseph, "Sophia," he tries to shake another breath of life into her, "Please, don't leave me," he cries into her shoulder, holding her as close to his heart as possible.

Atticus falls to his knees, but can only feel anger. He quickly fills the emptiness with it, hoping that the pain will go away. But it doesn't work. His head throbs until it's numb, his throat chokes, and tears begin to stream from his eyes.

"No! This cannot happen," screams Atticus. He pushes Joseph away, and kneels over Sophia. Using all of his might, he tries to heal his mother with his own powers, straining with every ounce of strength. But there is nothing; only a glow of blue light. Sophia remains still. Atticus tries again, and again, crying uncontrollably. Everyone around him is silent. He feels an arm on his shoulder.

"She's gone, Atticus. Let her go, my boy. Let her go," Joseph says, and lifts his son.

Atticus grabs onto his father, sobbing into his shoulder. Everyone gathers around, giving them as much time as they need, in silence, and sorrow.

Chapter 29
Goodbye

One week has now passed by since the battle. Atticus stands in front of the mirror in a room deep inside Wysardian Manor. He checks to make sure his black suit is tidy. He wipes a small tear from his eyes and tries to will away the redness.

"I miss you mum," he whispers under his breath.

"There you are," says Joyce as she pops her head around the corner, "It's time."

"Joyce, wait," says Atticus, knowing he must do this. He has lost too much, and does not want to risk losing again.

Joyce pauses, sensing what is coming, and she doesn't like it.

Atticus holds her hands, "We have to end this, Joyce," He says. He grabs her hands tighter, "I love you with all my heart, but I could not take it if another life I cherish so much were to leave me."

"We are in this together, Atticus. You do not need to do this; I know the risks," replies Joyce.

"No," says Atticus, "Just by loving you, being with you, I put you in danger. The demons... they will use this. They will target you harder than anything else, all to distract me. I can't allow that... I can't. Please do not ask me to."

A tear forms in Joyce's eye. Atticus softly wipes it away, he kisses her cheek and whispers, "I will always love you."

Joyce hugs him tightly, and walks away.

Atticus follows her to the Majjai Hall. He sees her wipe away another tear, but he knows this is right, that he must do this to protect her as much as he can. And deep down, he knows Joyce understands.

This walk to the Majjai Hall feels like eons, but they finally arrive. The room is filled to the brim with other Majjai, all dressed in black. At the front of the hall is a coffin. Joseph is standing next to it.

Atticus joins him at the front of the coffin. Khan, Olof, Ju Long, and Mage Callan meet them at the sides. Together they lift the mahogany casket and slowly carry it to the large private gardens at the rear of the Manor. *'It's peaceful,'* Atticus thinks; he can feel the warmth of the winter sunlight as it shines on his skin, "She'll like it here," He whispers to himself. A butterfly flutters into view and lands on Atticus's shoulder; it just sits there, waiting, the sun glistening on its wings. The oddness of a butterfly at this time of year does not strike him at first.

Elric steps next to Atticus, "Your father told me she loves them," before the butterfly darts to the coffin and disappears.

They reach the freshly dug grave and slowly lower the coffin into it. One by one they each place a handful of mud on top of the casket until Elric gives the nod to Safaya who magically fills the rest. She then covers the top with grass and moves an arrangement of flowers around it.

Atticus puts his hand on Joseph's shoulder, comforting him; he can see his father trying to hold back the tears and it pains him.

"You kill him Atticus, this Razakel," says Joseph, "An evil like that has no right to exist."

"Do not worry, Dad," says Atticus steadfastly, "I will."

A gust of wind swirls around the garden, making itself known to all present. Khan looks to Safaya.

"This is not my doing," replies the Princess.

The wind swirls faster and the dust gathers around the grave, a beam of light shoots from the newly created mound of earth above the casket into the sky, and the few clouds blotting against the light blue background begin to congregate. The butterfly that was sitting on Atticus' shoulder earlier flies back into view, joins the wind, and soars on top of the invisible wave up to the clouds, disappearing into a tiny flash of light.

The clouds swirl even faster and a face begins to form. It's Sophia. She looks down towards Atticus and Joseph, smiling softly.

"She goes to a better place, my friends," says Olof to Atticus and Joseph.

The clouds disperse as quickly as they gathered, and the light fades away.

Atticus wipes away another tear. Joyce hugs him.

"You ok?" she asks.

"I'll be fine," replies Atticus, "But I promise you this, Joyce: I will not rest until every last demon festers in hell."

"If we can't *be* together, we will damn well *fight* together until we can. We will win this, Atticus," says Joyce.

"Thank you, Joyce," replies Atticus.

"And we'll be with you too," says Khan, who holds out his hand, "The demons will not know what hit them. We are the Majjai Six, and together, no force can stop us. No Demon, no beast!"

Atticus grabs Khan's outstretched hand, followed by Safaya, Olof, Ju Long, and Joyce. The Majjai Six unite again, for they know this war is far from over.

Chapter 30

The Prime Minister's man

General Crawford rushes through the doors at Number 10 Downing Street with a video disc. No one gets in his way as they can see the urgency in his walk as he heads directly to a particular room. Two men in black suits stop him at the door, question him, and ask for his I.D. before letting him through.

Once the formalities are completed, he enters the room. Two men are ahead of him; both standing steadfastly, partaking in what appears to be a very intense conversation.

"General Crawford?" says the right-most figure in a distinctly British accent, "You do realise we are in the middle of a very important meeting."

"Forgive me, Prime Minister," says General Crawford, "But it has begun."

"Are you sure?" asks the Prime Minister.

"Yes," replies General Crawford, "Our satellite picked up these images after our seismic monitoring stations went into overdrive. As soon as I saw it, I knew I had to bring it to you straightaway."

"Should I stay for this?" says the other man in the room, his voice distinctly American.

"Yes, Mr President," says the Prime Minister, "This concerns us all."

General Crawford runs the video for the two leaders to observe. He knows by their reaction that he is right to do so.

"They cloaked much of the area, it seems," says the General, "But... is that what I think it is, flying through the air?"

"A dragon!" says the President, "So the rumours of the Majjai are true?"

"It seems that way," says the Prime Minister, "But which side are they on is what is more important."

"We'll need to monitor this *school* more carefully," says General Crawford.

"Yes," replies the Prime Minister, "And also its elusive headmaster, Elric Griffin."

Epilogue

I sit here, waiting. So long have I waited, yet the answers escape me.

This wait bores me.

I am my only source of conversation, yet I feel the presence of others. I sit and listen; I try to hear the voices of the other damned souls, but they are pitifully weak. However, they dare to share my prison.

I have learned to see through this darkness. The fabric of it tears and reunites, creating a doorway, perhaps? I question my sanity, yet it is that questioning which saves me from going insane. For Millennia I sit and wait. My chance will yet come.

Wait — another tear. I see a battle, and what is this? Asmodei's pet, he leads his army. Ahhh, I sense Majjai here.

They control the opening. Asmodei's pet is trapped. I see it. I cannot reach the opening. It is too far.

I need to be free; the darkness blinds me more each day. Arrrrggghh! I smash these walls! This invisible ground, I SMASH YOU! The rage! Asmodei will pay for his trickery!

I hear something; a voice perhaps?

No, a presence. I sense it, this mist, it has power; it has knowledge. This red mist surrounds me; I feel it. It joins with me. The power, the knowledge! It is MINE! I know you! I know him, I know of them all! The evil taste stings my soul. ARRRGGHHH!!

The pain! I feel it, the evil, my soul it is tortured by it. NO!

I am more powerful. I know the secrets of the cosmos, yet I struggle to escape its cell. I struggle no more. The answer, it comes.

I feel something else – the void opens tears throughout time; the canvas is torn, who dares meddle with the laws of time? The meddler has a purpose. I sense something else, a kindred? A son? But how? Unless… it worked?

The path, the path to freedom, it is clear now. I am Razakel! No! This evil must be contained!

I am Kazmagus!

I am free!

14397927R00210

Printed in Great Britain
by Amazon.co.uk, Ltd.,
Marston Gate.